W9-ACU-660

THE ONES WHO MATTER MOST

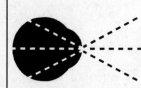

This Large Print Book carries the
Seal of Approval of N.A.V.H.

THE ONES WHO MATTER MOST

RACHAEL HERRON

THORNDIKE PRESS

A part of Gale, Cengage Learning

GALE
CENGAGE Learning

Farmington Hills, Mich • San Francisco • New York • Waterville, Maine
Meriden, Conn • Mason, Ohio • Chicago

GALE
CENGAGE Learning·

Copyright © 2016 by Rachael Herron.
Conversation Guide copyright © 2016 by Penguin Random House.
Thorndike Press, a part of Gale, Cengage Learning.

Thorndike Press® Large Print Women's Fiction.
The text of this Large Print edition is unabridged.
Other aspects of the book may vary from the original edition.
Set in 16 pt. Plantin.

LIBRARY OF CONGRESS CATALOGING-IN-PUBLICATION DATA

Names: Herron, Rachael, author.
Title: The ones who matter most / by Rachael Herron.
Description: Large print edition. | Waterville, Maine : Thorndike Press, 2016. |
  Series: Thorndike Press large print women's fiction
Identifiers: LCCN 2016017442| ISBN 9781410491756 (hardcover) | ISBN 1410491757
  (hardcover)
Subjects: LCSH: Large type books. | Domestic fiction.
Classification: LCC PS3608.E7765 O54 2016b | DDC 813/.6—dc23
LC record available at https://lccn.loc.gov/2016017442

Published in 2016 by arrangement with New American Library, an imprint of Penguin Publishing Group, a division of Penguin Random House LLC

Printed in Mexico
1 2 3 4 5 6 7 20 19 18 17 16

This one's for Dad and Lola, with love

CHAPTER ONE

Abby Roberts tucked a sachet of allspice and thyme — for healing and courage — into her jeans pocket and mouthed again the words she'd thought she'd never say to her husband.

She'd practiced them all day. "I want a divorce," Abby had whispered to the over-wintering kale, her knuckles darkened with dirt. "It's not you; it's me," she tried on the bag of bone meal. Poking her fingers into the ground around the baby broccoli starts, she said, "No, wait. This *is* about you. How *dare* you?"

Divorce.

Unthinkable.

Not that she was against it for others, of course. There were seasons where divorce seemed to be contagious, roaring through couples they knew like wildfire, burning up carefully decorated homes and meticulously wrought child-care plans. And even though

7

it was commonplace, the word was always a shock of ice water to the face. No one was ever casual about that kind of gossip. "The Quinceys are getting divorced? Well, they never seemed to be that happy. Want to get a coffee?" No, the response was always abject horror. "You're *kidding*. I can't *believe* it." Seventy years after feminism made divorce something that could be both borne and afforded, it was still mentioned in a dropped voice, with a moment of silence, an invisible crossing of the body, a warding off.

The fact that Abby needed a divorce was flattening. She was a bruised pansy pressed between the pages of a book she never thought she would have to read.

Scott's truck pulled into the driveway. His quick footfalls came up the porch steps. The door opened — he was often late, but he was always cheerful and apologetic. "Look! Yellow roses! It's not Valentine's Day yet, but I thought I'd surprise you early."

Had he felt her anger across town? While he was rounding up his gardening crew, buying his latte, settling in at the office, and putting his dirt-worn fingers on the Mac keyboard, had he somehow known what the doctor had told her? Had he thought then of buying her flowers?

No. They'd never had that kind of connection. So many other kinds of connection, yes. Humor, sex, fun. But he'd never been able to read her mind.

"Thank you." Ten years together — she was thirty-six; how the hell had that happened so quickly? — and he'd never seemed to remember that she didn't like roses. She loved their hips, for their myriad uses, but not the flowers themselves. "I want a divorce." Her voice was loud. Too loud.

Scott froze, one arm out of his jacket, one arm still in. His face went carefully blank, as if she were a difficult client, one who wanted the newly laid sod ripped out and Astroturf put in. "Sorry?"

It was exponentially harder to say it a second time. "I want a divorce."

There was a stillness after that, a muting of the sounds that usually traveled through their big old house. She couldn't hear the whirring of the ceiling fan or the rumble of traffic that drifted down from Solano Avenue. The house was as numb as Abby.

Scott squinted at her. His mouth moved strangely, twisting sideways.

She wanted to reach forward and take her words back. *I was kidding. Never mind. Bad joke, I'm sorry.*

But she didn't.

9

Scott finished taking off his jacket and hung it on the coat-tree. The knot in Abby's throat moved up until her jaw was clenched so tightly she wondered whether she would break a tooth waiting for him to say something.

"Honey," he finally said. "What?"

"I want a divorce."

His face was red. "No."

Fear bit at her hands, gnawing at the last bit of bravery she had clinging to her fingers. "Yes." She wouldn't tell him why. Not now. He deserved to sweat. To hurt.

Scott walked out of the living room and into the hall bathroom. He shut the door gently behind him. The exit was his statement, and Abby had no idea what to do next. She'd spent hours trying to predict which way tonight would go, but she hadn't ever wondered what she would do if he left the room altogether.

She stood in the hallway, leaning against the wall. She listened to her husband — the man who would soon be her ex-husband — urinate. He would make sure not to drip, as usual. He'd put the seat down afterward, because he'd always been considerate that way.

Then there was a crash.

Had he thrown the framed picture of Vernazza? Scott wasn't a thrower when he was mad, but Abby didn't know what else it could be — the sound was loud enough that it traveled under the door and through the hardwood, up into the soles of her bare feet, into her knees, through her empty stomach, traveling to her chest, where the sound waves battered her heart.

Or — had he fallen? That wasn't likely, though. You didn't just trip in your own bathroom, did you? But Abby froze at the thought, terrified into solid ice. She was glaciate, the frost in her blood too thick to allow motion. Instead, she listened as hard as she could for any sound at all.

There was nothing.

Bastard. Was he messing with her? Again?

She pressed her ear to the door.

Still nothing.

She knocked. "Scott?"

The house, all of it, was silent. The only thing Abby could hear was her own heart pounding and tripping over itself.

She smelled lemon balm, sharp and pungent, and only then did her brain finally — *finally* — allow her feet to move, her hands to hit at the door, beat at it (why had he locked it? who did that in their own home?). Eventually, at the urging of the 911 dispatcher, she knocked the door open with

11

her shoulder.

He was on the floor, his red face now green-gray. His eyes opened and closed slowly. He looked vaguely pleased to see her. *"Scott."* She scrabbled at his arm, which was twisted under his body at an awful angle — he must have broken it as he fell, as he partially wedged himself between the toilet and the sink. "Scott, get *up.*" She tugged at his shirt, patting at his face, scrubbing his skin with the tips of her fingers as if she could bring the redness back. There was no anger in his eyes, none at all. There was no fear. He only gazed at her, blinking with an interested look of confusion.

Then he closed his eyes. For good.

CHAPTER TWO

"Found anything yet?" Kathryn called from the kitchen. "Only keep the good memories, remember."

Abby jumped. She stared at the living room bookshelf as if she'd never seen it before. "Almost!" She was supposed to be finding something to give away. Kathryn said it would help her. She wasn't sure how. She wasn't sure about anything.

Every time Abby thought of her husband lying in the funeral home, the twisted mass of manzanita lodged in her chest sprouted three or four more sharp red branches. At some point, she was pretty sure it would grow up and through her esophagus, and she'd die.

Good memories.

Memories were sharp, a razor blade dipped in cayenne powder. It had been only two days since she'd dialed 911, since the ambulance had called the coroner, since her

13

husband's body had been rolled out of the house on a gurney, a dark cloth over his face as if they'd been suddenly transported into an extremely boring episode of *CSI,* one in which the person died just because he died. Just because Scott's heart — his large and loving and careless heart — had decided to shut down like a computer monitor. He'd been only thirty-eight. If his heart *had* been a computer monitor, it would have still been under warranty.

Scott's handkerchief in her hand, a can of Pledge in her other, she looked for things to dust in the living room, but their house-cleaner — *her* housecleaner now — was too efficient. Dust didn't settle for long.

"Are you sure it's going okay in there, girlie?" Kathryn poked her head out of the kitchen.

"Great!" Lies were ready in her larynx, eager to spring out. She had agreed with Kathryn that decluttering might help. One of many recent lies, it just stacked on top of the assertions she'd made to the funeral home (*I'm fine, thank you*) and to her next-door neighbor (*Yes, I actually did sleep okay last night*). Yesterday, the day after Scott had died, her entire house had been full of friends. Brook, with her almost-painful hugs laced with the smell of the soap she made;

14

Therese, with that way of listening that made you want to tell her the truth; Vivian, with the wine; Simone, with the Scotch. Abby had lied to each one of them, one after another. *I'll make it through this. I'll be all right. You're making all the difference in the world, just being here.* And Kathryn, of course. Kathryn was always there, in the background, holding things together. Abby didn't lie to Kathryn. Much.

What Abby wanted she couldn't say to anyone, not even to Kathryn.

She wanted to get the fuck *out.* To move. To leave through the front door empty-handed and not even bother to lock it behind her. No looking back. If Abby's garden hadn't been behind the house, if she could have slipped it into her pocket whole — onion sets and perfect compost (such *gorgeous,* sweet-earth-smelling dirt) and all — she thought she might actually have done it.

Today, though, Kathryn had arrived with a plan of action instead of another kind of tea. She'd reached forward and taken Abby's hands in hers. "Darling girlie. Let's look at clutter today."

It was an excuse, Abby knew it was. The house was tidy. There wasn't much clutter anyway (except in her potting shed, and she loved that just the way it was). This was Kathryn helping her *do* something instead of letting her lie in bed in shock.

"Okay."

"So, let's get rid of a few of the extraneous things."

"Wait —"

"Not throwing his things away. Nothing like that. This will just make you feel lighter, give you another place to store a little of your sadness."

Maybe it would work. Darling old hippie Kathryn, with her perma-scent of Nag Champa and weed, often knew what was best.

"You go work in the living room, my girlie. Get rid of a few things that are just pretty, a couple of things you're not passionate about. Keep the good memories only. Don't you worry about me — we'll go through everything I think you can get rid of. I'm only looking for things like fondue sets and heated ice cream scoops. Things you don't use, that you don't care about."

Funny, thought Abby, they (no, *she*) owned both those things. Wedding gifts, as useless as emoticons in a voice mail.

She ran the handkerchief over the mantel clock. Scott had always wound it. It had stopped at one twenty-three. She hadn't even noticed the chiming stop.

Everyone *said* Abby hadn't actually been the cause of Scott's demise, everyone from Scott's GP to the priest she'd confessed to yesterday. (Abby wasn't Catholic and the priest had seemed irritated behind the red wood panel. She'd left feeling very small and even sadder than when she'd garnered the courage to pull open the confessional door.)

And while in the smart, sensible forefront of her mind, she knew she hadn't killed Scott, in the back of her mind — the part that held old bits of Latin from college and an exact memory of the first time she'd ever smelled wisteria — she knew she had killed him.

But he'd started it.

He'd gotten a vasectomy. In secret. She'd gone in to talk about her fertility, and the doctor had looked so confused. *But I assumed you knew.* Then there had been a terrible, awkward few sentences while the doctor explained he'd just violated medical privacy rules, and he shouldn't have accidentally told her.

She was his *wife.* She wasn't supposed to *know*? The whole last year of hope (silent, secret hope), the whole time she'd been clocking her ovulation, making sure they

17

had sex, living in hope that turned to familiar disappointment again and again, almost (incredibly) missing the miscarriages (at least she'd been pregnant a few times, life inside for weeks at a time), the whole last year of non-conception wasn't her fault. It was *his.*

So she'd killed him by asking for a divorce. His damaged heart had just stopped beating.

Her fault. All hers.

"Um." Kathryn cleared her throat behind Abby. "Is that a handkerchief? You don't have a rag somewhere?"

Abby held up the light blue striped linen. She'd bought them, classic and soft, for Scott to keep in his pocket. She thought he'd like the old-fashionedness of them. But after folding the first one with a smile and shoving it into the pocket of his chinos, he'd never used one. She'd taken to keeping one in her purse, or in the pocket of her sweater. They came in surprisingly handy. She'd used one just the other day to wipe off the inside of her car's window. The heater had been spitting that invisible film that obscured the world, and the expensive handkerchief of Scott's was just right to make it clear again. They were nice to wash, too. They came out clean and ready to go. The opposite of a Kleenex gone through the wash — handkerchiefs were there for you after the dry cycle ended. Intact. Still strong.

"Abby?"

She'd been staring again. "Laundry," she said, and moved around Kathryn, dodging her concerned gaze. "I love laundry. You know?"

Kathryn just nodded, her long, mismatched crystal earrings jangling.

Abby dropped the handkerchief into the washer with satisfaction. She wished she could keep the feeling, wring it between her hands and smash it into her thighs, push it into her cheeks, keeping it for later when she'd really need it, when she was alone. Alone. *Shit.* The breath went out of her again. Scott was gone. She'd lost him.

But she'd wanted him to leave.

Where did that put her? What was she supposed to feel?

Abby turned on the washer, adding the still-clean kitchen rug to make the cycle worth it. She choked, and swallowed what felt like a mouthful of dryer lint.

Kathryn said, "It's grief, honey. Let yourself feel it."

Feel it? Oh, no. No, thank you. She wasn't strong enough for that. When her grandparents died, the grief had been terrible.

When her parents died, it had been so much worse, ripping her out at the roots.

This new grief was different. Unexpected. This was bodily, enormous, too big for her. It was grief for Scott, and also, secondarily but just as monumentally, for the children she would never have with him. The names she'd never use. The grief was the monster in the washing machine when the cycle went off-balance, that house-jarring thudding that made her feel like the walls were about to come down around her ears.

Abby propped her hip against the washing machine.

Kathryn said something behind her, words that didn't add up to a sentence in her brain. Then, "Abby?"

Against Abby's thigh, the washing machine gave a warning grumble.

She turned to face the machine, and put one hand on either side of it. She would damn well try to hold it in place if she had to. She would figure out how to be strong enough. For once. If the machine started to judder and thump across the floor, she would sink her fingers right through the metal, ignoring the blood that mixed with the wash water. If the house rocked on its base, she would try to hold it — all of it — in place.

"Abby. I'm right here."

What she wanted to do was turn and grab Kathryn by the shoulders. *I can't do this. I can't do any of this.* The sharp, breathtaking pain of grief warred with something else, a feeling she wouldn't — couldn't — acknowledge.

My fault, my fault. My fault.

The other feeling, the one she could never admit to, was the slip of relief — a newly bloomed silver lupine — vulnerable to air itself. Abby knew if she brushed her fingertips against it even once, it would die.

So she stood and held the washer as it shook the way she wanted to so badly.

CHAPTER THREE

Abby had believed in *Till death us do part.* She had believed in it so *hard.*

For two years before they died, Abby's mother (ovarian) and father (prostate) had made chemo appointments together, each refusing to let the poison drip into only one of them. They held hands while the nurses wiped away furious tears at the injustice of it. Hospice took over. The volunteers couldn't stop crying. Their doctors conferred and agreed: neither of them had much time left. Abby's parents had gotten dispensation from the mortuary on Green Avenue in Berkeley to be buried together in a coffin custom-made to fit them both. Abby's mother died first, and her body was held at the mortuary, cold and chemically prepared, until Abby's father finally let go nine days later. The inside of their joint coffin was lined with blue silk the exact same shade as their bedroom walls. A faux headboard matched the one they'd commissioned from a Santa Cruz woodworker for their first anniversary. At the funeral, the twenty-two-year-old Abby would have crawled in bed with them as she had so many times before if Kathryn, her mother's best friend, hadn't slipped her a limb-dulling Ativan just before they walked into the church.

When her parents died, she was left with only Kathryn for family. In the billions of people on the planet, she had no one related to her by blood at all. She'd had a sister, once. Well, that wasn't exactly the way she thought of it. Her mother had given birth to a baby girl who'd lived just one day, a year before Abby came along. She'd been raised knowing she was missing something she couldn't understand. Her sister, Meg. Gone before she really existed. She'd always thought the loss didn't really count.

(Now, of course, she understood the loss better.)

Scott had been her landscape architect. As a trained botanist, she shouldn't have needed one, but while good — no, excellent — with plants, she'd never had a knack for lawns. The house she'd bought in Berkeley with her inheritance had a vast expanse of green velvet that came with an equally vast set of neighborhood expectations.

The first time Scott kissed her, they'd been talking. Just talking. About . . . she could hardly remember now. Something about a problem with Bermuda grass? Whatever it was, it had just been an excuse, for both of them. He'd smelled like the lawn itself, strongly green, like herbal tea made from an apple Jolly Rancher. He was smart (so much smarter than she would have guessed, just from watching him ride the riding mower like it was a long-legged horse). He was carefree. Self-effacing. And when he kissed her, she lost all knowledge of where her feet were — she was floating, they were together, and that was all that mattered.

They started dating.

He wanted to know everything about her, but he hid parts of himself from her, which only made her more interested in what she couldn't see. He said his apartment was too small for her to visit, that he'd be embarrassed if she saw it. He wanted to do so much, change the world to a brighter, greener place. *Roberts and Sons,* he'd say, looking at her, as if she could help with the last word. And god, she wanted to. She could practically feel the eggs in her womb lining up, readying themselves. He had no family, and seemed ashamed of that, too.

"I have no family, either," Abby whispered to him, the old loneliness of the words choking her. "Not anymore."

Three months into their relationship, he couldn't afford a ring, so he made her one out of red clover stems. She wound one for him out of six braided pine needles, and then they lost the rings in the sheets.

Marriage meant family. *Her* family.

When Abby and Scott married, Kathryn walked Abby down the short aisle at St. Edward's Episcopal. Abby wore a mermaid-style pale cream, raw silk dress with just a few carefully placed beads. She felt her mother smiling down at her from somewhere above the transept.

Till death us do part. Abby's voice shook as she said the words, but Scott's confident voice rang all the way up to the rafters.

CHAPTER FOUR

Abby lifted out the load of dry clothes and put them into the laundry basket. So much less of it now. She wished she wore more clothes, more often, just so she'd have more to fold.

"Have you eaten today?" From behind her, in the kitchen, Kathryn opened the fridge and then tsked. "Even one thing? You haven't touched the roast chicken I left you."

"I think I ate some of it." Abby brought the basket out of the laundry room and set it on the kitchen table so she could fold it. "Yesterday."

"Today, sweet girl? Tell me what you've eaten." Kathryn's hair was falling out of the braid she'd put it in. Her T-shirt was black, and torn right above the Grateful Dead bear's eye. It might have been ripped lower, too, but Kathryn's favorite overalls covered the worst damage. A few years more than sixty, she always looked like a hurricane survivor. If anything, though, she was the force of the hurricane itself. Kathryn had been Abby's mother's best friend, and she was the rock to which Abby had clung when her parents died. After the joint funeral, Kathryn had moved into Abby's spare room for two weeks, saying only, "Your mother was my best friend for most of my life. Let's work our way through this together. Come with me to the nursery tomorrow. I'll teach you how to garden." Abby's pale blond thumb had been vibrantly jade by the time Kathryn had gone back to the house she shared with her wife, Rebecca. Abby had gone back to school for biological science, and the day Abby was hired at the Berkeley Arboretum, Kathryn had been thrilled. *I'm only in it for the free plants you'll give me, my girlie,* Kathryn had said, but Abby had felt her own mother's pride coming through Kathryn's radiant smile, too.

Right after she and Scott had married, the arboretum had a major budget crunch and they had to let half their staff go. Abby didn't need the money, thanks to her parents' property investments. Instead of going after another job, she'd fallen in love with the patch of dirt behind the house. There, with her hands in the soil and the sun on

27

her face, she could forget for hours how much she missed her parents. Her full-time obsession became her carefully tended beds. Every year that passed, her plants became as important to her as Scott's clients did to him. As Scott's business thrived, so did Abby's garden. Her bear's-foot hellebore was so precious to her she would have counted it among her friends, and while she knew she needed to pinch off the lime basil's flowers to keep it from getting leggy, she did it gently so the plant knew it was appreciated.

Then she started infusing oils with herbs, selling them in small batches to herbalists and soap makers locally. Kathryn sold them from a countertop at her nursery. Abby knew she could do more with it, but the business end of things made her cranky. She didn't *want* to invest time in a Web site or marketing. What was the point of a Facebook page, the upkeep of which would keep her out of the garden? She just wanted to grow things, to transform them into oils and tinctures that brought out their healing properties. Rue flower for headache and arthritis. Ginger for PMS and joint pain. It made Abby happy to see the oils darkening in their bottles. Her potting shed, where she worked, smelled like heaven: dirt and spice and dried burdock and calendula.

Scott had been dead for only two days.

She wondered idly if there was an herb for loneliness. Water violet, maybe, since it encouraged warmer relationships.

She wondered if there was an herb for penance.

Now Kathryn's silver eyebrow jumped. "Will you answer me, please? Or are you just going to do fake laundry all day?"

"No."

"Okay, then, what about sleep?" Kathryn put a hand on her hip, an unstoppable loving force, an embrace wrapped in a train crash. "Huh?"

Abby twisted a dryer-warm washcloth in her fingers and cast her thoughts back to her afternoon nap. Unable to stay awake after two phone calls from the mortuary, she'd gone back to bed and pulled the covers over her head, dropping into a heavy slumber. Hours later, she'd rolled over in bed and had felt for a moment, before she came back to full consciousness, a burst of pure happiness. That feeling — an unforgivable lightness in the center of her chest — kept hitting her out of the blue. She'd forgotten, again, that she was a new widow. All she'd known was that the bed was empty, and that sun spilled over the windowsill and onto the new duvet she'd found herself buying at Nordstrom. Before Scott died — the word was still so foreign to her as it pertained to him, *died, dead, deceased* — she'd kept the bedroom well-appointed with gender-neutral grays and taupes, highlighted by eggshell and dove accents. At the department store, shopping for something appropriate to wear for the memorial service, she'd shocked herself by spontaneously buying a lemon and pink duvet cover.

It felt like a new bed.

"I slept. I napped today."

"And food?"

Did thirty drops of Saint-John's-wort tincture in a cup of ginger tea count as eating? "I think I had a yogurt."

Kathryn, never one to avoid confrontation, kicked the foot lever of the garbage compactor and slid it open. "Really?"

"Really."

"Where's the container, sugarplum?"

"Are you calling me a liar?" She was one, of course. "It was mango peach."

"Aren't you allergic to mango?"

Abby pulled open the drawer that held her napkins and touched them, enjoying their flat green smoothness. Last night she'd washed a whole load of clean ones, just so she could justify washing her bathroom

30

towel, used only once. "I'm not. I don't know why you always say that."

"Mango made your mouth itch that one time."

"Once. I was six. Thirty *years* ago."

"Oral allergies are nothing to mess with. They can change quickly. Do you have an EpiPen?"

"Of course I don't."

"Have one of mine." Kathryn dove into her huge jute purse and came up with a yellow tube.

"Come on."

"I have two spares at home and one in the car even though the doctor warned me they shouldn't get too hot."

"But . . . what are you allergic to?"

"Nothin'. But I swear to the goddess, every customer who walks through the asters and marigolds seems to be deathly allergic to bees, so I keep them handy. One guy bought a bare-root lemon tree last week and then came running back in with his hands swelled up like fat little balloons. He knew he was allergic to citrus, but he didn't think the tree would hurt him."

"You would stick a person with one of those without knowing if they had a prescription?"

"Sure. I'd probably save their lives."

"Wait, how did *you* get a prescription?"

Kathryn shrugged. "Lied."

"Don't they test you for that?"

"With what, a lie detector? Nah. Powers of persuasion."

"Well, maybe your dream will come true and you'll save a life someday. Be the hero." Scott had needed a hero. When she'd dialed 911, the dispatcher had talked her through CPR. Abby hadn't done it well enough, or fast enough, or something. She hadn't been enough to save him.

Kathryn slid the still-open garbage bin closed quietly, the opposite of the way she usually slammed it. "Not the hero," she said. "Just a helper." She held out the EpiPen.

"Fine." Abby put it into the junk drawer next to the scissors with the broken handle that she kept forgetting to throw out.

Kathryn moved back to the refrigerator. "Here." She held up a raspberry yogurt.

"No, thank you."

Kathryn peeled off the foil top and plucked a spoon from the drawer. "Eat, please? Make me happy?"

"I hate raspberry."

"No, you don't. It's in your fridge. Why would you have it if you didn't like it?"

Abby didn't feel like pulling the punch.

"That was Scott's."

"Oh. Shit." Kathryn blinked hard. "I'm so sorry, girlie."

Abby shook her head, ignoring the silver sparks that swam at the edge of her vision. "It's fine. I ate his disgusting pistachio ice cream last night just because it was the only sweet thing in the whole house. Except for that yogurt, apparently, but I'd forgotten about that." Tears thickened the back of her throat. *Scott.* Scott and his stupid taste in disgusting ice cream. He liked rum raisin, too, and no one in the whole world liked rum raisin.

Kathryn pitched the yogurt into the garbage. "Fuck raspberry. I'm sorry."

Abby said, "It's fine." And it was. Grief as thick as mold coated her soul, but at the very bottom of it, if she had scraped off the greenness, she knew she would find a bit of light.

She'd find a bit of relief. She'd find a bit of desperate and totally unforgivable hope.

CHAPTER FIVE

Abby's phone buzzed with a text while she was crouched over, fighting with the lowest drawer on Scott's desk. She was *sure* she had the right key — it matched the patina on the brass drawer pulls. And it almost fit. She jiggled it harder.

Her phone buzzed again.

Abby fell backward onto the Berber carpet. "Damn."

The text was from Kathryn. *Don't get too carried away. Take your time. You don't need to go through everything now.*

Abby snorted. Too late. Kathryn's decluttering encouragement had stuck a windup key in Abby's back. She was wound to the edge of snapping, but if she kept moving, she'd be able to soldier her way right through this. It was *good* to get rid of things. It felt great. His stuff — that would be easy to pitch, right?

Abby jiggled the key again, then turned it

upside down and tried for the fourth time. Stupid key.

Stupid *desk*. It was the size of a small cow, and — Abby was just guessing — probably just as unwieldy. She'd always thought the huge rolltop would look better a foot to the left, closer to the light of the window, but once the deliverymen had dropped it into place (a gift from her to Scott on their third anniversary, when he was busy enough with the business to have to work from home some nights), she and Scott couldn't move it, not even a millimeter.

Abby had never opened even one drawer of it. She'd never had a reason to. She had her own desk, upstairs, in her bright office, where she researched gladiolus and spearmint varieties. She didn't need to go through his files. She didn't care about his clients' needs for drip irrigation or the perfect succulent to complete their desert landscape.

So when the key finally persuaded the largest bottom drawer to open, when she was finally staring down into it, she was shocked by what she found. There were no files. No paperwork. Not even a stapler. There was just a pile of *Urban Garden* magazines, a half-eaten bag of white cheddar popcorn, some paper towels, and a white box.

Abby's mouth went dry, her tongue sticking thickly to the roof of her mouth, as if she'd balled up one of the paper towels and placed it on her tongue, a bulky Communion wafer of fear.

She scrabbled at the other, smaller drawers, the ones that hadn't seemed important enough to start with.

He worked in here at night. Often. He would have paperwork somewhere, right? Work stuff.

But the top drawer just held three boxes of Nerds. The wood itself smelled of fake blueberry. What the *hell*? Nerds weren't even a *candy*. Not really. They were just pressed sugar, in the flavors of red and green and yellow. She hadn't had any since she was in her teens, but could still remember exactly how purple (not grape, just purple) felt in her mouth. Abby tried a pink one. The flavor exploded in her mouth, as pink as a little girl's shoe. Nothing about the flavor came from something she would recognize in nature. She held up the small box, twisting it in the insubstantial light. *Double Dipped Lemonade Wild Cherry.*

Abby tossed a palmful more of the pink rocks into her mouth and crunched hard.

Sugar felt amazing. She could practically

feel the sugar receptors in her brain light up. She'd been trying to go easy on it recently, keeping it mostly out of the house, eating raisins when she felt the craving. Scott had been trying, too, indulging only in ice cream when he needed a fix, saying it was lower glycemic and therefore okay. Where had he even bought these? When had he sneaked them in the house?

On a hunch, she moved the mouse on his Mac, and the screen lit up obediently. She brought up his Amazon page, his password conveniently autofilling. They had separate accounts, both linked to the joint checking account that Abby had never bothered to pay attention to. She hated to admit it, and wouldn't do so to her friends who shopped responsibly and locally, but in the middle of the night, she'd sometimes remember that they were out of toothpicks, or salsa, or paper towels. It was easier to open the app on her phone and hit one-click-purchase than it was to find a pen to write it down to add to the shopping list the next morning. The boxes would show up, jars of mayo and bottles of white vinegar triple-wrapped in plastic bubbles and multiple layers of cardboard, both of which Abby would carefully recycle to at least be able to pretend that her order, delivered right to her door, had a carbon footprint less than that of a Humvee.

Maybe Scott had done something similar.

And there it was. His last order had been two boxes of MoonPies and a bottle of Jack Daniel's. Sent to his office.

Of course. It wasn't like she checked his work bag when he got home. After a healthy dinner of lean chicken breast and fresh broccoli from her garden, it would have been easy for Scott to squirrel MoonPies into his desk drawers. The meals she made for him with thought and love and the freshest herbs possible, weren't enough for him.

The worst part of the hidden candy was that if Scott had brought a package of MoonPies into the house under his arm, if he'd held them up and announced, "Look what I brought home!" Abby would have laughed. She loved it when he satisfied himself. He bought expensive, locally brewed beer, and liked to talk his way through a bottle, discussing the flavors (cherry! anise! vanilla!) with her. He'd been the one who'd insisted on the raised spa tub in the master bath when they'd done the last renovation, and she'd loved watching him run the taps, adjusting the water, playing with the different buttons, showing her the action of the jets. She'd used the tub itself way more than he did. He loved to sit on the fluffy blue bath mat, laughing at her as she sank under the water and blew bubbles. *I love you,* she told him from underneath the warm weight. *I love you* in bubbles, light as air.

With every miscarriage, they'd moved further apart. Not that either of them had admitted it. They'd moved from lying in bed locked in a love jail of their own making, both of them delightedly fascinated by every tiny facet of each other's bodies and minds, to living separately, so alone that not even their online accounts talked to each other.

Abby unrolled a Tootsie Roll and popped it into her mouth. Damn. She could eat all this sugar herself if she wanted to (and she kind of did).

The sudden slight thrill that rocketed through her to the tips of her fingers was probably caused by the sugar high. That was all.

She rubbed her eyes and took a deep, shaky breath. Back to the job at hand. She checked the pigeonhole drawers at the top of the desk.

Empty.

How did a person leave drawers *empty*? Jobless? If this had been Abby's desk, she'd have used one of the tiny drawers for the hair bands she was always trying to find while she was working. She'd use one drawer for the orange mechanical pencils she loved. Another drawer for lip balm. These drawers were empty. Wasted.

Her hand went back to the biggest drawer. She hesitated before opening it again, the hairs on the backs of her arms prickling. She shivered once, hard. Then she slid the drawer open again and pushed aside the bag of cheddar popcorn. Scott was lucky they didn't have mice. (No, that wasn't okay to think. He hadn't been lucky in any way at all.)

She pulled out the white box.

Photos.

Relief swamped her as she deliberately exhaled. Just photos.

Abby smiled as she flipped through them. A younger, thinner Scott grinned at the camera. He'd been so *gorgeous* and young and gloriously cocksure. She could almost hear the boom of his laugh, feel the bottomlessness of it. There were shots of him in what looked like a shared house filled with old sofas and bongs propped on coffee tables, him leaning on various girls. Playing beer pong with guys whose faces were frozen in perpetual whoops. Shooting pool in a garage under a garish orange lamp, looking as confident as he had waiting for her to walk down the aisle.

And then there was a short stack of pictures of him with a dark-haired woman.

Abby felt her jaw tense. It was such a small sensation that she almost missed it. She could still dump the pile of photos back into the box, close it, and put the whole thing into the recycling even though photo paper was probably technically too glossy.

But she didn't. She flipped to the next picture.

Scott's arm was around the woman as they stood in front of a large white column. They were dressed up, as if at someone's wedding. Scott was in a suit. The woman was pretty in a simple kind of way with large, wide-set brown eyes, and teeth that looked strong and useful. She might have been Latina. Her long dark hair looked heavy, and though it was straight in the picture, it frizzed into a dark halo around her head, as if it curled naturally, and her skin was a dark olive. She wore a light peach dress and a lacy cream shawl. The setting was familiar, but she couldn't put her finger on it — Abby *knew* that the bay was just out of sight, the Golden Gate close by. . . . The Palace of Fine Arts?

The next picture confirmed it. There was the rotunda and the lagoon, the gorgeous green stretch of lawn flanked by eucalyptus trees.

The funny part, the really *weird* part, was that Scott and the dark-haired woman looked as if they were the center of all the pictures. There were no pictures of the bride and groom, if they were indeed at a wedding. Or had this girlfriend been so important to him that they'd scheduled a real photo shoot?

The most incomprehensible picture of all was the one in which Scott was kneeling on the ground in front of the woman, his hands on her flat belly. They were both laughing into each other's eyes, and neither of them looked at all conscious of the person holding the camera.

Why would they pose like that? It almost looked like one of those cheesy pregnant couple poses. Abby peered into the photograph as if she could get close enough to hear what Scott was saying to the woman.

So odd. Abby shook her head. Another chill ran down her arms.

She should stop going through the box. She should toss it. Right now. It wasn't her business. Scott was gone. She rubbed her bottom lip. Then she looked at the next picture.

Two hands, a man's and a woman's, on

top of each other's. With brand-new sparkly rings.

One of the hands was Scott's. She knew his work-worn knuckles like she knew her own. Only his thumb crooked that way. He was almost double-jointed and proud of it.

That peach dress the woman was wearing — it was the woman's wedding dress. The woman and Scott weren't *at* someone's wedding. They *were* the wedding.

Jesus.

Married. He'd been married.

Before her.

Married.

Abby stood, unable to stay in his chair. She walked backward until her calves ran into the low sofa. She stood in place, the photos gripped in her hands.

How . . . how had she never known? How had he never *mentioned* it? Wasn't that something you *had* to tell the person you were engaged to marry? She scanned her memory, searching for some kind of law, something she could have had him arrested for. Back then. Before she married him.

She flipped through the pictures faster, her larynx so tight she coughed.

A photo of them kissing under a colonnade. The woman fit into Scott's arms in a way Abby had once thought only she herself did.

She covered her mouth and stared closer at the picture of Scott and the woman driving away in a shiny black Honda. It was decorated with *Just Married* on the windows and tin cans tied to the bumper. Just like Abby and Scott had. The car decorating had been Scott's idea. Abby had thought it was retro and clever and adorable.

Holy shit.

Then Abby came to the last photo. The color of the paper was different, the feel of it thinner. Less substantial. She let out a low, strangled cry.

A gobsmacked-looking Scott held a ridiculously red newborn. From a narrow hospital bed on the other side of Scott and the baby, the dark-haired woman was radiant, tears in her eyes, hope lighting her face like sunlight.

CHAPTER SIX

Abby didn't sleep, even after half a Benadryl followed by the second half an hour later. Even though the bed still felt new under the pink and lemon (Nerds-colored) duvet, her brain spun, whirring faster and hotter like a disk drive about to die.

Scott had a baby. A *baby.*

A child. Of his own.

Scott had a child of his *own*?

When dawn came, when the clock crept past five, then six, and finally seven — an almost-decent time to call someone — Abby shook the ache from her clenched fingers and reached for her cell. But when she lit the screen and looked at her contacts list, her mind went blank. Kathryn would . . . God, she'd be wrecked. She'd be furious, the spitting mad she got at misogyny and terrorist acts. She'd stage a protest march or something. And then she'd try to take care of Abby. Abby wasn't ready for that.

She could call her friend Yvette, but with four kids under the age of five, Yvette was always at her rope's end. She didn't need Abby's problems. Lisa had been around so much already this week, and today she'd been going to her sister's house. . . .

Brook. Brook had problems. Man problems, kid problems, money problems. Brook wouldn't judge. Every time Abby sold Brook a case of herb-infused oils to use in her soapmaking, she ended up staying five hours. They'd met because of Abby's business, but they'd become friends almost instantly.

But she just got Brook's voice mail. "Leave a message and I'll — Oh crap. *Put your sister down, Danny!*" For once, the recorded message didn't make Abby laugh. She hung up without saying anything after the beep.

Abby kept her eyes dry, locked onto the ceiling fan. Waiting.

At eight, Abby let herself rise and dress. She made coffee and toast. Then she went back to Scott's desk. Yesterday, when she'd started going through it, she'd gone slowly, jiggling the key with care so as not to harm the lock. Now she let her body go feral. She was a crime scene in action. She ripped out all the drawers and dumped them upside down, in case he'd taped anything to the wood bottoms. She reached inside, searching for false backs. One drawer was stubborn about lifting from its tracks, so she yanked out the metal with nothing but brute force.

She pulled every single thing out of his office closet, throwing shoes and ski equipment over her shoulder without looking. A snowboard hit the top of the side of the roll-top, driving a deep gouge into the wood. She threw a ski pole at the wall clock, which hit the floor with a satisfying crunch. She moved the sofa away from the wall and banged on the paneling, ignoring the voice in her head that told her she was crazy. She wouldn't even know how to tell whether there was a hidden cache of something. . . . No, Scott would never have a hidden panel.

Not when he had a whole office to himself a ten-minute drive away in South Berkeley.

She was wearing red yoga pants and a pink T-shirt that read, *Is this a garden? All I see are hoes,* a shirt Scott had given her, one that she never would have worn out of the house. She was so very far beyond caring. In the tiny pocket of her pants meant to carry nothing but a car key, she stuffed dried feverfew (for protection) and lilac (for luck). Then Abby was in the car so fast she almost forgot shoes.

At the small office of Roberts and Sons, Scott's assistant, Charmaine, gasped. "Oh, my god." She came out from behind her desk, her hands outstretched. "Abby. I didn't expect to see you here. Not so soon. I was going to call you, but I figured I would be more help just being here. . . ."

"I need to get in his office."

"Oh, no . . . Truth? I haven't put it in order yet. I was going to call you after . . . I'll let you know when I'm done."

Abby walked past her toward Scott's door, feeling her pulse speed up. She was scared of Charmaine, always had been, ever since Scott had hired the brunette with legs that went for days and an attitude to match. Not that she didn't trust Scott. She did. She had. What an idiot.

"That's okay. I don't mind a little mess."

Charmaine moved quickly and put herself between Abby and the door. "No. You have so much to deal with now. I'll let you know when I've handled it."

Abby sucked in a breath. She'd never stood this close to Charmaine before, and the heavy scent of her too-sweet perfume made her dizzy. "I . . ." She faltered.

Putting a hand gently — understandingly — on Abby's arm, Charmaine said, "It's so hard. I know. I feel it, too. He was a good man."

Abby had always vaguely wondered if Scott and Charmaine had ever been attracted to each other. Now, she realized, she didn't care, both a shock and a relief. A potential past wife trumped a possible fling like the sun trumped a flashlight.

Charmaine stood straighter. "There are things I need to handle in there."

"I found out his secret." Five words, five short words, words she didn't even know for sure were true. She hated that she ran out of breath so quickly she could barely finish them.

"Shit." Charmaine stepped to the side. The fact that she moved meant Abby's fear was justified, and terror ran through her blood like frozen acid.

It took Abby fewer than five minutes to scuffle through his hanging file folders to find the one marked *Fern Reyes*. The other files were labeled with addresses, alphabetical by street. Hers was the only name.

Fern? The woman had a specific name now, a name shared with a creeping, invasive, gloriously robust rhizome. Abby had always loved ferns. She'd taken a whole seminar in leptosporangiate ferns at college — they were vascular, reproducing by

49

spores instead of seeds or flowers. Fiddle-heads and fronds, fascinating and tropical.

Abby sat heavily in Scott's chair, and then — feeling the way the seat had conformed over the years to his body (his now-dead body) — sprang to standing again. She reached forward to pull up the file and spread it across the top of the desk.

There they were. Divorce papers, naming Fernanda Reyes as his once wife. And the paper that should have howled like a Hog-warts screamer: a dog-eared photocopy of a birth certificate.

His son. Matias Wyatt Reyes-Roberts.

Fernanda and Matias.

Scott's other family.

"Charmaine!"

The woman popped out around the corner as if she'd been standing right there, wait-ing. "Um. Yes?"

Abby would have liked to have yelled and screamed, to have carried on like a woman freshly scorned, but her moment of bravery had sunk four inches below the thick moss-like carpet beneath her feet. "Did you know about Fernanda and Matias?"

Charmaine's pink-frosted lids dropped for a moment. Then, "She goes by Fern. And he's called Matty, I think. That's what Scott called them."

Matty. It was adorable. A sweet name. A name that had been on her short list (from Matthew) for a while. With a sickened pang, she remembered passing her list to Scott once, asking him to cross off names he didn't like. How the hell had he not struck off Matthew when she'd given him the pen and made him go through her dreams? *He already had a Matty.* He'd known that. She hadn't. "I need the address."

Charmaine opened her mouth as if she was going to protest, but then she just nodded. A moment later, she handed Abby an oversized yellow Post-it.

"Thank you." That was as much as Abby could give her.

"You're welcome." There was a pause as Charmaine watched Abby putting the file with its contents into the spare fabric shopping bag she always carried in her purse. "You'll want this, too, probably." She held out another file, thicker than the first.

Abby's heart sank as she reached to take it. "What is it?"

"Finances."

"Scott's?"

"Um." Charmaine looked down at her peach-colored nails. "Theirs? I guess?"

Abby nodded as if she understood.

Inside was a large stack of business-sized

51

check duplicates. Each was for fifteen hundred dollars. Abby didn't think her legs would hold her much longer. "Monthly support."

"Um. Yes."

"Well." She wanted to curse, but no word was strong enough. She wanted to throw the file, but she wouldn't be able to bear stooping to pick up his shit. She wanted to hurt someone, a very particular someone, but he was assholically dead, and wasn't that the whole problem? She felt like taking Scott around his neck, that deliciously corded and muscled neck of his that used to turn her on just to look at. She felt like choking that same neck until she made him stop breathing. Again. "Well." Such an impotent word.

"Yeah."

Finally Abby found the exact words she wanted. "Son of a bitch motherfucking son of a motherfucker *fuck.*"

"Yeah," said Charmaine, and this time it sounded like she meant it.

CHAPTER SEVEN

Seven hours later, after digging four holes in the garden for no good reason (yet — she'd put something in them eventually) and a fruitless attempt at a nap that did nothing but amp her up even more, Abby exited the freeway at the Oakland Zoo. The GPS, as if stunned to be out of its everyday zone, stuttered and then blurted to life, telling her to turn left. It sounded doubtful. Abby took a too-quick sip of the passionflower tea she'd bought at Peet's (she'd gotten it for its ability to help with emotional balancing and hysteria relief — she tried to ignore the fact that passionflower also heightened libido).

In the years she'd been with Scott, she'd never seen a single place he'd ever lived. Not one. Now she finally knew why. Her stomach clenched harder than her hand on the wheel did. Rage burned in her stomach like she'd chugged a shot of jet fuel.

Motherfucker.

Scott, of course, had heard about each place she'd lived in over the years. There had been only three, after all, not counting college dorms. He'd known specifics about the Potrero Hill Victorian she'd grown up in, where she'd spent her first eighteen years, where her parents had spent their last. He knew how it creaked in the winter and how those creaks sounded like happy groans in the guest room they'd never used. He knew that her mother had thought it was cheerfully haunted. Abby had sold the house after they died, so Scott hadn't ever been inside it, but they'd once broken into the backyard on a quiet Wednesday afternoon and Abby had cried when she'd seen that the new owners had turned her father's little woodshop into a yoga space. Her mother's kiln still stood, and Scott had tried valiantly to talk Abby into letting him steal it for her, brick by brick, before the residents turned it into a wood-fired pizza oven or something.

Scott knew all about her first apartment in the Mission, the one she'd moved into after she graduated from State. Her parents had hated that place — its triple locks, the homeless sleeping in the doorway of the lowest unit — but they were too sick that year to fight her much. Every time Abby and Scott had gotten burritos at Taqueria Cancun, she pointed it out. "See it down there?"

He would nod. "You had the room with the broken stained-glass window. The landlord refused to fix anything, and your neighbors wanted to sue. But you loved it and you wouldn't move because you're stubborn as hell."

"I wouldn't move because it was amazing." She'd loved that rattrap apartment with its glorious light and its colder-than-imaginable foggy summer mornings and its clubbing throb on Friday and Saturday nights. She didn't move until after her parents died, until after she found that her bank account was so full it was just plain stupid of her to continue to rent anything, let alone a cheap, run-down studio. The enormous 1914 Craftsman in North Berkeley was the first place her Realtor had taken her. She'd barely noticed the high crown moldings and the built-ins and its proximity to Solano Avenue — she'd just been drawn to the jungle of the backyard. Left untended for at least a dozen years, ancient-looking ferns had tangled with blackberry. Pandanus had encroached on the old pond, and a bamboo stand threatened to take over the entire lower quadrant. The Realtor had been apologetic. *We can stipulate they clean this up. Burn it. Something.* But Kathryn, who had just opened the nursery, had been overjoyed. *I'll make sure you have everything you need. Imagine raspberries right here! Your mother would have loved this.*

Abby turned left on MacArthur and double-checked to make sure the doors had auto locked while she'd been driving. This wasn't anything like her part of Berkeley, where Alice Waters lived around the corner. Abby could walk to three different cafés with fair-trade coffee, and the local schools had on-site gardens that sent organic vegetables to the cafeteria.

This neighborhood, on the other hand, appeared to have only liquor stores and churches bracketing the small wooden houses. Nothing else. She hadn't seen a doctor's office or a grocery store. Not even a bank.

The sun was out, and people were taking advantage of it. A group of older men sat on a stoop and shook something small and white onto a red blanket. A woman wobbled past them on high heels, wearing a long fall of cherry cola–colored hair. The men ignored her, and she kept her eyes on the street. Abby caught her gaze accidentally and then didn't know what to do with it.

She yanked a hard left and winced as the GPS on her phone caught her mistake. "Rerouting. Rerouting." How did a computerized voice hold that much judgment? Two more left turns and another right at a fork in the road and she was on the correct street, at least.

The houses here were tiny. Most couldn't be more than two or three bedrooms. In Abby's neighborhood, when residents upgraded their homes, they literally dug them up and lifted them skyward, leaving them perched precariously on stilts while they added a story or two below the original body of the house, getting additional bedrooms and garages out of the remodel. If people couldn't go up, they went out. They went out to the very edges of their property lines, out to the back fences, pouring foundations over old lawns, adding loggias and outside barbecue pits, their outside living rooms complete with fountains and widescreen TVs protected from the elements by environmentally responsible reclaimed lumber.

In this part of Oakland, though, the houses remained small. Narrow side gates led to backyards that, by the signs hanging from almost every one, held guard dogs, not wide screens. Abby felt herself guessing the interior square footage as she slowly drove past. A thousand. Eleven hundred. Eight hundred. Could that one there be any more than six hundred?

She watched address numbers on the sides of houses. The numbers rose in direct proportion to her heart rate. Still, she was startled by the GPS when it announced, "Your destination is on the left."

God. The house she'd been staring at, without realizing that it was the one she'd been looking for, the house she'd automatically slowed in front of.

Of course.

She'd recognized the boy.

CHAPTER EIGHT

"Hi."

The boy looked up at her suspiciously and said nothing.

Matty.

His skin was five or six shades darker than Scott's summer tan, but in every other way, he looked like every kid picture she'd ever seen of her husband. He was skinny, with a wide jaw that didn't fit his face. His hair wasn't Scott's red blaze, but the rust was there under the brown. Holy hell. "I . . ." Scott's son was half-Latino. What did that *mean*?

The boy ignored her, dropping his eyes back to the notebook in front of him. Good for him. She was a stranger. He was an eleven-year-old. He shouldn't talk to her.

"Is your mom home?"

The boy didn't even blink.

"Do you mind if I open the gate?"

Now he looked alarmed. His colored

pencil stopped moving.

"I'm not —" Not what? If she said *I'm not going to hurt you,* she'd sound like a child predator or something. "You're Matty, right? I'm looking for your mom. Fern." It was the first time Abby had said the woman's name out loud, and the softness of it surprised her. It didn't *look* soft in Scott's file, and it didn't feel soft in her mind. It should sound pointy and dry, a heap of old sticks. But said in the open air, the name felt like the plant itself, light and rounded and brushed.

The boy's face was a mixture of relief and apprehension. His eyebrows stayed close together. "You know my mom?"

"I don't," Abby said, still on the other side of the latched gate. "But I'd like to meet her. Is she home?"

He narrowed his eyes, back to wary.

"I . . ." This was stupid. This was ridiculous. This wasn't respectful, of Scott (although, really, *fuck* Scott) or of his ex-wife or, maybe most important, of his child, the one in front of her right now. "I just have some of your mail." That was true, after all. So it had been returned by the boy's mother. It was still Fern's.

"Oh. We got some of Joe's mail last month."

"Is Joe your neighbor?"

He nodded. "Mom opened it accidentally and it was some kind of crazy big bill, so she said we had to pretend we never saw it. She fixed it with a glue stick and put it in his box." He clamped his mouth shut as if suddenly aware that wasn't for sharing.

"Makes sense."

Matty assessed her, his eyes still. "Did you open it?"

"What?"

"Our mail."

"Well, actually, it was already open. I have quite a bit of it in this bag." Abby looked up at the windows. Dust and spiderwebs danced at the corners of each old pane. She glanced at Matty again. "What are you drawing?"

"Leaf."

"Can I see?"

Suspicion lit his eyes. "Why?"

"I like leaves."

"Do you know how to draw them?"

"Yes," she said. How many veins and petioles and stipules had she drawn in college? "I really do."

Matty stood up and opened the gate. Then he sat back down on the stoop again. Sunlight made the top of his head glow. He scrubbed an eraser over the beat-up page in his notebook.

"Is this for class?"

"Yeah." His tone was miserable.

The blood moved faster in Abby's veins. This was weird — this was much too weird. You didn't just meet a child and sit next to him on a step in the sun; but what were you *supposed* to do when you met your husband's child?

She sat. She looked at the page. He'd drawn a circle in black pencil and then he'd added lines bisecting it in brown. "That's a leaf?" she said.

Around the eraser of his pencil, he said, "Yeah. I guess."

"Because it looks like a dying hedgehog."

He snorted. "You're not supposed to say that."

"Why not? I think it's a very good dying hedgehog. I wouldn't want to run into it in a dark alley."

"I hate art. And this isn't even art — this is for science and that just makes it worse."

"Well, art is one of those hard things. You can't really add it up, you know? Two plus two doesn't always equal four when you're dealing with colors and lines, right?" Abby was proud that her voice didn't shake. She couldn't remember the last time she'd talked to anyone under the age of twenty-one. And she'd never spoken to anyone this important, maybe ever. "Where's your leaf, anyway?"

"Huh?"

"You're out here because this is where the leaves are, right?"

He frowned and jerked his head back as if he'd just remembered he had a shell. "No. I'm out here because Elva baked that curry-lentil thing she makes and it smells dis*gust*-ing in there."

Who was Elva? She couldn't ask. *Don't ask.* "So you're not drawing from life?"

Matty just stared at her. His eyes — Jesus, his eyes. Scott's eyes met hers. Brown with dark green on the edges, smart and sweet and holding just that little bit back. He said nothing.

"Well. If you don't have a leaf, you're not going to get it right. Let's find one."

Matty's skeptical look was so clearly written on his face that he didn't need to say anything.

"Come on. Let's do this."

He slouched upward with a sigh and followed her onto the tiny unkempt lawn. "I sure hope you're not an ax murderer."

Abby patted her yoga pants, front and back. "Awfully small ax."

"You never know these days."

It was so unexpected and so *funny* that Abby felt an adrenaline rush spike through her.

Matty's head was down. He scuffed at the overgrown grass with the toe of his sneaker. "What kind of leaf?"

"You're the boss," said Abby. "Pick one you like. No, pick two. Just in case you get mad at the first."

"What do you do then?"

"Rip up the page and then pull the leaf into tiny bitty pieces. Let both of them blow away into the wind."

Matty gave a surprised hoot of laughter.

Abby bent down and picked up an oak leaf that must have blown in from the neighbor's yard. It pricked her finger, and the sharpness of it felt just right. If she were going to draw a leaf, she'd pick this one. Ragged at the edges. Brittle, but still strong. At least for now.

A few minutes later, Matty held five or six leaves in his hands.

"Got some? Okay, I'm going to show you the magic trick now."

"Really?"

Whoops. "I mean, it's not a *magic*-magic trick."

Reasonably, Matty looked confused.

"All I mean is there's something I do

when I'm drawing, and it works pretty well. Okay, you like this one?" It was a fat sycamore leaf, bright green with one bug-chewed edge.

He nodded.

"Turn a page in your notebook, that's right. Put the tip of your pencil on the page, yeah, like that. Now, with your other hand, pull that first piece of paper back over your hand."

Matty looked so flummoxed that she wanted to laugh. "Huh?"

"You're trying to hide your hand from yourself with that piece of paper. Get it?"

"No."

Abby held up one finger and traced the top of the leaf's edge. "Your eyes are talking directly to the tip of your pencil. Move your eyes slowly, *really* slowly, along the edge of the leaf. When it turns, your pencil turns under the page, but you can't see the tip of it. All you can see is the leaf. Look — really look — at the veins of it. Follow each one. Be as detailed as you can."

"But not look *down*?"

Now she did laugh. "Yep. Just try. I'll hold it really still."

Matty nodded once, though his eyes still telegraphed skepticism. Then he plastered his gaze on the leaf.

It was quiet as he drew. Or, at least, it was as quiet as this neighborhood could be. Abby had always thought her neighborhood in North Berkeley could be a little noisy sometimes, with planes taking off from SFO rising overhead and the perpetual whine of lawn mowers in the distance.

But the sound here in Oakland was different. Even though the freeway was on the other side of the low hill, she could feel its rumble in her chest. As soon as one siren died in the distance, another took up the wail. A solid *thoomp-thoomp* beat from a car's bass sound system somewhere close by. She heard two screams. Matty didn't even blink. He kept his eyes on the leaf, his hand moving under the paper. The screams resolved into wild laughter and a group of teenagers on foot loped past the gate. Now that she was really listening, she could hear a hundred other sounds: at least two TVs from the apartment building next door, the rattle of a dryer with spare change caught inside the drum, and, astonishingly, in all that sound, the low throb of a humming-bird's wings as it buzzed them, heading for the early jasmine she'd seen in the yard next door. Its wings flashed green and gold. Matty didn't so much as glance toward it.

After perhaps four minutes, he said, "Can

66

I look now?"

"You're done?"

"Yeah. I think."

"Let's see."

The image on the page was a scribble of intricate pencil marks, woven lines making a fine mesh.

"That's *horrible.*"

"It isn't! Look. It's amazing!"

He jabbed a finger at it. "*This* is not a leaf. *This* is a big old fat pile of dog caca."

"But it is a leaf. Look close." She scooted on the step so she was closer to him. "It's like this wild jungle, and you drew it."

"It's a mess."

"But did you know a leaf looked like that?"

He stopped rolling his eyes and narrowed them, first at her, and then at the paper. After a moment, he said, "No. There's a lot of wiggles. Veins."

"You know what it reminds me of?"

"What?"

"Look at the palm of your hand."

He glanced at her, and then back at his hand. "I guess they're kinda . . . huh. That's weird."

"Isn't that cool? By drawing the leaf, you were sort of drawing your hand, too."

He sighed. "That doesn't make any sense."

"Okay. But was it fun?"

"Yeah. But I don't think my teacher is gonna believe me, that this is the leaf."

"So bring the leaf in, too."

"She's really mean. She didn't say to bring it in."

"Did she say not to?"

He grinned, and Abby's heart suddenly starting beating as rapidly as the hummingbird's wings had thrummed. What would it have been like? If she'd been able to have Scott's child, a boy, a brother to this one? What kind of life would that have been, the one that had passed her by?

"My mom's not home, by the way."

She'd almost forgotten she'd asked. "So . . . Elva?" Was that the housekeeper? His nanny? How old was a child supposed to be before you let him be a latchkey kid? Abby had exactly zero experience with children, and she would have guessed sixteen, but good grief, at that age they could wield two-ton vehicles on the freeway, so, yeah, kids probably got house keys earlier than that.

"Elva's in there. She lives here." He jerked his head backward, toward the front door. "And Grandpa Wyatt."

An abyss yawned in front of Abby and the ground dropped away behind her. *Grandpa Wyatt.* Scott's father had been named Wyatt, but he'd died years before she and Scott met. *I wish you could have met him,* Scott had always said. *He would have loved you.* Abby teetered on the tiny square of solid ground she stood on, unsure whether to step forward or back.

This wasn't right. Everything about this was wrong, so wrong.

She carefully balanced the leaf on the open page of his sketch pad. "It looks good there," she said. "Next to your awesome drawing. Anyway. I should —"

"Hey," Matty exclaimed, making her jump. "My mom's here!"

Behind her, the gate opened.

The woman said, "Holy." Then she said, "Fuck."

CHAPTER NINE

Fern Reyes had never, ever expected to find Matty talking to the enemy in her own yard. The day's exhaustion fled her bones and if Abby Roberts had flown straight upward like the *bruja* she was, Fern would have been able to follow even without a broom. "Why are you talking to my son?"

"I . . ." Abby's eyes blinked blue innocence.

Fern turned to Matty, trying and failing to keep her voice light. "Did you let her in the gate?"

He hunched forward, a pencil in his hand. "She said she knew you."

Fern's arms had been killing her — three paper bags from the grocery store and her purse — but the pain went away with the burst of adrenaline. "Well, honey, she doesn't."

"Oh, my god," said the woman. "You know who I am."

70

She would have known Scott's wife, Abby, if she'd boarded her bus wearing a burka. The eminently Google-able Abby Roberts née Crowley, the subject of way too many late-nights-with-red-wine image searches. She was even prettier in person. "Why are you here?"

Abby stepped backward and almost tripped over a broken hose.

"I was just . . ." Her voice trailed off, the way Matty's did when he didn't want to answer a question truthfully.

Sweet baby *Cristo.* Was this really happening to her today? She'd been looking forward to one thing — *one* thing — a hot bath. She was going to let Matty have pizza pockets for dinner after letting him get out of doing homework, because god knew they all needed a break. Tonight she needed to balance her bank account (like, *really* balance it, make sure no stray debit charges were going to sneak through before payday, which wasn't for another four days) and she needed to clean both bathrooms, and there were probably four more loads of laundry waiting for her even though she'd done laundry till eleven the night before. But screw all of it. She'd been planning on taking a bath, bringing with her a glass of wine and the latest copy of *People* magazine, which someone had left on the bus that afternoon (a regular perk of the job — fresh, read-only-once magazines). Maybe, if she felt really frisky after the bath, she would call Gregory and have phone sex. He was good at it, good at getting her off, listening to her use her vibrator while she laughed and kept her voice as low as possible in her bedroom.

But no.

Tonight was *this* now.

Her.

Scott's wife was still staring at her. A skinny *güera* ghost. She was pale, even paler than she was in her (unlocked) Facebook account. Thinner, too. Bony. There was a blue vein under her chin, and Fern could almost swear she could see it pulsing. Lord.

"Are you planning on passing out on me?"

"Pardon?"

Who said that in real life? Fern sighed, the bags heavy in her tired arms again. "Matty, take one of these, would you?"

Matty and Abby both stepped forward, each putting out a hand.

She gave Matty the lightest of the bags. She kept the other two. "Come on in. Let's do this." Fern felt something like tears form at the back of her tongue, and as she pushed her way inside her house with Scott's wife on her heels, she cleared her throat angrily.

"This way," she said, thankful that Elva drew the curtains at the first sign of afternoon sun. At least it was dark inside, and the woman wouldn't be able to see how many dust bunnies lurked under the TV and in the corners. It had to be three weeks since she'd had time to vacuum. Grandpa Wyatt wasn't in his easy chair, so that meant he was napping, thank god. She couldn't deal with Matty's grandfather right now. "Put that bag in the kitchen and then go to your room."

"But . . ." Matty had that look on his face, the one he still got sometimes when Fern changed the channel on something that was about to go too naked for an eleven-year-old. "What . . . ?"

"Your room. Go play Minecraft."

Matty jolted. "Without finishing my homework?"

"Now." It was her *Off my bus* voice and it worked on her son like it did crackheads. He went.

In the kitchen, Elva was stirring something at the stove. "Oh, there you are! I'm making lentil soup." She peered inside. "Or lentil curry. Or maybe chili."

Fern watched Abby's eyes widen as she took in the elderly woman still in her slippers. Elva was fully dressed, Fern knew that — she dressed every morning as if she were going out even if she wasn't. But in the afternoons, after her nap, she got chilly and she said the ancient blue terry-cloth robe warmed her legs and knees, something a sweater wouldn't do. So, yeah, Elva kind of looked like a homeless person shambling around Fern's kitchen, but that was Fern's business. Besides, very few homeless people had their hair set every Monday morning.

"I was going to give Matty pizza pockets tonight." Way-too-freaking-expensive but blessedly easy pizza pockets.

"Fan*tas*tic. I'll stick this in Tupperware." When Matty got pizza pockets, so did Elva and Grandpa Wyatt. It really was like having three kids. At least Matty's grandfather and his girlfriend didn't eat that much. And they paid her. That was nice. Fern wouldn't make the mortgage without their tiny rent checks. But she wished she knew a polite way to ask Elva to stop helping in the kitchen. A couple of years ago, when Fern hadn't been able to get much overtime, she'd tasked Elva with cooking on the cheap a few nights a week. It made her boarder feel good to be needed. Elva, though, took a bit too much liberty with the sale bin at the back of Safeway. Fern had pointed out, more than once, that there might be a very good reason that particular brand of oysters had been discounted to nineteen cents a can, but Elva adored making something brand-new. "Getting honey from wax," she called it. Sometimes Fern was pretty sure she'd rather eat the wax and leave the oyster-flavored honey alone.

Elva looked interestedly at Abby. "Hello. I'm Elva Schwartz. I'm a dancer." She didn't mention she hadn't been a dancer since the fifties. "And you are?"

Scott's wife put out her hand. "Abby Roberts."

"So nice to meet you. I'll put away the curry later, and let you two have some time together in here."

"Thanks," said Fern.

"You're welcome. You probably have quite a bit of" — Elva looked from one woman to the other — "catching up to do?"

Huh. Elva might be getting forgetful, but she was no dummy.

Fern sighed and heaved her purse onto the table next to the shopping bags. This morning she hadn't minded that the table-top was covered by mail and mostly empty boxes of cereal, but now the whole kitchen looked cluttered. The clock on the wall was an hour fast — she hadn't changed it since they fell back, months ago. Soon they'd spring forward and it would be on time again, and she wouldn't have to bother. She made a half hearted swipe at some crumbs with her hand. She hoped Abby just wouldn't see the dirt. It was dark in the room, after all — only two of the three overhead bulbs were working. She was going to buy some more, just as soon as there were a few dollars in the grocery budget, as soon as the bulbs were more important than pizza pockets and a single bottle of three-dollar wine. She pushed the hair back out of her face. She hadn't had time to dye the roots in more than a month, and she had at least a quarter inch of salt-and-pepper showing at her part. The cheap incandescent bulbs did her no favors.

Abby said, "Matty. He's lovely."

She didn't have the right to say that. "Mmm."

"I know this is weird."

"Weird? You think this might be *weird*?" Her voice was so sharp she reminded herself painfully of her mother, which wasn't normal or at all comfortable. Fern was known for being chipper, not strident. At work she was the funny one. Always cheerful. Well, fuck that right now. Fuck that right off. Fern put the bottle of sale wine on the

76

door of the refrigerator. The freezer might still be broken, but at least the wine would be cold. And no, she wasn't going to offer this woman any of it.

"So, Fernanda? Or Fern?"

Fern wanted to say *Ms. Reyes to you,* but she'd never liked her last name. For that matter, she wasn't that fond of her first. "Fern is fine."

Abby bit her bottom lip. "Fernanda is so pretty."

Was she criticizing Fern's choice of preferred name?

"Is it, um . . . Spanish?"

"Mexican," said Fern bluntly. Is that what she wanted to hear?

"Ah."

Fern could almost see the thought bubble over Abby's head as the woman wondered if she was illegal. She couldn't decide whether to laugh at the woman or cuss her out, so she just went with simple. "I was born here."

Abby flinched. "I didn't know anything about you until yesterday. Fernanda and Matias. That's all I knew. And your picture."

"My picture?"

"Of you and Scott getting married. And in the hospital. I found them yesterday. You looked . . ."

Fern thought her heart might pound right

out of her skin. She took a deep breath and tried to rid her mind of the image of pushing this woman bodily out of the kitchen and — preferably — into traffic. "Seriously, what the fuck is Scott trying to pull, sending you here?"

Abby looked over her shoulder. "Is Wyatt . . ."

"*Wyatt?* Is he what?"

"He's . . . alive?"

Fern laughed, even though humor was the last thing she was feeling in the tight band across her chest. "He told you he was dead, huh? That's rich. Of course he did. His father's fine. Probably napping in his room." *He chose us.* She wanted to say it. She wanted to say it *so* badly. "What else don't you know about us?"

"I don't know anything."

Fern weighed the words, balancing them against the woman's paleness, the way her fingers opened and closed on empty air. "You're serious."

Abby nodded.

"You know nothing."

Abby shook her head, still wordless.

"Did you know Scott and I bought this house together before we got married? Did you know he got me to put just my name on the deed because of his credit score? Did

78

you know I was stuck with it when he left? Did you know I'm still driving the piece-of-shit car I had just bought when we met? Did you know I've worked overtime every week since I can remember just to make the house payment, to keep a roof over his son's head, to keep peanut butter on his bread? I don't even know what my regular salary looks like on a check — it's been that long since I worked a forty-hour week."

"I — I don't even know what you do."

"Driver." Fern crossed her arms. Did she actually feel *shame* admitting her profession? Bullshit. "AC Transit."

"You're . . . a bus driver?" Scott's wife bit her lip.

Fern kept her arms crossed and squared her body to face her. Screw this woman and whatever she came here to find out. "What do you want from me?"

"I'm so sorry. I didn't mean to . . . I'm doing this all wrong. Can I help you put away the groceries?"

"No!" Fern surprised herself by following the question with a sharp laugh. Nerves. They were about to kill her.

Abby looked frightened, her light blue eyes so wide Fern could see the whites all the way around.

Fantastic.

Feeling a level of exhaustion so deep that her very bones wanted to lie down and sleep with or without the rest of her, Fern said, "Look. Can we skip the niceties and just get to the point?"

"The point? The point is . . ." Abby's eyes went to the ceiling as she bit her lip.

Fern leaned against the sink, willing Abby not to notice that it was dripping as usual.

Abby bit her lip harder, as if she wanted her teeth to go right through her bottom lip.

Fern really didn't feel like dealing with blood. "Okay." She used the softer voice she used on the ancient tweakers, the ones who didn't look like they'd make it through another night. "Let me guess. He's cheating on you. Possibly with someone you know. And you want advice."

Abby shook her head. Tears swam in the lower half of her eyes, threatening to spill but somehow staying in place, like clear mercury.

"He hit you?" He had never laid a hand on Fern — didn't seem the type — but who knew how he'd changed?

"No!"

"Spent all that money of yours." Whoops, that came out a little cold, but after all, if Scott had gone for Abby *because* of the money, he'd probably skate when the well ran dry.

Abby stepped forward and raised her hands as if ready to catch Fern if she fell forward. "He's dead."

The inside of Fern's head went fuzzy and dark. "Excuse me?"

"God, I'm so sorry to tell you this."

"Holy . . ." Fern couldn't find an expletive good enough. Big enough.

Dead.

Scott was *dead*?

She'd imagined Scott dead so many times. In the worst months, she'd lain in bed and put herself to sleep with cheery images of him strapped to railroad tracks, screaming for her to let him loose. She'd imagined his parachute not opening, his hot-air balloon burning up, his car crashing through a guardrail. She thought she'd be happy to hear the news. Thrilled, even. She thought she'd throw a party and invite everyone she'd ever complained about him to, and her small rooms would overflow with good friends congratulating her.

Instead, Fern burst into tears in front of Scott's goddamned skinny little wife.

CHAPTER TEN

Abby had no idea what to do.

If she were at home, she would have brought Fern a box of tissues. She would've opened a bottle of sparkling water and brought it to her with a straw. She would have moved her to the couch and put a pillow on her lap. Everyone needed a pillow to hold when they cried.

Instead, she was in the kitchen of a woman she'd never met — a woman she hadn't known existed until the night before — and though there was a six-pack of paper towels still in plastic sitting on the floor next to the refrigerator, she saw no tissue box in the clutter that rested on every flat surface.

Still, every house had cushions.

"Here." Without stopping to worry about whether what she was doing was wrong or right, she took Fern's hand and led her to a kitchen chair. "Sit for a minute." She placed Fern's hand on the top of the table, because if she let it go, it would just smack down into Fern's lap. Tears rolled from Fern's closed eyes, and she was making a terrible small noise, a tiny mewling.

Abby ripped open the plastic that encased the paper towels and tore off a sheet. "Take this."

Fern groped for it, her eyes barely opening.

"I'll be right back. Don't move."

Abby darted into the living room and grabbed a cushion at random from the sofa. Back in the kitchen, she thrust it into Fern's hands. She took a clean-looking glass from the dish drainer and filled it with tap water before setting it next to Fern's purse on the table. Then she paused, putting her hands on her knotted stomach. She wished she had a pillow, too.

Fern gave a sob that ended on a strangled intake of breath. She clutched the pillow. In a constricted voice, she said, "Fuck."

Abby sat in the chair next to Fern. She carefully looked forward. Sometimes the best thing you could do for someone was to look away.

Fern cried almost soundlessly for another minute. Maybe two. The only sounds were from outside: a radio blaring something in Spanish and a woman yelling something about how a kid better come in or else. The inside of the house, except for Fern's choked breath and a faucet's drip, was almost completely silent.

Abby sat next to her and waited.

When Fern stopped crying, she stopped abruptly. She gasped another half sob and then, to Abby's surprise, broke into what sounded like a laugh. "What an *asshole*." Fern glanced sideways at Abby, her face wet from the eyelids down. "Sorry. But, you know. I'm not sorry. What a totally shitty thing for him to go and do."

"I think so, too," said Abby, and it felt good to say even through the wave of guilt.

"How did he die?"

"Coronary. Massive."

"Where?"

"In the bathroom."

"Oh." Fern sat back, still hugging the pillow. It was brown, decorated with a yellow stitched giraffe. It looked hand embroidered.

"Did you make that?" Abby reached a finger forward to touch it.

"This? Are you crazy? No. Goodwill."

Abby wanted to run right out the door, hit the sidewalk running, and not slow down till she was back in her car and on 580 headed home. Scott's ex still had feelings

for him. Obviously. Why had Abby thought
this might be easy? That she could come
over and get a simple explanation, something like, *Married to him? Oh, that. It was
annulled; the baby was mine from someone
else. I'm sure he just didn't want to upset you
with something that was really nothing.*

Instead, Fern seemed demolished, the
eleven-year-old was definitely Scott's, and
Scott was just the biggest asshole that had
ever lived (or died) for keeping such a
devastating secret for so long.

"You said in the bathroom?"

Startled, Abby said, "Yeah."

"Taking a shit?"

"Would it help to know that?"

Fern closed her eyes as if she was thinking
for a minute about the correct answer.
"Yeah," she said slowly. "I think it might."

"He was done with whatever he'd been
doing in there. He was buckled up. Standing when he fell."

"Were you home?"

Abby nodded.

"Did you . . ." Fern's voice trailed off.

Abby had no idea what Fern's next words
might be. *Did you try to save him? Did you
run? Did you cheer? Did you cry?*

Did you love him?

But Fern didn't finish her sentence. She

just looked at Abby.

"I called 911. The dispatcher talked me through CPR."

"God."

"I'm not sure how much . . ."

Fern sat straighter. "Tell me all of it."

"I don't need to —"

"But I need to hear it," Fern interrupted. Her fingers dug into the giraffe's neck.

"We'd had a fight. No. A disagreement." About the end of their relationship. "I thought he'd thrown something. I thought he'd taken the heavy picture off the wall and thrown it to the floor." Later that night, she'd wondered why she'd ever thought that. When Scott got angry, he raised his voice, but she'd never felt physically threatened by him. Why she thought he would take down the huge framed photo of the Vernazza terrace, the photo she'd taken on their honeymoon and spent seven hundred dollars getting framed, she'd never know. It was what she'd heard.

But then she'd heard nothing else.

Fern stared. "You heard him fall —"

"No. Like I said, I thought he threw —"

"There's a difference between something falling and a body hitting the floor."

There was. Abby didn't want to know how Fern knew. "After a few minutes —"

"How many?"

Abby paused. An urge filled her, an urge she hadn't predicted. She wanted to tell this woman. "Three. Or maybe four."

"Wow."

"Yeah."

"So . . . you heard him hit the floor and didn't go to him for four minutes?"

"I was listening. The picture — I thought — maybe . . ."

Fern just looked at her. "I don't blame you."

Abby's throat was tight. "Maybe you should."

"I would have waited an hour."

The air left Abby's lungs in a rush. Was Fern kidding? Was she supposed to laugh? But Fern just made a go-on motion with her hands.

"I knocked on the door. He didn't answer. I didn't know what to do." She tightened hold of her fingers in her lap and wished Fern would pass her the pillow to hold. "I swear I didn't do it on purpose. I don't know why I waited. I thought —"

"I know." Fern's voice was soft. And then, as if she'd read Abby's mind, she passed over the cushion.

It was warm from Fern's lap. Abby dug her thumbs into it. "I pounded on the door.

I was terrified. I yelled through the door at him —" She cleared her throat. "I yelled that I was going to call the cops. The dispatcher asked me if I thought he was okay, and first I said yes. Then I realized I didn't know. I told her so, and she asked if I thought I could break down the door. I didn't think I could, but I had all this . . . fear, I guess. It only took one hit with my shoulder, and the door broke in." The corner of it had struck Scott in the leg with such a sick thud that she'd wondered at first if breaking down the door was what had knocked him down. Nothing had made sense to her. Nothing at all. The dispatcher's words, *Place the heel of your hand on his breastbone in the center of his chest, right between the nipples.* For a wild second of disbelief, while she knelt next to him, she'd thought the dispatcher had made a mistake. *No, it's my husband.* Only women had breasts with nipples, she'd thought, literally forgetting basic anatomy. Nothing had made sense.

"I did CPR for a long time. It felt like forever." They'd already e-mailed her the medical report for her insurance company. When she'd read the terrible words, it showed she'd been on the phone with the dispatcher for just six minutes total. A couple of those had probably been spent not understanding what the dispatcher was saying, another one spent breaking down the door and rolling him from his side onto his back. "I heard his ribs crack. She told me that meant I was doing it right, but it was — there was air going in and out of his lungs, I could hear it, but — god. I should stop. This is terrible."

Fern's eyes were twin blackened marks of heat. "No. Go on."

"His lungs wheezed. No, that's not it. His lungs sounded wet, like something old and damp peeling apart. The operator kept telling me that was what was supposed to happen, that I was keeping the oxygen moving around in his blood, but I *knew* it wasn't helping. Maybe that's just what they say — maybe it helps some people to hear that. . . ."

Fern nodded.

"But I knew it was a lie. I wanted her to tell me that I should stop. That he was beyond help. That I was just making it worse."

"You weren't, though. You were doing everything you could."

"No. I was doing everything I could to guarantee that I'd have nightmares every night since."

"Then what?" Fern seemed impatient now, the tears almost dry on her cheeks.

"The ambulance came. They took over. They used their defibrillator. Shocked him." The real shock had been hers. If they'd been able to hook him up the way her own heart had pounded in her chest, they could have brought him back. Instead, they'd pushed her out of the way, two of the men barking questions at her that she couldn't seem to follow. *When did you last see him, what are his medical conditions, does he have an advance directive?* She'd stood in the hallway, and somehow, even though she knew he was dead, she was surprised when they'd stopped pumping. They'd peeled the sticky paddles off Scott's chest gently. (Why gently? Why didn't they just rip them off? Scott was gone. Everyone there knew he was gone by then.) They'd put away their gear, and then one of them, a very young man with not even one single crease on his face, not even a laugh line, sat her down on the couch in the living room and asked her if they could call anyone for her. She'd given them Kathryn's phone number, and she'd sat in numb silence. Pre-grief. Pre-everything.

Now she said to Fern, "It was my fault."

"Bull." Fern rubbed the back of her neck

90

as if it ached. "You can't tell yourself that. It's not true. When I was with him, he had blood pressure that was sky-high, and he was practically a kid then. Did he ever get that treated?"

Of course he hadn't. All the blood pressure medicine the doctor threatened him with would have jeopardized his ability to function sexually. Abby had — ridiculously — taken this as a strange kind of compliment. Her husband wanted to make love to her so badly that he'd risk his health.

I asked him for a divorce. She wanted to say it, wanted to see the look that would cross Fern's face.

"God. It's been so long. . . . I don't remember what he wanted. Burial?"

"Memorial service. Then cremation." The words didn't apply to Scott. They couldn't. "Sunday."

"*This* Sunday?"

"Oh, damn." Abby had no idea how bus drivers' schedules worked. Of course they drove on weekends, too. "It's . . . maybe we can —"

"I'm off." Fern wiped her face with both hands. "I work tomorrow and Saturday, but I'm off on Sunday. Oh, god, I have to tell his father. And . . . Matty. My poor Matty." Her voice broke on the last word.

91

Scott's father. This was worse, so much worse than she'd thought it could possibly be. If she'd known what it would feel like to be in this small, dark house with the people Scott had once loved, would she still have come? "Let me know if I can help. With anything."

Fern stared at her as if she'd just appeared in the kitchen. "Do people keep saying that to you?"

"Yes."

"Does it help?"

"No."

Fern tore out a piece of paper from a battered notebook she pulled out from under a pile of place mats. "Here." She wrote something. "My e-mail. Send me the time and place. I'll try . . . I'll see if we can be there. Can you please . . ."

"Yeah." Abby knew how the sentence ended. It was fine. She couldn't breathe in this small kitchen, which was literally the size of her pantry at home. She felt like the asshole Fern obviously saw her as. A sob was crawling up her esophagus, but she managed to say, "I'll go."

There was gratefulness tangled with something else — anger? grief? — in Fern's gaze. "E-mail me."

"Yes."

Abby left. The old woman, Elva, silently raised the remote at her as she made her way through the living room and out the front door. There was no sign of Matty or his grandfather. The front door opened with a creak and closed with a snap that Abby felt somewhere near the bottom of her soul.

CHAPTER ELEVEN

Fern predicted the stop request and was already pulling over at Fortieth when the ding ran through the line, singing up from the back along the wire. The sound went into her seat and up her spine. It was her song, her jam, her holy bell, the one she heard ring in her sleep. She pulled her coach over smoothly, just another wide ripple in traffic.

But the guy in the back row yanked it again. And then again. "Hey!" he yelled. "I gotta get off!"

Why did so many people not believe that she was going to pull over when they rang the bell? A good twenty percent of people yelled at her to stop, even after they'd pulled the request, even after she was actively pulling to the curb. That was about nineteen percent too many.

But she called, "You got it, pal!" That was her shtick. She was the nice one. You couldn't piss off Fern. Even when she had to physically put hands on people, "encouraging" them off the bus, she could make them think she was being polite. *No. Hell, no. Put that away — grab your pipe and go. You have to get off my bus, but you have a nice day, now, okay? Gorgeous day out there.* Some people, the ones who boarded wasted, the ones furious with their lives in general and her in specific, would call her names — *"pendeja fea,"* "you fuckin' fat cow," "stupid cunt" — but it wasn't like that was anything new. Some tried to fake-swing at her occasionally, but the guys riding her line were usually too tired to swing at her for real.

"Hey!" the man in the back yelled again as her front right tire kissed the curb with a whisper.

"No problem, my friend," she said in a loud voice over her shoulder as he disembarked at the middle doors. "You have a nice day, now."

Four more stops till she picked up Matty from the skate park. Fern smiled at the older woman who climbed on board with her even more ancient mother. "Afternoon," she said. "Good to see you again." Sixteen more stops before she finished driving for the day and told Matty his father — his shit-tastic, absent father — was dead.

Back on the road, she dodged a silver kamikaze Honda while keeping her eyes on a guy in the fourth row who seemed like he was about twenty years too old to try to be hitting on the girl behind him who couldn't have been more than thirteen. At the next stop, a bicyclist loaded his bike, obviously for the first time. He pulled down the front bar awkwardly and struggled to get his wheels in line. Three more stops.

Patience was just counting. Up or down, it didn't matter. You were going to something or away from something else. She'd been counting routes till she got this one, the one she needed, the one that ran in front of Matty's middle school, right in time for him to start. Grade school had been fine — they'd lived so close that she'd trusted him to walk the four doors home and then text her as he spread peanut butter on saltines — but his middle school was too far from home, too many blocks across an urban wasteland where bullets flew too fast and too often for her to let Matty walk home alone. It had taken years to work this out, years of counting trades and tallying favors for other drivers, getting to the point where she could hold this route. It was hers now. *Hers.* Now she picked him up every school day she drove.

There was more math to be done, and soon, but it wasn't the kind of counting she could do while driving. She'd need to pick up more overtime to make up for the lost fifteen hundred a month in child support. And since the winter hiring, when they'd finally trained enough drivers for the first time since she'd worked for the agency, overtime was in short supply.

She could do it, though. She could make it work. Worst case, she could double-bunk with Matty and rent out her own room to another boarder. No, that wasn't fair to Matty. She could sleep on the couch.

Her bell's ding brought her out of imagining the slimness of her bank account and back into the driver's seat. Later. She could figure that part out later.

Three stops left, the same number of Canadian dimes that had gone into the fare box today. Then two stops left. Fern made herself unclench her grip on the wheel. That was the way Shirley Broadmore had gotten her carpal tunnel. No one was going to take care of her if she didn't, and if she couldn't drive, who would take care of Matty? Relaxed fingers were key. Her epilepsy was under control. She always took her meds. Her hands were strong. She could be more physically active, but her blood work always came back great. There was nothing that could take this job away from her. Fern breathed as deeply as she could, given that the man in the first row hadn't taken a bath in a year that began with the number two.

The smell didn't matter. The closer she got to Matty every day, the lighter her heart got. It was that simple. It didn't matter if she had a load of loud, swearing teenagers, the kind that littered as she drove, trailing bits of candy wrappers and soda cups out the cracked windows like they were leaving a line of bread crumbs behind them to find their way home. It didn't matter if, like today, the only person at the penultimate stop before Matty's was a thirty-something guy, jittery and jumpy, obviously strung out, the kind of guy who was going to argue with her about how much he should have to pay.

And of course he did. "Fifty percent?" he said.

She shook her head. "Sorry, buddy."

"A dollar?"

Oh, that was good. He was going down, not up. The fare was $2.10. It had been for years. "Sorry, friend. Two ten it is."

"But I got a dollar."

Fern drew her sigh back into her chest. This was the problem with bending the rules sometimes. The information spread.

You let an old lady get on board for a dollar once, and everyone in five miles knew about it. Ralph, he never had these problems. He'd been driving for AC Transit for longer than God had been making light, and he never let a single person skip fare, not once. Most drivers didn't worry about that stupid extra dime. Who had two dollars *and* a dime? People stuck two dollars in the machine and then moved along, giving Fern that look, the one that made her feel the pain they obviously had in their feet, in their backs, in their necks. She let them slide. It wasn't fair, anyway, that the Clipper card gave that ten-cent discount to people rich enough to have computers at home, people who had enough money to *have* a bank account that issued them a debit card and direct withdrawal. *They* didn't need those two-dollar rides, not like her regulars, who could use the slim weight of those dimes resting at the bottom of their threadbare, repaired pockets.

"A dollar?"

He was a repeater. If she let him on board, that was probably all he would say. A dollar, a dollar, a dollar. She was going to stick with no. This time, she would hold out. She would respond in the negative and mean it.

Then she looked in his eyes. Most people

met her eyes, if they did so at all, with just a flicker. Just a half second of connection. That's all anyone had time for, not including little kids and the seriously ancient ones.

Fern met the guy's eyes, and they were empty. Under his wrecked, ruined skin, above the slit of a mouth that wobbled, his gaze held hers, and the awful thing was that there was nothing in it. No one should be able to hold a look that long without communicating something — anything — and this man had nothing left to give. Probably hadn't for years and years.

"All right, buddy. Come on." He didn't give her a dollar, and she didn't ask him to.

Matty was the next stop. That was all that mattered. Then she was there, the door opened, and the jittery no-dollar man swung himself off, jangling down the sidewalk.

Fern scanned the flock of kids waiting to board. Three boys, two with skateboards, and one girl dressed in black, carrying a longboard. Matty was behind them. She could tell he was trying to fit in, to eavesdrop. He wanted to be a skater — it just wasn't ideal that he fell off his thirdhand skateboard more times than he stayed on it. He wanted to listen to them, to think of something cool to say — she could see it in the way he kept his shoulders high and tense. The kids paid no attention to him. They climbed on board the coach without glancing over their shoulders once at her boy.

Matty swung himself into the seat that Fern always kept for him by putting her coat over it. Funny, how there was obviously no one *sitting* in the seat. It wasn't like a passenger had nipped to the bathroom or something. This wasn't like a café, where someone might lay claim to a chair by leaving a sweater on it, by putting her sunglasses on the table. If a seat on a bus was empty, for sure there was no one coming back to claim it. But when Fern put her coat on the seat, no one ever touched it. Over the last two years she'd been picking up Matty on her route, only one elderly man had pointed out that someone had left a jacket behind, and in thanks, she'd given him a coupon for three free rides that she was supposed to save for people who gave up their seats.

The rumble of the bus ran up her legs to her seat. She glanced over her right shoulder. Matty held his skateboard on his lap, absentmindedly spinning a wheel with his thumb.

"Pizza when I finish my shift?"

He frowned. For about a month at the beginning of middle school, when every-

101

thing had changed, he hadn't wanted her to speak to him at all when he got on the bus. *You can't,* he said. *You're the bus driver. The* other *bus drivers don't drive their kids around.*

The other drivers weren't as lucky as she was, that's what Fern always told him. *What other job,* she'd ask Matty, *would let me hang out with my best kid for the last hour or two of my shift every day?*

I'm your only kid, he'd say back.

Best kid, she'd repeat.

Free day care. That's what Fern never told him.

Once, Matty had admitted he didn't actually totally hate riding her bus. She hadn't planned on eavesdropping, but she'd been putting towels away in the hall closet and she'd eavesdropped on what her son and his friends were talking about while they played Minecraft. "Your mom seriously drives a bus?" River had said scornfully. That was rich. Even though River was white as a Safeway receipt, even though his family lived on the north side of 580, River's mom, Heather, was a night waitress at a diner that got regularly raided for having a cardroom in the back.

"Yeah," said Matty.

"You *have* to ride her bus home from school?"

Fern's heart had lodged uncomfortably right underneath her tonsils.

"Yeah. It's cool, though."

"Yeah?" River hadn't sounded convinced.

"I get to see her fight with people."

"Whoa. Like with weapons?"

"Nah." Matty had paused for effect. "Not that often. Only sometimes."

"What kind?"

"A guy had a knife once." Matty had made a squeak then, as something went wrong in the game. "And once maybe a gun."

"You saw her use a gun?"

"No. She told me, though. She didn't use it, though. The guy had one."

"A real one?"

Fern, even though she couldn't see into his room from the hallway, could almost see his small shoulders lift and fall. "She told him to get the eff off her bus. That's all." Hearing that had made Fern feel like she'd won something huge. Something better than the lottery, maybe.

A bike darted in front of her left wheel. She swerved and gave a long blare of the horn, making sure the bicyclist would live another day.

"Hey, kiddo. You didn't answer. Only twelve stops left. Wanna get pizza with me?"

So I can break your perfect hopeful heart.

While keeping her eyes on the road and her left hand on the wheel, she stuck her right fist out behind her.

"Okay." Matty leaned forward and fist-bumped her. He'd picked it up from Fern's brother, Diego, and on these streets, it was as good as a kiss. Matty, her baby boy who wasn't a baby anymore. He was eleven, and someday he'd be a man, and he'd want to go by "Matias" instead of "darling Matty" or *"mijo,"* and then he probably wouldn't let her kiss him good night, but Fern had this idea that she'd sneak up into his house on a ladder like the mother did in *I'll Love You Forever* and kiss him good night. Grown-up Matias would never know she'd been there, but maybe he'd sleep better because she had been.

But all she had right now was this minute, and that's just about all she had, so with her boy tucked safely in his corner seat, Fern made her coach dance.

CHAPTER TWELVE

The first time, Abby had been fourteen weeks along.

Fourteen weeks was long enough to have had the colors for the nursery picked out (a yellow that reminded her of thinned sunshine, as if they'd put it in the can and mixed it with unclouded well water and then added the warmth of a light blanket).

Fourteen weeks was long enough to have a short list of names. Hannah, Timothy, Mabel — old names, and all of them probably too trendy, but she couldn't help it — they were sweet and warm and round, exactly the way she felt about the sweet, warm, round thing she was growing. She was better than a plant. She was stronger than a tree. She was growing a *human.* Someone had cast a magical spell on her, liquid and preternatural. At night, lying next to Scott, she felt sorry for him, and that made her generous. She would share as much as she could of this with him. He would never know what it was like to feel like a mystical being. While he slept, she pressed the low bulge of her stomach against his back, trying to share the glorious warmth of her skin, the strength of her bones.

After all, the miracle had all started right there, in that bed. The embryo had begun to grow inside her one night, as she slept. Her body had made it happen, and she hadn't had to think about it. Abby — who had to make notes on her calendar to remind herself to change the filter in the water jug and when to fertilize the tomatoes — hadn't had to think about making a *person.*

It had ended there, too. She'd felt a cramp in her sleep, and had twisted once. Then twice. Three times, she'd stretched her legs out straight in the bed, pushing her toes against the top sheet. Cramps. She'd have to get up and take an Aleve, or she'd be miserable for the rest of the day.

It wasn't until she tried to stretch out the pain a fourth time that she remembered, still wrapped in slumber, that she wasn't getting her period — she was pregnant.

During any earthquake, big or small, Abby had always found herself in a doorway so fast she couldn't remember getting there, couldn't remember making the conscious decision to move. It was like that then, the first tremor of her body's betrayal. She was in the bathroom before she knew she was moving, before she'd even totally worked through what might be happening.

"No, no, no, no." If she said it enough, it would be true. "No, no, no, no, no." If she'd imagined a miscarriage (which she carefully hadn't, not once letting it slide through her hopeful mind, not even reading that section of her pregnancy book), it would have been bloodier than this. It would have been a hemorrhage, a red war, a sea of blood that would rush through her bathroom, carrying her out of the house and straight to hell.

Not this. There was just a streak of blood on her panties. Not enough to terrify her. Definitely not enough. Thank god. The pain was low and dull. She wiped, the blood bright on the tissue, and left the bathroom to get the book. She took it back into the bathroom and sat on the toilet again to read. She didn't have to pee, just felt that solid ache, but she wanted her legs bare, parted, open. She wanted to be able to reach down to feel, to push it all back inside, if she needed to.

It had stopped, though. The tissue was clean.

She sat, and found the sentences she needed. "Spotting is normal — as many as one in five mothers-to-be experience it in their first trimester." She clung to the words, memorizing them.

Then the cramp twisted, moving to pain. Real, actual pain. Pain that would have required more than Aleve to fix, if she'd been willing to actually admit that it was happening. *NO* wasn't a strong enough word, but as flimsy as it was, it was all she had. It was a shout in her head, but only a whisper in her mouth, and it slid sideways, *ohhnn-ohhnn-ohhnn,* the beginning of the word bleeding into the end of it as the blood trickled again, this time increasing to a rush that nothing could have stemmed.

And even though Scott said she would be okay, even though the nurse who'd checked her in had said she'd be just fine (she'd been such a *pretty* liar with eyes the color of blue borage), Abby had known.

Scott held her hand. He'd looked upset. So sad. And no matter how sad he'd looked or felt or said he was, it wouldn't have been enough to match her grief.

Abby hadn't been strong enough to hold all that life inside her.

Abby, who could unroll chicken wire without wearing gloves, who could carry two large bags of Black Gold potting mix at once, who had always had small biceps curled under her skin, wasn't strong enough.

She'd always thought Meg, the lost sister who'd lived only one day, was a bit of an exaggeration. Her mother cried every time she thought about the (nonexistent) baby. They celebrated her birthday every year with as many strawberry cupcakes as she would have been turning in age. As a child, Abby had always thought if they *had* to celebrate an intangible birthday, they should have at least done it with chocolate cupcakes. She didn't like strawberry. She never had.

But then, with her first miscarriage, still twenty-six weeks shy of how long her mother had carried Meg, she understood. How had her mother ever stood up again?

And even though she'd gone home that night (that *night,* they hadn't even kept her overnight to see if Abby would live, which, obviously, she probably wouldn't), even though she still had sensation in her limbs and familiar air in her lungs, there was a part of her that had never gotten up off that bloody soil. She'd felt the shot to her gut, she'd lain down in the battlefield, she'd closed her eyes, and she'd died. Then she'd had to leave that part of her behind, harder

than petrified wood, useless even for com-
posting.

CHAPTER THIRTEEN

Matty should have been more suspicious.

When Zingo, their old Siamese, needed to be put down, Fern had brought Matty to Itza Pizza to tell him. When his first-grade best friend, Hawk, was moving to Chicago, she'd brought them here on their last play-date. Not pizza pockets on sale, not frozen pizza from Target's sale section, not even takeout. The real stuff, eaten in the parlor. Soon her poor kid would equate pizza with pain. *Dios.*

She should have thought about it harder. Next time she had something bad to tell him, she'd take him to the dentist. At least that kind of association would make sense.

"You want quarters for the video games?" If they were really smart about their business, they'd put in both an ATM and a coin changer. They had neither, and Fern knew that the person at the counter never had enough quarters in her till, either. You had to remember to bring them in with you, and what about the parents who didn't know that? They had the *cool* games here, the old-fashioned ones, the ones she'd grown up with — Frogger and Battlezone and Tron — the ones that made a holy racket of blips and beeps that you thought would drive you out of your mind until you realized that they'd been pinging behind you for a half hour and you hadn't heard a thing. Their noise was awful and soothing at the same time. Exactly like the noise of an eleven-year-old boy.

Matty took the quarters and raced off. He didn't ask her to play with him like he did with Diego. Fern ordered the pizza and took a picnic table in a corner. It was deserted this afternoon, just them and another mother with two children that she was keeping close to her side. Maybe that woman was sharing bad news, too. Maybe those children's grandfather had just died in his sleep. Maybe the woman lost her job and this was their last pizza until she graduated night school and got a better job. Oh, god, maybe her oldest had been killed by a stray bullet — but as Fern watched, the woman put her head back and laughed, twisting in her seat and rubbing her very pregnant belly. No, that woman wasn't telling bad news — she was hoarding all the good news in the room. Maybe on this side of town.

That was okay.

Fern could do this.

She could probably do this.

The stuffed Roadkill came, with its five different kinds of cured meat. Even though it gave Fern heartburn, she got it because the name made Matty laugh. He sat across from her, saying something about a new board someone had had at the park. She should be listening to him — she should be completely engrossed in whatever it was he was saying about Raul's new wheels, Santa Cruz somethings.

"Yeah?" she said. Fern didn't know crap about skateboard wheels. She put another slice of pizza on his plate. Inside her mind, she practiced the words she would say in her head, slipping them like abacus beads across a string, counting them, one by one.

"You're not listening to me," accused Matty.

Fern jumped. "I *totally* am."

"Tell me what I just said."

Quickly, she rewound what she'd just heard. Something he wanted her to buy for him. "You need a new pair of . . . shorts."

"Nice try," he said.

"Gym socks."

"Nope."

"Jockstrap?"

Rewardingly, Matty fell sideways laughing. A jockstrap was always, always funny to him, along with farts and diarrhea and wet burps.

"Hey, *mijo.*"

In response, Matty straightened and took a bite of pizza. Around his mouthful, he said, "Yeah?"

She chickened out at the last second, swerving hard. "Mrs. Hutch wants to see me."

He hunched his shoulders. "I hate her."

"It's just life science."

"It's *stupid.* And she's mean. She hates me, too."

"You don't know what it's about? What she wants?"

A shrug. He didn't meet her eyes. "Maybe she's talking to all the parents."

That's not what the e-mail had implied. *Matias might need help more specialized than we have discussed in the past.* Fern hadn't been able to help the knee-jerk thought: *Bullshit.*

But then again, that's not why they were having pizza. It was so much worse than a difficult teacher who didn't like kids to talk in any voice above a whisper.

"Okay. Anyway. Your dad . . ." Oh, god. She'd meant to be strong about it. *Your father died. Let's talk about what that means.*

Matty's jaw slowed. "Huh? Is he coming *back?*"

As if Scott were Jesus or Santa Claus or some other perfect and completely mythical white guy.

"Sorry," Fern said. "No. It's just really hard to say. Your father died."

Matty swallowed his bite of pizza, his small Adam's apple working hard, as if it had the whole job of pushing the food downward. Then, instead of asking anything, he took another large, deliberate bite.

"It was a heart attack. It was no one's fault." Of course that wasn't true. It was Scott's fault for not eating right and keeping his arteries clear. It was Abby's fault for not making him exercise with her. It was Grandpa Wyatt's fault for giving him faulty genes. Something. There had to be a reason. "It happened four days ago."

Matty swallowed. Then he took another bite.

Fern accepted this. "I'm feeling really sad about this. Your dad and I split up, but he gave me the best gift I've ever gotten."

Matty blinked and then frowned as if confused.

"You. He gave me you."

Matty chewed harder. Behind him, a video game sounded like it was going to come to life and hop across the crooked wooden floor, shooting lasers at them. The two children with the pregnant mother laughed and laughed.

This was so much more difficult than she'd thought it would be.

"You can ask me anything. Anything at all."

Instead, Matty took yet another bite, as if eating were a new video game fight combo and he was going to get it right. He choked for a brief second, and Fern's whole body froze — Heimlich. Did she remember it? Sheer, naked terror flooded her limbs and she couldn't remember how to breathe. Then he coughed a little and cleared his throat and the world came back to her. The picnic-table top was rough under her fingertips, and she pressed harder, hoping for a splinter. Something to feel, something immediate.

A thin muscle jumped in Matty's jaw, the echo of his father's. Scott got that jump in his cheek when he was upset, just like that.

Then his eyes filled with tears.

"Oh, baby . . ." Fern didn't get up. She didn't move around the table to hold him.

That would have made it worse. Something in her son's watery eyes told her that.

He leaned forward and spit out the mouthful that had defeated him. "Why?"

"A heart attack." She'd tell him as many times as it took him to understand, even though every time she thought the words, her chest pulled with the tightness of the irony surrounding the circumstances. A heart attack. That implied Scott *had* a heart, and if Fern had come to doubt anything about her ex, it was that. "You know how my car used to stall sometimes before I got it fixed?"

Matty nodded.

"A heart attack is like that. The engine just stalls." She paused. Matty's jaw still worked even though his mouth was empty now. His face was so thin. Was that new? Was that to go along with his growth spurt?

"They can jump-start a heart," he said finally. "Like a car. With jumper cables. They showed us in health. There's one in the cafeteria. It's a blue box and once Simone pulled it out and an alarm went off and she got in trouble."

Fern imagined the stocky metal clips attached to Scott's heart, red and black leads clipped to a Honda battery. "You're right. A defibrillator."

"They didn't have one?"

"They did. They put the thingies on his chest and they gave him a jump start, just like Mr. Hayes used to do to the car. But you remember that morning it didn't work even with his cables? That morning we had to call a cab to get you to school on time?" She remembered that morning, the panicked wings beating in her lungs, Matty's small worried face, the phone call to Friendly Cab, the searching for her emergency twenty-dollar bill that she *knew* she'd stashed somewhere once, after a strangely flush payday. After ripping apart her address book and her calendar, she'd found it behind the small stack of business cards she'd been collecting from speakers in her night business classes.

"Does Grandpa know?"

That had been bad last night. Fern had woken him from his nap. He'd laughed at first. *Thought you were coming to tell me I was late for work!* The man hadn't been behind the wheel of a tow truck in seven years.

Scott died.

Wyatt had sat on the edge of his small bed, already in his pajamas even though it was barely eight at night, his hands on his lap, palms up. He'd looked over Fern's

118

shoulder, his gaze blank.

I thought he'd come around. I really did. I thought he'd come around. Tears had dripped down the old man's face as if the loss was new.

Fern bit the end of her straw and tasted plastic. She spoke around it. "I told Grandpa last night."

"You didn't tell *me* last night."

"That's because you were harder to tell."

"Why?"

Because Grandpa gave up hope a long time ago. You lived in it. "Because."

"Is there . . ." Matty pushed away his plate, his second slice uneaten.

"Yeah?"

"Is there gonna be a funeral?"

Fern bit the inside of her lip. "A memorial, yes."

"Are they going to put him in the ground?"

She took a breath to try to slow her racing heart. It didn't work. "Cremation."

He scowled and picked up a fork. He poked at the crust, then stabbed it. "When?"

"Day after tomorrow. Sunday."

"*Sunday?* Can we go?"

"Do you want to?"

"No."

"Okay."

"Wait. Maybe."

"It's okay not to know what you want to do. Grandpa is going. You and I can decide later. We can stop at the store to get some clothes, if you want." She meant the thrift store. She meant funeral-appropriate clothes.

Matty was still catching up. "He'll *burn*?"

Fern wanted to reach out and stroke his hair, but she knew he would just bat away her hand. "When you think about it, it's kind of the same as being buried. It's just your atoms rearranging. . . ." The church used to think you shouldn't be cremated, but Vatican II said it was okay, like God suddenly figured out how to pull the dust back together in the atomic age. God got smarter as man did, apparently. What a crock. Matty was eleven. He shouldn't have to think about this. Ever. He was bad at science already. He shouldn't have to —

"No, that part is okay. Would we get to watch?"

Fern stared. "What?"

"Burying people is disgusting. Maggots and worms and stuff. And stinky. Like when we found that possum under the house. Cremation is just like . . ." He held the blackened end of his crust in front of his eyes. "At school, Asman was talking about

120

it. For his uncle. He thought it was cool."

Fern wanted to parrot the last word incredulously but stopped herself just short of uttering it. He was eleven. He didn't know his father, didn't know that the shape of Scott's wrists was identical to his bony ones, and after he burned, the comparison would be impossible. Forever. She'd bet As- man Singh had made cremation sound macabre and amazing — that kid could talk the rest of them into doing or wanting anything. He was the reason Matty had wanted a skateboard, come to think of it.

Matty started to say something else, then stopped.

She waited.

"I just . . ."

Fern felt fear spike at the back of her head, right where a headache was starting.

Matty's voice was tiny. "I just thought I'd get to . . . that he would come back for —"

Back for me.

"I know, baby."

"*I* would have." He started to say some- thing else, but the noise stuck in his throat like the pizza had.

Fern's breath juddered. "You are nothing like him." Except for those wristbones.

"Grandpa says I look like him. Sometimes he says I act like him, too, but that's usually when he's mad at me."

Last spring, Fern couldn't completely get the toxic green abandoned-vehicle sticker off the front of her car window (it had *not* been abandoned — she'd just left it in the same spot for three days and it wasn't like she had time to wash the old beater). She'd been chipping and peeling at that sticker for almost a year now. The cheap paper stuck forever and ever. It would go to the junk-yard with traces of it left on the glass. But Scott could erase a whole family from his life without ever getting in trouble for it. He hadn't even told his new wife he had a *kid.* He'd sent them money, which was *not* being a father. (God, the money. She should have gotten a smaller pizza.)

"Trust me, Matty. You're not like him."

Deep down inside, Fern had known Scott would someday get his comeuppance. She'd yearned for it in a way that wasn't right — anything that hurt him might end up hurting Matty somehow, so she was wrong for wanting it. But she imagined it sometimes. How he'd come to the door and Fern would slam it in his face. She could almost hear his voice sobbing on the other side of the wood. Or later, years down the road: he would want to be near his son, and Matty wouldn't meet him. He'd be denied. He would hear he had a grandchild, maybe, and wouldn't be allowed to meet her.

But no. Scott had gotten away with it. He'd gotten away with all of it. She picked a flake of red chili off her plate and put it in her mouth. She bit it in half, and let the heat spread over her tongue.

Matty's gaze turned suspicious, his chin angling southward. "Is this about that lady who came over last night?"

"Abby. Yeah. It is."

Matty nodded and stabbed his pizza again — it was oozing bloody tomato sauce all over his plate. Then his hand stilled. He looked up. "She *said* she knew you." His voice was fractious, like he was a feverish toddler.

"She's your dad's wife." Was. Damn it, Fern should have said *was*.

"Oh."

So much in that one word. Fern's heart, already small and weak, shriveled even more inside her chest. "Did you like her?"

He shrugged. His default move.

"She thought you were nice." *Lovely* had been her word. Fern had to admit, it was a good word for her boy. He was lovely.

Matty frowned, but his pizza jabbing slowed.

Fern waited.

More jabbing. He sprinkled chili flakes from the shaker on top of the perforated pizza crust and then used a tine to shove them more deeply into the bread.

"I don't get it."

"She . . . she loved your dad."

"So what does that mean to me?"

"Nothing." Why had she told him that? Scott couldn't even manage to love his only child. "It doesn't mean anything, *mi pollito.*"

Matty groaned and leaned backward. "I *hate* it when you call me that. I've *told* you that a *million* times."

"Sorry. *Hijo* —"

"I don't want to talk."

She swallowed the words she wanted to say, all of them, one by one. "Okay. Eat some more."

Another stab of his fork. "Mom?"

"Yeah." She swallowed the endearments, all of them, that rose in the back of her throat.

"I'm pretty mad at him."

"Me, too. Matty —"

"Can I have some more quarters?"

"Honey, we should . . ."

"God." Matty threw himself over the bench to standing. "If I knew we were coming here just to *talk* and *talk,* I would have said I didn't want pizza. I still have a dollar

anyway. I don't *need* any more quarters."
He stomped away, dragging his heels on the
wood like he did at home.

Fern felt the happy-looking woman looking at her. At her son who yelled, at her
table now empty of anyone else. She
wrapped her hands around the pint glass of
root beer she'd ordered because it sounded
like fun when Matty had said he wanted
one. It was still half-full, now warm and flat.
It was sickly sweet, too sweet for an adult to
tolerate.

Kind of like that Abby, with her pillow
pressing, her big eyes, her damned concern.
Lovely.

Fern tipped the glass, slowly. The edge of
the liquid slid toward the lip. She let a little
fall onto the picnic table. It ran through the
crack and dripped to the already sticky floor.

There.

She'd poured one out for Scott.

That's all he would get from her. He
deserved no more.

CHAPTER FOURTEEN

Abby was being handled. If she hadn't been so aware of it, she might have welcomed it more. But from the woman at the front desk who greeted her with a soft handshake and an even softer gaze, to Isaac, the "memorialist" in charge of the service, everyone was ushering her around like she was in danger of bolting.

She wasn't.

She *might* have run, another day. Two weeks ago? She would have bolted like her intransigent arugula had last month, shooting up spikes of green and white flowers faster than stars streaked across the night sky.

But today, her skeleton had been replaced by wood. Teak, probably, strong and fast-growing. The wood was twisting under her skin, moving through her veins, replacing the calcium in her bones. It would take more than a lightning strike to weaken her.

"Here you go," said the woman named Perla. Her voice was ready to empathize. "There's a box of tissues here, under the registry. And there's a box at the end of each row of chairs."

Now that they'd been pointed out to her, Abby couldn't see anything but the ubiquitous pale blue boxes. They jumped into her vision like bunting at weddings, gaudy and ready to do their job.

She'd cried for days, on and off. At first, she thought she'd swallowed the sea. She would never run out of water, out of salt. But since her drive to Oakland on Thursday, since meeting Scott's son and his son's mother, she'd run totally dry. Even when she tried to make herself cry, she hadn't been able to conjure up so much as a sniffle. It was numbness, she knew that. There would be more tears where they'd come from. That's what Kathryn had said, "Normal. Sometimes we don't feel things all the way through till we grow smack into 'em. Like a tree root, you know? It doesn't hurt the plumbing till it tears out a pipe."

Normal.

Abby knew one thing: normal was *not* a room like this. Dark wooden chairs lined perfectly along a deep maroon, plush carpet. The vacuum lines were so straight at first

Abby had thought they were a pattern on the carpet. Who pushed the vacuum that carefully? A young man, she imagined, some stoner kid who couldn't find a better job than cleaning a funeral home at night. Did he take pride in his straight lines? Or were they something he had to do so he didn't get fired? Did he listen to heavy metal on his iPhone as he worked? Did he have to clean the back rooms, too? Were spilled fluids his responsibility?

What about the burning machine? (Abby had Googled it: it was called a cremulator, which made it sound like something to be used while baking. *Use the stand mixer to beat the dough, then use the cremulator until desired texture is reached.*) Whose responsibility was getting all the ash out of it and into the boxes or urns? What if they didn't get it all? Was that even policed? Abby felt a burst of nerves — oh! decidedly not numb — in the pit of her stomach. At least with burying bodies, like she'd done with her parents, there was a comfortable level of deniability as to what was going to happen to the people. They were made to look pretty. They were put in a solid box that would take a long time to degrade. No one had to imagine what they would go through when you turned and walked away.

Burning, though.

Scott would be gone, physically, within a couple of hours, according to the tasteful pamphlet Isaac had given her when he'd run her credit card. It would take two to four hours. Nothing left but smoke and ash. She didn't ask about metal fillings. The screw placed in his wrist after he'd broken it right after they'd met. She didn't want to know.

Abby went to the bathroom (Perla ushered her carefully to the private one marked FAMILY — so thoughtful of them to provide a private place for a widow to sob and scream and wail, Abby thought dispassionately). She didn't have to use the restroom — it was just someplace to be that wasn't out there, standing with Kathryn. Kathryn — wonderful Kathryn — who would have taken all the pain for her if she could have. She'd even put on a dress and makeup for the event, her lipstick chalky and her foundation unevenly applied. She was trying so hard to help, and it almost physically hurt Abby to stand next to all that love.

Abby sat on the closed lid of the toilet and clicked open the small black purse she owned expressly for going to funerals. At home she had at least two more small black purses with equally specific uses: she liked the one with the black-on-black embroidery for night weddings, and the one with sequins was for charity galas.

What *bullshit.* Black, expensively made purses. No one — *no one* — needed to own three. All she had in it was her phone, her credit card, the single pine needle for strength, and one of Scott's handkerchiefs.

Next to her knee was a metal sign that read FOR YOUR SANITARY NEEDS. Perfect. She took out one of the opaque plastic bags and dumped in the handkerchief, the credit card, the pine needle, and her phone. She set her empty purse carefully behind a display of yellow roses next to the sink. If they found it somehow while she was still there, she would deny it was hers. Later, they could donate it to some widow charity, whatever thrift store specialized in ugly black dresses and hats with small black veils.

Clutching the top of the plastic bag, Abby let herself out and followed the vacuum track marks back to the Celebration Room.

The seats were mostly full. It was almost time. Abby knew most of the people. There were Roberts and Sons clients and there were families from their neighborhood. Scott had been active in Berkeley's Small Business Association, and most of them were here. Guys he golfed with stood in a small clump, awkward in suits rather than polo shirts. A tight cluster of her friends sat near the front, a polite two rows back. At the sight of Abby, Lisa waved, and Simone started crying. Even this far away, Abby could tell that Vivian was furious at Simone for starting the waterworks too early, but she also knew that later on, Vivian would be the one who wouldn't be able to stop sobbing.

Then she saw them.

The older woman who'd been at Fern's house, Elva, and an old man wearing a scruffy brown suit. He didn't look like Scott, not exactly, but he held his spine the same way, slightly sideways, as if looking for a wall to lean against.

And next to them, Fern and Matty.

Thank god.

CHAPTER FIFTEEN

"All these people knew Dad?" Matty's head was on a swivel and his eyes were huge.

Fern hated it when Matty called him that, like it was a title Scott had earned. "Probably not."

"Huh?"

"Sometimes people just come to funerals to be polite. Even though they didn't know the person."

"That's stupid."

Fern agreed. She didn't point out that's what Matty was doing, too. Goddamn it. What were they doing there? This wasn't the place for them. These weren't people they knew. The plush chapel smelled of the kind of perfume that never got on Fern's coach. All the expensive clothes, the perfect peach lipsticks, the men's gleaming shoes: all of it was freaking her *out*. The last funeral she'd been to had been Earl Stanton's, and that had been at the First Baptist on Adeline. The rollicking service had been followed by a catfish fry-up, his favorite. There had been paper plates and Costco napkins and a keg of Corona that got tapped before the sun went down.

This place probably spent more on furniture polish than the First Baptist paid their pastor.

There was still time to leave, still time to usher Matty to the car. She'd leave Grandpa Wyatt and Elva to pay their respects and take Matty to Fentons, to get him an ice cream sundae bigger than his head and make him forget all this. Like he was five instead of eleven.

Eleven goddamned years Scott had ignored his son and they were *honoring* him by being here? A sudden punch of fury made the inside of Fern's head feel as if it were made of tin — lightweight and hollow. She looked at her watch, counted backward. Had she taken her Carbatrol? God, she didn't remember taking it, didn't remember swallowing the glass of milk she took it with. . . . Was the tingling in her arms from anger or part of a seizure aura? Because if she fell down and started seizing right here, in front of Scott's people? Oh, *hell,* no. When she came out of it, when she looked up at these terrified faces staring down at her like she was an animal in the zoo, she would just have to kill herself, and wouldn't that be something for Matty's therapist in twenty years, watching his mother stab herself to death with a ballpoint Bic at his father's funeral?

She put her hand on Matty's shoulder.

And there she was. Abby.

She looked so relieved, so happy, as if she'd been waiting for no one but them. It was just weird. Fern couldn't help looking over her shoulder as if there was someone behind her who'd made Abby's face light up like that. But no. Abby was coming to them, to Fern and Matty, like they were the reason everyone was there, like they were the ones she'd been waiting for.

Fern decidedly did *not* want to hug Scott's widow. She took one protective step backward, but it was too late — Abby swept in and went high. Surprisingly, it was a good hug. Tight but not uncomfortable. Fast, but not a hit-and-run. It felt like a friend hug.

"I'm a hugger," Abby said, as she released her. "I hope that was okay."

Fern was a hugger, too. She just didn't quite want to admit it.

But Abby must have felt Fern's hesitation, and she didn't fold Matty into a hug. Thank god. Matty's eyes were wide, the way they got when he was nervous about where to put his feet next. She nudged his shoulder. "Say hi to Abby. You remember her."

"Hi," he mumbled.

"Hi. Oh, hello. I'm so glad you're here. All of you." Abby folded her hands under her chin, and in the black dress that was a little too big for her, and her hair pulled back simply with a black ribbon, she looked like she was a child from a picture book. A confused, clueless child with dark circles under her blue eyes. "Hello again, Elva. And you must be . . ."

Grandpa Wyatt stepped forward and held out his hand. "I'm his father."

"I'm sorry I didn't know about you before."

"I'm sorry my son was a jackass. And I don't give a shit about talking ill of the dead. I loved him. But he was a jackass."

Abby's shrug was graceful. "I'm glad you're here now. Will you all sit with me?"

"Sit?" Fern looked around, as if a chair would suddenly materialize next to her knees. The back of Matty's hand brushed hers, and if she didn't know him so well, she would have thought he wanted to hold her hand. He was eleven. He didn't.

Abby gestured to the front of the room. "Up there."

"Oh, no."

"Please."

The room was already full of people who looked like they belonged there. Fern could feel their curious gazes crawl over her softly, like spiders' legs, ticklish and unwelcome. She could feel them wondering. Judging. Who was the brown woman and the light brown boy? Their maid and her son, perhaps? Why was Abby standing so close to them? Was the boy a charity case of the family's? That would explain the black sneakers instead of the expensive, shined black shoes everyone else wore. Fern stood straighter, wishing again that she could have afforded to buy Matty a whole new outfit from Kohl's — even Macy's — instead of scrounging for a black button-down and black twill pants at the thrift store. She had bought herself a black blouse that she'd thought was nice, but it wasn't until they were leaving the house that she'd noticed the buttons on the front gapped. She hadn't been able to find a safety pin, and had finally decided it wouldn't matter.

Now it felt like it mattered.

No. Fuck that. She was here because the man who donated half Matty's genes had up and died, letting her son down for the very last time. There was an unexpected relief in the thought.

"Okay. We'll sit with you."

The tiny lines at the corners of Abby's eyes creased happily. "Thank god. Kathryn's here. I'll introduce you. But I have no . . . no other . . ." She paused, and it seemed as if all the low, polite chatter in the room just stopped.

No other family. That was obviously what Abby had almost said.

The unspoken — the *incorrect* — words hung in the air and Fern brushed past them as she walked up the aisle.

She raised her chin. Hell, yes, they'd sit in the front. She whisked invisible dust off the back of the chair before she sat, making pointed eye contact with the old white lady sitting behind her.

Hell, yeah. She'd make them all wonder about the maid.

The service was nice. Nicer than Scott deserved, Fern knew, but hey, whatever.

Kathryn, who was apparently Abby's deceased mother's best friend (a maternal stand-in? Fern felt jealous for one brief, unpleasant moment before giving her a California nice-to-meet-you hug), seemed kind and concerned. She sat on the end of the aisle and passed things down throughout the service. Mints. Gum. Tissues, drawn from a pale blue box. At one point, she'd handed down a ziplock bag containing granola, as if they all needed sustenance. Fern let Matty have a little and Grandpa Wyatt wolfed down two handfuls.

The casket was closed in that strange Protestant way. The wood was ruby red and gleaming, decorated with gold accents. Fern would bet it was the nicest one the place sold. In the same way she used to wonder what would happen if she stood up and yelled *Curse God* during Mass when she was a kid, she wondered what would happen if she ran to the coffin and shoved the hideous floral arrangement off the top of it and opened it. What would she do next? Spit in Scott's cold, waxen face? Kiss his stiff lips? She shivered and wrapped her arm around Matty, who couldn't take his eyes off the casket, either. Later tonight, she'd call Gregory, see if he could meet her on Wednesday afternoon, her early day. She needed warmth. She was cold inside, chilled to the bone, and she wasn't sure if even Gregory would be able to warm her up, but she'd let him try. Three days away. *Three.*

Fern, Matty, Abby, Wyatt. All of them Scott's people at one point, all of them in one place. *Four.*

Counting helped. *Five.*

Five people spoke after the minister's generic address: two men who had worked for Scott and had good things to say about his entrepreneurial spirit, one guy who had apparently golfed with him (golf!), a man from a board he'd sat on (Fern's mind boggled), and Abby.

Abby said only a few things, her words rapid-fire, as if she'd memorized the sentences a few minutes before and was trying to spit them all out before she forgot them again. *A good man. A loving companion. A thoughtful husband. Funny. Sweet.* Her voice didn't shake. It didn't break in that way guaranteed to choke everyone else up. She told a story of a time he'd taken an elderly woman back to her care home after she'd gotten lost — he'd lied to the staff, pretending to be her nephew, so the woman wouldn't get in trouble for wandering away. He'd stayed with her till she slept, holding her hand. He'd gone to visit her twice a week until she died three months later. In a rare lucid moment, the woman had rewritten her will, leaving Scott her storage locker, which was full of nothing but junk: useless lamps, old newspapers, and school yearbooks. He'd kept the unit for an extra year, paying the fees while looking for a relative who might want her old, broken things. Abby laughed, self-deprecatory, as she confessed the worst lamp of all, the pink one with the shredded gold shade, was still in pride of place in her husband's office.

She sat down again. For a second, Fern wondered if Grandpa Wyatt was going to stand and take the podium. He stirred as if he might. Then he sighed slowly, and the pain of it compressed a part of her own lungs.

Damn Scott. It would have been so much easier for Fern to *truly* hate him if he hadn't been loving when he'd been around. If he'd screamed at his father when he'd left. If he'd shouted epithets at Fern. In a hidden spot in her belly, just behind her navel, she wished — really wished — that he had hit her. That he'd thumped her just once. If he'd screamed at her in the middle of the night — the way her mother used to scream in Spanish at Diego and her in a voice thick with emotion and tequila — she could hate him from now until forever. Fern knew how to handle an enraged drunk and poorly aimed curses — it was easy. All you had to do was get out of the way so if they needed to hit something, it wasn't you or your brother. Fern's mother had spent a lot of time hitting the door of the refrigerator with a flyswatter because Fern learned to put it into her hand and suggest it. Not once had Fern's mother said, "Why? What good does this do me?" She'd just done it. She'd broken three flyswatters one bad winter, and luckily, she never protested when Fern put another one in the basket at the corner store. "Flies are bad this year," was all she'd say. Fern never knew if she remembered how they broke.

But Scott. He'd come into her life happy, and if he'd been sure he could have left them without hurting them, he would have departed happy, too. At the end of the service, the overhead speakers played "What a Wonderful World" and a series of photos scrolled across a tastefully framed screen. In every picture, Scott was smiling. He didn't know how to take one straight-faced. He'd been delighted with the world, but somehow he'd managed to let go of his only child, the boy who sat next to Fern, his eyes glued to the rotating photos, a child just as suscepti-ble to delight as his father had been.

Matty blinked hard and jerked his neck backward. A noise rose among the people behind them — not so much a gasp as a collective sound of surprise. Of curiosity.

Fern looked away from Matty's face to see a picture of herself up on the screen.

She was in the hospital. She was red, her face sweating. Scott was smiling with tears in his eyes. (T-minus one hour to liftoff — had he had a plan then? Or had he just run, spontaneously? She'd never found out. Now she never would.) Matty, wrapped in a thin blue hospital blanket, had just been placed in Fern's arms. It had been, literally, the happiest moment in her life, up to that point.

"Mama, that's me!" Matty's voice filled the room, as clear as if he were wearing a lapel microphone. And in that second, Fern had never been prouder of anyone. She leaned her shoulder against his. "It sure as hell is, *mijo.*"

Next to her, Abby said, "I hope you don't mind?"

"No. It's . . ." Fern held a quick breath and then released it. "It's nice to be included." In one million years, she would never have predicted she would say that at Scott's funeral.

"Speaking of included, would you come with me into the back when this is over?" Abby touched her bottom lip and looked at her finger, as if she were checking for lipstick. Or blood. "I mean, not Matty, just . . . Oh, I suppose you can't do that."

And leave her son out here with Grandpa

Wyatt and Elva? Not a great idea. At least one was guaranteed to wander off, and it probably wouldn't be Matty. "Why?"

The usher, perfectly suited to his profession with his long, sad face and long, pale fingers, was trying to lead them from their row, but Abby waved her hands at him. "Show everyone else out first, please."

"Ma'am, the widow goes first."

"Sir." Abby's voice was bright. Still friendly but very clear. "The widow pays the bill. Show the others out first."

A low murmur rose again as people gathered their belongings. "What's in the back?" Fern asked again. Next to her, she could feel Matty's ears get bigger.

"Oh. Yeah. They said . . ." The whites showed around the blue of Abby's eyes again. "There's a button."

Fern thought for a moment, scrabbling in her memory for anything about a funeral button. "I don't know what that means."

Matty leaned forward around her. "The button. It starts the fire."

"*Cállate,* Matias!" Why would he say something like that?

But Abby nodded. "It's the ignition button. Or something. To start the cremation."

"You're serious. They want you to . . . Matty, how did you *know* that?"

143

"I told you. Asman Singh, at school. He told us."

She stared at him. Fern had only ever worried about what blow job myths Matty might pick up on the playground. She'd never thought to worry about funereal horror stories.

"Remember? He said the oldest son in the family gets to push it. He pushed it for his uncle because he didn't have kids."

"No." It was too macabre. Even worse than standing at an open grave.

Abby twisted the handles of a plastic bag. "They said it was an option."

"Well, it's not."

"Mom." Matty looked around the room and then back at her. "I'm the oldest son."

"Holy shit." It was the only thing she could think to say. "No way."

"I'm sorry," said Abby. "I shouldn't have . . ."

No. Abby shouldn't have. "We have to go."

"Mom." Matty used to call her *Mamá* at home. That was a long time ago now. "You're going to make her do it alone?"

Fern tugged her blouse down again, trying to close the gap. "Honey. It's not that easy." But really, it was. That was the problem.

"I . . . of course. That is . . ." Abby seemed

to be fumbling for words. "Silly idea."

"Jeez, Mom." And it was that, that grown-up tone in Matty's voice, that told Fern what to do. He knew what was right. "I'll stay here with Grandpa." Wyatt and Elva appeared to be bickering over the last few raisins in the bag of Kathryn's granola.

"You'll be okay? They'll watch you." By that, she meant, *Watch them. Don't let them wander.* Poor Matias.

Solemnly he nodded.

"You're the best." Fern said it all the time. She'd never meant it more.

CHAPTER SIXTEEN

Fern had said yes. Abby had hoped she would, but she had automatically walked through every reason she would say no. First, it was creepy. Second, it was weird. Third, it was creepy *and* weird.

But she'd said yes.

Isaac seemed thrilled. "Of course you both may come into the viewing room. No one else?"

Abby watched Fern fold her lips tightly and shake her head.

"Very good."

Isaac in front of them, Perla behind them, Abby and Fern were ushered down a long burgundy corridor. Heavy-looking carved wooden doors hid what was behind them, and Abby fantasized for a moment about pushing one open. Just to see. Was this where they worked on bodies? Would she see a young man using sewing thread to close recalcitrant lips? Would the rooms behind these ornate doors be white and cold, full of medical supplies and liquids meant to stave off decomposition?

Questions battered at her like dark moths. Was this where they'd worked on Scott's skin? Where they'd brought color back to his cheeks? He'd had such natural color when they'd shown him to her — that terrifying green shade had been gone entirely, and while he looked a little too matte and a little too tan, he'd looked so *healthy*. Then they'd closed the casket. Forever. She'd wanted to touch him. Isaac had said she could. But when she'd tried to reach out to brush his face with the tips of her fingers, she'd quailed. (She'd realized too late that she should have slipped the pine needle she'd brought into the casket with him. For strength, pine should burn.)

With a murmured apology, Isaac pushed open the last door on the left. "Just here, to the right."

Fern was completely silent behind her, her footsteps not even making a sound in the deep blue carpet. They were ushered into a small, well-appointed room. A long red sofa was flanked by two burgundy wingback chairs. A pale blue tissue box sat on a glass coffee table next to yet another arrangement of Easter lilies. "Lovely flowers," said Abby.

Isaac beamed. "Aren't they? Locally sourced, of course."

"Of course." A patch of them had popped up in her garden — unasked for, a gift from a previous gardener — every spring since she'd moved into the house. They flourished with no attention, to the point that she'd thinned them the year before, guiltily tossing the bulbs into the green-waste bin.

Perla pulled back a floor-length red drape to display a large picture window facing the seating arrangement. On the other side of the glass stood an enormous machine, silver and industrial and frightening in its appearance of usefulness. That was it, then. The cremulator.

To the left of the window were two square buttons, one green, one red. She'd thought there would be just one.

Isaac gave a jaunty Vanna-like flourish at the window. "State-of-the-art, only a year old. The top of the line in efficiency and automation."

Was that supposed to make them feel better?

Fern made a small noise in the back of her throat. Abby felt her bones strengthen.

"You'll understand, of course, that we are . . ." *Distraught. Confused. Terrified.*

"Of course. I understand. It can be over-whelming, I know. Rest assured, though, that your husband" — he blankly refused to look anywhere near Fern's face, Abby noticed — "is in a better place now. And we'll take excellent care of his remains."

Why didn't they call them cremains? Someone must, right? It would make a good band name. The Cremains of the Day. Hor-rifyingly, Abby felt a bubble of amusement threaten to rise into her chest. It was just that Isaac's face — he was so *earnest*. He had a huge machine that *burned people to dust* and he was excited and proud of it. Unreal.

"Beyond unreal," murmured Fern, as if she could read Abby's thoughts.

"Now, Mrs. Roberts, the choice of how to proceed is yours." Isaac gestured at the sofa. "You may rest comfortably here while your husband's body is moved to the opening. I am happy to push the button for you, if you'd both prefer not to. Our assistant, Es-ther, will remain with the body until the operation is fully complete."

The operation. As if they were doctors, fixing Scott. The same inappropriate urge to laugh rose again. She choked it back. "You said there was a choice?"

"Or, once we load the casket into the

machine, you may start the process yourself." He pointed to the red button. "In many cultures, this is a method of honoring the deceased, and it's gaining more mainstream popularity every year." Isaac folded his hands over his belly, one stacked on top of the other. He was settled, his weight resting evenly on both legs. He looked ready to catch either of them, ready to hold out his arms should one of them start to sway. His expression was set to neutral kindness. He reminded Abby of a tax accountant she'd once known. February 1, the start of tax season, was Katie's favorite time of year. As people brought her their worrisome columns of numbers, Katie expanded and grew into the best, most useful version of herself. Isaac had the same look on his face — a deep contentment as he sank into what he knew, what he loved.

As soon as Abby got home, she'd rip out those unasked-for, unwanted lilies. She knew gardens. Easter lilies belonged in a funeral home. Not in her garden.

"What does the green button do?"

Isaac blinked. "It opens the machine. You won't need to push that."

What was it there for, then? "The red one closes it?"

"And starts the process."

Red, like flame. Of course.

"I think we'll do it."

Fern cleared her throat.

Abby turned to her. "That is, unless you can't. I totally understand that. But I'd like to . . . Oh, god."

"Okay."

"Really?"

Fern nodded sharply, as if she was worried she would change her mind. "Can we do it now?"

Isaac inclined his head, and on cue, Perla disappeared out the heavy door.

Abby stared at the red button. It was unlabeled. How many fingers had pushed it? What stories had it swallowed? Her heart clenched again. Was she doing it all wrong, all of this? "I'm —"

Fern said, "Don't worry."

"But —"

"I mean it. Look at me."

Fern's face was strong. So strong, like marble. She was solid stone next to Abby's suddenly flimsy wooden bones. "You haven't done anything wrong."

Isaac said in a voice that was almost a whisper, "I'll be right back, after I escort the casket in."

Abby breathed through her mouth, listening to Isaac's retreating footfalls on the tile.

She glanced upward. It felt like a warehouse, not a church. How was this possibly the right thing to do? "We tried for a family. I couldn't keep the babies." Fern could, though. She'd been able to.

"He was just a man." Fern's eyes were furious — blazing — but her expression was still solid. "Simple. He was just a guy. He loved you."

"I should have —"

"No." Fern's hand touched Abby's wrist.

Unable to stop herself, Abby turned her hand, grabbing at Fern's. "But —"

"No but." Fern held both of Abby's hands in hers now. Strong. Solid. "We just push the button."

Behind them, a whirring started, a jerky thudding that sounded like a luggage conveyor belt at the airport. And then the gleaming casket Abby had so carefully chosen rolled out through a door she hadn't noticed, next to Isaac. Isaac nodded through the glass at them, and a metal door on the machine rolled up. After the casket was pushed all the way into the machine by Isaac and a black-clad young woman with tattooed wrists, the silver door slid down.

Isaac walked out of sight and then back into the viewing room. He stood quietly, with his hands behind him, as if waiting.

For what? For them to pray? Wail?

She felt Fern squeeze her hands. Then Fern leaned forward, as if to whisper in her ear. Abby leaned forward to meet her. Whatever Fern would say would be the thing that would get her through this. She knew it.

Almost inaudibly, Fern whispered, "What is it about that guy that makes me want to fart, just to see what his face would do?"

Abby choked on her laugh, pushing it back down into her chest. But the joy rose anyway, tasting sweet in her mouth. It tasted like something she remembered. Something she wanted to grow in her garden.

And then Fern farted. It was the tiniest toot that could have been the squeak of a shoe or a mouse in the wall. Abby bit the inside of her mouth so hard she tasted blood almost immediately. Isaac's face stayed completely straight.

She gave Fern a sideways glance.

"Sorry," Fern mouthed with a tiny wink. *"No hay pedo."*

It should have been wildly inexcusable. It was completely inappropriate that either of them wanted to laugh right now. But Scott had been king of the fart joke, blaming his own on anyone nearby before walking away howling with laughter. Abby knew it, and

153

she knew Fern knew it, and if Scott were here (instead of just being *there*), he would have known it, too. He would have *definitely* made some lighting-his-fart-on-fire-with-the-furnace joke. At the thought, the delighted laughter rocked through her again, silently.

Fern had the same look on her face.

Abby tasted such sweetness in her mouth.

She wasn't alone. In this moment, she wasn't alone.

Isaac motioned to the red button. "Ladies. When you're ready." He sounded like the host on *The Bachelor* and then he faded back like smoke.

Abby stepped forward. Fern moved with her.

The tips of both their fingers (hers wood, Fern's stone) met on the button.

They pushed.

Together they made the machine on the other side of the glass roar.

CHAPTER SEVENTEEN

Three days later, Fern was naked, listening to Gregory rumble. Fern liked a lot about Gregory, but she *loved* his voice. It was low and dark and thundered as quietly as thunder could — it didn't even sound like it should come out as words. It was just a quiet roar. The fact that he did make words, good ones, was a bonus.

He'd just loosed that voice, loud and strong, a few minutes before. They'd lain on his bed, panting. Fern felt his mattress, so much firmer than her old one at home, hold her up, and she was grateful. "Redneck Woman" played on his stereo — she mocked him mercilessly for his addiction to country (she'd asked him, *You do realize you're black?*), but she loved the way the songs felt in her chest. Warm and familiar.

"You know I'm falling for you," said Gregory, still naked, sweat drying at his hairline. "Right?"

"A la verga," said Fern, and then she laughed. "No."

"You wanna call it Valentine's Day? A little late?" His voice was light, like he was joking. She knew he wasn't.

"More than a week ago. No." She'd been careful not to even text him that day. He couldn't be her Valentine, even belatedly. He knew that. They had *this* time. These few short, deliriously happy hours a week between her early shift ending on Wednesdays and her racing across town to pick up Matty.

The real problem was that she was getting so close to feeling something more for Gregory, and she didn't want to do that. She didn't have time. She didn't want, didn't have, *didn't need.* When she closed her door at night, she dead-bolted it. She counted the people safe under her roof (Matty, Grandpa Wyatt, Elva, and her — always four). She said or whispered or sometimes just thought, *"Estamos completos."* They were complete at four. She didn't need anyone else.

But when she was with Gregory, next to him, skin to skin, she sometimes forgot that.

"Oxytocin," she said.

"Bless you."

"No, it's a chemical. A drug."

156

"I know what it is, Fern. It's a hormone, actually."

"That's what we're feeling. That's all this is." She inhaled. The room smelled of the clove cigarettes he sometimes smoked. It reminded her of the way churches smelled, spice and smoke and hope.

He rolled onto his back. "Call it what you want. It feels really fucking good."

Fern laughed again. She couldn't help it. He was right. It did.

"Tell me I'm right."

She pressed a kiss to the inside of his forearm. "It does feel nice."

"You're adorable."

She snorted. "I am many things, I know." Fern was wide-bottomed. She laughed loudly and broke tension inappropriately (the dirty joke she'd told Matty's principal at Open House, the fart at Scott's funeral). She thought people were fascinating in their sheer *range* of different. Coworkers wanted to pick up buses from her, saying boarding an in-use coach with her leftover and cheerful passengers was always a relief. "Many things. But I'm pretty sure no one has ever called me that. Adorable is for kittens and knitted baby hats."

"What if I say it in Spanish? A-dor-a-blay?"

Fern grinned. "You're fluent! I had no idea!"

"What if one of us changes our mind about getting serious?"

"Mmm. We just won't." It was all she could manage. As surreptitiously as she could, she scoped the room for her clothing. It had come off as fast as usual, and she caught sight of her bra hanging over his exercise bike. Her jeans were at the foot of the bed — she could feel them balled up, right where she'd wriggled out of them. She would give up her panties for lost if she couldn't locate them with her toes. (Gregory loved her wide, white underpants, thinking they were a turn-on. They might not have been as fashionable or sexy as a wiggly thong, but they were practical, the best kind for wearing under the poly uniform pants — they breathed.)

"Fern. Say something."

"Your job," she said. It was all she could come up with. "You would lose your job, and I would never do that to you."

"My job? I get paid seventeen dollars an hour. You think I give a shit?"

He did, though. Some of the teachers at the adult school were just phoning it in, too old or too tired or too jaded to even try to pretend that they wanted to be there, teaching subjects that their students should already know. But Gregory . . . he'd been different. He never stood behind the lectern, for one thing. Most of the male professors held on to it like it was a prosthetic penis, stroking the wood as if they were in charge of keeping it hard.

But Gregory had started off the first night of Business 203: Microeconomic Theory class by having everyone move their seats into a circle. He put his papers and his pen on top of the little desk in front of him, just like they did. He was excited about the allocation and supply of limited resources. When he'd rolled up his shirtsleeves that first night, even with as tired as Fern had been after a nine-hour shift of driving through the rain on a route she didn't normally run, she'd felt something stir inside her. His dark wrists were narrow, but the planes of his hands were wide. She wanted to see more, to see if the hair on his chest matched that on his arms, dark and thick. When he started getting really excited about micro-scarcity models, she decided to try smiling at him. She liked the slight gap between his teeth.

Later he'd told her that when she'd smiled at him that night in class, apropos of nothing at all, he'd been so startled that he'd

159

lost his place in his notes. That had felt good, to watch his eyes slam back down to his desktop, to hear him stammer. On the third night of class, she'd come up with two good questions to ask him after class. The first question had been designed to be boring and to require a long answer: something about the measurement of elasticities. That gave the rest of the students a chance to gather their things and leave.

He'd answered, at length. Fern hadn't listened to a word of what he'd said. She'd just watched his mouth.

"You said you had two questions. What's the other one?" He'd moved his book bag from one shoulder to the next. He smelled like honey, warm and sweet.

Fern had the ability — she knew she did — to act as if she had nothing but confidence. Even when she didn't. "Will you fuck me?"

He hadn't answered for a minute. For the first time all night, he grabbed the lectern. He stroked the wood for a moment, his eyes going darker as he looked at her. "I can't adjust your grade for it."

"I'll get an A anyway," she said, raising her shoulder the slightest bit. She knew she would. Numbers didn't scare her. The way his eyes heated did, a little. In a good way.

"It's against my contract."

She shrugged again, liking the way his gaze followed the movement of her breasts. "I'm thirty-eight. Not eighteen. I won't tell. Besides, do you love this job so much you won't take a little risk?"

Gregory shook his head, slowly. "No. No, I certainly do not love it that much." Then he'd kissed her, and they hadn't even made it to his place that time.

She wished they were back there now, in the classroom. After desk fucking, you just had to stand and pull up your panties and limp your jeans up your legs. It was always just a little too cold, and there was no place to cuddle. She should have kept all of it there, but one night they'd almost been busted by the janitor and it had truly freaked Gregory out, and he'd taken her home to his tiny apartment, to his bed that smelled of spice. Now she'd been there so often she knew where his extra toilet paper was stored. Even though she never stayed the night, or even into the evening, she knew what he sounded like when he slept — heavy breathing that slipped into a soft snore, a sigh as he rewrapped his arms around her body.

"Don't worry."

Fern felt disoriented, as if the mattress

below her were floating. "Sorry?"

"There's nothing to worry about. Not here."

Fern wriggled her toes under his soft sheets. For one long second, she let herself imagine what it would be like, not having to leave. Being able to wake with him in the morning. To arise slowly, to make love again, to cook bacon and eat it in bed, to move to the couch with the paper and coffee, to laugh without worrying about waking anyone up. She hadn't had that kind of lazy day for so many, many years.

Gregory wasn't Scott. Not by a long shot. Gregory was a good man.

He might be a really good man.

And god, she didn't want to hurt him. "What about the women you're giving up because I'm keeping you from them?"

Gregory laughed again. "The hordes beating down my door right now, you mean?"

"I can't give you more than two hours on Wednesdays. Sometimes an hour or two on Sundays. That's not fair to you."

"Stop." The laughter was gone from his voice, and he turned to face her. He caught her hand and pressed it against his chest. She could feel his heart beating under his skin. She imagined it: the muscle extra strong from its slow, well-timed percussion set to beat in time with country guitars and fiddles.

A pause. "How did you meet Scott?"

The sudden topic change felt like a splash of cold water. She sat up while Neko Case sang that she was a man-eater. "Did you play this song on purpose?"

Gregory smiled that lazy smile of his. "That's the sweet genius of iTunes, baby. Now tell me about Scott. I don't know the story."

"In a line."

"What kind of line? Club? Starbucks? Bread line?"

"Closer to that last one, I guess. It was a job fair. He was in front of me." It had been at the Cow Palace on a foggy, cold morning. Fern had thought she'd be the first in line, because she was getting there an hour early. Instead, the line was hundreds deep. Yawns spread like the wave at a baseball game. Children ran in and out of the forest of legs, and Fern, still clueless then, wondered why people would be dumb enough to take their kids to a job fair. Now, of course, she understood.

"What were you there to apply for?"

"Anything. Everything."

"What had you been doing?"

Now she needed the pillow. Fern pulled it

into her lap and fluffed the top of the case so that her nipples were hidden, too. "Same." She'd bused tables at Ensenada out of high school and moved up to waiting tables. Even though she was good at it and made good tips, it didn't quite cover her rent, so she worked as an artist model in San Francisco. In one hour, she made enough to cover the BART ride there and back and a Subway sandwich to go (veggie six-inch, the cheapest thing on the menu). Every subsequent hour was money she could put right in her pocket, the pocket that even then was lined with dreams. Someday she'd have her own business. She'd sell something that helped people. That made them happy. She just didn't know what that was, back then.

Shit, she still didn't.

But even working seven days a week, she still didn't make enough. God knew she couldn't afford college, even the local JC. She needed a profession. At the job fair, she'd find one. It would be busting at the seams with careers. She would go claim one.

Scott had been in front of her in line. He'd grinned at her, and she'd smiled back even though he wasn't her type. She liked a big, dark, muscled guy, someone who drove too fast and might be familiar with the inside of a jail cell (Fern could admit she'd been more ambitious than smart back then). She wasn't into a skinny white dude with reddish brown hair, a guy who didn't even look like he'd jaywalk without needing to go to confession. He was handsome, yes, but in a pretty-boy way. He probably didn't even *go* to confession — he looked like the kind of man who went to a church with naked walls and a bare, Jesus-free cross. If he went to church at all. But he must. Scott looked so *good.*

"He flirted with me for an hour while we waited for the job fair to open. I thought he was sweet and harmless. I thought he was some kind of college geek, a computer guy. He wouldn't tell me what he was going to apply for when we got inside, kept turning the conversation back around to me instead. It made me curious. I got this idea to follow him around and see if I was right, if he'd go right to the tech area first. So we go inside, and I tell him I have to pee, that I'll see him later. He tried to ask for my number, but I was fast. I saw him when I came out. He was just wandering. Like, aimlessly. Hands in his jeans pockets. Smiling at everyone." Fern dug her fingers into the pillow. "With that charm of his? He could have had any job, I think. But he just walked around and didn't talk to anyone. I followed him up one aisle and down the next, and then he just headed for the front door. I caught him then. I asked him what the hell he was playing at. I accused him of slumming." Fern's face heated. "I think I said something about overprivileged, entitled white boys whose mamas could afford to keep them in gasoline for their late-model muscle cars."

"So you were flirting."

"Basically."

"What did he say?"

Scott had listened to Fern's rant (she'd been a pain in the ass back then, too — excessively fiery for her own good) and then he'd said, all in one breath, "My mother just died of an aneurysm. My dad drives a tow truck. We're losing the house I grew up in because she was the only one who knew how to pay a bill on time. I have no idea what I'm supposed to do now."

Fern had told him that he was an idiot. That he could do anything he wanted. That she would help.

"I fell in love with him," she said, feeling the edge of the pillowcase, worrying the loose thread. "Probably that very second. He followed me back in, and he decided he might like to drive a bus for AC Transit. I applied, too, just to stand nearer to him for a while. Even with the epilepsy, I got the job, but he didn't pass the drug test. Just marijuana," she felt compelled to clarify. "Nothing hard-core. Then, instead, he got a job with a landscape guy out in Livermore. That's where he learned he liked to mow grass, not just smoke it." She shrugged. "I got pregnant. Then he left."

"So you fell in love with him because he needed you?"

She gave Gregory her fiercest look. "Don't you dare. Don't."

"What about your friends? Do they have to need you, too?"

It wasn't like she even needed friends. She had her coworkers. And her family. She didn't need more than that.

He touched her kneecap softly. "I barely know how to boil water, you know."

"Stop it."

"Sometimes I forget to pay the phone bill and I get late charges." He ran his hand up her thigh, nudging the bottom of the pillow.

"Cut it out."

"Mmm. I know what'll get you." Gregory leaned forward and whispered in her ear. "Last week, I couldn't balance my checking account. I was off by a dollar ten, and *I didn't bother to find it.*"

Fern groaned. "I have to go. I've been here

too long already."

But then Gregory slipped his hand up her thigh and his hand started doing that thrumming thing that drove her out of her mind every time he did it, and she forgot to protest. That was all she could do, after all. Forget. She could forget what he'd said, she'd forget to worry, and for this long moment of being in this bed that smelled like a church, Fern could do nothing but feel every inch of her skin the way she used to feel it when she was younger and she had a whole lifetime of feeling ahead of her. Martina McBride sang "Let the weak be strong, let the right be wrong," and Fern laughed out loud at the joy of it.

Gregory's mouth, while she came, tasted like leisure, like luxury, like all the time in the world.

Chapter Eighteen

Rue oil.

Abby gathered the buds early in the morning, just as they were starting to bloom. She snapped them off with her fingers, taking with them three inches of stem, dropping them into her garden colander.

All the other women who had done this stood behind her as she plucked the flowers, quietly invisible, but there. Centuries of women before her, women of all ages, all body types. Witches, maybe — certainly women who had been *thought* to be witches. Mothers and daughters. Sisters. Probably very few of them had worn a red spandex yoga top and a Title Nine skirt, like Abby was, but they were doing the same thing.

Combating pestilence.

Fighting disease.

Battling pain.

Just by reaching forward and pulling off a few flowers.

She looked up. The sky was a pale, unconvinced blue. It would be the first truly warm day of spring.

Scott wasn't here to see it.

It was the strangest thing, that fact. So fucking strange.

In the potting shed, Abby ran the flowers under the tap and then dried them with a Florida orange tea towel that had been her mother's. She chopped the rue with her garden knife and then used the flat of the blade to bruise it. The broken blooms smelled sharp and acidic, a potent promise.

She combined the rue with olive oil and a little vodka in her biggest nonreactive pot. She heated it, low and slow. *Warm bathwater.* Years before, when she'd first been experimenting with herbal infusions, she'd learned the hard way that when oil got so hot it smoked, the infusion was ruined.

Heat could ruin things fast.

As she stirred, Abby kept her gaze out the small window. Her lower back ached slightly, and she was grateful for the twinge.

Last night, she'd felt nothing at all. Literally nothing. It had been terrifying. Just as she'd been drifting off, she realized she couldn't feel any part of her body. None of it. Her body had been as numb as if she were drunk — no, it had been worse than that. Even when truly, staggeringly drunk, you could still feel the blood pounding in your veins. This was different. It was as if she were a mind suspended in a jar. Nothing but a collection of thoughts, all smoke and no substance.

Terrified, Abby had twitched her arms and legs, to make sure she *could* feel (she could — the sheet was light, the duvet cover heavier; a hair tickled her forehead), and then, as soon as she'd stilled, the numbness had taken over again.

Over and over, she'd twitched to make herself feel. At one point, she'd bitten the inside of her wrist, hard, but the pain had lasted less than a minute.

Was this why people cut themselves? Abby finally understood the motivation.

She'd given up, following the numbness into sleep.

In the morning, she'd stood and stretched, intending to do yoga, to do *something* that would make her feel. But then she'd checked her e-mail — a shop in New Mexico who'd been buying her stuff (who knew how they'd found her? through a Brook soap connection, maybe?) had ordered ten bottles of rue oil. She had only one on the shelf, but rue was just starting to bloom, and it was the right time to harvest it.

Now Abby stood in the shed, stirring. Her back ached. She could feel the spot on her wrist where she'd bitten herself the night before.

And, as the oil warmed, she let herself cry. Slow, thick-feeling tears slid down her face. She didn't stop stirring to wipe them away.

Rue was good for arthritis and headaches. It eased pain. In ten days, the oil would be full-strength. She'd strain it then and pour it into bottles. She'd tie a ribbon around each. She'd mail them to New Mexico while wishing the recipients good health.

But for now, it would sit. The oil would rest.

And even though the potion was weak, Abby took a spoonful and blew on it until it had cooled. She poured it into her left hand, then rubbed her hands together. She pressed the oil into her hair, slid it across her forehead and down her wet cheeks and throat. She ran her fingers down her arms, and then bent, rubbing what was left into her bare legs.

She stood straight.

It was silly. It was just flowers and oil.

But she didn't feel like crying anymore, and she could feel the nerve endings of her skin again. Rue, used for grief. Rue, for regret and remorse. She wasn't surprised. But she was grateful.

CHAPTER NINETEEN

Fern, just across the threshold and not even all the way out of her uniform jacket, froze in place and stared. "Wait. What? What did you *do*? You broke the couch? Since this morning?"

Elva made a face, pulling her eyebrows together, wrinkling her nose. She looked closer to a guilty eight-year-old than her actual age of eighty-two. "We just ripped it a little." Then she disappeared back into the kitchen.

A jagged flap of blue fabric hung off the front of the couch, exposing a yellow pouf of what looked like wall insulation. It had always been an ugly thirdhand couch, but now it looked like something that should be left on the sidewalk for the garbage truck or an arsonist, whichever came first.

Matty's grandfather had to be involved somehow. He always was. "Grandpa Wyatt?"

Wyatt shook the newspaper in front of his

face. "I was showing him how to fence."

"You what?" Fern felt the tension Gregory had untangled with his talented fingers and lips creep back inside her, twisting its way up her spine.

"Every boy needs to know how. Necessary in every trade."

In the sixteenth century, yes, probably. Wyatt had been a tow truck driver before he retired. The only fencing he'd ever done was fixing the barbed wire that ran around the tow yard where they kept the impounded vehicles.

Matty raced into the living room with a whoop. He stuck what looked like a sharpened dowel into a helpless pillow trying to make a run from the newly pathetic sofa. "On guard!"

"Hey!"

Grandpa Wyatt harrumphed and rattled his newspaper, lifting it higher. "My grandson is a natural."

Most days Fern was happy that Scott's father had picked them, but there were the occasional days she wanted to throw Wyatt back.

Fern scooped up Matty's backpack from the floor with her left arm, adding it to the other things hanging there: her purse and her coat and the paper bag from the drugstore. She made her way into the kitchen, sniffing suspiciously.

Tonight was a stew night, apparently, since her largest pot was actively bubbling on the stove. The air in the kitchen had a metallic scent tinged with an undertone of tomatoes and something sickly sweet.

"What are you making, Elva?"

"SpaghettiOs with a surprise protein addition."

"Hoo boy," Fern managed.

"Oh, the washing machine broke, too."

Fern pressed her elbows into her sides. "Broke, like it made that puddle again?"

"Broke, like it blew up. Black smoke."

"Smoke?" Now that she thought about it, maybe the acrid smell was coming from over by the laundry room and not the stove.

Elva pinched the air in front of her face. "*This* much fire. But I put it out! Baking soda worked like a charm, but we need more. Just in case. I unplugged it and cleaned it up best I could, but we're out of paper towels now."

From the living room, Grandpa Wyatt yelled, "Washer's a goner!"

Fern's knees felt shaky. Even a cheap washer was four hundred bucks at the Sears Outlet. The bank account wouldn't be able to cough that up for a while, especially now that she'd lost — she did the math quickly in her head — thirty percent of her income. She brought home thirty-three hundred dollars a month. She had *needed* that fifteen hundred from Scott. She would never have accepted it if she hadn't.

Matty raced through the kitchen, dragging the dowel on the tiles with a clatter. "I am *not* eating whatever that smell is." Then he ran for his bedroom. In a minute, he'd be plugged into Minecraft, his headphones on, his jaw slack as he thumbed the controls.

Grandpa Wyatt kept yelling, "Hey! The fridge isn't staying cool, either!"

Hasta la madre, the fridge, too? The freezer was already on the fritz, but this was new. She needed to get into bed with her Excel budget and make it work, find the money, pull it out from under the rocks she was going to have to start putting in Matty's sandwiches if she didn't figure out a way to come up with some more cash.

Wyatt shouted, "You wanna hear my best one of the day?"

No. She did not want to hear his best one. He made an almost full-time job of writing letters to the editor about how roads could and should be fixed. It didn't matter that he couldn't drive, hadn't been able to drive since he hit a power line and brought it down, draping it across his tow truck, trapping him inside an electrified metal box until PG&E got on scene to save him. He walked now, walked everywhere, noting potholes and fading road paint. He and Fern had that in common.

She yelled, "Maybe later!"

Elva gestured at the huge pot on the stove with her spoon. "This'll feed us for days."

Fern kept the sigh where it started, held tightly at the top of her sternum. *Focus.* She could manipulate the budget and aim for a miracle later, when she was by herself and could allow her face to relax into fear. Maybe this was the time she could finally go through her mother's Mexican coin collection. She could part with a few of them, surely? She had done some research once, and back then the 1959 twenty-centavo piece had been worth like eighty bucks. The 1940 one-peso coins were real silver, her mother had said, and had to be worth even more.

But they were her mother's treasure, the only thing left of her. Playing with the coins her mother had brought with her from Mexico was one of the few good memories Fern had of childhood. She'd learned to count from them, learning the numbers in Spanish first, then English. She got her love of math and talent for numbers from her mother, who'd never used her own talent for anything more than always being able to haggle the lowest rent in town (a not-small skill, truthfully). Fern had used the coins to teach Diego to count, and much later, she'd used them to teach Matty his numbers, too. On really bad nights, when she couldn't sleep for worry (tonight might be one of them), Fern would fold the 1945 fifty-centavo coin into her palm and hold it there while she slept.

Elva gave a mighty sniff and appeared satisfied with the scent of her dinner.

Fern was still suspicious. "Main ingredient? Besides SpaghettiOs?"

"Love."

"Well. How am I supposed to argue with that?" Fern dumped the bags onto the kitchen table and rummaged through Matty's backpack. He'd left half his bologna sandwich in its plastic bag, and the rank smell rose from the depths. Old, warm bologna. No wonder her poor thin kid didn't finish lunch. Well, at least SpaghettiOs were pure sugar — maybe there was a chance he'd eat some of it.

"The inspiration comes from the motherland, Italy." As far as Fern knew, Elva had a German heritage. "I added basil from the garden —"

"Come again?" said Fern. The only things growing in the backyard were weeds, some weird black-and-white tulips, and one artichoke plant that the previous owners must have put in twenty years ago. Fern neglected that plant completely, and every year it came back in the same place, giving them one or two huge artichokes, which she tried to remember to cook before they burst into purple bloom.

Elva rubbed her hands on her apron. "You know."

"You mean the *Silvas'* garden?" Maria Silva's backyard was perfectly plotted, weeded, and fertilized. Maria was visibly horrified every time spring rains made the weeds on Fern's side wave over the top of their low fence.

Elva folded her lips and gave the pot a mighty stir.

"Elva?" It was like having three kids.

"She has so much basil back there. It's completely overgrown. Kind of a weed, if you ask me."

Nothing in Maria Silva's garden was a weed. "Did you ask her, at least?"

"I knocked." Elva slurped at the wooden spoon and then stuck it back in the pot. Fern turned her mind firmly away from germs. "But she wasn't home. I *would* have asked."

Fern doubted that very much. There was a good chance that Elva had waited until Maria's old Pontiac had pulled away from the curb before she knocked, if she had at all.

"Anyway," Elva continued, "like I was saying, in honor of my heritage, I made meatballs and added some extra spaghetti and some cannellini beans and some oregano. I think you'll love it."

Fern peered over her shoulder, something that was easy to do since Elva seemed to lose an inch with every one that Matty grew. "What are the black things on the surface?"

Elva looked mildly worried and poked one with her spoon. "Croutons."

"Oh, god."

"Scat," said Elva firmly, waving her spoon. Red sauce dripped to the floor. Her eyesight was bad enough now she wouldn't be able to see the carnage to clean it up. That would be Fern's job. It usually was. Grandpa Wyatt always offered to wash the dishes, but every time he did, he broke at least one plate or a glass. It was as if he juggled them while they were still wet for fun. To save money, Fern just did them. Matty helped — his job was to dry and put away, but sometimes, on late nights, he looked so tired with those dark circles under his eyes that it was easier to just send him to bed and do it all herself.

Tonight nothing felt easier at all. Every single knot in her neck that had come undone in Gregory's bed was back, tighter than ever.

While Elva muttered about whether it was right to commingle oregano and thyme in her Italian masterpiece, Fern finished poking inside Matty's backpack. She confirmed he really had done all his homework while they were on the bus — he'd lied about it a few weeks ago, and she hated the mistrust she felt now, but if he didn't stay caught up in science now, he never would. Mrs. Hutch was a nightmare of a teacher, and god knew *she* wouldn't help him.

But there it was — Matty had done it all. He'd put a careful check mark (he loved that part of his homework, that heavy black doneness of it) next to each of his assignments in his homework folder. Good kid.

She pushed the mail around on the table. Junk, junk, three bills, more junk. She had no idea how she was on so many catalog mailing forms, since she hadn't ordered a piece of clothing online or otherwise in at least four years. Work provided her uniforms, and the thrift store provided both her and Matty their jeans. T-shirts, socks, and underpants were cheap enough at Target. Luckily Oakland rarely got colder than a shrug of frost in the winter, and Fern had learned years ago to shop at Thrift Town in May for sweatshirts and boots a size or two too big for Matty. By the time the weather changed again, she could wrap them up as Christmas presents, and pretend that he hadn't helped pick them out months before.

He was *such* a good kid.

Fern raked through the mail two more times before she realized what she was looking for. The thin envelope from Scott wasn't there. She usually got it on the twentieth, and today was the twenty-second — oh, shit.

Of course it wasn't there.

Fern could practically still feel that red button under her finger, next to Abby's. Scott was ash, like — apparently — the innards of her washing machine.

She'd held out for a year after Scott left, refusing his financial help. The checks he mailed then were smaller. They were whatever he could afford (she'd never taken him to court, never thinking he'd have a real job anyway). When the checks were a hundred bucks, they were easier to send back to him, ripped to small pieces.

That first winter, before Elva and Grandpa Wyatt moved in, she'd used the stove to warm the house, turning on all four gas burners and propping poor coughing Matty up in his car seat on the kitchen table, making sure she never took her eyes off the blue flames, that she never forgot they were on. Gas was so much cheaper than electricity, and all the house had was electric wall heaters. It had taken three years of overtime, but she'd finally been able to put in the central heating. Even now, just hearing the *whoomp* of the gas heater as it kicked on gave her a visceral joy in the pit of her belly.

It wasn't until she didn't have the copay for her seizure meds that she deposited that first check from him. That one had been $537. Such a strangely specific amount. And always in the memo line, always: *Take care.*

The amounts had risen slowly. Once he'd added a Post-it that said, *I finally started my business.*

He'd been married to Abby then. She hadn't been happy for him.

Her phone pinged as an e-mail landed. Probably next week's schedule. She dropped into her seat at the kitchen table and opened the app.

It wasn't work.

It was the mortgage check.
Bouncing.

Chapter Twenty

When the cramps woke Abby in the middle of the night during her second miscarriage, she knew what they meant. She went in the bathroom and called the advice line on her cell phone, keeping her voice low. She could have woken Scott, but she didn't want to. The nurse told her either she could go in then to the ER or she could collect the blood (the "blood," as the nurse called it, was so much more than blood) and bring it to the obstetrics office when they opened at seven. They would determine then whether she needed a D and C like last time.

Abby couldn't face the brightness and noise of the emergency room again, so she let Scott sleep until six forty-five. He drove her to the doctor's office, and she tried to forget — to erase from her mind completely — the quick look he'd had on his face when she'd said, "I need to go to the hospital." On her lap she held a paper grocery bag, folded over at the top. Inside was a kitchen measuring cup that held what she'd been asked to collect. The other two women in the waiting room held their round bellies while they waited. Abby held the paper bag.

Nothing hurt very much, not compared with the shrieking in her head. The D and C removed the rest of the dead tissue and a good chunk of her soul. Pleasantly sedated, Abby wondered if they'd seen that part of her. Small and green, a tendril of curled hope and so much love it shouldn't have fit inside her body, but it had, it really had. The baby, her baby, her perfect boy, had made it to only ten weeks this time. He'd had a name, but she hadn't told it to anyone, not even Scott.

They gave her drugs for the pain. They said they would do genetic testing, just to rule things out. (What things? Things that could change the past?) The medicine made her stupid and slow. Less than eighteen hours after it had started, she was back in bed at home. They told her moving was good. She knew walking to the kitchen to make a cup of tea would make her limbs ache less. She made up her mind and swung her legs to the left, but when she felt the air outside the duvet, she shrank again. She shriveled back into nothingness, into blank space. Blankness required only darkness, not tea.

That night, Scott came to join her in bed, like it was any other night. He brushed his teeth like normal. He changed into his boxers. He slid into bed, slipping his phone into the charger as if it were any other night. He put his arms around her and she could smell his toothpaste. It smelled like relief, and it was unforgivable.

Instead of breaking, Abby felt like moving. Slowly, the drugs making her movements thick and heavy, she stood, taking her pillow with her.

"Where are you going?"

"Spare room."

"Abby." His voice, concerned, and there, she heard it, right at the bottom of the well he dug by saying her name, the slightest tinge of annoyance. Pique.

"I just need to be alone." She hated how her voice broke at the end of the last word.

"Come on. Stay here with me. Honey."

Childish.

He was childish.

She was *childless.* Didn't he see that? She was empty. She was nothing.

She slept alone in the spare bedroom that night. And the next. That bed, the one no one ever slept in, absorbed tears better than her own. It was dry, had never cradled grief. As sterile as she was, the bed was good at holding the pain.

On the third day after her second miscarriage, she heard Scott whistling in the bathroom and she wanted to kill him with her bare hands. She could have done it if she'd been able to make herself move. The rage was better than the grief. The sadness felt like her flesh was being torn by teeth, all rips and snarls and shredding, but the anger was a clean slice of relief.

The fury passed, though, a tornado that left nothing but wreckage and exhaustion in its wake. Twenty-two days after they scraped the hope from her uterus, Abby got into bed with Scott. Still mostly asleep, he reached for her gratefully. His arm curled around her waist, his hand tucking under her (empty) belly.

She allowed it.

Abby didn't let herself get excited the third time she was pregnant. She wouldn't believe it until the baby socked her in the jaw with a tiny, angry, perfect fist.

Eight weeks into the pregnancy, she was helping Kathryn at the nursery on a busy afternoon when one of Kathryn's employees had called out sick. Abby placed three quarters into the palm of the woman who had just bought a packet of tomato seeds. She felt her body twist, shifting sideways inside her. "Fuck," she exclaimed, and the woman dropped the change.

"Sorry, excuse me. Let me get that."

Abby carefully picked up the change and smiled at her customer. Then she carried her purse into the bathroom and took out the ziplock bag she'd been carrying with her. She pressed two enormous overnight pads into her already spotted underwear, wrapping the wings carefully around to the outer fabric. She slapped her right cheek hard, and that felt good, so she did it again on the left side of her face. Her face flamed, but she didn't feel like crying anymore.

She ignored Kathryn's looks of concern and loaded questions. No, everything wasn't all right. No, she didn't feel well. Of course she didn't. But Abby wouldn't say why. She wouldn't name it. Kathryn had been so upset by the last one. Abby couldn't take care of Kathryn today.

She called her doctor, who had been monitoring her closely — so closely — this time. No genetic problems had been found. They didn't know why it had happened twice before. And now, god, a third.

Her doctor said to come straight in.

Maybe it was a false alarm. Abby drove herself to the hospital, knowing it wasn't.

And it barely hurt at all. God knew, she was so scarred by then they could probably do it without any anesthetic at all. It felt like she was a melon, like they were scooping out the flesh, scraping out the seeds. Melons didn't ache inside, so — resolutely — she didn't, either.

The bitchy outtake nurse wouldn't let her drive herself home, though. She had to produce an actual person to take her. She didn't want to call Scott and wouldn't call Kathryn. She presented Pharesh, the cabdriver, to the front desk with a ridiculous amount of sarcasm. She held on to his sleeve. "Here's a person. Can I go *now*?" There at the hospital desk, her insides dripped out onto the winged pads they gave her, the ones big as a diaper. *Diaper.* Everything that could have been was lost. She'd lost it all. Again. She didn't care if she bled through the pads with wings.

Wings held up nothing at all.

From the spare bedroom, she told Scott she had a migraine and that these curtains blocked out the light better than the curtains in their bedroom (they didn't). She said that she'd left the car at the nursery (it was at the hospital), that she'd get it tomorrow (she wouldn't, because she'd never move again).

Scott believed her.

That was the worst part, that he couldn't look into her eyes and know that she was empty. That he couldn't see that she was broken, that she was lost, that she had lost everything again.

He should have been able to tell.

He didn't even look into her eyes, anyway. He just nodded and said quietly, "Let me know if you need anything," before closing the door.

Need?

Need?

She needed rue oil (she hadn't known about it then, hadn't gotten into infused oils yet). She needed a priest to bless her, or a witch to curse her. Or vice versa. She needed help. She needed magic. She needed a map.

Three days later, she told Scott while she poured him a cup of coffee. Her hand didn't shake, which made sense because her blood was made of the same granite they'd just picked out last week for the new counter-top. Pulling her to his chest, he said, "You didn't do anything wrong. You did nothing wrong."

Abby wanted to slip the sharpest kitchen

knife they owned between his ribs for saying that. For assuming she thought she had
done something *wrong*. And all of her, every
cell of her failed body, hated herself for
needing his arms to stay around her forever.

CHAPTER TWENTY-ONE

"Shit, shit, *shit.*" Fern looked over her shoulder to make sure Matty hadn't come out of his room. He didn't like her swearing. "Damn." Of all things to bounce. Of *all* things. Why not the gas and electric bill? Why not the car insurance? The check she'd written to the grocery store with her fingers crossed behind her back? How could it have happened? She'd counted. She'd counted everything, always. She hadn't bounced anything for years, even though sometimes only a single, careful column of numbers prevented the ricochet.

God, the sheer goddamned *cash* it took to come back from a bounce. The overage fee that could, in itself, bounce. She pulled up her bank account on the phone, her fingers shaking. She bet people with a well-padded savings account didn't have to hand-carry a cashier's check to a mortgage office to pay a late fee. They probably just made a phone call and moved money around.

It *was* that check to Safeway that had done it. A six-dollar check for tampons because she knew her paycheck wouldn't hit her bank till midnight that night. A six-dollar check that had exploded through the barricade, blowing up her home.

"What's wrong?" Elva started to turn in place, the spoon still in her hand.

"Stir. No. Don't drip. *Please.*"

"What's wrong?"

"Bounced a check."

"An important one?"

They were all important, weren't they? Always one step away from losing everything. Fern didn't answer.

"Are we okay?" Elva's voice was thinner than an EBT card. "Do you need help?"

"No. No, sweetheart, we're fine." Fern kissed Elva's cheek quickly with a smack. She drove Elva to the bank the first week of every month. Elva could afford her portion of the rent, her vitamins, and her slow-rumba class. She had just enough left over for her and Wyatt to go gamble quarters one afternoon a month at the Indian casino. That was about it. Because of her perennial eye problems, Elva always asked Fern to look over her bankbook to make sure the teller hadn't stamped the wrong amount. Fern never had the heart to tell her that she was pretty sure that tellers didn't even *use* stamps anymore. The tellers apparently had other pensioners they were used to dealing with, though, because they took the time to handwrite her deposit and withdrawal in her ledger, which they certainly didn't *have* to do anymore. God bless a credit union. When Fern went into her big-name bank, all she got was a printed slip and a fake smile.

Fern would never have asked Elva for money, even if she had money.

Elva still looked worried.

Fern repeated, "No. It's fine. It's nothing. Honestly. Overreaction, that's all. Sorry." She shoved all the mail into her purse. She tossed Matty's half sandwich into the trash can, which was, of course, too full. Could no one in this house see when the bag needed to be taken out? She was the only one with trash superpowers?

The kitchen door opened just as she hit it with her hip.

"Hey!" Diego took the bag out of her hands and chucked it into the outside can for her.

"Why don't you live here?" It was a grumble, not a compliment.

"Because brothers don't live with sisters unless they're total losers."

"But you are a total loser," she said as she followed him back into the house. "Your apartment is the size of my bus."

"I meant the sisters."

"Ass."

"Whiner. Speaking of which," her brother said, "I brought wine."

"In that case, you're amazing and you're my favorite."

"It's cheap. Trader Joe's *and* on sale."

"Just my style."

"Diego!" Elva stood her spoon in the spaghetti-mystery-stew and clapped.

"You're looking spry, young lady."

Elva smoothed her hands down the front of her green checked apron, which was carefully tied over her bathrobe. "Well, I've been getting my steps in."

"It shows."

Elva turned pink and grabbed the spoon's handle. "Dinner soon."

Diego opened the wine while Fern got out the glasses. She'd found them at the local Salvation Army — a matched set, etched with *Tim's Divorce Bash, 1997.* She'd thought they were hilarious at the time and had happily forked over a quarter each. Now she wished she had plain wineglasses, ones that didn't celebrate Tim, who was probably happily remarried by now — Tim, who'd had to give all those glasses away to the thrift store because he had new wedding glasses to store on high, dusty shelves.

"Do you think Tim got a stripper for the divorce party?"

Diego splashed wine into her glass. "You think too much about that guy is what I think."

She fished out a piece of cork with her thumb. "Probably."

"Outside?"

"Yeah."

The backyard was a jungle, as usual, and the night was cold, but this was what they did unless it was raining. Diego was the kind of guy who didn't talk much about anything indoors. Nothing real, anyway. Get him outside, under his beloved trees, he'd bust open like a parking meter.

She lit the gas fire pit (one of her better Freecycle scores) and then sank into a plastic chair with a sigh.

"Long day?"

Fern nodded.

"How's Matty doing with everything?"

For the last two nights, he'd woken up screaming. Night terrors. Lots of kids had them, Fern knew.

But lots of kids hadn't buried their un-known father the week before. Lots of kids didn't think about their dads burning to ash. Fern wondered for the twentieth time if she should have let Matty come in the back with them to push the button, to see where the coffin had been fed to the fire. Maybe he wouldn't be having the dreams. . . .

"He's okay. Couple of nightmares."

"Damn. Sorry."

"He's tough." Her poor tough little guy. He shouldn't have to be. Last night, when he should have been sleeping, he'd crept out of his bed and stood with her at the front door. As she checked the dead bolt, he'd said it with her like he'd loved to do when he was little: *Estamos completos.* She had wanted to cry. Instead, she'd swallowed the lump in her throat and rubbed the top of his head, sending him back to bed with a kiss.

"It is what it is," she said.

"And you?"

"Fine."

"Hmph." He didn't believe her, she knew. That was okay — she didn't believe herself.

"How's your boyfriend?"

"He's not my boyfriend." Gregory was a fuck buddy. That was all she needed. All she had time for. "And he's fine." She relented. "Okay, he's *really* fine."

Diego laughed.

Overhead, the box elders danced, their still-bare branches making dark silhouettes against the lighter fog. Some nights the city lights were so bright against it that the night sky was white. Tonight, though, it was a pale gray. A car's bass thumped at the end of the cul-de-sac, and the stupid rooster that never knew the time crowed. The noises of the city filtered down, resting in her lap. Fern could almost run her fingers through them, clinking them against one another like their mother's old coins. An impatient horn. Two sirens. A hoot of laughter followed by a mariachi trumpet punch, quickly silenced. The air smelled of dirt and night air and, faintly, of hot plastic.

Diego spread his knees and looked up at the trees. "I gotta get up there."

"No." She didn't want him working in her trees. It was bad enough he was an arborist. She hated thinking about how high he went, the risks he must take.

"The top of that acacia has to go."

"So I'll hire someone."

"People as good as me are expensive."

"I'll get a day laborer over at Home Depot." It was an old joke. Long ago, before

200

he'd gotten certified as an arborist, Diego had stood with the day laborers. He'd helped as a translator when he could, or on really bad days, he'd pretended he couldn't understand a word of English. He and the other men had laughed and waited for work, standing in the parking lot with their eyes hidden under ball caps, never admitting how desperate they were. Grunt labor (house painting, fence repair) paid for kids' lunches and toilet paper, but sometimes the jobs just didn't arrive. The rainy days, Fern remembered, had been the hardest on Diego. What about the men who didn't get out of it like he had? What happened to the ones who were passed over again and again, like the last kids picked at volleyball? What about the man with the scar that ran down his face from the top of his cheek to his collar? Who hired him?

"You put a guy up there who isn't me and I'll show Matty how to hot-wire any car made before 1986."

Fern laughed. The familiar argument was as comforting as the sound of a Susan B. Anthony dollar rolling into the fare box. "You were lucky you were a kid, that it's not on your record."

"What record?" Diego locked his arms behind his head and peered up at the sky.

"Stars won't be out tonight," she warned him. Too much fog. Smog. Whatever it was that rolled in so often in the flats of Oakland. They got the haunting sound of the trains from the south, but they didn't get the stars that twinkled above Piedmont.

"Can't see 'em if you're not looking."

In her pocket, her phone beeped. She pulled it out — work. Her heart sank. Dispatch never sent an all-page unless something big was happening across the board. When the union needed them for a vote, a text went out. When the main schedule was pulled and adjusted, a page got sent.

Sure enough, *CHECK E-MAIL FOR MAIN SCHEDULE.*

Another text came in, this one from Judy, a woman she'd trained with back in the day. They'd been friends since then, looking out for each other. They traded day care and sob stories. Judy was an extreme couponer, and at least once a week, a ziplock bag of coupons Fern would never get around to sorting ended up in her work mailbox.

Well, that wasn't what you needed.

"What is it?" asked Diego.

"Work." Fern texted back, *Can you just tell me? Matty's on computer inside, I'm outside.* Her stupid crap phone wouldn't ever let her log in to the work schedule.

202

You got put on the 57. Sorry, friend. I'll do trades if it helps.

"Shit." The word was quiet but no less heartfelt for its softness.

"Tell me."

"I got the 57. I'm off my route."

CHAPTER TWENTY-TWO

"No more."

That had been Scott's response to her third miscarriage, when she'd finally told him, those long three days afterward. (*Her* miscarriage. Never theirs. He'd never felt involved enough for her to think of it as their loss, only hers. That's when she started to know for sure.)

"What?"

"You can't keep going through this."

"Yes, I can." Abby had been cried out, as dry and thin as the onion skins she collected in a paper bag in the shed.

"I think we should stop trying."

"Oh," Abby said. "You're saying . . ." He was okay with adopting? Years before, she had told him that would be her next step. He'd really listened. She'd asked, back then, and he'd said that when the time came, they could talk about it. He'd said he knew how she felt. He'd held her as she cried.

"Yeah," he said. "It's time."

"Oh." They'd been in the kitchen, sitting at the island. Sun streamed through the glass, over the yellow mugs she'd so carefully chosen when they'd gotten married. She felt the color seep into her skin, into her blood. "Oh, Scott. This makes me so happy. You — *you* — make me so happy."

He'd carefully set his mug of coffee — black in the yellow, a liquid bumblebee — on the countertop. He'd wiped away the drop he'd spilled. "What?"

"You'll see." Abby's thoughts tumbled in her head like a boxful of wildflower seed. All of them — each one — would bloom somewhere unexpected and gorgeous. "It'll be wonderful. How old, do you think?" She had a million ideas. A baby — *an emergency baby,* they called them in the system — would be riskier, since any family member could show up out of the blue (and, from what she'd read, sometimes did) to take the child back. An emergency baby, tiny and squalling and perfect and she hoped theirs to keep. Or they could foster-to-adopt an older child. A little boy with dark eyes and a hopeful lilt to his high-pitched voice. A girl with dark skin and hair that Abby would learn to braid (she would *really* learn — she'd become a pro at it, astonishingly adept at beads and tiny elastics — she wouldn't let strangers laugh at her child's hair).

"How old? I don't know what we're talking about here. I thought we were going to stop."

Abby was confused. That's exactly what they were talking about — stopping trying. "I know we talked about adoption, but the county's fost-adopt program is really wonderful — I know it's a risk, but I've had friends it's worked out for —"

"Abby." He placed a hand on top of hers. "Honey, no."

"What?"

"I don't want to be a father."

One breath of icy air blew down her spine. She drew her hand back. "Don't say that."

"I know I've been putting on a good front with the whole miscarriage thing, but every time it's happened, I've got to admit that I've been relieved."

"That's not true." She could make his feelings up for him like the bed they slept in. She could pull him tight and firm, bounce a coin off what she needed him to do.

"I never would have told you. I knew it was important to you, so I went along with it."

Went along with trying to make a *baby*?

"Are you serious?"

"But I just don't think I'm cut out for it. There's a reason that our bodies — together — don't make babies. Your body knows it, that's all, so it doesn't let it happen."

Abby wrapped her arms around her belly and slid off the stool, out of the stream of sunlight. Her bare feet were cold on the tile floor. She knew every millimeter of Scott's face, the way his nose dipped, and the crinkles under his eyes that had deepened in the years they'd been together. She knew the six freckles on his forehead, which turned to fifteen every summer. Last year there had been sixteen, and she'd become more militant about his sunscreen. "Who are you?"

"I'm the man who loves you."

She used to believe that.

He went on, "I know it's hard. You're still recovering from this one. We'll go to Hawaii when you feel up for it. Take some time off."

"Hawaii?" She wouldn't go anywhere with him. Ever. "You said you wouldn't mind adopting."

"I was wrong." His voice was shaking. "I didn't know I didn't want to be a father."

"But —" He'd *always* wanted to be a father. Always.

Oh, god, unless it had just been her saying that, over and over, until it was easier for him just to go along with her? Was that possible? Not only that he could deceive her like that, but that she could delude herself?

"You know the other day when I was two hours late getting home from the office? That Saturday afternoon?" He didn't wait for her nod. "I went to a . . . a friend's house. It was the kid's fifth birthday."

"You spent two hours at a kid's birthday party?"

Scott shook his head. "I didn't stay. They had a raccoon piñata in the front yard. So many kids, just hitting things with sticks. And the idea — just the idea of the kid and all the stuff that came with him, the piñata and the sticks, and all the *shit* that would come with a kid of ours — I left. I spent two hours just driving. I knew I had to tell you, but I haven't known how. Then you told me about this miscarriage. . . . We can't. I just can't, Abby. I'm sorry I told you I could."

Abby had walked out of the room a moment (a lifetime) later. She went up the stairs. She sat at her computer.

She would have to change his mind, because hers never would. Ever. And if she didn't change his mind . . . She would learn actual magic. She was halfway there already, right? She would wish on heliotrope and mugwort. Her healing powers would turn to the dark side, a thing she hadn't believed in an hour before, a thing that had to exist, didn't it? She would *make* him want a child. But . . .

Just as a test, a breathless dare to herself, she typed the words "no-fault divorce California" into a Google search bar.

Pages of divorce results scrolled past her eyes: companies that wanted to make it fast and clean. *No-fault.* Why did the term even exist? Abby needed an at-fault divorce. A full-fault one, as full of fault as anything had ever been before.

Then she closed the window.

Abby didn't need a divorce. She just needed to try again. Even while hating Scott, she knew she could get over that feeling. She just needed to have more sex with him. So much sex. She'd tell him she was on the pill if that's what it took.

And she'd get pregnant one more time. That one would stick because she'd do everything right, and Scott would *see.* He was born to be a father.

Abby made the plan and tried to summon hope from it. But her heart wobbled and

tilted slowly, then disintegrated, slanting to
dust.

CHAPTER TWENTY-THREE

Diego stared at Fern, the whites of his eyes bright in the porch light. "Off your *route*? But the 40 is yours. You worked so hard to get it."

"I didn't have enough seniority to hold it, I guess." Fern cleared her throat. "Next time."

"Shit. What are you going to do? About Matty?"

Four hours on his own in the afternoon. She wouldn't be able to pick him up, wouldn't be able to cart him around on her coach. And with the overtime she was going to need, it would be even longer. "We'll be fine."

Diego opened his mouth, but Fern cut him off. "Before you say it, no. You can't help. No more than you're already doing. You need to be working."

He sighed. "I feel like I'm always working. He could come with me. . . ."

"No," snapped Fern. Diego winced, and she felt terrible. He was only trying to help. "He can't be on a jobsite."

"He's good at climbing trees."

"And you have the insurance to cover that?"

"No *way* do I have that insurance," said Diego. "Are you kidding me? There isn't a policy in the world that would cover an eleven-year-old on a tree job."

"I'll work something out," Fern said. Again. It was like her theme song. She needed a dance to go with it. *I'll work something out,* tip of the hat, step-ball-change, jeté into the air, land in the splits for a big finish.

Diego narrowed his eyes but nodded once. "I'm going to help in spite of you. Did the bastard leave you anything?"

"Me? I'm sure he didn't leave anything to me." But what about Matty? Fern suddenly remembered the text that had landed while she was driving home from Gregory's place. "Abby texted me. Earlier. She wants to meet."

"See?" Diego crossed his arms across his chest. "That's what I'm saying. He left you money. I know he did."

Scott was dead. It hit Fern all over again. She'd never again wonder if he'd appear at their door, demanding rights that she might have to give him. She'd never feel that fear, never have to worry about proving to a judge that she — with her epilepsy and crappy work schedule and run-down house in a shitty neighborhood and no money in the bank — was the better parent.

She was free.

"If he weren't dead, I'd kill him." Diego reached forward, drained his wine, and then set the glass down again. He thumped a fist into his palm. Her brother was a big man. He was broad in the same places Fern was, but wide shoulders looked better on a man, especially a tall one. A thick waist just made him look like a lumberjack, which, essentially, he was. "You need a damn break, Fernandita."

The words were unexpected coming from him, the guy who worked as hard as she did. God knew she thought them to herself all the time, but that was her just being weak. Hearing them out loud made those stupid tears rise right to the tops of her cheekbones. She would *not* let them spill, so they sat there, little hot lakes just under her lashes, ready to betray her.

If he hadn't died, she would have gotten his check. It would have covered the fridge, at least. The washer — well, that was what

Laundromats were for.

The wine was so strong it was almost thick in her glass. It was her turn to search the pale night sky for a star. Just one simple twinkle, even of a plane's headlight, that would be enough.

It hurt to even think about that check, the same way it had always hurt to get it in the mail. Scott's damn handwriting in the memo box: *Take care.* He'd meant it — she knew him well enough to know that. He probably thought his way through the words each time. *I really hope she's taking care of herself and of Matty.*

Take care. That's all she ever *did.* Of everyone.

All he had to do was write a check while she raised a man.

"Besides the money, he never did *one thing* for that boy." Diego's voice was low.

She wouldn't look at him. "No. He didn't."

Not one damn thing since Matty's birth. Those had been the happiest moments of her whole life, those first ninety minutes while she and Scott held their perfect son, counting and recounting his toes, admiring his astonishingly bald head. Even the birth bruises on his head caused by the forceps — purple and shocking — seemed somehow

214

gorgeous, like immense storm clouds. Impressive. Something to be proud of.

Then Scott had gone home "real quick." She'd been stupid enough to think Scott had a birth present for her. They'd spent every cent of both of their savings for the down payment on the old house, and then they'd gone into credit card debt to put together the baby's nursery. But still she'd thought maybe he had a surprise for her.

It had been a surprise, all right. When she woke again later that night, Diego sat in the dimness in the too-small chair where she would have expected to see Scott. "He hasn't come back."

"How long have I been sleeping?"

"Almost four hours." Her brother had been vibrating with rage.

She'd checked her phone. Nothing.

Twenty-four hours went by. Enough hours that she'd talked to every hospital and jail in the Bay Area, looking for him. She spoke to the police officer posted to the front of the hospital. "I'm sorry, ma'am. It's not uncommon."

Other women had this happen to them, too? They pushed a human being out their *conchas* and then their men went for a walk and never came back?

Scott's father, Wyatt, sat in the waiting

room, flirting with the nurses, bragging about his parking abilities. He pretended he wasn't concerned, but when he bent over to kiss Fern's cheek and brush his fingertips over Matty's warm bald head, she could smell the fear on him. Wyatt knew his son wasn't coming back. They both did.

When the message bounced onto her phone, her hand shook too much to see all the words. Texting was still so new then. A text wasn't casual yet, and Scott had never sent her one before. She knew it would mean something huge. Terrified, she'd asked Diego to read it to her. Her poor brother. They weren't kids anymore. Fern had always protected him from their mother's drunk rages against whatever she was out to get — the blinds that rattled too much, or the sofa that needed to be dragged out to the curb — fury spit in Spanish they could barely understand, fury that too often turned on them. Fern had shielded him as much as she could, and when Diego became a broad tree of a teenager, he returned the favor, threatening the boys she dated by looming in the dark near the Dumpsters as they dropped her off, by showing up at the same parties and just *being* there in the dark background. Being him.

But he couldn't protect her from the first

and last text Scott would ever send her. Every word Diego spoke was a punch. *I'm sorry. I thought I could be a father. I can't. Let me know what I should do.*

Fern started to cry and tiny Matty, resting on her chest, gave a startled whimper. Wyatt, who'd been shifting from foot to foot by the door, said, "That little fucker." Wyatt hadn't wanted Scott to date her, not at first. *I tow a lot of Mexican cars, son. You think maybe there's a reason for that?* When Scott had admitted what his father had said, Fern had said she would never meet the man. Then she was pregnant, and Wyatt's whiskered chin had trembled the first time he'd asked to touch her belly.

"He'll come back," said Wyatt. "Or he's no son of mine."

"He'll come back," said Diego. "And I'll beat the living shit out of him, but I won't kill him."

"No son of mine would abandon his child. His child's *mother.*" Wyatt had fat tears rolling over the gray sand of stubble on his cheeks. It looked like his face would crack apart, his skin a ceiling, a leaking faucet on the floor above — soon the plaster of his skin might disintegrate and crumble. "I'll choose you," he choked. "I swear to Christ if he doesn't come back, you'll be my daughter and I'll have no son."

Diego said, "I'll try *really* hard not to kill him."

It had been an unnecessary threat.

"He won't come back."When she'd shown Scott the first ultrasound (she never told him about the pink plus on the pregnancy stick, just like she'd never told him about the first two doctor's visits), Scott had said *"No."* A visceral knee-jerk response. He'd never wanted to be a father, or at least not until he was old, "not till I'm thirty-five or something." They were just twenty-seven then. "I love you, Fernie. Of course I love you. But I don't think I can be a dad. Not ready. I'm *so* not ready."

She'd hoped he'd get over it. He said he would try. They got married outside the Palace of Fine Arts. He wrapped his arms around her at night and sometimes his palms drifted to her belly as it grew. He'd been there for the birth, the whites of his eyes wide the whole time she screamed, but he'd cried — sobbed, really — when they first held tiny Matias. *Ninety minutes.* For that hour and a half Fern had no pain even though the epidural had long worn off. There was nothing inside her but light. Hope. No fear. Just the baby and Scott and her, safe inside a perfect bubble of iridescent joy. She felt sorry for the nurse who checked on them, sorry that she wasn't in the bubble, never would be. How terrible that must have been for her, to witness that kind of happiness and then have to go do her job, snapping on lifeless, loveless rubber gloves.

She'd thought that Scott's tears were of happiness. Of falling in love with his son. She'd never been more wrong.

In that moment as she held Matty with his tiny wrist ID that matched the wider one on her wrist, as Matty's lips worked sideways in a brand-new way, as a woman yelled something in Tagalog out in the hospital corridor, Fern made up her mind.

Scott could be all in or all out.

He'd chosen all out.

All the way out. Fern had always wondered who her father was — she wasn't even sure she and Diego had the same one. Every night of her childhood, Fern had fallen asleep listening for an unfamiliar car door slamming, an unfamiliar tread outside the front door, wondering if he — whoever he was — would show up one night, open arms, waiting for his daughter to run into them. Fern's child wouldn't wonder. She wouldn't raise her son's hopes. Matty would know who his father was, but he would never expect him to be present in any way.

She would never let Scott change his mind and step back through the door, even if he wanted to. He'd lost that right.

Now, under the pale night fog, her hair heavy and curled with moisture stolen from the air, Fern felt something cold snake into her soul. She held up her wineglass. "More."

Diego said, "What about the child support? You're not going to get that anymore?"

"Abby shouldn't have to pay for his sins." She gave a hollow laugh. "I bounced the mortgage. It's going to cost ninety bucks, and that's only if I get the late fee in this week. After that, it goes to two hundred and ten."

"I'll give you the money."

Diego couldn't afford it any more than she could. "I need a new washer, apparently. And a fridge."

"Shit." He dropped his head and then raised it. "I got two grand on a new credit card. You can have it all."

"*Mamón.* You know I'll never take your stupid money."

He grimaced. "Do me a favor, then. Meet his wife. See what she wants."

Fern stayed silent.

"Just do it. Don't be a fucking idiot."

She gave up. "Fine."

He nodded. "Good."

"But if you show up with a washer, I'll kick you so hard in the balls you'll wish you were born with ovaries."

It was the same thing as *I love you.*

Diego smiled and kept his eyes on the ceiling of the sky. That was his way of saying it back.

CHAPTER TWENTY-FOUR

Abby gave a small scream as the blind closest to the bed whipped upward with a clatter.

"Okay, my sleepy girlie. Up and at 'em." Kathryn yanked the cord of the next blind.

Kathryn's habit of stopping by early in the morning had never been a problem before. Scott got up at six to go to the office, and Abby had always been a lark, better in the first hours of the day than she was at night, when she became a yawner. So when Kathryn let herself in, neither of them had minded. (At least Abby hadn't — the corners of Scott's lips had always gone taut, but when asked, he'd said that it was fine. "She's the closest to family you have." She had been unreasonably irritated by this answer.)

Since Scott died, though, Kathryn had caught Abby in bed more than once. For the first time in her life, Abby was good at sleeping. It had been only two and a half weeks of sleeping alone, but her nights were almost dreamless now. She went to bed early and got up later than she ever had, and she sometimes took naps, too. Grief, sure. Everyone told her grief would make her tired. But she didn't feel tired, exactly. She just couldn't keep her brain sparking for as long as she should be able to. She was reading a thriller chock-full of chopped-up people and heart-racing intrigue, and almost every corner was folded over. She could only get one or two pages before the book would drop. Sometimes she didn't even get a whole page, and she'd refold the corner of the page as sleep dragged her under, feeling worthless.

Was it grief that let her sleep? Was that where sadness fit in her body? Was it terrible to admit she loved having the bed to herself? (She knew it was. No one knew she'd asked him for a divorce. She could barely admit it to herself.)

"I made coffee, but you have to come downstairs to get it."

"Hey!" Abby held up her hand to shield her eyes from the sunlight. "My eyes don't adjust that fast." Her words were thick, as if she were hungover.

"Sure they do. Open them wider."

Abby pulled the bright new duvet over her face. "You chirp louder than the damn birds."

"Best time of the day. Come on. I have two azaleas I saved from being put in a wood chipper by some fake gardener over near Point Isabel. They'll look great over by the rhododendron. And Brook called me. She said she left you a message, but you haven't called her back."

Abby groaned. "You're in cahoots. You can't steal my friends. I've told you that."

"I adore your friends. They keep me young. Get me some more. Now up with you! Meet me in the garden! Keep moving! We'll dig holes!" Kathryn left the bedroom door open as she left, clattering down the hall and thumping down the stairs.

Abby dragged a brush through her hair. She'd shower later, after Kathryn made her dig whatever it was she needed to dig. Her limbs felt heavy with grief, her blood thick with concomitant guilt — she knew she wasn't grieving the right way. Her heart should be shrouded in black. She shouldn't have felt the rush of happiness she had when Kathryn yelled at her about digging holes. She didn't deserve it — she had loved Scott less every time she lost a baby, every time that flash of relief shot across his face. How could a woman deserve to mourn a man she was leaving?

And yet she did. She ached with missing him. It wasn't right. But she didn't know if it was wrong, either.

Keep moving.

T-shirt on. Jeans up. Sunscreen slicked. Garden clogs on.

Before Abby put her phone in her pocket, she retrieved the message. Brook, constantly frazzled, sounded even more frantic than usual. "Girl. If I don't get some more of that spearmint bergamot oil from you, I swear to god I will have to make my own from toothpaste. This is not a drill. I repeat, *not* a drill. Can you swing a couple of bottles by this afternoon? I'd come get them myself, but I have two kids down with strep. I promise they won't touch you. Except . . . shit." Abby could almost hear the second Brook remembered about Scott. "Holy *shit.* I forgot. I don't know *how* I did that. Fuck me. You looked beautiful at the service. Everything was beautiful. I'm so sorry Jason started screaming at the end, but Wayne kicked him and I had to fight World War Three as quietly as possible in the back row, but I'm sure you heard them. Germany probably heard them. Sorry about that. So sorry about bugging you. What a dick

225

move." Another pause. "No, wait. I'm not sorry. I love you. I love your oils. I love what they do for my soap business, and I can't fulfill this order to some New York boutique hotel until I get a gorgeous bottle or three from you. So get to work, if that's what will help you feel better. Also, call me back and tell me to fuck off, if that will help you more. Love you."

Abby thumb-typed back. *I'll be there this afternoon. xo.* Brook was right — she needed to *do* something. She had at least four orders that she had to fulfill that had come in from her Etsy site. Thank god Brook had called — thank god she'd sounded so *Brook* about it all. The nicest part was knowing that later she'd go to Brook's house, where no two plates matched and there was usually a cat hair ball or two puked up in a corner. And no matter how much Brook felt sorry for her loss, there would be a moment when they'd be sitting in the living room and Brook would dump all her problems out, unpacking them in front of Abby like a too-full, broken-zippered suitcase. *He says he's got a crush on the receptionist. I told him to try to sleep with her, and he got all upset with me, can you believe it? I love him, I swear I do. I just want him to know he's not gonna be able to get in her pants. And lord, if he does, then at least I'll get a little break. And Danny got diagnosed with ADHD, tell me something I don't know already. You know how many bars of soap I gotta ship to make the copay on the Adderall?* Scott had always wanted Abby to be happy — sometimes it had felt like her job. Other friends, too, seemed to need Abby to remain strong and competent. Vivian and Lisa talked about mutual funds and politics over organic, Paleo lunches. They were aggressively cheerful, and needed Abby to be, too. It was a job she was normally good at. But everyone needed a break. With Brook, Abby had always been able to be herself. She could cry when she felt like it and not explain why she was sad if she didn't want to. Brook would pass her peanut-butter cookies in a plastic tray and rub her nose unself-consciously. Then Abby would listen to Brook's complaints and empathize.

Sometimes empathy was all you needed.

Abby looked out the window and saw Kathryn striding across the backyard carrying two shovels.

It was good to be loved. To be supported.

What about Fern? Had she had support when Scott left her?

In the garden, Abby came back into herself. Kathryn was right to bring her out here, to get her in the dirt early. If she could make herself do this every day, maybe she'd be able to figure out her next move. A Brewer's sparrow chirped and bounced from branch to branch of the ironwood. Next to it, the ginkgo tree was just coming into yellow bloom, a month too early. Last year the too-early blooms had made her worry about it and global warming and climate change. This year she was obsessing about other things.

Like how she wanted to see Scott's eleven-year-old son again. Like wondering what the routine was like at Fern's house.

"What is it?" Kathryn's voice was soft.

Abby put her hands to the small of her back and stood straight. Digging holes deep enough for the root balls of the full-grown azaleas normally wouldn't be a problem this time of year, but the six-year drought combined with the fact that Abby hadn't ever put anything in this corner of the huge yard made the dirt as stubborn as Kathryn herself. "Nothing."

"You're not here."

"Hey, I'm shoveling as fast as you are."

"I'm twenty-five years older than you are and I've moved double the dirt." Kathryn looked pointedly at their respective piles.

"You do this every day at the nursery."

"You kidding me? This is what I pay the boys to do. I don't have to dig *holes*."

"You love it."

"What's on your mind, girlie?"

"Them." Matty. Fern. She didn't have to say their names out loud for Kathryn to know.

Kathryn wiped her face with a green bandanna she pulled from one of the million pockets of her overalls. "What are you going to do about them?"

"What can I do?"

"What do you want to do?"

Be with them. Know them. She wanted to learn what they liked, what their favorite in-jokes were. She wanted to learn what Fern's face looked like when it was relaxed, figure out what made Matty laugh until he toppled over sideways. "Nothing. I guess. None of my business. They don't owe me anything."

"True."

Disappointment shot through Abby's legs, straight down into the dirt at her feet. She picked her shovel back up. It was even heavier than when she'd dropped it two minutes ago.

"But maybe you owe them something."

"The life insurance. I know. I'm going to give her a check." She tugged on the neckline of her T-shirt, suddenly too hot even though the sun hadn't managed to push its way into any part of the garden yet. "A really big fucking check. I texted her to see if we could meet last week, but she hasn't responded."

"Will she *take* a check?"

"Of course she will." It hadn't crossed Abby's mind that Fern wouldn't. "Without the money from his business, it'll be a little tighter than I'm used to, but one of Mom's investments just exploded. I'll have enough money, and I own the house outright." She looked up at the siding, up to the high window of their bedroom. It was just a shell. A very nice shell with a magic garden in back. But still just a shell. "I honestly don't want to keep his business running on my own. Maybe this will give me the motivation to really get my own business off the ground." Her Etsy site kind of sucked, she knew it. Great ratings, poor photos. She could work on marketing. Promotion. Maybe there was a business class she could take that wouldn't suck the life out of her.

Kathryn rubbed a streak of soil across her nose. "I don't know. From what I saw of her at the funeral, she seemed proud. Strong. I can see her refusing."

"But . . . what do I do then? She has to take the money. For Matty. How would I make her, if she says no?"

Kathryn leaned on her shovel, looking like a cheerful hobo gravedigger. "Offer her something she needs."

"Like I have any clue what that might be."

"She's a single mother. There's only one thing she needs, besides money, I'm guessing, and that's time."

"Um . . ." What step had she missed? "The money will buy her time?"

"Offer to help with Matty." Kathryn leaned down and picked a rock out of the dirt. "Two birds. One of these."

The idea was huge. Presumptive.

Abby suddenly wanted nothing more. "To, like, babysit him? After school?"

"How does she do it now? Does he take care of himself?"

"I have no idea. I don't know where his school is, or how he gets home. He has his grandfather, and the older woman who lives there, too. Maybe they pick him up? I'm not sure they drive, though." For the first time, Abby wondered if Fern *needed* to have the elderly pair there. Were they paying rent? She looked up at her huge house again. Thirty-one hundred square feet. Five bedrooms (two of which had been made into offices, leaving a room for their workout equipment and only one spare bedroom —

she'd always thought of it as a reasonable amount of space, if a little large). Empty except for her.

"What can it hurt to offer?"

"Yes. You're totally right." Abby brushed off her hands as if she would go now, as if she'd track Fern down on her bus right this very second.

"Wanna finish this first?" Kathryn's eyebrow was a sharp upward slant.

Abby nudged the soil with the toe of her garden boot. "Okay. Yes." She smiled. A ray of sun found its way through the ginkgo tree's blooms and landed on the top of her head. She closed her eyes and felt the warmth, letting it soak into her. Just a second or two.

It felt like absolution.

"All right, then." She picked up her shovel, but Kathryn spoke again before she could take another spadeful of dirt.

"Do me one more favor."

Abby felt magnanimous. She had a new plan, a big one, an important one. "Anything."

"Do things that feel good."

"Yes! Look!" She stabbed the side of the hole. "I'm doing that now! With you!"

"When I'm not making you do it, I mean. When I'm at work, when I can't see you."

"I will."

"Eat. Take a bath. Remember your body."

"I know. I'm trying." She'd lost weight — she knew she had.

"Get laid if you can."

Abby blinked and rewound the words in her mind. Kathryn couldn't have just said what she thought she'd heard. "Like, rest more?"

"Like fuck someone."

"What?"

"If you get the chance."

Abby didn't know whether she should laugh or cry — both reactions felt imminent. "I loved him. I know you think I didn't —"

"I know you did, sweetheart. I also know you were desperately unhappy."

Abby had never told her that. She'd been so *careful* to never tell Kathryn that.

"Just remember that your body needs ways to grieve. Different ways. You need to sing and cry and dance and shovel dirt, and maybe get touched by someone else."

Anger spiked, as real and as sharp as the splinter that had just bitten her thumb from the shovel's handle. "Scott and I had *great* sex. *Hot* sex."

"When you had it."

"I should never have talked to you about

it. About anything."

"Just remember. If it comes up." Kathryn's upper lip twitched. "As it were. Get it over with."

"Like you would." Kathryn had been married to Rebecca for twenty-seven years.

"Absolutely. Rebecca and I both would, in that situation. We were talking about it last night. You've lost the one person you could trust to hold you. A bit of holding wouldn't do you wrong."

"No."

"Just keep it in mind. Craigslist has Casual Encounters, you know."

"Kathryn!"

Kathryn raised that eyebrow again. Sunlight winked against her tanned cheek. "Sometimes I read 'em for fun. You never know. Just remember I said it, if it comes up. It's nature's way. Get it over with if you can, and have fun doing it." She pointed downward. "Now, my darling girlie, dig that hole."

Chapter Twenty-Five

As Fern entered the café, she kicked herself for feeling so nervous. She felt like she'd shot a can of Mountain Dew and then jumped up and down, like Matty used to do to feel the fizz in his stomach (before that throwing-up-at-the-movies incident). After four more texts, two e-mails, and one very long phone message from the suddenly quite-pushy Abby, Fern had finally agreed to meet Abby: *Okay.*

The response had come almost immediately. *Great. Zocalo Cafe, 1 p.m., Friday?*

Who in the whole world got to go hang out at a café at one on a weekday? Women who didn't have jobs, that was who. And, more worryingly, women who had a newly fluctuating work schedule. Fern was free at that time, and she hated that she was. *Zócalo.* It meant public square in Spanish, but she'd only ever heard it used casually, as an interjection of surprise. *Oh, my god.* It seemed appropriate.

The café was quiet. A few scattered men sat at dark wooden tables, tapping on computers. One man with a beard to his chest was sketching, casting quick non-subtle glances at the pretty blond barista. The art on the walls had changed since Fern had last been there, and showcased an artist who apparently liked blue skies and the small San Leandro bungalows that surrounded the café.

Abby was there already, papers spread in front of her on a larger round table. As if she felt Fern's gaze, she looked up and waved. *Dios,* she was too eager. Fern wanted to pull her internal e-brake and U-turn out the way she'd come in, but instead, she took a breath and made a gesture toward the counter. "Coffee," she mouthed.

In line, Fern looked up at the café's board, staring blankly. A coffee. She just wanted coffee. Why couldn't she see how much that was? If she'd been in charge of writing out that chalkboard, she would have kept it clean and simple. The names of the simple drinks with clear prices next to them. Instead, all she could make out on the busy signboard were things like Paraguayan mochas, low-fat caramel steamers, and Mexican Borgias, whatever the hell they were. She had a dollar seventy-five in quarters. That had to be enough for a cup, didn't it? She'd be damned if she had to put a four-dollar latte on her debit card.

She ordered. A dollar sixty-five, just a dime for a tip. They used a point-of-sales unit that looked ten years old. If she'd been running the café, she would have put in an iPad Square system. Easy. Cheap.

Fern stepped to the side to wait, ignoring Abby's smiling face half a room away. She pulled her shirt away from her body and flapped the edges of her cardigan as surreptitiously as she could. She'd had to park three blocks away, and the sun, for spring, was hot as hell.

She stole another quick glance at Abby, who was looking down at her phone.

God, she looked so *sweet.* Abby had the kind of face that half the mothers in the PTA had. Matty's school straddled an Oakland zone that was smack-dab in the middle of a gentrification sweep (a fancy word for whites discovering things that weren't theirs). So the mothers who came to the PTA meetings were split right down the middle — half stay-at-homes, half work-all-the-motherfucking-timers.

Those stay-at-homes. It was funny, they always looked the most worn-out. From what? All the driving they did for their children? A rough day was a day they volunteered *and* had to drive their kids to soccer. One of the rich moms had once thanked the mothers who donated the most time to the PTA because "stay-at-home mothers are the hardest-working mothers in the world."

Such bullshit. Fern had wanted to scream, but instead she dug her embarrassingly non-manicured fingernails into the palms of her hands and didn't say a word, just went along with the group on the vote for gluten-free nut-free (flavor-free) cupcakes for the bake sale. Single mothers who worked full-time, *those* were the goddamned hardest-working people in the whole world, and Fern would bet her house on the fact that this was true the world over. In India, single mothers lost sleep trying to hold the world together with their bare hands. In Australia, single mothers worked their asses off, just like they did in Japan. In Iceland, single mothers probably had excellent health care and vacation benefits, but when they got off shift, they still had to do the laundry, clean the house, clean the children, and make dinner so they could do it all again, alone, the next day.

Stay-at-home mothers. *Madre.*

But like Grandpa Wyatt always said, being

238

smug was a well-paved two-way street. If she felt smug for working long hours because she was strong enough to do so, that was fine, because stay-at-home mothers got to feel smug about making healthy food choices for their kids, something Fern didn't have the time to do. Homemade bread was a luxury, and yeah, it was probably way better for their growing bodies. And it was *never* going to happen in her house unless Elva decided to embrace a new art. God help them all if that happened.

"Ma'am?"

Fern jumped. "Yeah?"

The barista pointed to the stacks of mugs in front of her. "You can just take a cup and fill it yourself. Right there."

Embarrassment flooded her. She tried to nod like she'd had a plan, standing there, motionless.

Her cup full, she moved to Abby's table. "Hi."

Abby smiled, and Fern swore to god, her eyes sparkled. "Fern! Oh, hi! How are you?"

Fern sat, ripping off her sweater, cursing the fact that she was now sweating at her hairline. She could feel how red her face was.

She ignored the question. "So." She took a sip, carefully not making a face when the liquid, still too hot, burned her. "What did you need?" That was good. Making it clear that she knew Abby was the one who needed something. That this wasn't her idea.

"Okay." Abby looked down at the paperwork in front of her. "Yes. Okay. We'll get right to it." She sounded nervous. "I've been working on this for days. It's the only answer I can come up with."

Answer? "What's the question?"

"What to do about the money."

Fantastic. Finances, brought up within twenty seconds. "What are you talking about?"

"The money Scott was sending you."

Confusion slowed Fern's synapses. "What?"

"The checks."

"The checks," she repeated. The heat moved from her face down into her chest, and she felt her brain snap to sharper focus, the way it did when a group of the wrong kind of teenage boys got on her bus, the kind that felt threatening in their quietness, the kind of group that didn't bluster harmlessly like the rest did. She settled one hand flat on the table next to her coffee mug. "If I'd taken him to court, he woulda had to pay more."

"Oh. No, that's not . . ."

240

"He got off easy." Would Abby want the money *back*? Was that possible? Legal? Could they subpoena her bank statements? What would that prove besides the fact that she was broke, that she was always broke? That was fine. It would be humiliating, yes, to have to show off her slim checking account and her empty savings, but she would do it if she needed to prove that she hadn't gotten rich from the checks.

"Fern, slow down. It's okay. I want you to have his life insurance. With just one catch."

Chapter Twenty-Six

The only word Fern heard was *catch.* She stilled, conserving her energy. A catch. "Sorry?"

"I'm so nervous. God. I hate this."

Abby looked young, *so* young. Years ago, some embarrassing but inevitable Facebook stalking had revealed to Fern that Abby was only two years younger than she was. Abby was thirty-six now. But Abby looked no more than thirty, while Fern felt like her own bones were in their mid-fifties, at least. "Go on, then." Fern kept her hands carefully wrapped around her mug. She would not agree to a catch, money or no money.

"I want to spend time with Matty."

Fern just stared. The café quieted around them, as if listening. Or maybe it was the roaring in her head that muted the rest of the world. She could hear her own breathing.

Abby — insanely — kept talking. "I mean,

not *much* time. Just whatever you say is okay. Like, if you ever need babysitting. In the afternoons after school, maybe? If there are . . . other times like that? That you might need help? I'd love to —"

"Spend time with *Matias*? No. He's my son. He's not a chess piece."

"No, not like that. Of course not. I thought — in exchange for the life insurance —"

The base of Fern's spine heated as if she were sitting on the plug-in seat warmer she used on the coach in winter. "You thought I'd sell you time with him? With Matty? That you could *buy* him?"

Abby pressed her fingers against her cheeks. "No. God, no." She coughed once and went red. "No, no. I didn't mean it to come out like that."

Fern gritted her back teeth together for a moment. "What you said was that you want to give me money. In return for letting you spend time with my son."

"Shit," said Abby. Her hands dropped from her cheeks, and she laid them, palms up, on the table. "I did. I said that. Exactly. I didn't think it through, not to that conclusion. I thought — I thought —"

Fern stood, the wooden chair clattering backward. She gripped her sweater with damp palms. "I don't need his money." She thought briefly how Abby had been inside her home. She'd seen the broken blinds in the living room. She'd seen the couch, the way it sagged in the middle like an old wooden bench. The scuffed linoleum in the kitchen. The way the wall paint buckled above the sink. "And I sure as shit don't need yours."

Abby shot to her feet. "He owes you. Scott *owes* you."

True. But that would *never* make her beholden to this woman. "He did. But I didn't want it. And you don't owe me a thing." It hurt to say. In her deepest heart, maybe she'd thought that, yeah, this Abby woman, with her perfect brown oversized handbag that looked as light as if it had nothing more than keys and a wallet inside, with her perfectly matching brown boots that didn't have a single scuff, maybe Abby *did* owe her, like Diego said. Maybe the thought had flitted through her mind. Once. Okay, a few times. In her rational mind, the one that controlled what she said, what thoughts were put into words, she had known Scott had owed her. And Scott was dead. So she said it again, to convince herself. "You don't owe me a goddamn thing."

Abby said, "Then I'll just give it to you."

"Did he leave it to his son?"

Abby's face fell. "No. I was the only beneficiary."

Exhaustion made Fern's legs feel weak. "So you want to give me money that belongs to you and then extort me later?"

Abby shook her head. "I promise you, Fern, I never thought it would come out like that. I'll give you the insurance free and clear. I'm sure it will take a while for it to pay out, but I can advance it to you from my own money." She pointed out the window to the credit union across the street. "That's our bank. I mean, *my* bank. That's why I asked you to meet me here. We'll go put your name on that account and take mine off."

Fern hated herself for asking. "How much?"

"Well, okay. It should have been more, but when we bought it, we were only thinking about protecting his business. When we had kids, we were going to up it — we were going to up both of ours. If I'd known about Matty . . . I would have made him buy more." She glanced at a Post-it note. "Five hundred thousand. Plus twenty thousand from an old policy he got online a long time ago."

Abby thought it should be *more*?

A half a million. So much money.

So much fucking *money.* She could pay off the house and still have half left over. No mortgage payment, and a safety net in the bank. All of it for Matty, for his *life,* his extraordinary life, because it could be that, with that kind of cash. College, anywhere he wanted. Her mouth went dry at the astonishing thought. She tried to breathe — she tried to remember why she was saying no. No, no, *no.* No.

Abby glanced down at the floor, and Fern saw a silver hair glinting at her temple. Just one. A promise. She probably had her hair highlighted and dyed every six weeks. She probably happily forked over hundreds of dollars to stay looking as young as she did.

Fern, on the other hand, had Googled her way to learning how to mix her own hair dye when she'd gone prematurely gray at thirty-two. A whole box of dye cost fifteen dollars at CVS. Instead, she bought the color in six-packs meant for professional hairstylists on Amazon. Developer was literally cheaper than bottled water, two bucks for an amount that lasted her two years. Plastic gloves were only pennies if you bought them in bulk at the SavMart on High Street. She used one of Elva's royal wedding shot glasses to measure one ounce of each into a chipped ceramic bowl she kept under the sink for exactly that purpose. Total cost of each touch-up: $5.37.

She *had* this. She knew how to live. What to do.

She didn't need this woman's money. Ever.

But there was . . . Something about Abby was heartbreaking, something other than the fact that her husband had just died, what, three weeks ago? Not just that single gleaming silver hair. It was bigger than that. Fern tried not to look for what it was but couldn't help scanning her face again, one more time.

Abby laced her fingers together at her stomach. "I'm so sorry. I didn't think it all the way through. I wasn't trying to buy time with Matty, I swear. Not like that. I'm ashamed of myself." Her voice was disconsolate.

"I won't take your money." Fern's voice was softer now, but she was still on guard. She could still fight.

"But . . ."

Fern stuck her hand on her hip. "And here it is."

"I promise, no condition. I swear. But I . . . I'd love to ask you as a favor. To let me spend time with Matty."

Fern blew out a breath sharply. "Why?"

Abby's words were rushed, as if she was scared of them. "I asked Scott for a divorce. A few minutes before he died."

Fern couldn't help it — she laughed.

She shouldn't have. The look of sorrow on Abby's face wasn't worth it.

But that, combined with the silver hair she'd just seen. It was . . . time. That was all. Scott's second wife. Leaving him. Finally.

"Why?" Abby's voice was small. "Why would you laugh at that?"

"I'm not laughing at you," Fern said, trying to catch her breath. "I'm sorry. It's just . . . Well. Good job, girl. You should have told me that earlier, don't you think?" Then she sobered. Why, then, if Abby had been going to leave him, would she want to spend any time at all with his son?

As if Abby were reading her mind, she said one word, "Family."

Fern waited.

"It's all I wanted from him. Family." Abby pressed her hands to her stomach again, and now Fern thought she knew why.

"And he never told you about us."

"He *had* one." Abby's fingers were shaking. "And I didn't know that."

If she'd been anyone else, a passenger on

the bus, a customer in front of her in a checkout line, Fern would have known what to do. She would have just grabbed her in a hug, wrapped her in her arms, and given her a few reassuring thumps on the back. She would have held on until Abby let go. Then she would have cracked a dirty or otherwise inappropriate joke until Abby's face relaxed.

But this was Abby.

"He had a family," Abby said. "He never told me. He never saw you two even once, am I right about that?"

Well, he'd shown up out of the blue on Matty's fifth birthday, but he'd stayed less than ten minutes. The *pendejillo* hadn't even been able to make himself come in off the sidewalk. He'd clutched the fence and watched the children run around, shrieking. Fern had been pretty sure he wasn't positive which kid was his. "Once. He came by and watched Matty and his friends smack a piñata. He freaked, and left. Didn't even talk to his kid."

Abby gasped.

"What?"

"A raccoon? Was it a raccoon piñata?"

Fern jolted, and her knee knocked the table leg. "Yeah."

"He told me about that. Not about Matty,

249

but that he'd gone to a friend's kid's party. It was his response when I told him I'd just had my third miscarriage. He said he didn't want the . . . the *stuff* that went with a child. I was so shocked I didn't quiz him about who he'd gone to see. It never crossed my mind to wonder."

"Motherfucker."

"He had a *family*. He had the only thing I ever wanted, and he threw it away."

"So you . . ."

"I want to know you. All of you."

"You can't have it." The words were harsh, but this woman needed to hear them. *"You can't have my family."*

"I know. God. I'm so sorry." The words sounded ripped from Abby's throat. "Can we just go to the bank? Can you let me do this for you?"

"No. Never. I won't take the money." Fern was going crazy — she was losing her mind right here in this coffee shop. The money could change everything. She needed more time to wrap her head around it, around the rightness or wrongness of it. She needed to count in her head, up and down, from penury to wealth, with Matty's face at the front of her mind. "But you can babysit him."

"What?"

Fern's stomach leaped. "It turns out . . . that I might need some help. My schedule got changed at work. And I . . ."

"Anytime. I'm free every day." Abby's words tumbled over themselves. "Every single day. I mean, I volunteer with a botany group on Tuesdays, but I was thinking about quitting that anyway. I'm free anytime at all."

Why was Fern even considering this? She shouldn't make any rash decisions. She should go home and think about it. She shouldn't agree to anything concrete. But goddamn it, she felt sorry for Abby. So she said, "Wednesday. Three o'clock?" It was still her early day even on the new route — she could see Gregory a little longer than normal if Abby took Matty. Was that too selfish of her?

"God, yes. Thank you. Yes." Her voice was a gasp.

"Jesus. Breathe, okay?"

Abby gave no sign of hearing. "Where? Where will I go? Where will he be?"

Fern frowned. "Have you ever babysat before?"

"*Oh,* yes."

"When?"

"I was fourteen the last time, but I was *very* good at it. I'm still CPR qualified. I

251

make sure of that. You never know."

Lord have mercy. Matty wasn't that good with exuberance. It made him nervous. "Well, I hope like hell you don't have to use it on him. He's a pretty healthy kid. No epilepsy."

"Oh, *god.* What?"

This was insane. "I have it. It's controlled. He doesn't have it, that's what I'm telling you. He's a healthy kid. Pick him up at the school. I'll put your name down for him, and you'll have to check in the first day so they know you are who you say you are. Bring your ID."

Abby scrabbled at her purse as if she would prove who she was right then, right there. "Yes. Let me write this down. Yes."

Fern told her the name of the school. She gave her the address and told her where Matty would be waiting.

Abby smiled so brightly she could have lit up downtown San Francisco. "This will be amazing. We'll have fun. Wednesday."

Zócalo. "Yeah."

CHAPTER TWENTY-SEVEN

The birdlike woman at the school's front desk who checked Abby's ID didn't even look at her face. She just glanced at her license, and then returned to pecking at her computer. "You can wait outside for him."

"How will the yard monitor know that I'm allowed to take him?"

The woman pursed her beaklike lips and twitched. "She'll know."

"Do I need to show her my ID, too?" Abby wanted to get it perfectly right, from start to finish.

"No."

"But —"

"Outside." The woman flapped the tips of her fingers in the direction of the door.

Abby was half an hour early. The school yard filled and emptied twice already while she leaned against the fence trying her best not to look suspicious, trying to look like a mother. Or, okay, at least a babysitter. She kept her face relaxed, a nonthreatening smile affixed.

There was an ebb and a flow to the yard, a tide of traffic and running feet. Cars pulled up, behind and next to hers, double-parking with assured nonchalance. The city buses wheezed up, doors flapping open. Women (and the occasional man) filed into the playground. There was some chitchat, but less than Abby would have thought. Most of the women kept their eyes on their phones, thumbs scrolling. As classes were dismissed, children launched themselves at their adults. They all hugged, as if on cue, and then the women ferried them away. The buses pulled out. The playground emptied. Then, five minutes later, the next classroom — or grade, or whatever it was — would let out and it started all over again. The waves of the tide were women, the ocean breeze was car emissions, and the sand dollars left behind were worried-looking kids whose mothers were late.

The bell rang again, and even from half a playground away, Abby could hear doors slamming. She could practically hear the backpack zippers, recalling the feeling of freedom that came with pencils sliding into cases, math books shoved into desks. She remembered the feeling of hair permatangled from hanging off the parallel bars during lunch. Abby had loved school, doing better in class than out. She'd hated summer break after the first two weeks, and within a day or two of a new school year, she was always deeply smitten with whatever teacher she had, bringing her bright cherries and the best caterpillars and construction-paper love letters.

She checked her compact mirror as subtly as she could and quickly reapplied a layer of gloss. It was armor. The playground monitor would see it and know she was well put together. More trustworthy. Where *was* the monitor? A harried-looking woman with frizzy black hair had patrolled the playground twice without saying a word, but Abby hadn't seen her in at least twenty minutes. Abby could be *anyone.*

Then Matty was there.

Even at a distance, she recognized him. He had Scott's walk, that steady rhythm, little pistonlike legs, regimented arms. The similarity was unexpected, and it took her breath away.

She waved.

Shyly, he waved back. He didn't smile. The distance between them felt like a mile though it was less than the interior of her regular Starbucks.

When he was close enough, Abby said, "Hi." Original. She should have had something planned. *Hi, tiger. Hi, cutie pie.* She added, "Matty," and then felt like an idiot.

"Hey," said Matty. He hitched his backpack higher on his shoulder.

"That looks heavy," Abby said, grateful to have something to say. "Can I take it for you?"

Matty's eyebrows slammed upward. "No!"

"Sorry."

Matty didn't answer, just trudged toward the open gate.

"I checked in at the office — do I need to check out with you?" Like he was a library book.

"Mrs. Perez saw you." He gestured at the harried woman near the double yellow doors.

"But she doesn't know me."

"It's fine."

Abby felt her driver's license burning through the wallet in her purse as they walked. It was the one thing she had to get right, she knew that.

Or she'd *known* that. Turned out what she had to get right might end up being much harder.

Just outside the gate, Abby stopped and Matty, two steps behind her, did, too. "This is *so* weird," she said.

Matty nodded.

"That's my car over there." She pointed at the champagne Lexus RX.

"Okay."

"Are you nervous, too?"

Matty shrugged. He didn't answer.

"I'm super nervous and I think it's because I want this to go right." She started walking again, and just behind her, he followed.

"Why?"

The question startled Abby, and she wondered if the rest of the afternoon would go like this: them startling each other until one of them fell over in surprised exhaustion. *Because you're more important than I ever knew you would be. Because I have no idea what to do with you.* "Because I've never had an eleven-year-old friend."

"Aren't you, like . . . babysitting me?"

Abby hit the unlock button on her car. The familiar chirp was reassuring. "Well. You're not a baby."

Matty looked at the sidewalk, apparently fascinated with the way the concrete cracked and buckled. He didn't move to open the passenger door, so Abby did it for him. He jumped up, tossing his backpack on the floor in front of him.

Abby got in on her side and started the car. "So."

Matty blinked.

"What should we do?"

He turned his head to look at her, and something about his unblinking gaze reminded her of an owl. "You're asking me?"

"Yep. What do you normally do?"

"Mom used to pick me up, but she's on a new route this week, so Diego has been doing it."

"He's your uncle, right? What do you do when Diego picks you up?"

"He takes me home and then goes out to work again."

"What does he do?"

"He climbs trees."

"Sorry?"

"He cuts them down. From the top."

"He's an arborist?"

"Yeah. He's cool."

Abby longed for Matty to say that about her someday. *She's cool.* "What do you do then? When you're alone?"

"Not usually *alone.* Usually my grandpa and Elva are there."

"So they watch you?"

Matty didn't answer. He unzipped his backpack and poked into it as if he was looking for something. He came up empty-handed, leaving the mouth of the pack open. "I'm supposed to do my science homework."

"What's the assignment?"

"Stupid."

"Ah." Abby didn't know what to ask next.

"It's for, like, a stupid science fair. We have to change something into something else."

All Abby could think of was Harry Potter. "Like magic?"

"I wish. That would probably be easier."

"What are you going to do?"

Matty thumped the back of his head into the headrest. "Die. I'm doomed. That's all. The teacher hates me."

Abby smiled gently. "I'm sure that's not true."

"She told me it was fine, that not everyone can be smart."

"Seriously?"

He nodded grimly.

"That's not cool."

"My mom was pretty mad about that. She had a meeting with the principal and everything."

"Did that help?"

"Made it worse. Now she's out to get me and won't let me use the pencil sharpener more than once a class." His mouth was tight. "But I break a lot of pencils."

"Okay, let's work on it."

"The pencils?"

"The science project." Abby's heart beat faster. "I have a garden. That's practically magic, right there."

He looked at her skeptically. "Carrots? Tomatoes? I think it has to be bigger than turning seeds into vegetables. Anyone can do that."

"You'd be surprised. What about using vegetables to dye something?"

"Like paint?"

"Maybe something that you made?"

"What?"

Abby felt a thrumming of excitement at the base of her throat, an extra pulse. "Let me think about it. I can help you. I want to help you."

Matty's sigh was so heavy it felt like the parked car would tip onto its side.

"We can think more about that later. What's fun for you?"

Matty looked at her seriously. "That's a very big question."

"Yeah. I guess it is."

"The comic book store is fun." He looked sideways out the front window, and then back at her. He expected her to call him on it. To take him home. To be boring.

"Lead the way."

"Really?" His smile was sudden and dazzling.

"Sure. Tell me how to get there."

Matty blinked again, his smile dimming. "There's one on . . . uh. It's the street where the Safeway is, the one with the stinky fish." He paused and thought. "I'm always the passenger. Not the driver." His *duh* wasn't stated, but it was definitely implied.

Abby got out her cell and tapped at it. "Okay. Comics Unlimited? That one's close. Is that the one you like?"

"I think that's the one." He lifted his shoulders and dropped them. "If it has comics, it's the one I like."

Turning on navigation on her phone, she pulled slowly away from the curb. The shallow fear she'd pushed back into her shoulders rose again, growing into her chest and throat. A red Ford truck came too close to her bumper as it drove around her, and Abby realized that never in her life had she transported more precious cargo. There was no insurance she could take out on her policy that would cover what she was carrying. Why had she offered this? She was driving her husband's *child* around. True, she'd packed dried figs in a ziplock in her purse as a talisman for safe passage. Seriously, though? She'd thought that would be enough? What if a drunk driver came around a corner and smashed into them? What if Matty was hurt? If she didn't die from the impact, she'd have to kill herself. She wanted to pull over, to call an Uber to take them to his house, where she would place him on the couch and then stand over him, making sure nothing with blades or bullets or poison came in the front door until his mother came home.

"Turn left," said the navigator.

"My uncle's GPS sounds like Chef."

"Chef?" All Abby could think of was Julia Child.

"From *South Park.*"

"Ah."

Another pause. "Wally thinks I'm a baby," said Matty.

"Sorry?" Abby had missed something, but she wasn't sure what it was.

"You said you weren't babysitting. But he says that I'm a baby every day." His feet didn't reach the floor of the footwell, and he kicked his heels backward into the leather. Abby found she didn't mind at all.

"He's in your class?"

"He's in seventh."

"So he's a year older."

"Yeah. He chases me up the jungle gym sometimes. I hate him."

"Well, I hate him, too, then. He sounds like a bully. Have you told your mom?"

Matty sighed.

"What?" Abby took the right turn so slowly a pedestrian almost outpaced them on the sidewalk.

"Grown-ups are always like that."

"Like what?" Abby felt strangely pleased to be lumped into a group in Matty's mind.

"Like you can do anything about them. You can't."

"I agree."

Matty swiveled, his whole body following his head's motion. "You're not supposed to say that."

Abby started. "I'm not?"

"You're supposed to say something stupid about how I should tell a teacher when he starts or tell my mom when I get home."

"Oh." She thought about it. "Yeah, well. I was bullied when I was a kid, and nothing made it stop."

"I don't think you're supposed to say that, either."

"Sorry." She wished she could see his root structure, like she could a turnip. Study it. Figure out what to say, what to give, what to do to get it all right.

But when she looked sideways, the smile was back on his face.

"Nah." He thumped backward into the seat again. "It's okay." A pause. "You got bullied?"

"Constantly." Abby had grown into her long, thin face, but it had taken a while. "Kids called me horse-face."

"Really?"

"It was true. I did have a horsey face."

Matty said, "Look this way?"

She did, reluctant to take her eyes off the road long enough to do it.

"I can see that," said Matty.

"Thanks."

"Well, now you're really pretty, too." He was matter-of-fact. "But your face is still long. So yeah." His voice changed and she glanced at him again. He was grinning. "Can I call you Mr. Ed?"

"Ow." Abby risked thumping herself in the chest. "That was one of the names. You wound me." But she didn't mind, not even a little bit.

He laughed.

Then a dog as big as a small horse raced into the street and launched itself at her front tire.

Matty screamed.

CHAPTER TWENTY-EIGHT

It wasn't bad, as accidents went. In swerving to miss the dog, Abby had only tapped the back bumper of a parked Scion, which looked like it was used to it. Her air bags hadn't gone off (thank *god,* what if the air bag had blown up and injured Matty?) and her car, sturdily built, barely suffered a scratch. It would probably cost more to fix than the entire Scion bumper, but who cared?

Matty wasn't hurt.

It was like a song in her head. That was the chorus.

Matty's not hurt.

The chorus was nice. The refrain wasn't as good.

I could have killed him.

She could have killed Scott's son. Fern's son. Scott and Fern's son. Matty. *I could have killed him.*

Then the chorus kicked back in.

Matty's not hurt.

He was very *not* hurt, in fact. The enormous dog who'd run in front of her wheels was currently pinning him down on the sidewalk, and the Great Dane — because that's what it was, a *large* black-and-white Great Dane with ears like tent flaps and sticking-out bones — seemed as happy as Matty did with the situation. He was very young, and dirty, and very, very thin, but he grinned at Matty, panting.

Frustratingly, the cops had refused to come. The dispatcher said if no one was hurt and if they weren't blocking traffic, then she had to make the report with DMV, not with them. "But I don't know whose car this is," said Abby.

"Leave a note," said the dispatcher.

"What's to stop me from leaving a bogus name and phone number?"

"Ma'am," said the dispatcher, sounding tired. "If you were the kind to lie about it, then you wouldn't have called us in the first place."

"What about the dog? It's huge."

"Congratulations. Make sure it gets its shots."

Abby wrote a note on the back of an oil change receipt. She left her phone number and insurance policy ID, along with the word *Sorry*.

Matty thumped the dog's side, as if testing a cantaloupe. "What are we going to do about him?"

The dog? No one was around, no one looking for a dog the size of a miniature pony. Abby felt as if, along with the Scion's bumper, she'd hit the wall of her ability to think like the adult. "I have no idea. He has no collar, so . . . What do you think?"

Matty was sure. "We keep him. He's so skinny."

"Um, not an option." She wasn't sure of much, but she was pretty sure that bringing Matty home with an enormous-pawed puppy would blow what preciously little babysitting credibility she had with Fern.

He only deflated a little. He knew the lay of the land, too. "Then we knock on doors."

"Good idea." Why hadn't she thought of it? "We need a leash." She thought of the inside of her car — nothing. It wasn't like she carried rope around. Her belt? She pulled it off and threaded the end through the buckle. Then she put the loop over the puppy's neck. The dog seemed startled and pulled away, but then relaxed again. His neck was so big the leftover belt had only a few inches to hold on to, but he didn't seem inclined to run.

"He came from that direction," said Matty. He pointed at the nearest apartment building, a run-down block of solid, unmitigated gray. The side parking lot was full of cars in various states of rusted disrepair. Over the main entryway was an incredibly ill-advised iron sculpture, all horns and demonically twisted spikes. It looked like it was waiting for the right curse and a full moon before it uncoiled with a scream and gored someone. A man shambled past, talking to himself, dragging a three-wheeled shopping cart full of cans.

After the first knock got them nothing but a muffled shout, Abby started to doubt the wisdom of what they were doing. This was *not* the kind of place she normally canvassed while volunteering for her favorite local politicians. In Berkeley and Albany, people usually didn't want to talk, but they nodded and took her flyers. There, the sidewalks were clear of dog shit and dime bags (Abby was startled to realize that's what the little cellophane packets were — startled to recognize them as such even though she'd never seen one before).

Here, in front of this building, no one seemed to want to answer a knock. All the doors faced the street, a small relief. They got two more grunted shouts, and one door opened an inch and then slammed shut again. A woman in a very short purple skirt darted out one door and in through the next.

Abby worried about Matty's backpack, which they'd left, probably unwisely, visible on the front floorboard of her car. "Do you want me to hold the leash? Is he pulling?"

"I got him." Matty sounded more grown-up than eleven. "What about those houses, back there?" He pointed to the single-family houses farther down the block. He didn't want to knock on any more of the scary apartment building doors, either.

Too relieved — *she* was supposed to be the adult here — Abby agreed. "Yeah."

The first house had probably once been bright yellow but was now a dirty shade of butter. The porch held two wicker rocking chairs, one with a busted seat. If they got one more grunt in response, they were out of here. Straight to the animal shelter. That was it.

But the door opened. On the other side of the iron door, a tall young man filled the doorway. He didn't look more than seventeen, but his shoulders filled the doorway. "Yeah?"

Abby got nervous again. "We found a dog." Her voice was small.

Matty's voice was bigger. "Do you know him? Can you look at him?"

"Aw. Yeah. That's Snickers."

Abby saw the naked hope on Matty's face only as it ran away with his fallen expression. But valiantly, he rallied in the space of only a few seconds. "He's yours?"

"Nah. Belonged to the dude next door." He pointed to the house that had four barbecue grills in various states of disrepair littered across the dead lawn.

"Okay. Thanks," said Matty.

"But he don't want it."

Abby turned. Through the iron door, she couldn't see much of the inside of the house, but what she could see looked old-fashioned. A curved upholstered blue chair. Something that looked like a sideboard filled with china. It looked like a place where a grandmother would live. It smelled that way, too. Fresh bread, and laundry detergent. "Excuse me?"

"They threw it out."

"What do you mean?"

"They don't want it. Been running the streets for a week."

The dog's spine poked out his back, his ribs visible. "They just let him go?"

"Yeah."

"You don't want him?"

"Have you seen those feet?"

Well, yeah. Abby looked at the pup's wide head and long ears. "Do you think it's possible he's still *growing*?"

"Sorry, lady. Good luck." The door shut with a polite click.

Abby faced Matty. "So."

His expression remained serious, the corners of his lips tucked in. "So now we knock on that door. Where he came from."

"What if they don't answer?" Why was she asking an eleven-year-old? "You're right. Let's try."

They walked next door and knocked. The door opened, wider this time. A boy not much older than Matty answered. He held half an apple in one hand and his face was blank. "Yeah, he was mine. But my gramma said he barked too much and was too big to fit in here."

"So you put him outside." Abby tried not to let the judgment she felt creep into her voice, but she knew it was there. What kind of an adult-in-charge didn't take a young dog to the shelter? It was less than three miles away. "You know he would have gotten hit by a car if he was just left out here."

Matty stayed where he was, kneeling on the wooden porch, petting the slobbery dog.

An older woman's voice said from behind

the boy, "You tell her to get out of here."

Abby and the boy stared at each other through the iron screen.

"Tell her the truth," the woman said. "Tell her I ain't buying food for both you and that damn dog."

The boy's face went even more blank, and he shut the door with a polite but final click.

Abby and Matty didn't look at each other as they filed down the short drive to the sidewalk. They walked together past the scary apartment building and back to where the car was parked. Abby was relieved to see all her windows were intact, and immediately felt shame for feeling surprise.

"So," she said as she hit the unlock button.

"We take him," said Matty. He rested his hand on the puppy's head.

"To the shelter."

"Or to my house."

"No way. Your mother would kill me."

"My dad wanted to get me a dog."

For the first time, Abby understood the phrase *caught flat-footed*. She stood in place on the sidewalk, the dog tugging away from her as he sniffed something in the gutter. She could feel her toes on the ground through her shoes — she spread them so that she could be more grounded, could use whatever the earth wanted to bring up through her legs. Sap rising, and she was the tree.

Scott hadn't even liked dogs. And how would Matty even know *that,* if he'd never seen Scott?

"Did your grandpa tell you that?"

"He always says boys should have dogs. He said he should have let my dad have one. But he never let him." Matty nodded firmly. "My mom, she's been looking for one."

"A dog." Fern hadn't seemed like the type of woman who wanted or needed to bring more chaos into her life.

"She's lonely. She has, like, no friends."

Well. That smacked of truth. What would a boy Matty's age know about loneliness if he hadn't been told?

"What about at work? She has friends there, right?"

"I don't know. I guess. It's not like she hangs out with them. I think she's sad."

The words hit Abby with a thump. "I suppose we could check. With her, I mean."

"Yes." Matty snapped his seat belt with a satisfied click. "Can he sit on my lap?"

Abby looked down at the dog. "No way would he fit up front with you. I think he's grown since we found him."

Matty laughed. "Please?"

"No. Dog goes in the back."

"Can I name him?"

Some remarkable small sense of preservation made Abby say, "Let's hold off on that. I'm sure that if you get to keep him, your mom will let you name him." She opened the back door and heaved the pup inside. As she walked behind the vehicle, she could hear Matty's voice but not his words. She could hear the delight that lit his words, little eruptions of happiness under each syllable.

Abby held her breath when she touched her door's handle and made a wish. A prayer.

May this work.

CHAPTER TWENTY-NINE

When Fern got home from an extra hour at
Gregory's place — her knees still as shaky
as an old articulated bus with a busted
suspension — she found a dog the size of a
refrigerator in her house.

While she'd been rolling around naked
with Gregory, while she'd been biting his
shoulder and trying (and succeeding) to
forget her son was being watched by her
ex's wife, that same wife had given Matias a
dog. Not just any dog, but a skinny-ass male
Great Dane.

Fern's entire household was sitting on the
floor in the living room playing with the
damn thing. Elva was sitting next to
Grandpa Wyatt (god knew how either of
them had gotten to the floor) and her
brother, Diego, was holding a tennis ball
that already looked drippy with saliva.
Matty was stretched out on his stomach
wrestling with the dog, who rolled ecstati-

cally on his back, flipping his huge paws in the air.

Abby was the only one standing, and Fern didn't blame her. If she were Abby, she'd be poised for a quick getaway, too.

"You did what?" Fern said crisply. She'd heard Abby's words. She wanted to hear them again.

Abby's voice was lower now. "We brought him here. Because . . ."

"Yes?"

Matty, who hadn't appeared as if he'd been paying any attention to them, said, "I told her it was okay."

"To bring a dog *here*?"

"Dad would have —" Matty's voice started out strong but faded almost immediately. "He would have wanted it. Um, Grandpa said?"

"Me?" Instead of protesting his grandson's obvious lie, Wyatt looked pleased. "Yeah! I probably said that!"

The air left Fern's lungs, and she set the paper bag she was still holding down on the ground. The pup immediately righted itself and ambled to her, sticking his head into the bag. Of course he did. She'd bought steak, which had been on sale. It wasn't a huge piece of meat, not one of those twenty-dollar slabs, but it was big enough that when it was cut five ways, each of them would get a little bit.

There wasn't enough for Abby.

And there *really* wasn't enough for Abby's dog.

"Let's get this straight, Matias."

Matty didn't meet her eyes. He knew what was coming. Of course he did. Her son was smart — too smart to try to pull this ridiculous stunt.

"You want me to get mad at Abby, is that right?"

That wasn't what Matty had expected. His head rose. "Huh?"

"Because you better be sure I'm not mad at her." It was a brilliant lie, glowing neon in the air in front of her. "I'm mad at you."

"Me?"

Oh, the aggrieved air he could pull off. "Yes, *you.*"

Matty ran his hand awkwardly over the angular bones of the dog's thin face. "But, Mom, look. He loves me. He loves me the best already." He made his eyes huge and round. "He's starving."

"He's six feet tall. We can't afford him." She softened. He was a boy. Boys wanted puppies. But puppies grew up into gigantic dogs who wanted steak, dogs who needed shots and collars and walks. "Honey, did you really think I was going to go for this?"

Abby started to speak, but Fern silenced her with her farebox face.

Matty stopped tugging at the dog's upper lip (which the dog strangely seemed to be enjoying). He stood. He'd grown again — Fern could tell by the way his jeans were too short. One more thing to add to the list.

"No," said Matty. "But I *hoped* that you would want to do something to make me happy." He paused and looked right at her. "For *once.*"

"It's not about your happiness. It's just . . . we have so many other things right now with higher priorities. A dog is not going to work. You know that, love. Did you figure out your science project yet?"

Matty scowled.

"You have to start. I don't care what you choose but —"

His tight fists were knots of fury. "I don't care, either! I don't care about anything but the dog, but you don't care about anything at *all.*" He stomped past her and then ran down the hallway, his feet thudding heavily on the wooden floorboards.

Even though she'd been expecting the slam of his bedroom door, she jumped. "So dramatic," Fern said. She kept her voice light, but she felt anything but casual.

278

"I thought —," started Abby.

"You thought he was telling the truth because you had no reason to think he would lie about it."

Elva and Grandpa Wyatt had a brief tug-of-war as they both stood, using each other for assistance. "I'll start dinner," said Elva, pushing a lock of gray frizz out of her face. Wyatt added, "I'll help."

"Chickens," said Diego. Fern's brother had been watching with interest, but this was the first thing he'd said.

"Chicken it is," said Elva as she drifted out of the room, Wyatt on her heels. Fine. If Elva made chicken, then there would be more steak later for Matty and Fern and Diego.

"I'm an idiot," said Abby.

Fern wanted to agree. But instead she said, "Any boy would lie about a dog." This dog, in particular. Fern sank to the floor, trying not to groan with tiredness. "He's cute, I suppose." She touched a long black ear. He looked like he was wearing an even bigger dog's clothes, wrinkles at his shoulders and hips. "His bones look sharp." His skinny black-and-white muzzle hung in velvet folds, giving him an older face than he should have had.

Diego said helpfully, "You should feed

him. He's hungry."

"Nice try," she said. "You feed him."

"Not a chance. *I'm* no idiot."

How had Abby introduced herself to Diego? *Hi, I ruined your sister's life.* No, that wasn't fair. Scott had done that. Abby hadn't known.

It was hard to remember.

"Can you go help Elva?"

Startled, Diego said, "Me?"

"You."

"I don't cook. Except with the waffle iron."

Fern nodded at the grocery bag. "But you grill. I got steak. Go light the barbecue for me?"

"But this is fascinating."

"Vete."

He shot his grin at Abby — shit, he *better* not — and headed toward the kitchen.

Fern stared after him suspiciously and then gave the dog another scratch. It groaned happily. Probably had fleas. Or worse. "I'll take him to the shelter, I guess." A puppy like him would get adopted, wouldn't he? He wouldn't be put to sleep? Thrown away like so many other dogs in Oakland? He was huge, yes, but cute. He would be saved. Surely.

"Now?" said Abby. "Won't they be

closed?"

"They have one-way drop boxes." At work, Bo was always scooping up loose dogs on his shift. They came to him, as if his coach blew the scent of bacon out the biodiesel exhaust pipe.

"No, that's too sad. Would he even fit? Look at him."

Fern was trying very hard not to. "You want to keep him, be my guest."

Abby's face lit up as if a small sun had burst into flames above her head. Then she sobered. "Me? I can't have a horse in my house. He's just getting bigger, I'm sure. I can't keep him."

Fern sighed. "You didn't think this through at all, huh?" Honestly, the woman didn't *seem* dumb, but come on.

"I feel like I did a lot of not thinking today."

Satisfaction prickled her skin. "Says the woman who picked up my child from school."

"I'm so sorry. It crossed my mind that Matty didn't have it quite straight. About the dog, about you wanting one. About Scott . . ."

Fern tugged on the dog's ear and he fell to the floor sideways, landing in a happy thump. "If Matias ever tells you anything about his father, you can be pretty sure he's lying." He'd gotten into that habit when he started school. Everyone else talked about what their dad did, and his best friend in that kindergarten had possessed *two* dads. Of course Matty had wanted to talk about his father, too. Fern had wished so many times that Scott were dead — it would have simplified everything. Then she could have lied her ass off about him. She would have told Matty that Scott had been an award-winning journalist, writing war stories that changed lives. A handsome risk-taking underwater welder, building bridges that would stand a century or more. An accomplished cellist, whose interpretations of Bach made battle-hardened marines cry.

And now she couldn't lie. Matty was too smart, and Fern was too late. "Matty came with hope built right into him. I'm sorry he fibbed."

Abby touched the dog gently on the head. "I'm not. I would have taken him right to the shelter if he hadn't lied. Or if I'd been alone. Instead . . ."

Something protective rose in Fern's chest. Abby was so young-looking, and so thin, and . . . No. Feeling the ridiculous protectiveness pissed Fern off. "You wouldn't have been alone in our neighborhood, though.

Not ever. You would have had no reason to come slumming down here."

Abby didn't rise to the bait, further irritating Fern. "I'm glad I was with Matty today. And I'll take the dog."

Fern narrowed her eyes. "For good? Or for the night?"

"I don't know. A normal dog, maybe. But I don't think Great Danes are normal. Are they?"

Fern remembered suddenly the image of a Great Dane she'd seen on the Internet. Standing on his back legs, the dog was taking something off the top of the refrigerator. The *top.* "You should know for sure. Whether or not you're keeping him."

Abby's chin rose. "Should I?"

Fern's irritation left her, leaving her empty. She was hollow without it. "Whatever." Abby could make her own flea-ridden bed.

"Matty named him in the car. I asked him not to, but I don't think he could help it."

"Oh, god. I'm scared to ask."

"Tulip."

Fern craned her neck and looked at the dog's rear end. "That dog has *cojones.* Literally. Big ones."

"I know."

"Tulip isn't the name for a boy dog."

283

Abby nodded. "Agreed."

"Where did he even get that name?"

"He said it was his favorite flower."

"Oh." They were the only flowers that came up in her yard every year, and only because she didn't have to do anything about them. Matty had always loved them. They'd come with the house, along with the cracked stair rail and the crown molding. They were strange, too — she'd never seen them anywhere else, white and such a dark purple they looked streaked with black-and-white stripes. Just like the dog.

Tulip was chewing Fern's fingers, his teeth sharp but gentle. She shouldn't let him, she knew that. It was teaching him bad habits. But it felt nice — the graze and pinch of it. A love slobber. "Tulip," she said. Then she looked up at Abby. "I guess you have a dog."

CHAPTER THIRTY

Abby punched the button that opened her Lexus. She opened the back door. "Up."

Tulip sat on the sidewalk.

"Wrong command. Get up, dog." She tugged on the makeshift leash, but Tulip sat firmly, as if it were his job.

"Pork medallions," she said to the dog. He stayed in his firm sit and gazed up at her with joyful eyes. "I'll make you pork. That can't hurt you, can it?" When she got home, she would defrost the tenderloin that had been in the freezer since before Scott died. (Would this be the way she classified everything now? Before and after Scott? Would there be a time she wouldn't date-stamp her life this way?) She had leftover jasmine rice from Thai takeout earlier in the week. "Pork and rice. Isn't that what you give dogs with upset stomachs? Or is that chicken?" God. What on earth did you *do* if a Great Dane got diarrhea?

285

This was crazy.

She had nothing for a dog at home. She didn't have a bowl, or food, or a crate. She didn't even have a collar. She'd have to stop at the pet store on the way home, some place she could get real food that wouldn't upset his stomach. Or . . .

Abby couldn't do this.

Then Tulip pressed his wide, rectangular head into her knee. As if to say she could.

"Looks like you got more than you bargained for today." Behind her, Diego's voice was low. Abby spun.

His shirt was dark green and ripped at the hem, as if he'd caught it on a branch, which he probably had, right? "I guess I did."

"I can help with Tulip. If you want."

Abby stilled. "What do you mean?" Did he want to keep the dog? In the few minutes since Abby had made her decision, she'd gotten attached to the idea of watching Tulip grow into a full-grown zeppelin.

But if Matty's uncle wanted Tulip, he should have him. It was that simple. It didn't matter that the dog had already started chewing companionably on Abby's purse, as if he liked the taste of the leather. She tugged it out of his mouth.

"Like," Diego continued, "when you're not home, I could come by and walk him."

"What do you mean?"

He squatted and leaned forward to touch the pup's huge ears, flapping one back and forth. Tulip closed his eyes and let his tongue flop forward. It was a smile. Clearly a smile. *What* a cute dog.

Abby bit her lower lip. Would it be setting a terrible precedent to allow the big dog to sleep in her bed that night? More than anything else about Scott, she missed his warmth in bed. She wanted the weight of the bed creaking next to her more than she wanted him. It was an awful thing to know about herself.

No, a crate. She'd have to get a crate. Dogs that size weren't for bed.

Diego looked up at her. His eyes were the deep brown of ground black cardamom. "What do you do all day, anyway?"

"I'm . . ." She cleared her throat. "I'm a biological scientist." Or she had been. A long time ago.

"Seriously? I didn't know that." He spoke as if he knew other things about her. He stood to his full height, which, Abby noticed again, was considerable. "I thought you didn't work."

For the first time in years, she ached to say that she still had her old job. *At the arboretum.* It used to be that people's eyes either glazed over or lit up when she said it. Diego's would have lit, she thought.

Polite. There was something she had to say here to remain polite. "Currently, I just work in my back garden. I sell infused oils, some tinctures. Herbal remedies, that kind of thing. Matty said you swing from trees. Tarzan, right?"

"Arborist, yeah. Same difference."

"What's your favorite tree?" She wasn't sure if she was genuinely interested in what it was, or if she just wanted to see if he had an answer.

He did. Without hesitation, he said, "European beech."

"Why?"

Diego smiled, and she noticed that he had a deep dimple in the stubbled brown skin of his right cheek. "Good branches for climbing. And for logical dismantling."

She winced. "Ah. You like to kill them."

"I hate to kill them. But it's part of the job. Right? Like a vet. You love 'em, you know? But sometimes you have to help put them out of their misery. Before they fall on the house."

Abby reached down and flapped Tulip's ear like he had. The puppy responded by twisting to nibble her fingers. "Tulip can hear you. And he would never fall on a house. Not until he finishes growing up, anyway."

"What's your favorite plant?"

She laughed, the feel of it rusty in her throat. "I don't have one."

"That's like a parent saying they don't have a favorite child."

"They don't!"

"Only child?"

Abby nodded slowly. She felt her dead mother nudge her in the ribs. Meg didn't count. (She did, she knew Meg counted.) She thought of the way her onion bed looked when the bulbs were still young scallions, their vulnerable green tops waving like delicate flags. The way the green was so dense, so full of flavor. Other garden crops — peppers and tomatoes and cucumbers — were full of water and space. But onions, whether harvested as green or globe, were layer upon layer of usable material, a gorgeous bulb. They were aromatic and assertive at the same time. Egyptians had sworn oaths on onions. Onion skins had been dyeing cloth for centuries. But no one would admit they loved onions best. *"Allium cepa,"* she said.

Diego inclined his head. "Ah. Of course. Sweet. But strong."

"Hey." He was smart. This pleased her

more than it should have.

"What? I like 'em on my burger, you know?" He stuck his hands into his jeans pockets and then looked over his shoulder at the house. "Seriously, I can help with the dog if you need it. I make my own hours. I run two guys who work for me, but they can do a lot of jobs without supervision."

The polite Abby who jog-walked with the ex-mayor's daughter wouldn't have prodded anymore. The responsible Abby who paid an inordinate amount of property tax wouldn't have pried. But Abby didn't feel like herself. She wasn't sure who she felt like, but it wasn't normal. Not anymore. So she said what she was wondering. "Aren't you supposed to hate me?"

To his credit, he didn't look surprised. Instead, he leaned against the bent white metal mailbox that looked as if it had been clobbered by something. "Nah," he said. "Well. I don't know. I don't think so?"

Abby felt unaccountably flattered by his ambivalence. "Oh. Well. I think I'm good, but I'll let you know if I need help. With walking or . . . something? Thank you."

Diego probably did want to help with Tulip. For Matty's sake. She could feel he meant it.

She felt something else, too. He held her

eye for a split second too long and she felt her spine heat. She heard Kathryn's voice in her head. *Get it over with.*

Diego had absolutely every reason to hate her.

And Abby would never even *consider* how hot he was — Diego was her dead husband's ex-brother-in-law. Oh, god, she still had those dried figs for safe passage in her bag. She tried to wipe from her mind the knowledge that they were also used in love spells.

"You bet," he said. "Let me give you my number. To help. If you need it."

Abby said, "Okay."

She took his number, punching it into her phone. Then she gave him hers.

For the dog.

Tulip finally jumped into the backseat.

Abby nodded at Diego. He nodded back. Something in his gaze caught and tangled in her throat, and she felt it there as she drove away through the darkening, unfamiliar streets.

CHAPTER THIRTY-ONE

Driving into North Berkeley with a carful of boys, Fern realized — for the first time — why people called their upper torsos their chests. Hers was full of things that would have been better stored away. Her feelings — trepidation mixed with confusion mixed with a strange, unfamiliar feeling that she couldn't actually name, but which reminded her of fear — were folded on top of one another, like heavy blankets.

Crammed next to one another on the backseat, the three boys were hopping up and down as much as their seat belts would allow them to. She'd told Matty to ride shotgun, but he'd wanted to be in the backseat with his friends. Neither of the other two boys was interested in sitting next to a mom.

"You guys! Chill! She only said she *might* have a trampoline." She never should have mentioned that part of Abby's text. How did someone only maybe have a trampoline, anyway? "It's a science afternoon. That's the important part." Abby had said she would teach Matty to dye fabric with plants in the garden. If that worked, then damn. Mrs. Hutch would have to get over her hate-on for Matty. Wouldn't she? The other two boys already had their projects on the go (Jorge was doing a project on how golf balls accelerated on an incline, and Bryson was comparing goldfish heart rates with human ones) — Matty was the last to start his.

From an inch behind her ear, Bryson trumpeted, "I've been on a trampoline before! I was really good at it!" It was such a Bryson thing to say. His mother was one of those touchy-feely women who praised their kids for tying their shoes correctly every day. Bryson got gold stars for saying good morning. He was probably applauded for how interesting his dreams were. "I'm like the best at it ever."

"I'm hecka good at jumping," said Jorge. "There's a place near my dad's house in Sacramento where it's, like, this warehouse? And it's full of bounce houses. You bounce out of one into another like you're Superman."

"Superman doesn't *bounce.*"

Jorge didn't care. "It's like you're flying. I can go five feet sideways or something."

Fern glanced in the rearview mirror and caught Matty's skeptical look. "No way."

"So way. There's, like, a hundred trampolines. All next to each other. So you don't fall off. And it's better because you can go higher. Like, you're flying and then you flip? And sometimes you can get a double flip. You're not supposed to, but I did it, and then the guy yelled at me, but I'd already done it."

Matty's voice was worried. "I've never been on a trampoline."

Fern wanted to say, *It'll be all right. You'll be wonderful at it.* But the truth was Matty usually didn't get things on the first try that took coordination. It had taken forever to convince him to take off his bicycle training wheels. The very first time he'd gotten on Diego's old skateboard, Matty had broken his wrist by flying off the board into the Silvas' garbage cans. "Maybe it's like skateboarding. Remember? You got better at it as you went."

She shouldn't have inserted herself into the conversation. In the rearview mirror, she saw Matty's shoulders rise.

"It's not the same," he muttered. "And I'm still not good at it."

The other two boys didn't seem to notice, and the conversation moved to the new deck Angel's brother had gotten with epoxy fiber reinforcement and some kind of new axle they couldn't remember the name of.

Fern stopped looking in the rearview. Instead, she watched the little girl in the Mercedes in front of her contort herself practically inside out, twisting around in her seat to make faces through the back window. It was obvious she was trying to do it without her mother noticing, and her desperate flapping was getting funnier by the second.

Did rich mothers notice less? Fern knew she would have been able to tell if Matty was flipping around in his seat behind her even if she didn't see him do it. She'd be able to feel her old car shake. And if she didn't feel it, she'd still just *know*. Mother's intuition. At the next light, she pulled up next to the sleek, black car. The girl in the backseat looked at them, then plastered herself against her window, her cheeks ballooning as she blew against the glass.

Jorge noticed, then Bryson and Matty. All three hooted and did what they could to match it. Fern would have to clean off their face grease and spittle later, and she didn't mind. That's what Windex was for.

The mother in the car still didn't notice. As they idled at the red, the woman kept talking on her cell phone, holding it to her ear in defiance of the law. A $165 fine probably wouldn't mean the same to her as it did to Fern.

Five hundred thousand dollars. Plus that twenty thousand Abby had mentioned in passing, the amount of the old policy that had seemed to hardly matter to her.

Fern could have all of it sitting in her bank account right now. If she had accepted it. If any part of it had been acceptable to her.

Did stubborn *always* equal poor? It didn't seem fair. Then again, Fern had always believed that people who wasted their time whining about fairness usually just needed more sleep. Fair was something that came and went. It didn't deserve stressing about.

She pulled around the Mercedes only to catch the light at Adeline.

That cash.

It was math she could do in her sleep — she could have done it in rush hour traffic while driving her coach, so it was easy to do while steering the small car around a stalled pickup truck in this early afternoon traffic. *Five hundred and twenty thousand.* Invested in a good S&P 500 index, bringing in a conservative five percent interest, it would earn twenty-six thousand dollars a year. Without doing a damn thing. Just sitting there. Dave Ramsey swore the stock market over the past seventy years had brought in an average of twelve percent, even with volatility. If that was true, the interest could come closer to sixty-two grand. Just *sitting* there.

She breathed through her mouth to slow her heartbeat and ignored the fact that every time Bryson bounced in the seat behind her, he kicked the middle of her seat.

Five hundred and twenty thousand dollars.

Fern had dreamed the numbers last night, the numerals gleaming bright yellow. She'd touched them. They'd been sticky like those plastic gummy decorations you put on windows at holidays.

They were just numbers.

They didn't *mean* anything.

Or, at least, they hadn't meant anything until she'd tried (again) to wring the money for a new washer out of the overtime check that had landed in her bank account on Monday. The life insurance hadn't meant as much until she'd gone to get a flat fixed at the tire shop on Tuesday night after work and found out she needed to buy new brake pads. They were — apparently — impera-tive, according to Esteban. "Look, *mami*, I told you you could wait the last two times." He'd looked pointedly at Matty. "You can't wait again. You hurt somebody if you do." In order to cover the cost, she'd ignored the second notice on the electricity bill. The new brakes stopped the car smoothly and quickly now, instead of mushing apologetically with a sigh to the floorboards. The car was safe again.

It was funny — she'd always been a grasshopper, believing in the best. She and Scott had that in common once, fiddling for fun instead of working, like the industrious ant. She knew she'd always make it — she used to feel that in her heart. It might be tight, but the money would be there, somewhere, somehow. She had a job. She'd had child support coming in, exactly enough. She didn't save, but someday she would. Someday she'd be a grown-up, but until then she'd have enough.

Now Fern didn't have enough. She hadn't seen it coming, hadn't planned for this rainy day.

There was an umbrella being offered to her. A huge one. A bright rainbow-colored umbrella, the kind that chased whole storms right out of the sky.

And damned if she couldn't reach for the handle.

"Mom! You missed the turn!"

"No, I didn't."

"It's back there!" Matty wailed as if it were too late, as if they would never be able to turn the car around, as if Abby and the science project and the maybe-trampoline would disappear because she would have to drive an extra three blocks because she'd been thinking of the power a thin piece of bank-issued plastic held. She could have bought a whole *car* with her debit card if she'd taken Abby's money. She could get a used Nissan Juke with that card. She could swipe it, sign somewhere, and drive out of the lot in that boxy clownlike car that made Matty laugh. Not that she ever would have. That money would have been for the house, and college savings, and, god, a tutor for Matty if science kept making him so furiously frustrated.

Fern took two more right turns and pulled into Abby's long driveway. Her brakes stopped firmly, and she tried to lock down her thoughts the same way, tried to fold them the same way she was folding her feelings, storing them in her chest, just above her breath.

It would be fine. She would just pick up a few more hours of OT and pay off the PG&E bill next week. She'd scrape the next mortgage payment out of the next paycheck. She always did. If Abby mentioned the life insurance again, she'd hold up her *Stop* hand, the one that had kept three different would-be robbers from demanding her cell phone in the last few years.

It was just that . . . Fern sighed as the boys threw themselves out of the car like it was full of poison gas.

The people who said money couldn't buy happiness had never thinned mustard with water to make the bottle last another week of ham sandwich lunches.

CHAPTER THIRTY-TWO

Abby was surprised by the boys' height difference. Matty seemed normal to her, a normal eleven-year-old boy height, coming to just below her shoulder. Bryson, though, had to be six inches taller than Matty, and Jorge was a good eight inches shorter. As if to make up for the disparity, they'd dressed in what seemed to be a uniform — each wore a blue shirt with some comic-book character doing something with a weapon. Matty sported a green man with an ax, Bryson had a red man with a knife, and Jorge wore a yellow man with what looked like a flare gun.

"Are your characters all on the same team?" she asked, earning only blank looks. She pointed to their chests. "Like from the same universe? Is that how you say it?"

Matty looked startled. "Yeah."

"Sweet," said Abby. Then she wondered if that's what boys said now. Maybe that was the equivalent of "groovy" by now. *Awesome. Dope. Sick.* She had no freaking idea.

Fern looked uncomfortable. She was wearing a black puffy coat that was too long on her — it came almost to her knees and looked like something an old woman would wear to the grocery store. "I parked in the driveway."

"Yay!" said Abby. "That's what it's for." What a dumb thing to say. "Anyway. I'm so glad you're here. Come on in."

She ushered Fern and the boys down the hall into the kitchen. She tried to see it for the first time, the way she had when they'd bought the house. The backyard and its raw potential had been what sold her on the house, but the kitchen's large open expanse of counter and its huge island with its own sink had been what got out her signing pen. She kept three vases full of flowers in the kitchen, always. The blooms varied by season, of course. Now, in March, she had blue statice and dark purple irises.

She pointed at the island. "I set up a taco bar."

The boys said, "Oh, *yeah,*" and *"Nice,"* as if they were ogling a girl in a bikini.

Fern frowned, her eyebrows drawn together.

"The salsa is my specialty, made with

cilantro from the garden and heirloom garlic, but I'm pretty proud of my guacamole, too."

"Let me guess. Avocado tree?"

Abby felt herself blush. "Yeah. Two."

"Damn. I was kidding. That's just . . . that must be great."

"It is. Yeah. Oh, god. Is a taco bar too weird?"

"Nah. It's great."

Were they still talking about avocados? Abby had no idea. She felt as off-kilter as she had when Hugh had helped her up onto one of the trampolines in the back to try it out.

She blinked in the hopes it would help her feel more focused. "Tulip did *not* help, by the way. He was, in fact, hugely unhelpful."

At his name, the dog nudged her waist with his nose.

"What did he do?" asked a delighted-looking Matty.

"He ate *all* the ground beef. I had to go get another pack. It was *raw.*"

It got the effect she was hoping for — the boys chorused, "Ewwww," thrilled and impressed.

Then Matty asked, "Did you get a trampoline?"

Abby clapped. "I did. My neighbor Hugh was getting rid of his. His three girls are in boarding school, and he didn't think it was getting enough use. He helped me set it up this morning. *That* was a chore. You want to try it?"

"Yeah!"

Fern raised a hand. "Don't forget. We're here for your science project."

"Just for a while, Ma. I want to try it." Matty shot Fern a half-excited, half-scared look and raced out the sliding glass door. The other two followed him, stampeding into the yard.

"I'm glad you brought him. Them." There was a polite thing to say, Abby knew, and a right thing. She knew the polite thing. She wasn't sure, though, what would take that look off Fern's face, the look that was throwing Abby off so much she wanted to hold on to the porch rail as they stepped down onto the grass. Tulip had already torn around the lawn twice, and was now trying to lick Matty's face. He didn't even have to jump up to do it. Impolite, poorly trained puppy. Abby wanted to call him back, but knew he wouldn't come, so she didn't even try.

"No problem."

Polite. They were so polite.

"Matty's such a great kid."

"Yes."

Abby's stomach clenched. "We went to the library this last Wednesday, did he tell you? I showed him how to use the Kindle app on his phone to get free e-books."

Fern nodded, her face still.

It wasn't a bad thing, was it? That she'd said *free*? Abby thought Fern would like it, the way Matty had.

"Mom! Look!"

Fern's face changed as Matty called her, her expression going softer, her eyes less guarded. If Abby hadn't been looking right at that second, she would have missed it.

And then Fern said, "Holy shit. *That's* your trampoline?"

"Um. Yeah."

Hugh's trampoline had actually been more of a trampoline complex. He and his wife had had triplets seventeen years before, and had been doing everything bigger than everyone else since. There were six trampolines in total, set up in a large rectangle. There were foam landing pads on all sides. On the farthest side stood a sort of fabric wall, lashed to sturdy posts now sunk deeply into her lawn. Abby had tried jumping earlier. These weren't like the backyard trampolines when she was a kid. These were tighter, bouncier. Better. Or was it that she was heavier now and had the weight to go higher? She wasn't sure, but whatever it was, it had felt wonderful. The falling down toward the trampoline — that had been fast and fun and exciting. But going up had felt like a slow, invisible elevator rise, one that she was making happen herself.

She'd wanted to flip. Maybe later she would dare.

But now worry filled her. "Is it too dangerous?"

Fern squinted.

Abby took a quick step forward. "I knew it. I'll stop them. I knew it was too much. God, the last thing I want to do is hurt them. Kids!"

"No." Fern pulled at Abby's elbow. "They're fine."

The boys launched themselves up without using the small set of steps. Jorge flipped immediately. Bryson flapped his arms and bounced to another surface and did his own flip.

Matty watched, bobbing gently, only his knees moving.

"Are you sure? What if one of them falls off?"

"Kids fall off things all the time."

"What if they *break* something?"

Fern lifted one eyebrow. "You never broke anything as a kid?"

Horrified, Abby said, "No!"

"Overprotected much?"

"Well. Yeah." Abby thought of the way she had had to wear a helmet when she went on the pony ride at Tilden Park, even though no one else but the really little kids had to. The wildly embarrassing way her mother hadn't let her take swimming lessons without arm floats until she was ten.

"Kids bounce. Literally. They're tough." Fern raised her voice to a shout. "You can do it, Matty!"

Encouraged, Abby yelled also. "Yeah! Do it, Matty!"

Matty jumped harder. He went higher. And then higher.

Then, almost in slow motion, he raised his arms as he launched upward, tucking his legs and folding forward, sailing into a flip. He didn't quite stick the landing, falling sideways on the second bounce, but it was close.

"Oh, he *did* it," said Fern so quietly Abby almost couldn't hear her.

Matty whooped, stood up, and did it again.

They all did. Like a trio of rubber balls, the boys bounced and leaped. They flew and flipped and glided. Every once in a while, they'd whack themselves into a post, or slap an arm against a side, but they just yelled and started leaping again.

Abby and Fern sat on the lawn in two of the Adirondack chairs Abby had moved down from the porch.

"They're good at it," said Abby.

Fern nodded. "My little Mexican jumping bean."

Abby snorted.

"Not that you could say that," warned Fern.

"Never," said Abby sincerely.

"Okay, then." Fern's face was softer now, the lines that had pulled at her eyes fainter than they'd been. "Yeah. So. Are you trying to throw him a birthday party or something? Because that's not till September. I thought we were here for his homework."

Abby looked at the boys, still flipping. Still flying. Her fingertips tingled, as though she could feel their adrenaline in her own body. "I just wanted to make it fun."

"They're kids. Drinking Coke out of plastic cups and chewing on straws is fun."

"Well." Abby watched Jorge flip himself against the back wall and then chest-bump Matty midair. Tulip watched from the side, barking with excitement. "Now I know."

Fern grinned. "It's pretty fun to watch."

"Fun to do, too. Wanna try?"

"Hell, yes, I do." She didn't hesitate. "Maybe when they're getting tired of it, if we have time." Fern glanced at her watch. "Thirty minutes. Then we work on his project?"

"Yes. Of course."

"Hey." Fern kept her face forward, looking nowhere but at the boys.

"Yeah?"

"Thanks for this."

Bryson sailed in a perfect arc, landed perfectly, and did it all over again. He looked like a tiny astronaut. All three were working on some routine, bumping fists while in the air.

They looked like they were flying. Happiness filled Abby like helium and she felt like she might be the next one floating into the sky. "You're very, very welcome."

CHAPTER THIRTY-THREE

Taco time was an unholy mess. Fern wanted to keep Matty next to her so she could undo some of the damage as it happened, but every time she reached toward him with a napkin, he laughed and dodged out of her reach. "I'm fine, Mom! Jeesh. It's just taco sauce."

Taco sauce that he could and probably would track out of the kitchen and onto Abby's white carpet (white carpet! who had white carpet except for people in carpet commercials?) if she wasn't actively watching him every second.

The boys mowed through their loaded plates while Fern tried not to show how impressed she was by the guacamole. Ensenada Taqueria had the best guac in the East Bay. But Abby's might come close.

When they were done, after Matty and Bryson had seconds and Jorge took thirds, after Abby had surprisingly let Tulip lick the ground where Bryson had lost half a taco, they went outside again. Abby gave a flourish toward the shed at the bottom of the yard. "Now you get to see my secret lair."

"Is there a dragon? Dragons have lairs." Bryson sounded hopeful.

"I have a dragon tree, and it oozes red resin when you cut it. Does that count?"

The boys made impressed noises.

"That's my potting shed. Well, that's what I call it, but I do most of the repotting out on that table." She pointed to a huge wooden table standing off-kilter next to a redwood with peeling bark. "The potting shed is where I make the magic."

The boys screeched and raced ahead, leaving Fern and Abby to follow.

The shed was painted the same cream as the house, but the paint looked older, peeling in places. It looked, like many of the things in Abby's pretty, pretty home, artfully distressed, only Fern got the feeling that everything else was supposed to match this. This building felt real.

Abby pulled on the wooden door, which opened with a low screech. She reached up and pulled a cord, and a single bare bulb came to life. She tugged back thick canvas curtains, and more light filled the shed. It was about the size of a two-car garage, but it looked like a room where magic potions were made. Long dark tables ran along two walls, and on the other two, shelves upon shelves reached up to the ceiling. Each shelf was full of bottles — cobalt, ruby, and clear glass with cork stoppers. Raffia ties were around their necks, small cards hanging from each.

On two of the tables were stacks of bowls, and underneath the tables were more shelves, full of larger glass jars, gallon-sized or more. These were labeled carefully: *Funnels, Dye pots, Mordant.* An industrial sink stood in one corner, next to a small stove that held an already-steaming pot.

"Are you a witch?" asked Bryson.

"Do *not* ask that," said Fern quickly. But she wanted to know the answer, too.

"No," said Abby with a smile. "But I feel a lot of sympathy for the women who were called witches, just because they knew things about plants and herbs. Think about it — lots of medicine comes right from plants. Aspirin is made of bark, did you know that? I always wonder who the first person was to chew on a piece of tree bark. And what happened next? Her toothache stopped? So she did it again?"

"What if it had been poisonous and she died?" Matty's eyes were locked onto her.

Abby shrugged. "A lot of people did die, testing things." She appeared to take their measure and then she leaned forward. "Gruesome, *painful* deaths. I hope *we* don't die, getting ready for the science fair."

The boys laughed, falling backward and jabbing one another in delight. Fern leaned back against a shelf, careful not to brush up against anything. You never knew.

"So this is an onion." Abby held up a big red one.

Matty yelled, "I knew that! That's not poisonous!"

Abby grinned. "Wait for it. What's on the outside of the onion?"

"Paper!"

"Skin!"

"Paper skin!"

"Right. You're right! This skin stuff is papery, and it comes right off after the onion has been dried. These are some that I grew last year."

"Ew. So old! Gross!"

Abby suddenly looked a little nervous. She blinked. "Not gross, I promise. I won't make you eat them, but they would be fine if we did. Onions are amazing. Remember when I left the tacos to run out here? I had to turn on the stove so the water would be ready for us. You see this here?" The water was boiling.

"Yeah."

Abby hunched her shoulders and stirred the pot with a long wooden spoon. "Boil, boil, cauldron bubble . . ." Her voice was just a creak. "Science classroom falls to rubble."

The door to the shed banged shut in the wind. Bryson gave a small scream. Matty laughed maniacally. Even Fern jumped. Then Abby straightened and laughed at all of them. "Oh, man, you should see all your faces right now."

She'd gotten them. Fern's spine relaxed.

"Come on, look. I've got boiling water in here. I'm going to add this onion skin, and a whole pile of more skins I've got here in this bag. There. We'll let those cook a little while. Here, Matty, poke at the water."

He stood next to her and swirled the spoon in the pot.

"Do you see what's already happening in there?"

Matty went up on his tiptoes. "It's kind of . . . tan. Like, maybe orange. Why isn't it red?"

"We'll talk about that. Now. What's this?" She held up a cream knitted hat, slipping it over her hair. Her honey-colored hair looked wonderful under it, like a smooth, expensive waterfall. Fern pushed at her own frizzed curls. If she put on a hat like that, she'd look like a homeless person.

"A hat!" they all said.

"Aren't you clever?" Abby grinned at the boys, and Fern saw them all grow at least an inch taller. She had them in the palm of her hand. Tacos and trampolines. The woman wasn't dumb.

"What happens if I put it in the onion water?"

"It'll get dyed!"

"Right! What color?"

Silence.

"Hard to answer, huh? Let's wait and see, and when we're done, we can talk about how Matty can make this magic happen all on his own to wow his teacher at the science fair."

Matty threw his nervous look at Fern. "But . . ."

Fern bit her lip. This was for Abby to handle. And if she couldn't, well, then Fern would come in and figure something out. She couldn't help the small hope that rose in her, the tiny wish that she would *have* to be the rescuer.

"But?" said Abby.

Matty did that quick tiptoe move he used to make when he was nervous. "I don't think it's enough."

A wrinkle creased Abby's forehead. "You don't?"

"Just, like, coloring a hat? Like an Easter egg? Mrs. Hutch hates me. She's not going to say that's enough."

"Not just that. You're gathering the onions, because we'll need more, a lot more, and you're learning how to tell when they're ripe and how to process the skins. Not only that, but you're taking yarn and making it into a hat."

"Huh?"

"You're transforming simple cream yarn into a useful object using just a couple of sharp sticks, and then you're changing that object's color with a natural chemical process. We'll show how it works chemically on paper, and then prove it in the dye pot."

Matty said, "Whoa. Wait. I have to *make* the hat?"

"Simple knitting."

The other two boys hooted with laughter. "Ha! You're going to be a knitter! Yeaaaah, Grandma Matty!"

But Matty looked okay with it. "Shut up, you penis-heads. I'm gonna make a skater hat. Yeah. Cool. I wanna do that."

Abby looked so pleased it almost hurt

Fern to look at her bright face. "Good. Oh, good."

Fern's upper chest thumped with a tiny, shameful jolt of disappointment followed immediately by a burst of pride. Those warm blankets of feelings, folded in her chest, rose up again. Muffling her voice. Burying her breath.

"Can you teach me how to knit on Wednesday?" said Matty. "Can we go back on the trampoline now?"

"Yeah," said Abby. Then she shot a quick look at Fern. "If your mom doesn't mind. We can totally start on Wednesday."

"Fine," said Fern. "That's fine."

The boys practically leaped over one another to get out of the small shed, their screams unintelligible and furiously joyous.

"Wow," said Abby.

"I know. They kind of move in and out like a hurricane but with way less warning." Fern looked around. "It's three times bigger in here now that they're out."

Abby picked up a rag from a folded pile and rubbed at the top of the small stove. "I know it's kind of a wreck in here, but . . . I love it more than any other place."

Fern picked up a bottle. *Tulsi Basil.* "You sell this shit?"

Abby blinked.

"I mean stuff," corrected Fern. "It's not shit. Obviously. It's very pretty." Wait, how did she get so off-balance again?

"I sell some of it. But mostly I just like making it. I give a lot away. I never have to worry about birthday presents, you know? I just pick something the person would like." Abby bit her bottom lip. "Like you. I would give you . . ."

Fern shook her head. "Nah. You don't have to."

"I know. Hang on." Abby ran her finger along one shelf of blue bottles, and then up to the next one, where small light blue sachets were tied with dark blue ribbons. "This one. Here."

"I don't need —" But curiosity got the better of her, and she raised it to her nose. "Oh, sweet baby *Cristo*. What the *hell* is that?" It smelled like beer and dirt.

"Sorry. It's not my best smelling. It's hops and mandrake root. I should really put a little lavender in there to even it out." Abby pulled a small notebook out of a drawer and scratched a quick note.

"What is it supposed to do?"

"Hops are for sleep. And mandrake is for protection and prosperity."

Fern snorted. "Well. I'll take it." She looked around again. "I'm surprised this isn't a full-time gig for you. People eat this up." *Right. Abby didn't* need *a full-time job.*

"I want it to be full-time someday. I'm just not that great at the business end of it."

"Do you have a Web site?"

"Just an Etsy shop. It's kind of lost over there, to be honest. There are a lot of people selling this kind of thing. You'd be surprised. I know I always am, every time some stranger randomly orders the lemongrass-basil tincture, or the vetiver oil. And I'm not that great at getting to the post office. I tried to sell some once at a farmers' market, but I kept forgetting to write the money down. Making change and standing upright at the same time is kind of like a miracle."

The way she put herself down grated Fern's nerves the way a broken blinker did. Abby was wicked smart — you could tell just by the way she reacted to things, cat-like, with quick, graceful moves. Smart people might miss their stop, but they realized it all in a second, calculating how far they'd gone past it, which line they were going to have to connect with to get back. *I need the 62, or the 41. Where does this line cross?* Dumb people blinked lazily out the window and mumbled, *What the hell?*

"I don't believe you."

"It's true." Abby tapped the side of her

head. "Bright but forgetful. That's what my teachers in grade school always said. Matter of fact, I think they said that in college, too."

"You can pay people to do all that for you. Hire a bookkeeper, a graphic designer, and a marketing consultant. You can do all that online now, and then you just make the shit." She corrected herself. "The stuff."

"Yeah. I suppose I should look for someone to help, if I'm going to get serious about it. And since Scott died, I'm kind of thinking that I should do it. You have any interest?"

Fern blinked once. Then again. "Sorry?"

A quick, crooked smile. Hopeful. "In helping me? Part-time work?"

"I *have* a job." It was so preposterous — and surprising — that it wasn't even that insulting. Abby was a different breed. A totally different kind of person.

Abby rubbed at her cheeks. "I know. I didn't mean to imply that you didn't. . . . I'm sorry. I was just thinking out loud. Sorry. The most important thing to me is spending time with Matty. That's all."

Abby and Matty — they had a connection. Fern could see it. She could feel it in the air between them. It wasn't too early for Abby to love her son — who *wouldn't* love

Matty? But Matias was smitten with her, too.

What if he came to rely on her?

No.

Abby couldn't . . . God, she was lovely. She was gorgeous. She was sweet. No one could argue that. But she couldn't just swoop in and *take* the family that Fern had built, the one that Fern took care of. Her family was her job, the only job that really mattered. Her family was *hers.*

"And that's still okay, right? Us hanging out, me and Matty?" Abby's face was as wide-open as an Oakland street at three in the morning.

Matty thundered into the shed, yelling something about a double flip and how Abby *had* to come watch.

Abby. Not Mom.

No, it's not okay. You can watch him, you can learn about him. You can help. But you can't have him.

Matty will not rely on you.

Matty relies on me.

At least, that's what she tried to say. It came out more as *"Mrpht."*

"Mom?" Matty's voice was worried, and she should reassure him, but the sound faded into the buzz that was inside her head, just behind her teeth somewhere.

"Mom!"

I'm fine, Fern said. She heard the words at least, knocking against the buzzing, but she wasn't quite sure they could hear her.

Didn't matter.

All that mattered was Matty.

"Fern?"

Abby's voice was miles away, in a tunnel. So far down the tracks and in the dark, and she could hear the thumping of the wheels and then Fern forgot to think about anything as she felt herself inside the train, inside the engine itself, rushing toward darkness that was quieter than anything else.

CHAPTER THIRTY-FOUR

Abby watched Fern fall. *Jesus.* She couldn't tell if she'd said the word — a sudden, unexpected prayer — out loud or not.

"It's okay! Move away from her!" Matty rushed at his mother like he could catch her, even though Fern was already down, already lying on the wooden floor of the shed. "Give her space. She needs space." He looked upward at the shelves, as if considering whether things would fall, like it was an earthquake.

Jorge and Bryson, standing in the small bright doorway, stared, frozen.

Fern made a noise that didn't sound human. It was a growl.

Abby felt fear rise from every pore. An ambulance, that's what they needed. *That* was it. "Jorge. Here's my cell, call 911. Matty, help me here."

Jorge took the phone and started dialing.

"Tell them we need an ambulance. Okay?"

Matty screamed, "No! She's fine! Just let her have the seizure."

"Jorge," said Abby, "call."

Fern's face was a rictus, her body a mass of twitches. Abby had never seen a seizure, but she'd had an idea of what they looked like, and this was *not* it. Fern wasn't flailing — instead, she was making the tiniest, tightest motions imaginable, as if every muscle in her body were bound by tight rubber bands. She made that growling noise again, a terrifying low sound that seemed yanked from her throat with every jerk of her body. She lay half sideways on the floor, one arm behind her. Her jaw jutted forward, her lower lip twisting along with her limbs.

"Matty." Abby knelt next to him in the space between the shelf and his body. "What can I do to help?"

"Don't call 911."

Fern's body was spasming now, going rigid, as if she were a woman about to be sawed in half on a stage, and then folding into softness, only to be pulled taut again. One eyelid was halfway open. That horrified Abby most of all. She could see Fern in there, could see her trying to get out. She was almost unrecognizable.

"Honey, we have to." Abby glanced at Jorge. "She's not — oh, *Jesus* — I don't think she's breathing. Are we supposed to do CPR or something?"

"No, just let her come out on her own." Matty's voice was full of tears, and he alternated between holding his arms above Fern and furiously scowling at Jorge. Abby felt a scream build in her lungs, but there was no place for it to go. The only person screaming should be Fern, and she was still a terrifying bundle of jerks and vocal clicks.

He dropped to his knees next to Fern. "Mom says no 911. Never 911."

Fern was softening now, her legs finally stilling. Her right arm was still bent and locked at a forty-five-degree angle, but her head lolled sideways.

Matty held his mother's head. "I got this. She's breathing again, see? We're fine." He pushed his fingers into his mother's hair. "It's just a seizure. *God.* She'll be fine in a minute."

Abby put one hand on Fern's shoulder, the other on her elbow. A fine tremor raced through her fingers, and it took a second to realize it was she who was shaking now, not Fern. "We need to get her — Matty, what do we do now?"

"She's totally *fine,* aren't you *listening?* She's fine. Look!"

Fern gasped. She was blinking and breathing now, but she looked like someone else. Her eyes were slitted, her mouth still open, her body curling like a question mark that had been stretched straight and then released.

She looked feral.

And terrifying.

"How . . ." Abby could hear sirens now. "How long does it take for her to come out of it?"

"She's out of it. Can't you *see* that? She's already out. She'll be fine." Matty didn't look up, keeping his hands on Fern's forehead. "Mom, tell them. Sometimes it takes a minute. That's all. *Mom.* Tell them to stop. Tell them not to come."

"They're just going to check her —"

"*No ambulance.* Cancel it!"

Maybe Abby could change the subject. "What about juice? Would that help her, if we could find some? I think I have some pineapple juice in the kitchen. . . ." It was Scott's — he'd liked it with vodka sometimes. Small cans, she had them somewhere.

Matty's eyes widened. "She's epileptic. Not a *diabetic.*" He brushed the hair back from Fern's forehead. "*God.* See? She's fine. Tell them to go away."

"Matty —"

He met her gaze then and his eyes were

full of tears. "Please, Abby? Make them go away? It'll make everything worse."

It couldn't. There couldn't be much worse than that half-opened eye, not much worse than watching a woman twitch grotesquely on the floor of her shed.

The siren stopped, and Abby could hear a powerful-sounding engine coming from the front of the house. "Jorge, go get them and bring them back here? Bryson, grab Tulip's collar. Hold on tight to him, okay?"

"Please? Abby?" Matty sat taller and with his shoulders straight, with his jaw set fierce, Abby saw for a split second the man he would become. But his face — his little-boy face broke her heart, the lower lip that was shaking no matter how much he tightened it, the big brown eyes that were swimming.

Behind him, two women in white shirts and black pants hurried across the yard. Bryson, off to one side, tried to make Tulip sit, but the dog was dragging him slowly forward, foot by foot.

"Honey," Abby spoke as softly to Matty as she could, "let them check her."

"How long has she been in seizure?" asked one medic, dropping to her knees.

Another said, "Is she epileptic? On her meds?"

Their voices established them as in command. Relief trickled down the back of Abby's throat. "Matty, come on, let's let them have the space."

Matty hit — whacked — her hand off his shoulder. "Don't *touch* me."

Abby gasped. "I'm sorry." The side of her hand burned. She'd have a bruise there tomorrow.

"What's her name?"

"Don't tell them."

But Abby said, "Fernanda Reyes."

Matty's eyes.

The look of betrayal he gave her just before he turned his back on her was a wretched burn, a pain that seared through her shoulders directly into her heart.

Nothing could erase that look.

"No, no, no," mumbled Fern as the medics, now multiplied to four, loaded her on the gurney. It was all she seemed able to say.

Abby and Matty followed them as they rolled her through the garden and out the side gate. The gurney wobbled on the rocky path.

"Don't let her fall." Matty's voice cracked as they lined the stretcher up with the open back doors of the ambulance.

One of the medics said, "Don't worry, she's strapped in tight. Oh, hey, wait, buddy.

You can't get up there."

Matty was in the back of the ambulance before they even slid Fern inside.

The tallest medic pointed at Abby. "Can you grab him?"

Matty's look was ferocious, his eyes narrowed, his top row of teeth bared.

"I . . . I don't think so." Abby's throat was so tight she didn't know how much longer she'd be able to breathe. "Matty, you wanna come with me? We'll meet her . . ."

Matty stayed perfectly still except for his chest, which heaved as he panted.

The medics slid in the gurney, the legs folding below it like magic.

Abby gave up. "I'm not going to be able . . ."

The tall woman addressed Matty again. "Kid, you're *really* not supposed to ride with us."

Matty strapped himself into a side seat and crossed his arms.

"C'mon, now."

"I'm not leaving her."

The medic attaching a blood pressure cuff to Fern's arm said, "Aw, whatever. Let him ride, Cindi."

"Liability."

"Fuck it. This kid's not getting out, and I don't feel like fighting him. My shoulder's still jacked from that dude last night."

"We don't have Mom's permission."

"Yes," said Fern, her voice suddenly clear, ringing through the vehicle.

"All right, then."

As they finished locking the legs of the gurney and moving equipment around her, Abby looked behind her. There on the porch were the other two boys, both of them wide-eyed, tears still streaming down Bryson's face. She would have to get them home. She'd have to do that before she met Matty at the hospital. *Shit.* "Which hospital — ?"

"Alta Bates," said the shorter medic, and slammed the doors shut.

The last thing Abby saw was Matty's eyes, so full of anger they almost burned.

CHAPTER THIRTY-FIVE

Fern couldn't remember much, but the sick dread in her abdomen told her everything she needed to know. The vague queasiness and the metallic taste in her mouth meant she'd had a seizure. The noises and smells around her, the thin blanket wrapped around her knees, the ugly blue and white curtain hung high around her tiny bed, meant she was in the hospital.

Those two things combined meant she was fucking *fucked.*

She'd started to come back to consciousness in the ambulance, and she hadn't understood a damn thing at first. She thought there might have been a car crash. Or maybe she'd tripped and hit her head.

God, it had been so *long* since she had gone out. Years, probably. And it had been fifteen years — more — since she'd had a seizure in public. Besides her daily meds, she didn't give her condition a second thought. It was under control.

Fern looked up at the IV pole hanging just to her left. Her heartbeat *bing*ed in time on the machine, right along with the thumping in her chest. Matty sat on a plastic chair, playing some game on his phone, the ER curtain resting on his shoulders. There was never enough room in these emergency room cubicles. He was being sweetly fierce. When the nurses thrust the curtain aside, he watched them carefully, as if he were their boss, evaluating their every move. He'd said Abby was taking the other two boys home. Thank god for that — thank god she wasn't here.

Fuck. Fern was so fucked.

Four years ago, when Matty was seven. That was it — that had been her last seizure. Scott had sent her a registered letter saying he wanted to see his son, and she'd panicked, the letter still in her hands, her fear fanning the flames of her anger. He threatened to take her to court if she didn't let him take Matty on the weekends, knowing, of course, that she'd never have enough saved up to fight him. She'd watched her hands shake, and then her vision had blotched. Luckily, the postman had left as soon as she'd signed for the envelope, and even more luckily, Grandpa Wyatt and Elva had both been home. Wyatt, whose boss at the tow yard had fits, just moved the kitchen table out of the way and let her have the seizure. Elva tucked her up on the couch and put a Band-Aid on the two cuts she'd gotten on her arm, probably from carpet tacks. And best of all, Matty had been at school. He'd missed the whole thing.

Scott had never even followed up on his request. His threat. Didn't care enough, apparently. He'd had a minute of caring followed by his normal apathy. Her terror had been wasted, the seizure pointless.

But bless Grandpa Wyatt and Elva. They'd known what was imperative they *not* do. They didn't call 911. They knew she didn't need an ambulance.

Matty had known that. Abby — obviously — hadn't listened to him.

Or had they been in on it together? Both of them, caring for her?

It was an intolerable thought, making her head rattle as if her brain were a fare box filled with only change, no paper money to muffle the sound.

A tall man in a gray sweater and jeans pulled the curtain back. He kept his eyes on his iPad, giving it a quick swipe. "I'm Dr. Antes. You're Fern Reyes." Did doctors not wear white coats anymore? What was to say that this wasn't just some guy on the street with an iPad, pretending to be a hospital employee?

"How are you feeling?" Still he didn't look at her, which was enough to convince Fern he was actually a doctor.

Matty glared at him, his phone beeping, the game unplayed.

"Like shit." Fern felt as if she could sleep for a million years.

He laughed. "Most people say fine, for some reason. I like your honesty. Well, I don't see why you shouldn't go home in a little while. I just want you to get a few more fluids in you. There were . . ." He swiped his device again. Fern wondered what would happen if his network went down. Would this man still know how to be a doctor?

He continued. "Ah, here. There were just a couple of questions you weren't able to answer when you came in."

She'd been foggy when they were checking her in. She remembered that she'd gotten impatient with a small, round nurse whose accent she couldn't understand. She was pretty sure the nurse had been even more irritated with her.

"Okay."

"I see your list of meds here. Are you still on all of them?"

"Not the Keppra, it made me too tired. But the carbamazepine, yes."

Dr. Antes tapped the iPad. "Got it. Could you be pregnant?"

She shot a look at Matty. "No."

Matty, though. Keeping his eyes down. Was that something he ever thought about? *Cristo.* He was too young to worry about her sex life. Wasn't he?

"Is there another adult you want to call to come pick you up?"

It came back to her then, an ice floe shattering, an iceberg cracking in half. What she'd been worried about when she went down.

Abby and her son.

Matty relying on Abby. In any way at all, even small.

Shit, Fern had let this happen.

She pressed her fingers to her top lip.

"Fern?" The doctor looked at her then, his eyes a muddy noncolor color.

"My brother," she whispered. She cleared her throat. "Matty, could you go get me a coffee from the vending machine? Get a dollar out of my wallet."

"No."

She turned her head slowly, deliberately. With the voice she rarely used (it was her mother's voice — she got it out only for

335

extra-special shitty situations), she said, *"Go."*

Matty mumbled something that might have been a curse, but he dug her wallet out of the pocket of her jacket.

When he was gone, the doctor said, "So. Do we have a different answer to that pregnancy question now?"

Pompous prick. "I just finished my period yesterday," she said. She hated admitting even that to him. She flicked the oxygen meter off her left forefinger and yanked off the tape that held the IV needle to the bend of her arm. "Tell your nurse I need to sign out."

"Don't pull that out," he warned her.

"What? I'm not qualified to know what to do with my own body?" She tugged out the needle and pushed her thumb against the bright spurt of red blood.

"If you're pregnant, your medications need to be changed, as soon as possible."

"I'm epileptic. Not pregnant, or stupid." She should have said *nor stupid.* That would have made her sound smarter. "I'm going home."

He shook his head, as if coming back to himself. "You'll need a ride."

Dickbag. What a shithead. "I'm calling my brother."

"And you understand I'm a mandated reporter." He flashed the front of his iPad at her, as if she could read it from four feet away. "Medical-reporting fact sheet."

Why had she bothered to hope anything at all? Hating herself even more than she hated him, she choked back tears. "I understand."

"Your profession is flagged on your chart. I'm sorry."

He wasn't sorry. *His* salary wasn't the one that was going to be immediately frozen. She'd be off the boards for three months, mandatory. If there were no incidents in six months, probation could be lifted with approval. Those were the rules, anyway. But most of the time? Once you were let go for a lapse in consciousness, no matter what kind it was, AC Transit didn't tend to bring you back from purgatory. It didn't matter if someone blacked out from too many tequila sunrises while driving a full coach through rush hour on the Bay Bridge or if it was just a short seizure while inside a private residence on off-time — the agency had been sued too many times, by too many people.

Crying would only make things worse. Crying would only scare Matty when he came back.

But she had no choice left about it. The

tears came then, hateful and hot.

She'd be lucky to ever drive again.

CHAPTER THIRTY-SIX

It took Abby forever to drop off Bryson and Jorge — they lived only nineteen blocks apart, but there had been traffic, and then Jorge's dad hadn't been at home, so she'd had to drive to Hayward to drop him at a place where they were holding some kind of wrestling match. It didn't feel at all acceptable to leave him there, not in the parking lot full of lurching groups of men yelling and drinking out of red plastic cups, but then a short man dressed in black tights and red and blue face paint darted out a side door and lifted Jorge, swinging him around. The man's red cape swirled around his son as they twirled. Just in time for his last match, he'd said, obviously thrilled Jorge was there. *Thank you for bringing him.* Another boy of a similar age waved at Jorge, then both of them yelled abuse that sounded affectionate at an older man dressed in a similar wrestling uniform. Abby figured it was probably okay to leave.

Fern had already checked out of the hospital by the time Abby finally made it there. No one under Fern's name in the ER. That was all the information she'd been told. *No one by that name.* The young woman had actually looked like she felt bad about saying it, but she obviously couldn't say anything else. Rules. Laws. All of it.

Abby drove home. She didn't know what else to do.

Matty wasn't answering his cell phone. Of course he wasn't. He was furious with Abby for calling the ambulance.

She'd had to call 911. Surely he could understand that.

He was eleven.

What had she understood at eleven? She'd had a best friend — Emily — who had a houseful of siblings that fought and laughed and raged and wailed. It was the place she'd loved best to be. She'd pretended she was just one of the kids who lived under Emily's parents' roof, trampled and overlooked and beatifically happy. That was the year she'd decided that no matter what, she'd someday live in a house full of people, instead of a house in which a dead baby's picture took pride of place on top of the grand piano. She loved Meg. Of course she did, as much as she could. But she'd never even met her sister. At eleven, Matty's age, Abby had just started to realize how embarrassed she was by her mother's tears every time they passed the cemetery on the way to soccer practice.

So basically, she'd understood nothing.

The doorbell rang, and Abby dropped the glass she was drying right into the sink, not caring that it shattered. "I'm coming! Coming!"

But it wasn't Matty. It was his uncle.

Diego was curt. No smile. "Matty forgot his backpack."

"Oh, sure. It must be outside. Maybe?"

And there it was, by the foot of the trampoline, lying on its side in the last rays of the setting sun.

"Here." Abby picked it up, surprised by its heaviness. "Thanks for coming to get it. I could have brought it to him."

He nodded and headed toward the house.

"Do you want a drink?"

He paused but didn't turn his head. "Sorry?"

"I feel like I need one." What did that make her sound like? "I mean, I don't . . . oh, fuck it. Yeah, I need a drink."

The back of Diego's neck was dark tan and thick. He dropped his head forward as if checking in with his feet. Then he said, "Okay."

While she poured the wine — a red that Scott had been saving for something special — she watched Diego's wrists. He twisted his wineglass at the stem. His wrists were thick, almost twice as wide as hers. The glass looked smaller than it was. Were his wrists the result of climbing trees all day? Was that where he got the ropes of muscle she could see at the neckline of his T-shirt? Or did he climb trees *because* he had that muscle and had to climb something?

They moved to the back porch. The light had almost left the sky completely, and a ribbon of rose fog unfurled itself, a night-blooming sky flower.

"You're sure she's okay?"

Instead of moving like most people did to the outdoor dining table on the deck, Diego sat on the top step. "Physically, I'm sure she's fine."

"I still don't . . ." She sat next to him and took too big a swallow of the wine. It burned, scratching her throat as if it were cask-strength whiskey. "I don't know why what I did was wrong."

"Doctors are mandated reporters."

"I don't know what that is." But it started to make sense. Slowly.

"She'll lose her job."

"Don't be silly."

Diego shrugged, keeping his gaze steady. Forward.

"She can't."

"Sure. Whatever you say."

Abby felt as if she might throw up. "That's . . ."

"Happens." Diego tilted his head back. "Your palm tree needs help."

She followed his gaze. *Fern.* She couldn't let this happen to Fern. But she said only, "I know."

"True date palms don't belong in North Berkeley. It's too cold. The only one that thrives here is a Bismarck, or maybe a cabbage palm. Poor thing." He sounded honestly sorry for it.

"The fronds are driving me crazy. I was going to try to get up there and do something about it, but I hadn't figured out how to climb it."

"Don't be stupid. Get someone who's trained. Licensed."

"Like you?"

"Yeah. But not me."

Of course not. She pulled at her skirt, tugging the hem toward her knees.

Then their glasses were empty.

Without asking, Diego took her wineglass

and walked inside to the sink.

"You don't have to . . ."

Diego didn't answer. He moved as if he'd been in her kitchen a million times, picking the broken glass out of the sink carefully. He washed both wineglasses. Then he dried them. When he folded the tea towel and hung it neatly on the handle of the oven door, the motion nearly brought Abby to her knees with a sudden gut-punch of lust. She hadn't seen it coming. And she didn't know what to do with it.

"Thanks."

"You're welcome." He stood in front of her, tall and steady as a tree himself. Unmovable. Not that she wanted to move him. He was just fine where he was.

Lord, was she this much of an idiot? Was that possible? He needed to go before she made some kind of ridiculous fool of herself. How was it possible that while her skin burned in confusion and fear over what she'd done (what she might have done, what she hadn't *known* she'd been doing) to Fern, that she could also feel this shaft of desire under the burn?

Diego reached out and touched the granite countertop. She had agonized over picking it out, choosing the color of it, the texture. He stroked it with one finger. All the while his black cardamom eyes didn't leave hers.

"Okay, thanks." She'd just said that. She was repeating herself.

"If you hadn't just lost your husband . . ." His voice trailed off, but his eyes stayed steady on hers.

Abby's stomach lurched as if she were on the trampoline. "You'd . . . you'd what?"

"Quiero besarte toda."

"I . . ." She swallowed the rock in her throat and attempted a laugh. "I don't even know what that means." But she knew enough California Spanish to figure out most of it. "I sent your sister to the hospital."

"Yeah. You did."

The words came out before she even thought them through. "After you kissed me. Then what would you do?"

His eyebrows jumped, and she liked that she'd surprised him. "You shouldn't ask what you don't want to know."

"Oh . . ." Her courage quailed. "Were *you* ever married?" she asked.

His surprise only registered in the corners of his mouth, where he relaxed, incrementally. Abby felt relief shoot through her — he was nervous, too.

"Yeah."

"Did you like being married?"

He rested the flat of his palm against the granite. It would warm under his touch. Would she?

"Yeah," he said. "I loved it."

"Why?"

"I liked being with her. I liked going to bed with her. I liked the way she smelled in the morning. I liked the way she laughed at me." Diego glanced down at his bare hand, then back at her. "She laughed at me all the time."

"What happened?" Abby pressed her thumb against the wedding ring she hadn't remembered to take off yet.

He shrugged. "Life."

"What kind of life?" Tulip wandered in the open back door and flopped himself down on the kitchen floor like he'd had an even more exhausting day than they had.

"She fell in love with someone else."

"She cheated on you?"

"No," he said. "She didn't cheat. She told me before she left me. We'd promised we'd never do that, never inflict that upon each other. She told me she loved him, and then, only when I understood, then she left."

"Damn." Was it strange they were being so honest? So transparent? It felt good to listen to him.

"Yeah. Fucking sucked, and that's an

346

understatement. When she said she had something big to tell me, I thought it was that she was finally pregnant. We'd been trying for a long time — I wanted so bad to have a cousin for Matty. A son for me. Or a daughter. I would have been a good dad, I think. Our dad wasn't around, so I guess I don't know that for sure. But I'm a *really* good uncle. When I see what Matty has meant to us, to my family . . . But that wasn't what she wanted to tell me that day."

"I'm sorry." And she was.

Shrugging, he said, "I'm glad we had what we did, for as long as we had it. We were lucky, I guess."

Lucky. That's what he called losing everything?

"She had a kid," he went on. "Within a year of leaving, she was knocked up with his child. I saw her at the café on Bancroft once. She . . ." His voice trailed off. "She broke my heart double, I guess."

"Do you regret the time you spent with her?"

"I don't regret anything I've ever done."

"I've never heard anyone say that."

Diego leveled his gaze on her, clear and steady. "Things I've done I'm okay with. But I've regretted things I've never had."

"Like what?" Abby leaned on the counter-top.

"Time and cash to travel. I'd like to see Peru. And the city in Mexico our mom came from, Huatulco. She left when she was little, but we still have an uncle and some distant cousins there."

The intensity of his voice made her skin prickle, as if she'd brushed against a nettle. "What else?"

Diego looked over her head. "Not much. Kids. I still really want kids. Anyway. What about you? Were you in love with him?"

Abby thought of Scott's chin, the almost invisible dimple at the end of it. The way his stubble grew faster and thicker in winter, as if it wanted to warm him. The way he'd laughed affectionately when she got left and right confused, something she'd always done. The way they fit, the way she slept better when she'd been in his arms. The way he listened. "Yeah."

"Yeah," he said.

"He lied, though. In the end." She paused. She could have stepped forward. She could have closed the distance between them, but she didn't, even though she was throbbing now. Finally, she said, "What did you think of him?"

Diego blinked. She could feel him pull

back even though he hadn't moved. "Hated him. He hurt Fern and left Matty behind. They both deserved better."

"I tried to give her the life insurance. Or the equivalent, anyway. It'll take a while for it to be distributed, but I offered to give it to her in advance, out of my accounts. I told her she could have all of it."

He laughed, low in his throat. "*Dios.* I would have paid good money to see that. What did she say?"

"What do you think she said?"

"For fuck's sake." Diego rubbed his eyes. "She's an idiot."

"I'll get her to take it."

"Good luck. He really left them nothing? In writing?"

Abby shook her head.

"What a *shit.* Well, it's your money." Diego's brows tucked together. "Not hers. There's no way you'll get her to take it. I know my sister."

"He paid her so little, for so long. If I'd known about it . . . It's not like we didn't have enough." Abby immediately felt shame for saying it out loud. But Diego knew it already. She didn't need to hide it. She didn't have the energy to do so even if she'd wanted to. "It's her money. Not mine."

He pushed his thumbs into his eyebrows,

as if to try to smooth them again. "You know? I wanted to kill him for what he did to Fern. For how he left them." Though his face was dark, his eyes shaded, his voice stayed casual. "I've never been more glad that someone was dead."

It was her husband they were talking about. "So fucking me would be a way of fucking him?"

Diego blinked, hard. Shock quickly faded to what looked like simple surprise. Then grudging respect. "I hadn't thought it through, to be honest."

"You should have."

"I guess it would be unforgivable."

Abby's heart stuttered and almost stalled. Then she said, "What if we were both drunk?"

When he smiled, the right corner of his mouth went higher than the left. He said, "I guess it's too fucking bad we're not."

Abby moved then. She went to the liquor cabinet and got out the bottle of Herradura Silver tequila and grabbed two shot glasses. She brought them back, her legs quaking underneath her. She was soft inside, molten. She felt dangerous.

"I'm sorry I don't have any lime left. We used it all on the tacos, I think."

A muscle jumped in Diego's jaw. He

reached for the saltshaker that stood next to the napkins. "Pour it out."

She poured two shots, grateful that her hand wasn't shaking.

"Here," she said.

And then she reached forward and took his hand. She raised the inside of his wrist to her mouth and licked his skin. Then she raised her own wrist to his mouth. His tongue was a slick warmth.

He salted their skin. They drank their shots. Abby's eyes didn't leave Diego's as they sucked the salt off each other's wrists.

A second's pause. The alcohol hit Abby immediately, striking her in the knees.

"Say no," Diego warned. "It's okay if you say no."

She didn't want to. All she had was yes, a great swarm of yeses buzzing under her skin. She had no voice left, but she didn't need it — her body was such a huge yes yes *yes.*

She didn't find her voice until much later, when she was roaring through her third orgasm, his mouth at her core, her fingers clutching the sheets she'd bought with Scott in mind, her brightly colored widow's duvet pushed to the floor. Her voice came back, and she screamed so loudly she felt him jerk below her, but his tongue never stopped, never paused what he was doing so well.

Then she locked her fingers into his shoulder blades and dragged him up her body. She slid herself down, bucking her hips to take him inside her again. When she started crying, though, when she started sobbing, he stopped. He stilled completely inside her. And even though he was hot and hard, and even though she was slick, and even though she was still bucking frantically underneath him, he moved his hand to her wet cheek.

"I'll stop," he said.

"Never," she said, and she meant it. She had nothing to do but this, nothing to do but fuck this man — this stranger who was somehow related to her — from now until they died of exhaustion, of dehydration, of starvation.

"But . . ."

She hit at the tears on her cheeks with one hand and gripped his side with her other. She tilted her hips so that he was inside her deeper again. "I'll stop crying. I promise. I'm fine. *Fuck* me."

"Hey." His mouth caught hers again, for the thousandth — the millionth, the first — time. Against her lips, he said, "You can cry. Don't stop for me. I just need to know you're okay."

So she tipped her hips again and ground against him. She cried harder, so hard it felt like she was raining. High black clouds parted in her chest, rumbles of thunder roared through her head. The sobs made the next time she came even bigger, and as she clenched around his cock, he yelled something in Spanish that she didn't understand and then before he stopped moving, he kissed every inch of her face, her neck, her breasts. When he reached her belly button and the soft part of her stomach, she stopped sobbing and started giggling, and by the time he'd dropped kisses down her inner thighs, to her knees, to the bottoms of her ticklish feet, she was laughing so hard she got a cramp in her side.

Still giggling, Abby said, "This doesn't have to mean anything, you know."

He laughed, too. His dark eyes were clear. "I know. But *fuck,* you feel amazing."

It was the perfect answer. Abby felt something in her chest break, like the glass in the sink, and then she felt the shards cut her inside, so sweetly. The pain was flawless.

She rolled under Diego, wrapping his arms around her shoulders, pushing her nose into the still-sweaty spot between his ear and neck. She didn't get that old feeling she used to get after sex with Scott, that feeling of being safe, that nothing could ever hurt them.

Nothing was safe.

Trust, the thing she used to think she needed for good sex, wasn't in the room anymore. Sex was just sex. And she was still alive.

Diego said, "Shit. Matty's backpack." He kissed her forehead.

"Go."

On the floor next to the bed, Tulip groaned and flopped over. In bed, Abby did the same.

Diego pulled on his jeans.

He let himself out.

Abby rolled again. And then, alone, she slept.

CHAPTER THIRTY-SEVEN

Sex was just sex.

And Fern needed it. She didn't have a motherfucking job until all this was fixed (*if it could be fixed — god, it had to be fixed*), so she didn't need to wait till midweek to get some.

She'd been in the hospital — spitting with fury — until six p.m. the night before. She had sent Diego over to get Matty's backpack at seven. He'd come back with it at eleven, not meeting her eye. If he'd had sex with her . . .

Abby couldn't have her family. Not after she'd been the reason Fern had lost everything. First the child support (okay, maybe that wasn't exactly Abby's fault, except that Scott had left, and then he'd married her) and then Fern's job. The two things she'd blithely thought would always be there until Matty was eighteen.

Fern had been so naive. So intentionally

cheerful, sure that if she believed hard enough, everything would always work out.

So she didn't ask Diego what he'd been doing for those four hours. She just took the backpack and texted Gregory. *Tomorrow. Any time you want. I've got the whole day free.*

Gregory was out of his class at noon. They met at his place at twelve fifteen. They barely made it to the bed. Fern dropped her jeans, shirt, and underwear in the kitchen, and if Gregory hadn't had a belt malfunction, they would have had sex on the floor next to the stove.

Afterward, he rolled over onto his back. With satisfaction, Fern watched the sweat slip along his hairline. She'd done that. She was the reason his eyes were glazed. *She* was why his lower lip was swollen. Was it possible to have this? To actually keep it? This gorgeous (almost) string-free sex with someone she really liked?

"I needed that." *Here's your one chance, Fancy,* sang Reba McEntire.

"Me, too," he said.

He had no idea. She had *really* needed it, had needed to know that her body still worked. There was nothing wrong with her libido, with the way she got wet, with the way she made Gregory lose his shit. So she'd had a seizure. It was her body's way of overreacting, that was all. Reacting to Abby. To her being in their lives.

"So," he said.

"Yeah?" She moved her head up his arm so that her temple rested against the muscle of his shoulder. He smelled like sweat, and she liked it. "Talk to me."

"You —" He broke off.

Uh-oh. Fern felt a cool draft on her stomach and wished suddenly that they hadn't pushed the bedcovers to the floor in their eagerness. She couldn't handle it if he went back to the whole love conversation. She just needed this — exactly what they had now — to keep going. A little longer. She could break up with him in a month or two. Maybe three. Three more months of Wednesday afternoons with this man, of sex like that, such perfect fucking sex it was ridiculous . . . "Yeah?"

"Is it real?"

Her stomach slid into her kneecaps. "Gregory . . . I can't —"

He tightened his arm around her and kept his gaze upward. "No, I want to know. Are you really coming when you make those sounds?"

"What?"

"You can tell me."

"Gregory —"

"No, really. Linda was the one who broke it to me." He gave a short laugh, but there was no humor in it. "On our seventh anniversary. She told me that all women fake it. I mean, I knew some of that. I knew women could do that. I just never understood why anyone would want to. You know? And since then, I've asked a few women." The tops of his cheekbones colored. "They've all admitted it. That they've done it. And it's fine. If you do. I just . . . I don't know. I just want to know."

"Gregory, I came so hard I don't think I'll be able to walk. Maybe ever again."

"You don't have to make me feel — I know that most women don't orgasm from vaginal intercourse alone."

"Whoa. Sexy talker." She rubbed her eyes. "I come that way." She wished she could leave it there. And she knew she wouldn't be able to. So there she was. Taking care of him. Of course.

"You really do?" His voice was brighter. Hopeful.

It made her want to jab her finger into his side, giving him a mostly innocuous but still unpleasant surprise. And she knew she was a shit for feeling that way. Gregory needed reassurance. He was asking for it, which was a damn sight more than most men could do. "I don't come *just* because your penis is inside my vagina." They were such ugly words for such amazing body parts. "There's sensitive tissue called the cavernosum near my vagina that is connected to my clitoris. When you're on top and I push upward against you, I'm rubbing my clit against your pubic bone." She pitched her voice so she sounded like a sex-education high school teacher. "My vagina also clenches, which is pleasurable. When suitably and persistently aroused in a regular pattern with either a male penis or an expensive but realistically shaped dildo, I can achieve a satisfactory and highly enjoyable orgasm."

"Fern. God."

"What the hell?" Fern pushed herself backward, moving his arm so that it was between them. "I just told you how I come in the most precise terms available. I thought you'd be happy."

"What's your problem?"

I'm on medical probation. I'm not going to be able to make the house payment. My son isn't going to pass science because his project tutor probably fucked his uncle.

"My problem? *Que madres.*"

Gregory sat up and scooted to the headboard, reaching for a clove. "I'm glad you come that way, don't get me wrong." He flicked the lighter, and with his first exhalation, the room smelled like church again. "But after, you push me away so fast, every single time. . . . I'm just not sure I can keep up."

"What is that? A threat?"

Instead of answering, he sighed and drew deeply on the clove. It made a crackling noise.

"God, I knew this would happen." She should pull a pillow over her body — she should hide her breasts, the vee at her legs. But no, wait a minute. She was fine like this. With all of her solidity on display. She sat up and faced him, crossing her legs, feeling the coolness where she was still wet. "I knew it." She would have to break it off with him. The thought — just the thought of it — made her gut feel empty. Then she'd have no job, no money, and no Gregory.

She laughed. Then, in a move that surprised her to her core, she said, "I'm out of work. That's why I can be here on a Monday."

"What?"

"Seizure."

"Shit, are you —"

Fern pushed back his hand. "In public.

Abby called 911. Because of her, I'm out for three months at least, on probation for six. If I get my job back at all." Sandy Taylor hadn't gotten hers back. Not after her seizure in Safeway. She never got behind the wheel again.

"What are you going to do?"

The laugh wanted to turn into a sob, but she choked it into submission. "Sell my blood? Do they still do that? Maybe I could take up tarot card reading. How hard can it be to tell a fortune?" It was easy enough to see into her future, anyway.

"Start your business."

"Pffft."

"I mean it."

"I have nothing to offer."

"You have time. Talent. You look at numbers and see patterns. This is why you've been taking classes. This is what you've been *waiting* for. I know you can do this." His smile was brighter than the afternoon slant of light coming through the blinds behind him. "I'll make some calls. I know a guy who's starting a wine distribution group. He'll need a bookkeeper. And a sales team."

"No."

"Let me."

"Don't you get it?" Her words were a metal file's rasp. "I want to accept your help.

But if I do, that would mean I need it, and that terrifies me." Just the admission of it struck such deep fear into her she thought she might burst into tears or something equally embarrassing.

His hands stilled. "Just *accept*."

"Fine." It wasn't fine. But she could try. Couldn't she? "Give me his phone number. Maybe I'll call him." She honestly thought it was enough. That she was trying.

"For god's sake, Fern." There was real anger in Gregory's voice — alive and hot — and it shocked her more than if he'd reached out and slapped her across the face. "Why do you make everything so hard?"

She felt her mouth twist, and even though she hated herself for saying it, even though the words felt dirty in a bad, soap-scummed way, she said them anyway. "Baby, I know what I could make hard again."

He stood. The slam of the bathroom door was her answer.

CHAPTER THIRTY-EIGHT

Abby went to the video game store, and it felt more like arriving in Las Vegas than it did visiting a shopping mall.

There were lights everywhere, flashing and strobing in neon. Abby didn't understand a single thing. Used-car sales words such as *pre-owned* and *trade-ins* jumped out at her, reaching to grab her legs from the stacked boxes. The store wasn't large, probably less than two hundred square feet, but it seemed like a million miles to the back wall of Hot Releases.

Research. Abby's body ached to turn around and run. Just a few doors down was a national chain that sold cakes of soap and bars of bubble bath. Once she'd gone in with Brook, and Abby had felt viscerally confused, as if every scent were a sound that she had to untangle and trace to its beginning. She'd left with a headache that Brook had put down to the smells that weren't natural, like their own soaps and oils, but Abby had known it wasn't that. It was the *volume* of the store. The sights, colors, sounds, and smells had added up to a cacophony of confusion.

She felt the same way in the games store.

But this was research, the kind that might help. Maybe. Someday. In the space of five weeks, Abby had gone from being a wife to a widow, from having no family to having . . .

Well. She still had no family.

What Abby had was a house. She had a garden. She had a tall, thin Great Dane who was probably at that moment chewing down a retaining wall, a dog she had thanks to Matty.

Matty wasn't returning her texts.

Neither was Fern, except for the one that read, *Don't need your help with Matty anymore since I'm off my bus. Thanks.*

Those six simple letters — each one an insecticide-soaked spike: *Thanks.*

Abby had fucked everything up. Unintentionally. But she had. And then she'd literally fucked Diego, a fuckup to end all fuckups. Guilt twisted a dirty rag in her chest.

Abby took another three steps into the noise of the store. It sounded like a war zone — blurts and beeps and whines of sirens —

enhanced by two boys bellowing war cries at a console to the right. The store smelled of ink, a bright chemical smell that couldn't be good for anyone.

This was wrong. She'd have to do her research another way. She turned to leave.

"The worst, right?" said a woman standing next to a spinning rack of what looked like electronic Ping-Pong paddles but probably weren't. She was short and round and blond, wearing a black skirt that was rumpled in the back and a red sweatshirt that was snug at her waist. "Those are mine over there. Where are yours?" She peered over Abby's shoulder as if she were hiding a kid or two behind her purse.

"I don't . . . I have *no* idea what I'm doing here."

The woman sighed. "You're spending too much money on something that's only going to rot their brains and probably ruin their lives in the long run."

"Ah." Abby nodded and tried to sound as if she agreed.

"So. The new COD?"

All Abby could think of was cash-on-delivery, something they'd stopped doing by the time she was old enough to have cash for any kind of delivery. "Sorry. What?"

The woman's red sunglasses wobbled on

the top of her head. She pushed them more firmly into her hair. "You *are* new to this, aren't you? Call of Duty. The new Xbox version just came out."

"Is that . . ." There'd been a *New Yorker* article on it. "Isn't that a violent one?"

The woman gave a descriptive shrug. "Eh. They say twelve, but you know. How old is the kid?"

This, at least, Abby knew the answer to. She was grateful for its nonambiguity. "Eleven."

"Mature?"

"Yes! I mean, I think he is. I don't know him that well."

"Oh." The woman looked Abby up and down once, quickly, as if she were judging Abby's birthing hips. "Yeah, so that's my eleven-year-old over there." She pointed at the two boys now hooting at something on a screen. "With his thirteen-year-old brother. And I've got an eighteen-year-old working at the barbecue place in the food court." The woman smiled as she pointed out the games store door down the bright sidewalk.

She was objectively cute. In a bar, she'd get drinks bought for her. "You can't be old enough," said Abby.

The woman brightened. "Aren't you

sweet? I was a child bride. And a child divorcée, obviously, or their father would be doing this errand, not me." Her green bag buzzed violently. She pulled out her cell and glanced at the face of it before dropping it back in with a grimace. "You want game advice?"

Hell, yes. She wanted everything advice.

"Are the games for keeping at your house or for your boyfriend's house?"

"Oh. No. Not a boyfriend. Matty's a . . . a friend's kid. So for my house. For when he comes over." If he ever came back.

"Get an Xbox. Other people will say PS4, and that's fine if your kid's into single-player games. They're cheaper, too, and so are the games. But I gotta tell you, the kids still want the Xbox. Better for playing with friends, too."

"Xbox. Check."

"They're not cheap. But in terms of keeping 'em busy, there's nothing else like it. If I let them, my boys would sit in front of it all day in nothing but their underpants. Add some Cheetos and you're going to be the best babysitter in the whole world."

"Underpants," Abby echoed. "Cheetos."

The woman walked briskly to a shelf, motioning Abby to follow her. The dark-haired clerk, who couldn't have been more than nineteen, watched them without saying anything.

"So, here you go. Games. Start with these. Call of Duty — we talked about that. Halo, here. Not too violent. Kids today are tough. Don't worry about that. And WWE."

Abby stared at the cover of the heavily muscled man wearing a Speedo. "Really?"

"Oh, yeah. They eat that shit up. That's Drake's favorite." She pointed at the shorter boy. "Oh, here. Final Fantasy. That's still big. And Minecraft. Does he have that one? They all have that one."

Abby vaguely remembered Fern telling Matty to go play it in his room. "I think so? But should I have it, too? What *is* it?"

"It's like solving puzzles. I even like it. And it doesn't make me motion sick like the others do. My kids keep talking VR to me, but I'd hurl for sure."

Abby held the stack carefully, as carefully as if Matty had picked them out himself. "Hey," she said. "I have a question for you."

"Shoot."

Abby arranged the words in her head before she said them. "What can I do that will make him happy?" *Besides getting a dog. Besides buying all the video games. Besides all the hope in the world.*

The woman's phone buzzed again. "Damn

it. I'm so sorry. Boys! Now!" Without saying anything else, the woman waggled her fingers and left the store, her cell at her ear, the boys trailing slowly and listlessly behind her, short sailboats with no wind.

The young store clerk swiped Abby's card for an exorbitant amount. He placed her purchases in an enormous shopping-cart-sized bag.

"Thank you," Abby said automatically, taking the receipt.

"Listen."

Startled, Abby stopped moving. She faced the young man. "Yes?"

"Not to me. To him."

"Sorry?"

"The kid you're babysitting. Just listen. Don't push. Everyone pushes boys to talk, and he won't want to." The clerk touched the top of the counter lightly with his fingertips, tapping lightly. "Just listen to him talk about the game. It won't seem to matter. But it will."

"Thank you." Abby meant it. This man had been a boy, what? Five minutes ago? "What about mothers?"

"Huh?"

"How old is your mom?"

He blinked and a game's siren howled behind him. "I think she's forty-two.

Maybe?"

"What does she want the most?"

His answer was too fast to be anything but true. "A raise."

"What does she do?"

The young man scratched his eyebrow and glanced over his shoulder. "This is, uh, weird."

Abby slid a twenty across the counter, feeling brilliant and idiotic at the same time. "I can't tell you how much I appreciate your help. What's your name?"

"Robby."

"I can't wait to Yelp how incredibly helpful you've been, Robby. So. What does your mom do?"

The twenty disappeared. "Answers the phone at a glass company."

"So she wants a raise. What else does she want?"

"A nap. She's tired, like, all the time. She has something . . . chronic fatigue? She takes pills, but they don't help, and the good pills aren't covered by her insurance, so she just sleeps on BART on the way home. Once she went all the way to Fremont, and our stop is Bay Fair."

A keen sense of disappointment sliced just above Abby's eyes. "Ah. A raise and a nap." There had to be more. She already knew that Fern could use both of those things. *And a job. To replace the one Abby had lost for her.* "Anything else?" Please, let the boy know the magic answer.

He shook his head. "She says she needs a *new* job, but there's nothing out there, and she says she needs more sleep but can't get it because my sister is only six and she's a little monster, I shit you not. Like, literally a monster. I was living with my girlfriend, but we got kicked out of the apartment, so now I'm back with my mom, but I can't even be in the same room with my little sister, no joke. She bit me the other day for no good reason." He poked at his arm as if testing it for soreness.

There's nothing out there. Fern might lose her job for good. She'd have no money. And she wouldn't *take* the money Abby wanted to give her. She wished she could slide it across a counter to Fern like the twenty that now rested, warm and folded, in the young man's pocket.

"What about school? Can she go back to school somehow? Change her job?" She knew as she said it she shouldn't have. People couldn't just take time off their paid work to learn a new trade, unpaid.

Robby stared, and then yanked the receipt from the machine. Her twenty was obviously spent. "Dunno. Anyway. Here's a survey. If you call this number and answer seven questions, you can get ten percent off your next purchase of fifty dollars or more." He gave her a slip of paper. "And here's your bag. Thanks for your business and, um . . ." He trailed off, his eyes focusing above her shoulder as if he'd remembered something important.

Hope battered the top of her lungs. "Yes?"

"Um. Have a nice day."

CHAPTER THIRTY-NINE

Dinner was a planned attack. Fern was staging it, special chicken mole and all. Their mother's sole successful recipe, it was Diego's favorite. Matty loved it, too, especially when she served it with corn tortillas fresh enough from Mi Pueblo to be steaming inside the plastic bag when she tossed them on the counter.

Nervous, Fern tied her apron tighter, made sure Captain America's shield was front and center. Matty had gotten it for her the previous Christmas. It was too big, obviously made for a dad, but that was okay. She liked the way the ties were long enough to double around her waist and tie in the front. And she'd always liked being the man of the house.

Until recently.

In the living room, she heard Matty yelp and then give a howl.

Thumping footsteps were followed by

Matty barreling into the kitchen. "He said I suck at Minecraft Parkour."

"*Do* you suck at it?" Fern said, stirring the sauce. It was perfect, thick and red-brown like dark clay.

"No!"

"Then why do you care what he says?"

"God. You don't *get* it. And it smells terrible in here."

"What? You love my mole." Even though it was her mother's, they'd never called it *Abuela*'s mole. The cirrhosis had killed Fern's mother long before Matty had ever come on the scene. He'd never had an *abuelita* of his own. One of many things he'd never have.

"I hate it."

"You do not!"

"You don't ever *listen* to me when I talk!" Matty's voice had hit its seriously upset range. "You say you hear me, but you don't remember *anything.*" His face was bright red, and he looked like he was about to cry.

"Dude." He was actually upset. What was this? "Is this about the game?"

"No!"

Diego entered the kitchen, looking guilty. Great.

"Honey, your uncle didn't mean to upset you. I bet he wants to apologize."

Diego nodded. "I sure do. I'm sorry you suck so much at launching off walls."

Matty went redder and his fists balled at his sides.

"Diego!" Fern wanted to throw a tortilla at him, the hotter the better. "Can you apologize to him, please?"

But Matty didn't wait for any apology from his uncle. "I'm not mad about the *game.* I'm not mad at Uncle Diego. It's *you* I'm mad at!"

Fern didn't point out that she wasn't the reason he'd run into the kitchen at high speed. "Okay." She softened her voice and made sure she turned her body to face him. She hoped that maybe her head on top of Captain America's shield and bemuscled body would soften Matty's emotions. "Tell me how I can help."

Matty made a noise of pure frustration, a guttural growl that a grizzly bear would have been proud of. "Chicken."

"What about it?" Matty loved chicken. He loved wings and drumsticks and chicken tacos.

"You buy factory chicken. They cut off their beaks." Each word was spit in her direction.

"Oh, honey. No."

"They do. If one gets sick, the others *eat*

375

them. And they're as smart as dogs, did you even *know* that?"

Fern doubted this. "I think you've been reading too much on the Internet. This is the same chicken you grew up on. The same we grew up on."

Diego, no help at all, flexed. "And look at me now!"

Matty ignored him, keeping his rage focused on Fern. "They can't even move in their cages. They're stuck in there. They hate it."

"Who told you this?" Who should Fern thank for this fight? Yeah, she would have bought the college-educated free-range organic chicken if she could have. But even if she could have afforded it, her supermarket didn't even carry the fancy kind. They carried cheap and cheaper.

"Abby told me."

Fantastic. "I thought you were mad at her."

"She didn't mean to do anything bad. She said she feels *terrible* about calling 911."

Fern's skin prickled. "Did you see her? When did you see her?"

"I didn't." He crossed his arms stubbornly. "But I want to."

"Then how do you know how she feels?"

Matty folded his lips.

"Matias." Captain America's chest broadened. "Tell me."

"Text. Whatever."

Fern blew out a quick breath, a barely concealed curse. "How does that even come *up* in a text?"

"She said she was thinking about getting some." Matty looked up at the ceiling as if he were getting his words from there. "Some chickens. For the yard."

"With that dog of hers? *Ffft.* The chicken is fine. It's just a freaking chicken. Right, Diego?"

Diego, no help at all, just shrugged guiltily and tucked a chip into the beans and crunched it over the stove. He *had* slept with Abby. Fern would lay money on it. Goddamn him. She couldn't even handle that. Couldn't think about it.

Matty was who mattered right now. "They're happy. They even say it on the package now." She remembered noticing that. "Happy chickens."

"Show me."

Fern took a deep breath. "Okay." Please, for the love of god, let her have gotten the right kind of fucking chicken. Whatever had been on sale, that had been the right kind.

But luckily, there it was. "See? It says they're happy. Right there. That chicken is fully smiling."

Diego chimed in, "They can't print it if it ain't true."

"Humph," said Matty.

But the fight was over, as suddenly as it had begun. Matty set the table without protesting. He woke his grandfather in the living room, and he knocked on Elva's door, inviting her politely to the table. Fern made plates bigger than any of them would be able to eat.

She was buttering them up. Pouring on the fat and the sweet, before she hit them with the bitter.

Elva sat carefully and poked at her hair, pulled back into a dancer's bun. One errant gray lock stood straight up, waving back and forth with every move. "This looks wonderful. Can we say grace?"

Fern sighed. "Okay."

Grandpa Wyatt said, "I got a grace to say."

"Please," said Fern. They just needed to eat. She needed to get this over with.

"Here you go. Dear Lord, please fix my broken molar and make this food mushy enough for me to eat." Grandpa Wyatt slapped the tabletop. "Amen!"

Fern was speechless.

Diego laughed, the traitor.

And Matty just grinned and started building a mole taco with a tortilla.

"Are you serious, Wyatt?"

Wyatt stuck out his neck like the chicken they were eating. "Broke plumb clean in half."

Matty said, "Doesn't it *hurt*? Show me!"

Mouthful of beans and all, Wyatt dropped his jaw. The broken dark space on the right looked awful.

"Oh, god."

Diego said, "Appetizing!"

"Wyatt. You have to get that fixed."

Grandpa Wyatt shrugged. "I checked and it ain't covered on the insurance. I'll just eat on the other side."

Carefully, Fern made the perfect forkful: heavy, mole-soaked chicken, dipped into the rice and beans. If she was cautious enough, if she stayed still, maybe everything would go back to the way it was two months ago. Before everything broke.

"Eight hundred dollars!" Wyatt held his butter knife into the air. "I could do a lot of things with that kind of cash and fixing my teeth isn't one of 'em. Me and Elva, we'd go gamble on the ponies, right, Elv? If I had it, that is."

Elva shook her head and rolled half a tortilla into something that looked exactly like the blunts the guys on the bus rolled.

"I'd make you fix your teeth, crazy old man."

"Once, at the tow yard, I used epoxy and wood glue to make a mouth guard for a fighter who drove for us. It worked good, and in his first fight, he only lost a couple of teeth. Wonder if I could craft my own tooth? You think Krazy Glue works in wet places?"

Fern needed to find the money to fix Wyatt's tooth. She wondered for the hundredth — the millionth — time how much money her mother's collection of Mexican coins was worth. It wasn't like they were in mint condition or anything. Every coin had been handled. Loved. But still, it had to be a lot of money. Thousands, probably. Enough for the tooth and to cover the next month's mortgage . . . If she could only bring herself to take them to a coin shop. There was one in Alameda — she'd gone as far as to look it up. She could just go get them appraised, right? They did that? The very thought made her soul ache. But if they didn't fix Wyatt's tooth, all the rest would fall out and then he'd probably get something terminal, too, for good measure.

Jesus. If she lost her job permanently, she and Matty wouldn't even have *health* insurance.

Diego caught Fern's eye. No. She wouldn't accept his help. If he wanted to put Wyatt's tooth on his credit card, that was his business, but she wouldn't take the money.

But he only said, "This is good."

"Good." Fern straightened, wishing she hadn't taken off the apron before sitting down. Captain America was pretty good armor. "Hey. Guess what? I've been offered a part-time job at Ensenada Taqueria. Tamales for everyone!"

CHAPTER FORTY

"Huh? Ensenada like the restaurant?" Matty gave that sideways head tilt that always tugged at Fern's heart. "Why?"

"Just till I get back on the bus."

"The place you used to work at? By the BART station?"

"You remember me telling you that?" She'd worked at Ensenada as a waitress when she was in high school. A million years ago.

"You tell me that, like, every single time we go past it."

She probably did. "Yeah, that place."

DMV would get the report of her lapse of consciousness soon enough, and as soon as she got the notice in the mail, she wouldn't be able to drive even her own car, let alone the bus. The restaurant was close enough to walk to in less than thirty minutes. She'd just have to hope to get off shift early enough so she didn't have to walk the sketchy part of Bancroft after dark. She wouldn't be able to risk driving — she'd researched it online, and the punishment for driving with a suspended license in California was a mandatory thirty-day impound on the car driven. Grandpa Wyatt had confirmed this was true, and had pointed out that with tow-yard storage at more than a hundred dollars a day, she'd never be able to pay to get her car back at the end of the month. *That's how my boss got all the cars he sold at auction. Rich motherfucker. No one could afford to pick up their wheels after a whole thirty days.*

Fern continued. "Just think about it, all the bean dip we want, right?"

Diego nodded. "Sweet. Like, doing their books?"

The heat that hit her cheeks was painful. "Kind of."

Diego's eyes narrowed. "Kind of?"

"I'll be handling money." It was true, after all.

"You're gonna *waitress*?"

Fern looked at his plate, then at Matty's. Their plates were still full. "Water? Anyone want some ice water?"

"Oh, good," Diego said. "Getting some practice in?"

"Don't be mean."

Matty just looked confused. "What's wrong with waitressing?"

Diego banged his fork against the tabletop. "She's better than that, that's what wrong. And she knows it."

"That's not true." Ciela, who'd inherited Ensenada from her uncle the year before, had spent twenty years waitressing before taking over as manager, and she was as smart as anyone who'd gotten any kind of degree. They'd started together there when they were both sixteen. They'd bonded over how they could make change in their heads, and laughed at the girls who had to use the sticky calculator next to the water station.

Elva said, "I was a cocktail waitress in the seventies. I could go home with five hundred dollars in ones. That was when I wore the heels. But boy, my dogs barked."

"Dogs?" Now Matty just looked confused.

"She means her feet hurt," said Fern. "Honey, waitressing is a good job. Your uncle is prejudiced for some reason, even though his last girlfriend was a barista at the airport, isn't that right?"

Diego ignored the dig. "It's a step down. You *know* that. You shouldn't have to do that."

The frustration on her brother's face was the hardest part to take. *"I'm a bus driver."*

"Yeah, well, you're unionized."

"Yeah. So are janitors. Makes you think, huh?"

"Why the hell have you been doing night school? What's the goddamned point? You're never going to use your bookkeeping skills? Not good enough? You remember when Mom got that waitressing gig at the diner by the jail?"

That wasn't fair. That diner had a full bar and a line of guys planted on their barstools who were always more than happy to buy the little Mexican waitress a shot of tequila when she got off shift (or earlier). Their mother had had a disease. Fuck Diego, and fuck his morals. "It's temporary."

"That's what she said, too."

"This is *exactly* why I worried about telling you."

"Because you know I think you're better than that."

Grandpa Wyatt and Elva had apparently tuned them out, and were shoveling mole-soaked chicken in their mouths while talking about a reality television show that either was or wasn't airing that night.

Matty was still listening to them, though.

"I can't *wait* to get back to it. I was a kick-ass waitress back in the day. I love making people happy." She grinned at Matty, hoping he bought it. "I love surprising them with ice cream when it's their birthday."

He blinked. "But if they told you it was their birthday, then it's not a surprise."

"Hey." Time for a counterattack. "What did Mrs. Hutch say about a new science project?"

"Huh?"

Did he always have to say that? With his mouth open like that? "Your *science* project, genius?" She regretted the last word as soon as it slipped from her mouth. Mrs. Hutch had told Matty once that not all kids got to be geniuses and that he shouldn't worry about it. Somehow the teacher had thought that was supposed to make him feel better, and had been aggrieved when Fern called her on it. She was as terrible a teacher as Fern was a mother. Awesome.

Matty blinked again, that hurt-owl look of his. "I don't have a new project. Just the old one. She told me it was too ambitious. And that I was too stubborn. I hate her. I really, really do."

If Matty was stubborn, he got it from her. Pride curled through Fern. "There's no such thing as too stubborn. But what old project? You're not still doing the onion knitting thing." With Abby. He wasn't doing that anymore.

"Yeah."

"Yeah, what?" Fern's bite was cold and she let the chicken fall off her fork in a glop. "You *are* still going to do it with her?"

He stuffed a bite of the mini-burrito he'd made into his mouth and said, "Yeah."

"Matty."

"I *told* you. She knows she got it wrong. She feels bad."

Fern's eyes stung, as if the cayenne she'd sprinkled so carefully over the mole had suddenly gone airborne. Had Matty forgiven Abby? So easily? He'd been so furious, and even though she knew it wasn't the right way to feel, it had felt *good* to have her little Captain America so righteously angry at Abby. "Have you . . . started already?"

He stared into his burrito as if the answer were tucked somewhere inside it. "We've just been texting. But I want her to help me. I want to knit and stuff. And then dye it. I *want* to. I'm supposed to ask you if I can go to her house tomorrow after school."

"Oh, yeah? So when were you planning on asking?"

"I'm doing that now." He jabbed his fork into another tortilla. "So can I?"

"Matty." Disappointment laced through her veins, a slow poison.

Diego leaned in. "She's kind of a witch,

y'know." He waved his beer bottle in a circle. He caught Fern's eye and corrected himself quickly. "Abby! Not you."

Matty's eyes widened. *"Huh?"*

"Una bruja. A good one, I mean. Like the stuff she does with the plants. Kind of magic."

Fern said, "I think that's still illegal without a card issued from your doctor."

The corner of Diego's mouth twitched. "Like basil. She said it could help you find love and guarantee fidelity."

"What's fidelity?" asked Matty.

"A convenient fiction," said Fern, hoping he'd forget to look it up online later. "When was she telling you all this, huh?"

Diego didn't answer, just took another huge bite. The way he was sitting, bent forward, shoveling food into his face, he looked like he had as a teenager — big, broad, always hungry, always wanting more.

He'd always liked the *güeras.*

"So? When? When you were over there getting Matty's backpack?"

"Yeah. Then."

"And?"

"And we went out for dinner last night."

He wouldn't.

But he did, and he had. The betrayal rose in her throat, thicker than the mole, and more slippery.

Matty said, "Camo-something."

"What?" She heard how thin her voice was.

"It's a white flower. Camo-something. Makes tea."

"Chamomile?"

"Yeah."

"Like Peter Rabbit. Remember that?" Once, when Matty was about five, he'd asked to try the tea that the mother rabbit gives to Peter and his siblings, but when she'd brought home the green box and brewed him a cup, he'd roundly rejected it, calling it grosser than cough medicine.

Matty's eyes slid to the left, as he made the connection. "Oh, *yeah*. That's it. The same thing. She gave me some dried stuff the first day we hung out, after we found Tulip. . . ." Then his face went guilty, his lower lip twisting, his gaze suddenly fixed.

"Wait. Was *that* what was under my pillow?" She'd found dried detritus, and she'd blamed Elva, who always insisted on drying the sheets on the line even though she dropped them on the ground half the time. "Why?"

"It's supposed to be good for . . ." Matty broke off. Then, defiantly, he continued, "You're always complaining about how bad you sleep. I was trying to *help.*"

"Oh, Matias. That's pretty adorable."

The word lit Matty like he was a firecracker. "It's not *adorable.* It was just *nice.* I'm just *nice.* But you don't care about me. At all."

"Matty —"

"You care about whether I'm happy about the same amount as you care about how happy a chicken is." He thunked out of the chair and thundered down the hall, slamming his door before she could say a word. Elva and Grandpa Wyatt barely glanced up, still arguing in soft voices about the television show, something about a naked person living in the woods.

The bass in Matty's room thumped with the sound of a video game, all guns blasting. Zero to a hundred in two seconds, and Fern couldn't do a thing. She couldn't chase him and drag him back like she had when he was six. She couldn't hold his shoulders in place anymore. She couldn't face him and demand he finish his dinner, or listen, or follow her instructions. She couldn't demand he love her. She couldn't tell him to never see Abby again. If she did, he'd disobey. She would have if she'd been him.

Fern would have to call Abby. Tomorrow.

She couldn't do it tonight. "Seriously?"

Diego dragged a last tortilla through the red sauce on his plate and said, "Well, yeah. The chamomile thing is pretty fucking adorable. I wouldn't have told him, though."

"You know what's not adorable?"

"Mmm?"

"One guess, smart-ass."

"Me being friends with Abby?"

"*Friends?* That's what you're calling it?"

"Know what? I'm not going to waste time justifying it to you because, with respect, it's actually none of your goddamned business," he said.

He was right.

And it made her want to run away from home, even though she sure wouldn't get that far on foot. So instead, Fern cleared the table as Diego argued with Grandpa Wyatt in the living room over which direction to face the old TV. When the dishes were dried and put away, she scrabbled through the big, low drawer next to the sink until she found that old green box of chamomile tea. Six years old. She should have gotten rid of it ages ago.

Standing in the backyard, she ripped open each dry paper packet, letting the tea fly into the wind, over the fence, and into the neighbor's perfect, perfect garden. The lopsided moon hung almost close enough to touch, and she said the only incantation she knew: *Estamos completos. Siempre vamos a estar completa. Siempre.*

But when there were no more tea bags to open, no more chamomile to scatter, she wondered if she was just plain wrong. Maybe they weren't complete.

She'd been wrong about so many things.

Maybe Abby was someone who was *supposed* to come into their lives. Maybe Scott, against all odds, had been the mechanism for that.

A younger Fern would have believed that easily. The old cheerful, open-armed, wide-eyed Fern would have embraced Abby faster, harder. When had she gotten so tired that she didn't trust a person who just seemed to want to know her sweet boy?

Fern raised her chin. She looked the yellow moon dead in the eye. "I'm listening." She waited a beat, the low roar of the city filling her body, weighting her so that she didn't float away. "I'm trying."

It was *so* close to true.

CHAPTER FORTY-ONE

"Can you park a few doors down?" Matty was poking and prodding at his backpack as if he was looking for something important.

Abby didn't want to ask, but she couldn't help it. "Okay. Why?"

"I can't find my key."

Tulip leaned forward from the backseat — an easy thing for him to do — nudging Abby wetly in the neck. "Ew. Stop. Attack that guy, not me," she said, pointing at Matty. As if the dog understood, he nosed Matty, ruffling the back of his hair with his sticky breath.

Matty giggled. God, Abby loved the sound of it. He'd giggled earlier when he kept dropping the second needle every time he reached the end of a knitted row. The wooden click of the needle hitting the floor made him laugh. That was a good thing, she told him. Most new knitters got frustrated and wanted to hurl their knitting against the opposite wall. *Nah,* he'd said. *I'm good with my hands. Mostly.*

Abby had slipped up then, saying he'd come by it naturally.

Really? His voice had been so eager. *My mom is a total klutz, except when she drives the bus.* He'd paused. *So, my dad . . . ?*

His father had been good at everything, she'd told him, and it was true. From mowing lawns like it was a sacred vocation, to the way he'd touched her in the middle of the night (she didn't say *that,* obviously). Scott had been good at things like car repair and hanging Christmas lights, all the typical manly things he was supposed to do, but he was good at unexpected things, too: bookbinding (they'd taken a class) and fixing her broken jewelry and dancing. He'd been such a good dancer. Abby's jaw ached with missing him, the pain surprising. She'd known she would keep grieving Scott, even though she'd been leaving him. That was natural, of course. But she hadn't expected the piercing shaft of old, leftover longing. She hadn't seen the sadness coming — the knowledge that they would never, ever fix themselves. Abby had thought she'd given up hope for them, but apparently, a pocket of it still lingered, deep in her lungs.

Now she turned off her car and focused

on Matty, the boy next to her. The boy who remained. "Why am I parking down the street? You said your mom was okay with you hanging out with me."

Matty dodged the question and held up a key on a blue lanyard. "Found it! Hey, did my dad ever try knitting?"

Abby's heart dropped, landing in a cool puddle of regret. "He did." She should have thought of that earlier. Maybe she'd been blocking it out.

"What did he make?"

Scott had lied. He'd lied so beautifully, and for such a good reason. One afternoon near Halloween, he'd asked her to teach him what she was doing with her sticks and string. His usually nimble fingers struggled at first with the basics, the wrap of knit, the backward loop of purl. When it seemed like he was getting it, a few hours later, he took his increasingly even stitches off the needle, pulling the yarn, balling it back up. *Yeah. That's not for me. I was just wondering.*

But he was so good at it, she'd told him. He should keep going.

Nah. She'd never seen him touch the needles again.

Then, that Christmas, he'd given her a red scarf. It was almost perfect, with only one dropped stitch near the edge. He'd worked on it in secret, stealing time in parking lots when he was between clients, knitting in his office, ignoring the mocking of Charmaine, of the guys he employed. It had been her favorite piece of clothing for years, until she'd been visiting a friend in New York and left it behind in a cab.

"He made me a gorgeous scarf. I lost it, and I'm still mad at myself for that. I'd love to be able to show it to you."

Matty's eyes were so disappointed by this that Abby almost wished she hadn't told him. But then he recovered. "You think that's why I'm such a natural at it?"

Abby laughed. "Probably. Yes."

"Next week we'll dye it?"

"Maybe. Sometimes your first attempt isn't the one you want to save. The science fair isn't for another two months. You have time. Lots of little attempts add up." She cleared her throat and wiggled the key in the ignition. "Speaking of attempts, I'm going to give it one more try and ask you why we're parked here. I texted your mom. It's not like this is a secret." Brief texts that said almost nothing. Such an awkward, unwieldy conversation. She'd wanted to apologize for calling 911. But she couldn't — she would do it again if she were in the same situation. What if something worse had happened?

What if Fern hadn't started breathing again on her own? Abby wanted to apologize for everything, but hadn't known where to start, using texts as a medium, and then Fern had texted Matty would be at Abby's house at three thirty, that he'd take the bus. *Take the bus.* The one Fern wasn't driving.

"Yeah." Matty yanked the backpack zipper closed and ripped it open again. "I know."

"What's up, then? I do *not* want to piss her off any more than I have."

"She told me to take the bus home. She, like, made me promise."

"But I . . . Why didn't she just come get you, if she didn't want me driving you?"

Matty looked at her like she was stupid, and perhaps she was. "She can't drive."

"I thought that was just the bus."

"At all. For three months, and that's just to start. It's like the law. They suspended her license."

"Holy crap. *Shit.*" She glanced at him. "Sorry. But damn. So, I bet she actually wants to kill me. Like, for real. With a pitchfork or something, huh?"

Matty appeared to think about the question, as if weighing methods Fern could rid the earth of Abby — guns versus knives, fire versus plague. "Yeah. I think so. But you know what? I think she understands why you did what you did. Like I do. But deep down, maybe — maybe she has to blame someone, you know?"

Abby's arms felt as heavy as garden pavers, her fists lumps in her lap. "That's pretty smart."

Matty sighed. "It's so boring when adults are always *surprised* by a kid actually being smart. Like we're either about to rob someone or we're smart like the Wise Men or something. We're just *kids.*"

"That's a genius thing to say." She waited a beat. "Kidding."

Matty laughed. "Get it? Ha."

She laughed again. "*Kid*ding!"

"Heh. That's just dumb." But he kept laughing.

"I know." It felt good, to sit with him in the dark, giggling. She didn't want to ruin the slim, sweet moment. But she had to know, so when his laughter died down, she asked, "What is she going to do now? Like, while she waits to get her license back."

Matty shrugged as if he was irritated. "Waitress. I guess."

The shock was a cold thud. "Where?"

"This Mexican place she worked when she was in high school."

"Is that . . . a good thing?"

"They have the best tamales in town. That's what she always says."

"Well," she said weakly, "in Oakland, that's saying something."

"I don't know. My uncle is mad about it."

She'd seen Diego for the second time on Saturday night. He hadn't said a word to her about his sister. Then again, they hadn't said much of anything, had they? There had been words, many of them. But none of them had really mattered. He'd asked if she wanted to go out to eat, but it had seemed prescribed, a question he had to ask. Cutting to the chase, she'd used TaskRabbit to deliver a pizza and a six-pack. They'd eaten on the patio and after the sun went down, she'd taken him to her bed. She'd loved the way he felt, but more than that, she adored the way his voice sounded in her ear. It didn't matter what he said and it didn't matter what language he said it in. She just wanted his voice to keep talking, to keep making sound, and he'd complied with her desire until she'd fallen asleep, lulled by the dark, comforting timbre of his words.

When she'd woken in the morning, he was gone. The pizza box was in the trash, the napkins in the washer, the beer bottles in the recycling outside. "Waitressing."

"I guess."

"Dang it. I have to walk you in, dude."

Matty jumped. "I'm *pretty* sure you don't want to do that."

Apprehension was a dull buzz behind her eyes. "Oh, you are so right about that."

Fern had a level of control over her face that Abby admired. Her expression appeared open. Neutral. Her lips were curved in a small (very small) smile, and her forehead stayed smooth. Even her hair seemed tamer than normal, as if she'd just run a brush over it.

Only in her eyes did her anger show. The normal brown of her irises was almost black, and heat snapped in their darkness. She sent Matty to his room with a flick of her wrist, and without a word of protest, he went. Abby planted her feet in the low pile of the threadbare carpet. "Don't be mad at him."

"I told him to ride the bus home." Fern's voice was as neutral as her body language — open hands, her hips squared to Abby's. "I'm not sure why he wouldn't tell you that."

"He told me." Abby didn't mention he hadn't told her until they'd pulled up outside.

Matty's grandfather Wyatt, sitting on the

couch, didn't even try to hide his fascination, setting his pad of paper and pencil on the table next to him. He rubbed his whiskers eagerly. From the kitchen, Abby could see Elva peering out.

"I didn't say it on the phone last night — I didn't know about your driver's license then." Abby shoved her hands into her jeans pockets as if she had something to hold that would steady her. "But I'm sorry."

"For what? Calling 911?"

She couldn't — wouldn't — lie to Fern. That wouldn't be fair. "No. I'd do that again in a heartbeat. I thought you were going to die."

"But Matty —"

"Matty's a *child*. You were writhing on the floor. I was the only conscious adult there."

Fern's mouth snapped shut. She blinked.

Abby wouldn't lie, but she could tell the truth, stripped down to its basics. "I *am* sorry my actions have had such a major repercussion in your life."

To Abby's surprise, Fern laughed. "Fancy words for the shit I'm going through."

"I know."

Fern blew out a breath and pushed a frizzy curl off her forehead. "I appreciate you helping Matty with his project." The words sounded heavy and expensive, as if she could barely afford to part with them.

"You're welcome. He's welcome."

"Okay, then."

Abby realized Fern was nervous. It helped her move forward with her crazy idea, knowing that.

"Hey, I need help."

"Sorry?"

"I mean, I would love your help. To sell my stuff, the stuff I make. Like you said I should."

"God, Abby. I can't keep up with you."

"I know it sounds crazy, but I'd pay you."

Fern looked over her shoulder at Wyatt. "Are you hearing this?"

Wyatt nodded. "Seems she wants to make you her employee."

"No —" The last time she'd half-assedly mentioned she could use Fern's help, Fern had gone into seizure. What the hell was she thinking?

Fern's face was storm-dark. "Come on, Abby. Can't you use oDesk or something for that? What did Diego say you called to bring you beer? TaskBunny or something?"

He'd told her? About that second night?

But that wasn't important. Abby scrabbled in her mind for the right words — any words — that wouldn't keep igniting Fern's anger, that wouldn't accelerate her overreaction any further. "First of all, calm down. Getting mad at me can't be good for you."

Fern's eyes widened. "You tell *me* to calm down? Let me tell you something, *mami,* the other day? That was not *you* that made me have a seizure. I need you to know —"

"*¡Cállate la boca!*" It was about fifty percent of what Abby remembered from high school Spanish, but it worked. Fern's mouth snapped shut, and Abby went on. "*Not* an employee. The opposite. My partner."

CHAPTER FORTY-TWO

Partner. The word knocked the wind out of Fern, like a big fist sailing into her gut. It had happened twice on the job over the years, the punch she didn't see coming, the one that left her gasping in shock.

The secondary feeling was the same — not pleasant.

"Did you hear me?" Abby's face was red.

"Yes." Had this woman actually told her to shut her mouth in Spanish? Where had that come from? "I heard you."

"And?"

"And give me a minute." She needed to breathe. "Jeez."

"Fine." Abby crossed her arms and scowled. Elva had scuttled in from the hall and Grandpa Wyatt was openly staring.

"Outside. Backyard, okay?" Fern gestured into the kitchen, through to the door. All the way out — she didn't want this conversation to happen in the kitchen any more than she did the living room. The kitchen was her safe zone, and this didn't feel safe. "Keep going. Out."

Abby looked over her shoulder. "Are you going to lock the door on me as soon as I'm out there?"

Fern made a *humph* in the back of her throat and said, "You want a beer?"

"Really?"

"Give me a second."

At the sink, Fern leaned on the cracked porcelain and took a breath. Then another one. She searched inside herself for what feeling she should carry outside with the beer bottles — fear? resistance? caution? — and came up empty.

So she popped the caps and carried them out. She held one out and said, "Interview."

"For you or for me?"

"Both."

"Yes," said Abby, and if she was surprised, it didn't show. "Go."

Fern took a long sip of the beer and looked up at the box elder's limbs stretching overhead. The setting sun streaked the one lone swatch of fog pink, and two planes lumbered across the sky so slowly it seemed they must fall, that the crash was imminent.

"What do you want me to do?" The words came out wrong, implying that Fern would just *do* whatever it was Abby wanted. And that was so wrong. "I mean, what do you — what are you talking about?"

"I don't know."

"Awesome."

"The idea just came to me in the car."

"Spontaneous charity? Even better. Did Matty tell you I was going to wait tables at the taqueria?"

"Could you just *not* be a bitch? Huh?"

Abby's voice was sharper than Fern would have imagined it could be, and she felt the scowl rip across her face like a strike of lightning. She couldn't have stopped it if she wanted to (which she didn't). The problem was that the urge to laugh followed straight after. Even she could see that Abby was trying. God knew *what* she was trying to do, but it was something. "Well, now. That's not very charming of you. Isn't that your thing? Charm?"

Abby looked chagrined, her knuckles whitening on the Corona. "Just listen to me, okay? Maybe it's a fucking terrible idea, but I could use the help."

"What kind of help?"

"You were right. I could sell a lot more of my product if I actually put more into it. More time, more investment. I have orders I haven't been able to process, and I got a request from a lifestyle magazine for an interview, but I need a proper Web site first."

"Why, though? You don't need the money." Better to be blunt.

"Because my pau d'arco liniment helped my friend sleep when her rheumatism wouldn't let her. Because the sage and burdock tonic helped another friend deal with chemo side effects. Because this one shop in Cambria sells my dandelion-burdock tea in bulk to a man who's dying of liver cancer and says it helps a little. Because what I make *helps* people, simple as that. And because you were right."

It would have been so easy to mock Abby then. To take her words and squash them, the way older kids did on the bus to the younger ones, socking her verbally until she cried uncle.

But Fern didn't want to. She didn't want to be that person. "Go on."

"I'm not trying to be trendy. I'm not trying to be all Pinterest about it — I don't make it because it's pretty or hip or because I'm trying to impress anyone. I make my stuff because I love learning what herbal remedies worked in the past, and I like trying out the old recipes with the things I grow myself."

Fern sighed. "You know we'll have issues

with promises?"

"I don't need you to promise me a damn —"

"Not me. In terms of packaging and liability, I mean."

Abby blinked.

"Have you even thought of that?"

"No."

Of course she hadn't. "What you promise your users matters. If you say it will ease certain aches or pains, and it doesn't, then you're in trouble."

"Of course."

"Wait, now that I think about it, you might be in trouble even if it does get the job done. I'm assuming you don't want to go the whole FDA route."

"Sorry?"

"No promises of health, then. Just the suggestion that such and such herb has been known to help shit."

"Um . . ."

"And if they turn out to be deathly allergic to the kind of ionized water you put in there, the liability lands on you, you know that, right?"

"I knew that."

"What have you done about it?"

Abby tilted her head. "I hoped really hard it wouldn't happen. And so far, that's worked."

"Just a matter of time. That's okay — we can get insurance for that. Easier if we incorporate — have you done that?"

"Are you kidding me?"

"LLC?"

"What?"

"Do you even have a brand name?"

"I've been calling it Abby's Alimentary."

"I have no idea what that even means."

Abby nodded. "I hear that a lot."

"If you can't spell it or remember it, you can't Google it. First rule of business. Be discoverable." Over the fence, Fern heard Maria Silva's hose snap and spit as it was turned on. The sound was as familiar to her as Grandpa Wyatt's snoring, as Elva's humming over a pot of something unidentifiable. "Okay, then. If we did this, what do you envision my role being?" That sounded good. It struck the right tone.

Abby set her beer bottle on the cold rim of the fire pit and pressed her palms together, as if she were going to snap a *namaste* at Fern or something. Her face was eager, her eyes bright. "Selling."

"Marketing," Fern corrected.

"See? That. I make, and you sell."

"And my cut is?" If she'd learned anything in her night classes, it was that you asked about compensation up front, that it was all written down in black and white, so all parties were safe.

"I thought — fifty dollars?"

Fern frowned. "For what?"

"An hour?"

"An *hour*?"

"You're thinking more?"

Fifty dollars an hour for labeling bottles? For putting them online? Abby lived in a whole different world. Or this really was her fancy way of doling out charity, and Fern wasn't sure which concept was worse. "Holy shitballs. No."

"What's reasonable, then?"

"You don't have any idea how the real world works, do you? How much was Scott billing when he died?"

Abby picked her beer back up and took a sip. She was stalling, Fern could tell. "I think it was double that. Ish."

Fern whistled. "Wow." She breathed carefully through her mouth, hoping her hands weren't shaking. "I make twenty-seven an hour." And she had thought that was a lot of money. It never went as far as it should — taking care of three other people would do that to you — but she'd always been proud when she thought of her wage, the hourly rate that rested in her hands, which didn't sit on the backbone of a college degree or anything else just handed to her. She earned her money. At Ensenada, she'd be lucky to take home thirteen bucks an hour, even with tips. It had been hard enough when she was a cute nineteen-year-old with sky-high tits and hopes to match, slinging four-dollar plates of rice and beans. Tacos were still a buck fifty each, but she was almost twenty years older. Grandpa Wyatt needed a new tooth. The hole in Matty's backpack was patched with duct tape.

Fern ached to just say, *I'll take the life insurance money.* It would make everything so easy. She could actually rest a little. Not waitress. She'd managed to take Scott's money, after all. But that was different. He'd owed his son that much. The life insurance was different. It was his wife's money. Abby owed them nothing.

But if she worked for — with — Abby, she'd be an equal. Accepting money for real, honest work, work she would be good at. *Running a business.* That was the goal, the reason she went to night school in the first place.

"Business partners. Not friends."

Abby pulled up her chin. "Why not both?"

Fern let out the breath she'd been holding. "Girl, I need money way more than I need friends."

"I'm going to hope for both." Abby tilted a crooked smile at her.

"Let's start with business partners, huh?" Fern was proud that her voice was as strong as she wanted it to sound. "And my brother is off-limits."

Abby tucked her lips in, briefly. Then she said, "I'm sorry about that. I really am. It just happened."

"Twice?"

She colored, but she nodded. "Yeah. It just happened twice."

"Well, he would have to be out of the picture." That had to be part of the deal. No negotiation.

Abby paused.

Fern counted one breath. Then two.

Then Abby nodded. "Okay."

"That was fast." In a twist of emotion she didn't see coming, Fern wanted to know why Abby could just give up Diego like that, that quickly. He wasn't good enough?

"It's not a problem." The look on Abby's face was unreadable.

"Huh. 'Cause he said he saw you Saturday night."

"We'll make that the last time."

"And I get twenty-five dollars an hour."

Abby blinked twice. "Are you seriously negotiating me down?"

"I can't believe you're insulting me by offering me more than I'm worth."

Abby nodded. "Fine. Accepted. Plus twenty-five percent of the profits."

"Now you've just lost your goddamned mind." Fern's arms ached with the weight of all of it. She wanted to ask why Abby would choose them, would choose Fern and Matty over a few more rolls in the hay with her brother. She wanted to know why they were so important to her. It couldn't just be about Scott, not anymore. But she had a feeling the answer might bring her too low to the ground, and she was scraping the earth with her bare knuckles as it was.

"I told you, partners. I meant it. I get twenty-five percent, too. The rest, after expenses, goes back into the business. Marketing, like you said."

"Why me?"

Abby looked at her like she was an idiot. "Because you're Fern. And your son is Matty."

"*Ay, madre.* You have to understand that there's a limit to generosity."

"Why?"

"Are you serious?"

Abby set the bottle down on the edge of

the fire pit with so much force that Fern was surprised it didn't break. "People think there has to be a limit. Why is that true? Why can't we just give as much as we can give right up to the point we can't give anymore?"

Fern didn't have to think before she spoke. "Because your house would fill up with homeless addicts. Because some people are made to give and some are made to take, and those roles don't change. If you give too much, you'll end up with nothing." Ask her how she knew. Fern would fight to the tooth for her house, for what it represented in terms of protecting the ones she loved. She cared for the people who got on her bus, the ones she was paid to protect during her shift, but the ones who lived in her home? Her family? She'd do whatever it took to keep them safe from everything — from burglars and fire and crazies and zealots and earthquakes and from the very hand of God if it came to that. God was big. But her love was bigger. She would die for the ones under her roof. That was how you knew you were alive. "Because you're living in the wrong kind of world otherwise. It's not fair to those who can't pay it back." Did she really have to explain this to an adult? "You have to live in the world that's in front of you, don't you get that? Not the one that you make, not the world that you think is better than it actually is."

"What if other people are just seeing it wrong? What if I'm the one who's right?"

For calling Fern an idiot, it wasn't a bad way to do it. "Abby's Aliment-a-whatsit isn't going to work. Have you thought of any other names?"

"I did think of something. Maybe." Abby kicked at the base of the fire pit. It left a black mark on the white toe of her sneaker. "Taking Care."

Fern saw Scott's scrawled handwriting in her mind, that addendum to every check she'd ever cashed. *Take care.* Did Abby mean it as a fuck-you to Scott? She searched Abby's face. Her gaze was clear. Open. But there was possibly the *slightest* hint of mischief behind her dark, curled lashes. It was, Fern knew, nothing Abby would admit. She might not even know it.

But it was kind of awesome.

"Okay, then," said Fern. "I guess I'm in."

Abby held up her bottle. "To Taking Care," she said.

Fern clinked her bottle with the neck of hers. "Fuck, yeah."

CHAPTER FORTY-THREE

Two weeks later, Abby leaned backward and groaned. "I could not possibly care less about a Twitter account." The chaise in her office was dark red and heavily pillowed, and each pillow conformed exactly to the shape it was needed for — under a knee or behind a head. It looked decadent and a bit slovenly, the velvet's pile ancient, and Abby loved it. "You make all this crap look easy."

"It is easy."

"Humph."

"It's just time-consuming." Fern pulled her curls back with a red rubber band. Two or three spirals sprang wildly to the side. Her nose was shiny. She was pretty. Abby wondered how much prettier she'd been in person when she was younger. Fern seemed to be one of those people who was probably growing into her looks. If Scott had stuck around, he would have known that. Fern continued, "That's the only reason you never got around to it before."

"You're giving me too much credit."

Fern bent forward, staring at the Photoshop window. They'd done a photo shoot earlier in the morning, when the light was bright and clear: the blue and green bottles gleaming on a wooden bench they'd propped over a stand of newly sprung forget-me-nots. The calligraphed tags (in blue ink, Abby's hand) fluttered in the wind. Now Fern was cropping and putting filters on the photos, and they looked more professional than Abby could ever have imagined. Fern frowned and swore, making a white box jump forward and then minimizing it again. "It . . . Oh, never mind."

"What?"

"Nothing."

"No, tell me. Do you not like it? I can tell by your face. Do we have to reshoot?" Of course they would — it had been too easy. "Should I go set it up? Move the bench to the irises, maybe? Tulip has probably chewed on the bench a little more by now, made it look even more authentically aged." Abby peered out the window, and sure enough, Tulip was happily gnawing on the leg of the picnic bench.

"It's not that. I just . . ." Fern turned in her chair to face Abby. "I wish you wouldn't say you can't do simple things. Matty says that when he's feeling lazy."

Abby pulled her legs up, the old velvet prickling the bottoms of her feet. "Oh."

"I don't mean it like that. You're not lazy."

Heat started at Abby's hairline. "I'm not an imbecile, you know."

"I know you're not."

"It's just I didn't know where to start. Or, when I'd started, where to go next. Instagram, Pinterest, Twitter, Facebook — you know you've set all those up within a week? That's just when you've been here. I know you've been working on it at home, too." Fern was keeping an Excel spreadsheet of her hours.

"I could have done it faster if Gmail hadn't been acting so stupid about confusing your computer with the new address. That took, like, half a day."

"It would have taken me a whole day just to figure out Instagram."

Fern rubbed her eyes. "That's not true."

It was an exaggeration. Wasn't that obvious? "I know it's not *true.* I know how to make up a password and open an account. It's just that when I'd set it up, I wouldn't know what to do with it. I don't understand hashtags, why you'd even need them in the first place." Fern had started posting almost immediately, adding *#TakingCare* to every picture, to every tweet. "Who are you talking to right now, anyway? Who's going to read these things?"

"No one."

"Awesome."

"But they will. One person will find the Etsy shop — then they'll search for your Web site."

"Which I don't have!"

"But which you will have in about an hour. Then they'll see your Twitter account, and click over there to see if you're active."

"Like yeast." Abby pictured the Web site growing in a bowl, bubbling under a tea towel. They would set it in a warm place and in the morning, they'd have to punch it down so it could grow some more.

"Like professional. Then they'll buy something, and when they get it at their house, they'll hopefully post something with our hashtag, and other people will click on that, and see our pretty things. Get it?"

"I *get* it. I understand the concept. I just don't think anyone will actually do it."

"Oh, they will."

"Your lips to God's ears."

"I hate that phrase," said Fern absently. Abby watched as she changed a blue bottle to faintly iridescent green and back again.

"Do you ever like anything? Right off the bat?"

Fern finally turned to look at her. Abby tightened her arms around her knees but stayed still.

"Yes."

"That surprises me," said Abby.

"I'm kind of known for liking things," said Fern. "That's who people think I am at work. Or who I was at work, anyway. I like my riders. I like my coworkers. I like driving in the rain, and I like driving in the sun. I'm the cheerful one. The funny one. I never take life too seriously."

"What happened?"

Fern looked back at the screen. "Do you prefer this photo? Or this one, with more of the yellow base?"

"You won't answer the question?"

Fern sighed. "Life happened. And I hate that I'm the kind of person who's letting that get her down. That's never been me before." A short pause. "You blew up my life. Twice."

"Yeah. I'm kind of actively trying to not do that right now."

"Did you and Scott ever want kids?"

The abrupt change in topic felt like a change in elevation. Abby could almost hear her ears pop. "Yeah. We tried."

"Tried?"

"They didn't stick."

"Oh." Fern's cursor stopped moving on the screen. "I'm sorry."

"Some women are made to pop 'em out. I'm not, I guess. I was getting okay with adopting, but he said no."

"That sucks."

"Then I was going to trick him. To try again for a baby, once more. But he got a vasectomy." The bitter laugh was more of a choked-off breath. "A secret vasectomy. That's why I was leaving him. I was furious. I guess I still am. But I think I was just as bad as he was. We were both trying to trick each other about the most important thing of all."

Fern spun in the office chair to face Abby fully, her palms flat on her thighs. "I don't — I don't even know —"

"It's fine," said Abby. "You don't have to say anything. Really. And I'm sorry I blew up your life, by the way. Twice. Both times unintentional, you know."

"Sure. Damn, girl." But Fern's voice was light. Something had shifted in the room, as if a cloud had scudded away from in front of the sun. "Eh, I've forgiven you."

Abby's blood warmed. "Really?"

"Mostly."

"And now you . . ." *Kind of like me. Don't hate me. Could see being friends with me someday.*

"No way. Don't make me say it."

Abby thought she could see something behind Fern's eyes, something she wanted to tease out, to put in a warm place next to her bubbling business bowl. "*Come* on."

"You're fine."

Abby cupped a hand behind her ear. "I'm what?"

"You're all right, I guess." The corner of Fern's mouth twitched.

"You don't hate me."

"At this very moment?"

"At this very moment. And don't forget I was about to go make you another cup of coffee."

"A cup of coffee with cream, you mean?"

Abby nodded, her heart unfolding. "With cream, of course." What she meant was *Everything, anything.* She would make her a loaf of bread, a bubble bath, an oil painting — anything she could figure out how to make, she would do it for her. "A cup of coffee with cream for my friend."

Fern laughed lightly, the sound warm and round. "Don't push it" — a comma's breath — "friend."

CHAPTER FORTY-FOUR

The bus was so full that Fern had to stand up for the first twenty minutes, something she hadn't done on a coach in too many years to count. She laughed and ignored Gilmore when he told her just to get on, dumping her money in the fare box just like anyone else. "What, my money ain't good enough for you?"

"Why you gotta do that, lady?" Gilmore had put on a few pounds since she'd seen him last, and his hips spread over the edge of the wide seat. They'd started together, in the same training group. He ate two egg-salad sandwiches for lunch every day, without exception. Once his wife had sent him to work with peanut butter and jelly because the store had been out of eggs and he'd been so mad he spent the next three nights at their coworker Rizelli's house, going home only when Rizelli's wife threatened to make Gilmore start cleaning the bathrooms for his room and board.

"Yeah, yeah." She could almost afford the $2.10. Kind of.

"Hey, how long you off work?"

"Another nine weeks or so." It made it sound as if she was coming back, as if they'd let her, when she cleared medical probation. Fern grabbed the pole behind Gilmore's head, ignoring the flash of envy that raced through her at the way his fingers fit around the wheel. She missed the sound, the smell, of the bus — the mixture of rubber and gasoline and weed and body lotion and lunch meat. It smelled like perfume to her. She wished she could ask Abby to bottle the smell somehow, but she'd be the only customer for it.

"So you hit that cush disability gig, huh?"

She smiled. "That what you heard?"

He winked over his shoulder. "Yep. I heard you pulled a fast one."

"That I did, my friend. I can highly recommend it. Good stuff."

A lie. She'd filed immediately with human resources, but they said the state could take up to six weeks to even *start* paying her out, and no one seemed sure about retro pay. Linda had an e-mail in to Ivy, who had called the state twice already, but every question Fern asked raised two more. The transit district lost people to disability all the time, she *knew* they did. How was it that they didn't know their asses from a timetable? Fern didn't have six weeks. What she had was a father-in-law with a tooth that needed work, and a mortgage that was still late, still gathering charges and writhing like a dragon.

The check Abby had just given her burned in her back pocket.

Fern had been in love with a boy in high school — Romano. He lit his smokes with a Zippo, the only kid who hadn't used a cheap plastic lighter. After he'd kissed her for the first time, he'd let her take the Zippo home with her. "For tonight. Think of me. Then bring it back tomorrow." It had seemed like a declaration of love, that overnight loan. She'd slipped it into the back pocket of her jeans, and it sat there, a small hard lump. By early evening, her right butt cheek burned. She thought that was love, too, but then it started to itch *and* burn. It had leaked, and the lighter fluid caused her skin to rise in teeny-tiny bumps. Romano had taken his lighter back without comment, and she'd wondered how many other asses he'd burned with it.

The check felt the same way.

She hadn't had the guts to look at it yet.

She needed a few more minutes. A few more turns on the bus, a few swings around a couple of tight corners. That would make the feeling in her body settle, would bring her back into herself so she could decide what to do next. (She already knew what she had to do — it was why she was on this bus going this way instead of the shorter way home on the 53.)

"How do I pull that off, you think?" Gilmore smiled at an old woman who took off a yellowed glove to extract the exact change out of a tiny pink pocketbook.

"I'll tell you how," said Fern. "Just fall over in the middle of something, the more public the better. If you can pretend that you're foaming at the mouth — that's good. If you bite your tongue, it's even more effective. Blood and foam is damn impressive. You know what I mean?" She knew he did. Because passengers were so often among the ranks of people whose medical ailments were untreated, seizures weren't uncommon on the coach. She had to get radio to call 911 for an ambulance at least once a month, from as minor as a trip on the last step to the old guy on the 61 last year who had stopped breathing in the back row and never started again.

"You know I do. No fallin' out, you hear

me? I ain't in the mood."

"I hear you, friend."

A long, slow nod. "Good." He eased the coach into traffic like it was the tongue of a zipper. Gilmore'd always been good.

A woman wearing a black cutoff sweatshirt that slid off her shoulder *Flashdance*-style spit angrily into her phone. "This bus is *supposed* to be the fast one. Seventy-two R — that's why it's *R*."

Fern caught Gilmore's eye in the bigger mirror and they shared a tiny smile. Restricted buses were technically supposed to be faster, with fewer stops, but in rush-hour traffic, nothing was sure. The normal 72 sailed past them on the left.

"They *came* at the same time. That's why I chose this one!" The woman was yelling into her phone now. "I could've been ahead of this bus, but this driver is so fucking stupid, he don't even know what he's supposed to be doing. Can he hear me? Yeah, he can fucking *hear* me. He's right in front of me. I'm sitting right up front. He can fucking hear me."

Fern would lay equal odds the woman wasn't even talking to anyone on the other end of the phone. She was probably just trying to make her point. There was something almost soothing about hearing the

427

abuse. It was a language she spoke, something that cheered her up in the way it never changed. She could tell by the jaunty way Gilmore saluted at a kid getting off that he was amused, too.

At the next stop, the woman swung angrily off the bus. Gilmore gave her a cheery, "Have a great day!"

"Fuck off! Do your job!"

The woman ran to catch the 72 that was stopped half a block up. Then, with a jolly honk, Gilmore passed it. Fern could feel the satisfaction in her very fingers, the way it felt when the universe was in order. Like that.

She needed her bus. Oh, god. What if she never got it back?

At the next stop, Fern was pushed farther into the bus by a large crowd of schoolkids headed toward the Coliseum. When two kids finally pulled their tongues out of each other's mouths and noticed their stop, hurtling out of the bus like they were horny crickets, she scored a seat.

Finally, thirty long minutes after Abby had pressed the check into her palm, Fern worked up the courage to pull it out of her pocket. When she'd accepted it, she'd only been able to nod and say, "Yep." She'd folded it in half and then in half again, casually, sticking it into her back pocket as if it were a receipt from the drugstore, the kind that was a million miles long, printed with coupons that never came in handy. It was working — the whole helping Abby out. It had only been a couple of weeks, but it was really working. Fern could even admit it was sometimes fun. At least once or twice a week, Matty rode the bus over after school and worked on his knitted hat in front of the TV downstairs. Then Fern rode home with him. He leaned on her if it was crowded. She loved that.

She unfolded the check. It was light blue with darker blue stripes at the bottom. Heavy paper. She could picture Abby writing it out, could imagine that it came from a leather full-sized folio kept in a walnut secretary, so different from the vinyl-covered checkbook Fern threw in the kitchen drawer next to the scissors.

Fern's full name was written out in Abby's pretty, careful handwriting. Six hundred twenty-five dollars. Twenty-five hours last week, at twenty-five dollars an hour.

In the memo line, it read, *Taking Care,* followed by a smiley face.

For a moment, Fern tried to imagine what she would have done if Scott had ever included an emoticon on his check. She probably would have ripped it into tiny pieces and then immediately regretted it.

Out the window, the neon lights of the Chinese gambling place on Broadway caught her eye. This was where she needed to get off.

"Excuse me. Coming through." No one in the pack of kids moved, and for a second, she imagined what it would be like to be older, feeble. Invisible. She tried again in a louder voice. "My stop, let me out." The kids seemed to huddle tighter, the passage impenetrable unless she crawled up and over them like Diego climbed trees. Gilmore heard her — she knew by the way he was holding the bus steady, doors staying resolutely open even though no one was getting on. "Hey, you little shits, *move.*"

A small gust of appreciative laughter breezed through the teens, and they split, letting her pass. She waved at Gilmore up front and stepped down onto the sidewalk.

Taking a huge breath in and holding it, she turned to face the bank's double doors.

She went inside.

She filled out the slip.

She deposited the check. It was money from Abby, but it was money she'd *earned,* doing the thing that she'd wanted to for a long time, using her business brain. It wasn't half as hard as she'd thought it would be. Actually, it felt damn fine, putting that money into the stripped-bare account. Simple, really.

She caught another bus home (a new driver she'd never seen before, a young guy who barely met her eyes) and was home an hour later, the door closed and locked behind her. She sat alone on the broken sofa. Her perfect, sagging, ripped-to-shreds sofa.

Taking care.

It was simple if you could breathe, and Fern could. It was still her air, the air that smelled like home, like dust and Matty's shoes and cumin and oregano and old wood.

She could breathe.

CHAPTER FORTY-FIVE

Abby sat in the waiting room of the emergency vet and tried to fight the urge to throw up.

Tulip was going to die.

The strong, young Great Dane whose muscles flexed like an Olympian's, who had seemed completely invincible as he thumped through Abby's empty house, thundering up and down the stairs with man-heavy footsteps — he was going to die and it was all Abby's fault.

He'd eaten all the onions. All of them. For days, he'd been snacking on them, and she hadn't noticed. He'd pried off the lid on the box behind the shed, where she didn't go unless she actually needed some of the stored bulbs. Pounds and pounds of them. It was all her fault.

All because she thought he was safe outside. He chewed furniture, yes, but that didn't seem hazardous. She'd been writing new labels with a fountain pen, watching the rain (unexpected and welcome) fall outside. She'd been trying to impress Fern with fresh-ground cinnamon in her coffee. She hadn't been trying to impress Fern with her extended knowledge about historically accurate dye recipes from the nineteenth century, or even with something like the ability to navigate her new Pinterest page. No, just a cinnamon-dusted *coffee.* Tulip's huge feet were muddy after he'd gone out to pee, and she hadn't felt like having to mop, so she'd left the dog out there under the magnolia tree. He didn't mind. He wouldn't get into trouble.

An hour after Fern left at six, she'd called him. He came, but he was slow to do it. He peed on a solar garden light, and his urine was dark red. Then he'd fallen sideways, heavily. He'd just panted after that. She'd loaded him into the car immediately, almost dropping him as she tried to lift his heavy back half — but by the time they got to the emergency vet clinic, he was barely moving. It had taken two interns to help her carry him in.

The waiting room of the clinic was cold and sterile, separated into two parts. One enormous yellow sign shouted CATS over a left-pointing arrow. Abby sat under the blue

DOGS sign on the molded plastic seat that clearly had never been meant for a real person to sit in — it was square, the back at a right angle to the seat. (Maybe it was supposed to feel that way, hard and cold and terrifying and guilt inducing.) The walls were white, their starkness alleviated only by a cat calendar — on the dog wall — which featured a cranky-looking Siamese caught in a wide-mouthed yawn.

The receptionist, somewhere in her forties with bright red glasses, had been professional enough, but her smile hadn't reached her eyes, and when she wasn't typing on the desk computer, she was whacking the touch screen of her phone. After each flurry of smacks, another ding sounded. Any minute she was going to hurl the phone through the small plate glass window that faced dark and rainy University Avenue.

Tulip was probably going to die. Abby's stomach roiled, and she measured the distance to the bathroom again, for the tenth time. She would make it if she had to. Just in case, she noted the placement of the trash can. Then she made the mistake of imagining what might be *in* a trash can at an emergency vet's office, and felt even worse, like the ground was heaving below her.

A phone's low buzz. A few murmured words. Then a few more anger-slapped texts, a couple of corresponding dings, and the receptionist looked up. "You can go in."

Was Tulip dead? Was that what they would tell her? Abby tasted acid at the back of her mouth. No, no, no. She hadn't planned on falling in love with the damned dog. She'd only taken him home to please Matty. To tempt him. Tulip had started out as a bribe, and she'd known it. But that first night, he'd let himself out of his crappily made though shockingly expensive crate. Abby had heard him breathing heavily at the foot of the bed. She'd lain still in the hopes that he'd just curl up on the floor. That would be okay. But then she'd felt the bottom of the bed dip. Curious and vaguely amused, Abby had kept herself motionless.

Tulip had dragged himself up on the bed, one paw creeping up after the next one. He'd pressed his long body flat at the bottom of the bed, curving himself so that he wasn't lying on her feet.

The fact that he'd sneaked his way on (and knew it) had struck her as sweeter than honey. She'd let him stay, resolving the next night she'd figure out a way to close the crate more thoroughly. Maybe a twist tie. Or a padlock.

But when she'd woken the next morning, Tulip had moved. He was lying next to her, right where Scott had slept. His big square head rested on the pillow like a person's. His back was to her, and she'd had her arm slung around him.

She had spooned the damn thing.

He was hers then.

"Is he dead?" Would the receptionist tell her if he was?

The interior door buzzed. "Push," said the woman. "Room three."

The little patient room was even worse than the lobby. The seat was metal, like at a bus stop. The sink looked scrubbed clean, but it was rusted at the corners. It smelled of bleach, and Abby couldn't help thinking about what they might use the bleach for. "Mint," she whispered to herself. "Ginger. Blessed thistle." Maybe just whispering the anti-nausea herbs to herself would help.

She checked her phone. Seven thirty-two p.m. She'd been waiting in the room for ten minutes now. She'd give it two more, and then she'd bust out and go looking for Tulip's body. They couldn't keep her from knowing the truth. Not one second more. What would they *do* with him? Cremation? Was there a red button somewhere for the bereaved? What about that huge head of his?

That nose that wouldn't jam itself impolitely and hysterically into her crotch every time she walked in the front door? No, she wanted to bury him. There should be a place where you could dig the earth yourself and put your pet in the ground. A pet cemetery. Then in her mind, she saw the cover of *Pet Sematary* by Stephen King, and that, in turn, made her feel like she was going to throw up again.

The doctor entered, gray-haired and slump-shouldered. The white coat over pink kitten scrubs seemed too young for her.

"Tulip's going to be fine."

Abby's mind went blank. How could an almost-dead dog become fine? "Sorry?"

The vet rubbed her temples as if she had a headache. "Just fine. We induced vomiting for the toxicosis, and you're right, that was a lot of onions. He also needed a blood transfusion. He's resting now. We've got him on IV fluid for a little longer — it'll help him feel better later, since we just assaulted his system pretty rudely."

"Yeah." Relief flooded into her system like she was the one hooked up to an IV — it was cold and delicious, and the nausea abated immediately.

"You okay? It can be pretty scary, I know."

"I can take him home?"

"Yep. Probably be about ten or fifteen more minutes, then a tech will bring him to you. Sorry it took me so long to get out here to talk to you. Busy night. Hey. Are you really okay?"

"Yeah," said Abby. Then bile rose and she clapped a hand over her mouth. She raced to the bathroom and only just made it.

Half an hour later, she gave the receptionist the equivalent of a double car payment. Tulip sat on her foot and made no sign of wanting to leave. He panted happily and drooled on her leg.

"You both look a lot better now," said the receptionist, whose phone was nowhere in sight. Abby wondered if it was outside in the rain.

"Yeah. Well."

"Pregnant?"

Abby tilted her head, as if she could reframe the word, make it mean something else, like plant or puppy or present. "No. Tulip's actually a boy dog. I know the name is confusing."

"Sorry. I meant . . ."

"Me?"

"So sorry. You had a look. I apologize. You came in looking like I did with my first two."

"What?" she said again stupidly. Something shot down into her knees, a metallic

438

adrenaline rush.

"Kind of green. But not like with flu."

"I'm not pregnant."

"Of course." The receptionist didn't look convinced as she pushed the receipt and the credit card across the counter. "Just one signature here, and then I'll get you a complete printed record to give to your regular vet."

"You thought I was *pregnant*?"

The woman blinked. "So sorry."

Abby loaded Tulip into the back of her car and hoped he'd stay there for once. It was hard to see around him when he sat on the passenger seat. "I'm not pregnant," she told him. He just panted, his breath antiseptic-smelling with an oniony afterburn.

"I can't be pregnant." She settled into the driver's seat and tried not to pant the same way. She pulled up the calendar on her phone.

She counted.

Then she counted again.

And once more, because counting was hard when you suddenly didn't have a single brain cell that seemed to be willing to be devoted to the task.

She was late. Two weeks, almost three. It had been only a month since she'd had sex with Diego the second and last time. Was that even possible? She would have been ovulating . . . yep. That was about right. Shit.

She had used condoms with Diego. She wasn't a fucking moron.

Abby wasn't pregnant.

It was what she said to herself all the way to the store. She said it to the cashier, because the more she said it, the better chance she had of forcing it to be true. "I'm not pregnant."

The sloe-eyed cashier just rang up her box, obviously knowing better than to comment.

Abby drove home, Tulip slobbering in her ear. The dog was alive. She had managed to keep the dog alive. That was something, wasn't it? Something important?

Abby wasn't frightened.

What she felt in her body, what pressed at her lungs and pulled at her gut, was so much bigger than fear. She was shaking with so much *hope* that it was rattling out of her body. She had to kick her way through it to the car, she had to shovel it off the sidewalk in front of the house, and when she sat on the toilet and peed on the stick and then stood to wait, trembling, the hope threatened to bury her alive and she knew she would willingly die underneath it, her mouth open to breathe more of it in, more hope, more hope, always more, even when it made no sense at all.

CHAPTER FORTY-SIX

Fern's cell phone rang twice. The first time, she checked that she didn't know the number and sent it to voice mail. The second time, she and Gregory were both recovering, sweat drying, hearts slowing. "Just making sure Matty doesn't need something."

It was Mrs. Hutch, Matty's science teacher.

Fern mouthed the word *Shit* to Gregory and rolled to a sitting position.

"I need to talk to you briefly about Matty's ambition."

Well, that was something, at least. Mrs. Hutch had never started out that way before. Maybe there was hope. "Okay."

Fern started to stand so she could move to another room, to do this by herself, but Gregory cupped her free elbow and made her feel caught in a good way, caught as if she'd been falling and hadn't known it until her downward trajectory had been halted.

"Well, you know. We've talked about this before. Not all children can be at the top of the class, and sometimes we have to help them help themselves."

Is he on welfare or something? "Okay . . ."

Gregory lit a clove cigarette, and before he could even inhale, Fern took it from him. It crackled, and the smoke felt thick in her mouth. Protective.

"It's the science project. I feel . . . he's taken on a bit too much."

Fern's brain felt light, a feather in her head. "He said you approved it."

"I did. I didn't quite grasp, at that point, how much he was trying to do."

"It's not that much."

"Mrs. Reyes." She pronounced it Ray-jus. A *güera* trying to affect an appropriate Spanish pronunciation. "Matty's trying to learn a new motor skill while proving a theory about chemical composition and transformation within a classroom setting he already finds extremely challenging."

Motor skills. Like her kid had trouble walking or something. "Matty's a smart boy."

Silence met her words, and Fern's blood pressure shot up to the top of her head. What was the damn teacher's first name again? "Jane. Can I call you Jane?"

Another pause. "Actually, I prefer Mrs. Hutch. It keeps it simpler in regards to the parent-teacher relationship. I'm sure you understand."

"Of course." Fern literally saw the color red against her eyelids, but she managed to keep her voice even. "My son is more than intelligent enough to successfully complete the assignment. I'm fully confident of that."

"I wonder, Mrs. Ray-jus, do you remember our pencil conversation?"

Of course she did. Mrs. Hutch had asked her to keep Matty supplied with a full box of sharpened pencils because his need for a newly sharpened one during the middle of class was distracting to the other students. "He has pencils every day. I've been making sure of that."

"Well, be that as it may, he's still getting up in the middle of class to use the sharpener."

"It's hard for him to sit still." *When he's in a place he hates to be, that is.* Of course Matty got restless. He was a kid and he knew his teacher didn't like him. What kind of motivation was that for him to sit quietly in one spot?

"Mrs. Ray-jus, I'm thinking we should get him tested."

"For what, fleas?"

Another silence was her punishment.

"I'm sorry. Go on."

"I'm concerned he might have ADHD." Was Fern imagining it, or was Mrs. Hutch enjoying this? The carefully dropped voice, the acronym almost whispered as if it were a dirty secret.

"He doesn't."

"Yes, I find that's normally the response parents have at first."

Something about the woman's voice made Fern want to hurt her, to resort to actual physical violence. A quick pinch to the upper arm, a knee to the crotch. Poor Matty, having to put up with her for five hours a week. This woman brought out the worst in Fern and she had adult levels of impulse control. "Well, I'd have no problem if he did have ADHD, but he doesn't. In fourth grade, his teacher actually thought he might have it, too. So we tested him. He doesn't have it."

"Oh."

Yeah, *oh.* Bitch.

"Well, I'm relieved to hear that. I didn't see that in his file."

Fern waited for the apology, but it didn't come.

"So I'd like to talk to you about assigning him an easier project."

She leaned into Gregory's thumb. He rubbed a spot on her shoulder she hadn't even known was tight. "Like what?"

"Germination. I think he'd enjoy that."

"Germination?"

"Putting seeds into dirt, watering them, measuring the results."

"I *know* what germination is." Sweet baby *Cristo.* "He loved that project when he was six. It was very exciting back then. We got radishes." They'd had radishes for months. Those damn things were the only thing her backyard had ever really liked growing besides those weird black-and-white tulips the dog was named after. Nobody in the house would even *eat* the radishes. "I think you're underestimating my boy. You're aware his father died recently?" There. She'd done it. She'd played the dead-dad card, and she hadn't even seen it coming — it was so inappropriate she hadn't ever bothered wasting time worrying she might do it.

"Yes. I'm sorry for your loss." Mrs. Hutch's voice was flat. "I'm also aware they were estranged."

Fury leaped through Fern's body — an electrical storm of anger, perforating her skin and bone. But there was no good answer. It was true. Matty was mourning a shadow. She took a shaky breath. "What you're obviously *not* aware of is who he's working with on the project. His stepmother is a renowned botanist. Great woman. I mean, Scott obviously had good taste." Gregory snorted next to her and grinned. "She's also grieving, of course, I'm sure you can understand. I think it's been doing them good to work on this together, even though it's hard for Matty to get to North Berkeley to work with her every day as he has been. But my kid's dedicated." *Gets that from me.*

"Ah. North Berkeley?"

It was sick, terrible, that she knew what to say, and how to play it. "Up by Solano, you know the area? *Huge* house, enormous garden, which has been a boon to the project. Would it help if she came in to talk to you? If we came in together?"

"Well. I didn't know he had an actual botanist in the family."

Of course you didn't. "I'm sure she wouldn't mind." And Abby probably wouldn't. She'd jump at the chance.

And then, in Fern's chest, something released. It relaxed the same way the knot in her neck was loosening under Gregory's hands. Abby would help.

More than that, bigger than that — Fern would let her.

The knowledge felt like being on Gregory's bed. It was one of those memory-foam mattresses, and when she'd first lain on it — okay, she hadn't noticed a damn thing the first time she'd put her back on it, because she'd been fucking Gregory. But the second time, she'd thought it was wonderful, the way it held her up, the way her body sank down only an inch at most. The firmness felt like strength, something she didn't have at home when she lay on her old, sagging mattress with the springs that squeaked no matter how quietly she tried to get up in the morning.

Fern hung up the phone, shoving it away from her. Curling into a tight ball, she turned so that her forearms were against Gregory's chest, her legs tangled with his. His breath warmed her forehead. "Bitch," she said.

"Sounds like it. What are you going to do about it?"

"Play the game." Fern shut her eyes. The darkness felt warm, there in the circle of his arms. *I want a comfortable bed that won't hurt my back.* Lucinda Williams wasn't wrong about that.

"Games are okay sometimes. They get the job done."

She imagined Matty, the way his face

looked when he was playing Minecraft. His jaw went slack, as did his shoulders, but his eyes stayed focused, his alertness high. He held both in his body — keen attention and total relaxation — at the same time. "I can't stand it that she makes these judgments and doesn't play fair. How the hell am I supposed to motivate him to keep fighting her? To keep winning?"

Gregory's lips touched her hairline. "You can tell a lot about a person by what he does when he loses. What does Matty do?"

The time he couldn't figure out how to make the tetherball work. Long division. That city-building board game that his friend James had loved but made him feel all thumbs. It had been impossible to motivate him to keep going, to keep trying at any of them. "He stops playing. It's not fun for him anymore, so he just stops, no hard feelings."

"So if he's playing a rigged system, he'd stop playing, right?"

"You think that's what's happening in her class?"

"Sounds like he can't do right by the teacher. Why would he keep trying?"

Because that's what you do. Even when you can't win, you keep driving the fucking bus as long as they'll let you, as long as your body doesn't let you down. You hold it all together.

Gregory was right. Matty was smart enough to know that the system was rigged. And he wasn't motivated to win the way some people were, like Fern was. Matty just wanted to have a good time. That was his motivation. There was a clean, sweet relief in the realization, along with the frustration that went along with it. "So, what, he just gives up as he goes along? Where does that leave you, if you don't play the game the right way?"

Gregory pushed the edge of the pillow farther under his cheek. "Well, if you get a master's in economics and don't want to go into the family business because your old man's a jerk and instead decide to move to the Bay Area, where you can rent a one-bedroom for an amount that would keep a thousand families alive in the Sudan, and then decide to become an adjunct professor at three different adult schools, guaranteeing you'll never make enough to pay off your student loans, well, then . . . You end up in bed with a pretty woman, sweet enough to make you fall in love with her and stubborn enough to try to stop you — well, I'm just saying. He could end up worse off."

Fern touched Gregory's face, traced the

450

line at his nose that ran into a dimple farther south, an inch above his jaw. "I'm not sure what part of what you just said is the nicest."

"Sometimes the ones you can't motivate turn out just fine."

"Says the guy who's in debt, in a rental, and in a couple of jobs he doesn't like."

"And in your arms." He grinned.

It was possibly the cheesiest line Fern had ever heard. And she loved it. "Technically, I'm in yours."

"Even better." He kissed her eyebrow again. "Let him be who he's going to be."

"What if that's a burned-out skater living in a squat?"

"He's a great kid. He'll be fine. The squat will be better for him being there."

"You don't even know him."

"So introduce me."

Chapter Forty-Seven

Abby hid. Rather, she dropped. Off the radar, out of sight — she was a chunk of concrete dropped off the Bay Bridge pedestrian walkway, invisible six inches from the rail, completely nonexistent by the time it hit water.

She wouldn't be able to hold this baby inside her body (who was she kidding, even trying to?), but she also wouldn't be able to keep it a secret from them, from Fern and Matty, the ones who mattered the most now. She couldn't keep that kind of secret. She just couldn't. They might hate her — they might think this had been her plan (it hadn't — god, who made a plan like that?). Abby felt in her bones that the knowledge of this baby might destroy every chance she had with them.

She had no idea what to do. All she knew was she had to figure it out — she had to find the time to determine exactly how she could hurt the fewest people, for the short-est duration.

She needed time to think.

She sent an e-mail to Fern: *Great news! I got a fellowship at a botany retreat. The bad news is I'll be gone for three weeks. If you could just keep track of the hours you work, I'll settle up as soon as I get home. Tell Matty to keep knitting. And to get some onion skins. He should be able to get some from any produce market, just by asking to clean out the bin. We'll do the dyeing when I get back.*

She hit send, even though she had no idea how she'd be able to stand being near Matty, knowing she was carrying his cousin, knowing she would lose it (kill it — her body *killed* babies) like she always, always did.

She e-mailed Kathryn: *Last-minute chance to get out of town. Will call you when I'm back in three weeks.* Kathryn would know a fel-lowship at a botany retreat was bullshit. The less lying, the better.

She didn't have to explain a thing to Brook. "I need to get out of town for a while. Can you take me to the airport? And can you watch Tulip for me while I'm gone?"

Brook only said, "Pack me in your suit-case? Please?"

The next morning, Brook drove Abby to

SFO. Tulip panted in the car's backseat, no worse for the onion wear. "Sorry it's so early," Abby said. "I appreciate the ride."

Brook looked pleased to have been picked. She parked in the white zone and touched Abby's hand. "I'm just stoked you're doing something to make yourself happy. Are you sure you don't want to tell me where you're going?"

"I told you, I don't know. I'm being totally honest. I want you to get a surprise postcard from me."

"Bora-Bora?"

"Maybe."

"Edinburgh? Reykjavík?"

"Wait for the postcard." Abby kissed Brook's cheek. "Thank you for taking care of Tulip while I'm gone."

She waved the car out of sight, and then she entered the international terminal. Inside, the ceilings soared over her, and the clamor of passengers made her hands shake. She held her suitcase handle more tightly. She'd packed for contingencies. She'd put four books on her Kindle, all travel memoirs (China, Italy, Antarctica, and Russia). She'd packed a bathing suit and a heavy sweater. Heels and hiking boots. She would just walk the terminal until she saw a sign that pointed somewhere she felt like going.

But what if a flight was enough to do it? To shake the fetus loose? Abby cupped her hands at her low belly, a move that she'd done so many times in the past it felt natural. And useless.

Abby turned and headed for ground transportation. She bought a BART ticket to North Berkeley. On the train, she closed her eyes and pretended to be one of those commuters who were so tired they fell asleep on their way home. She couldn't tell if anyone was looking at her, but with her eyes shut, she felt invisible.

She walked home from the station.

Then Abby dead-bolted the door and then drew the chain, something she almost never did. The house felt emptier than it ever had, even emptier than it had right after Scott died. She'd gotten used to Tulip's thumps and snorts, the way his nails sounded on the hardwood, the sound of his jaws chewing something inappropriate, the edge of a door or the top of a table.

She took off her clothes and got in bed, folding her hands again over her belly. It wasn't even noon. She had three weeks of aloneness. Maybe she could send a fake postcard or three and push it to a month. Working on this, the only important project in the world.

She'd have to tell Diego eventually. Abby knew that — she just didn't know how to *do* it. If she were a different person, she'd never tell him at all. If she could, she'd stay here alone, all biological needs paused except the need to grow this child.

Wishes.

Later today Abby would have to get up and drink water — the filtered water from the Brita. She'd have to eat — she would order organic fruit and meat from Andronico's and have it delivered.

She had no intention of hurting herself, which, she realized, was the way it might look to the outside world.

It was the opposite, in fact.

She wanted to take care of herself. She'd done it wrong the first three times. Maybe this time, if she stayed still and quiet and alone, maybe if she kept her feet up, maybe if she ate right and drank right and slept right and hoped right — maybe if she hoped so hard that the wish became a bright color, a sweet scent — maybe this would stick. Grief filled her limbs, old blue-green algae that threatened to swamp her body when she rolled from one side to the other. Had this been what her mother had felt after losing Meg, when she was carrying Abby? The surety she wasn't enough to make a viable baby? (But, Abby! So viable! Still viable, even after three miscarriages. Still breathing. Hoping.)

Maybe this time Abby would be enough for a baby. Or (just maybe) the baby would make her enough. Redemption. Poor thing, to have to hold such an enormous, inappropriate word in hands that were probably still webbed, a clump of cells that couldn't survive outside her body.

But maybe. Abby clutched the word in her hands, storing it at night under her pillow next to the sachet she'd filled with lemon balm and nettle leaf and hope.

CHAPTER FORTY-EIGHT

The trip to the farmers' market had been Gregory's idea. "Almost every stall has bins of onions. We'll ask for them. It's not like anyone else uses them, right?"

Fern had Googled onion skins — turned out they weren't just something you could go out and buy. "That's a good idea."

"And, hey. I could meet Matty then." Gregory said it so simply that it actually sounded that way. Uncomplicated. Sure, why not? Matty was old enough. He understood that she dated. He'd never expressed interest in meeting anyone before, but that was probably due to the fact that she'd never been serious about anyone before.

Not that she was really serious about Gregory. Fern might be clearer in her head about him if she didn't have Abby so heavy on her mind.

Damn Abby and her skipping out, just like that. Who promised to help a kid with a science project and then took off? Fern had been fine for the last three weeks — she had plenty of Taking Care work that she could do from home. But Matty looked worried when he held out his almost-completed hat (*Is this part supposed to look like this? Did I do this right?*), and Fern had no idea what to tell him. Abby had been supposed to be home three days ago, but she hadn't returned any of Fern's e-mails yet.

Disappointment split the lanes of worry in her mind like a motorcycle threading traffic. What if Fern had just been plain wrong to go into business with Abby? The worry was electric, reminding her of the way she felt before a seizure — a mental wind that kicked up tiny but devastating dust storms. After the first two weeks of Abby's being gone without a single text or e-mail returned, Fern had stopped putting Ciela off. She'd worked three shifts at Ensenada so far. Abby wasn't coming back, if in fact she'd ever even left. Botany fellowship. Fern had a built-in bullshit detector, and that sounded like nothing more than total crap.

The money was good enough at the restaurant, the change and dollar bills heavy in her pocket as she left, making up for the physical stress of the job.

She'd had a seizure after her first shift.

She'd been at home, blessedly alone. She'd come to alone, and she'd cleaned up the blood from her mouth alone. Diego had brought Matty home soon afterward, and even though he *thought* she'd had a seizure, he couldn't prove it. What could she do? They needed the money.

The worst part was that Fern knew she'd never drive her bus again — one seizure from stress was one thing, but two? She wasn't safe, not anymore. She couldn't take the job even if they offered it back to her. Fern could see this truth in the corner of her eye — she could *feel* it — but she tried not to look at it. It was too hard, too painful. Like staring into the sun.

"Fern?" Gregory was still there, still looking at her.

Then, because Gregory's eyes were soft, because he was there, because he seemed to really *want* to be there, to be wherever she was, and because all of those added up to something happy and warm in her chest, Fern said, "Yes. You can meet Matty."

On Saturday, the farmers' market at Jack London was in full swing. The first truly warm day of spring, there was an excitement in the air that had nothing to do with baby broccoli or the shilling of lemon-verbena handmade soaps. Leaves were full on the sycamores. Tulips, planted by the city, bloomed happily in the huge ceramic urns. (*Don't think of the dog,* willed Fern, watching Matty's face. *Don't think of that damn Tulip.*) The estuary sparkled, boats bobbing past Alameda on their way to the bay. The air smelled of diesel and salt and heated caramel from the kettle corn sold from every other booth.

At the dock, Matty hung over the railing and watched the kayakers paddle past. "Can I do that someday?"

He could do anything he wanted. Fern would give him everything she could. "Okay."

"This summer?"

"Maybe. If we can get the money together for it."

"Sweet. I can get a job."

"You don't need to do that, *mijo.*"

"Under the table, I mean. Sergio's brother is thirteen, and he's making like fifty bucks a night busing tables at his dad's restaurant."

"I think that's illegal. Watch your elbow." Something white and soft was smeared on the railing, a gift from a passing seabird.

"Ew! Bird caca! I almost touched that! No, he's just helping. His dad calls it his allowance."

Numbers spun sweetly in Fern's mind, a well-oiled wheel. "How many nights a week?"

"Is this a trick? Are you going to get him in trouble?"

"Do I look like a narc to you?"

Matty giggled, and a child wobbling past on shaky toddler legs laughed as if in agreement. "I think they let him work every night he wants to. Which is like every night, because he's saving up for a Mustang, one of those old ones, when he's sixteen. He's all responsible and stuff, I guess. I just want the new WWE. And to kayak. That's all."

Fern ignored Matty's puppy eyes. There would be no new video game, and if he thought about it, he would already know that. "So you're saying he gets an 'allowance' of three hundred fifty dollars a week? That sounds more like a paycheck to me. Which is, like I said, illegal."

"Whatever it is, it's good. He buys a Frappuccino every day before he comes to school and those are like five dollars or something."

The wind ruffled Matty's short hair and Fern stuck her hands in her jeans pockets so she wouldn't do the same. "You don't even like coffee."

"That's not even coffee, Mom. It's like a

milk shake."

Mom. It used to be *Mamá.* Before that, it was *Mami.* Did they send out little-boy memos? When would he get the one that said he had to turn sullen? When would he get the one that said he could no longer hang out with her on the water in bright spring sunshine, watching the ducks bob and dive in the oil-sheened water?

"Where's your boyfriend, anyway?" Matty looked at his phone. "He's late."

"By like one minute. And there he is." *He's not my boyfriend.* She should have corrected him.

But damn. In that second, as she saw Gregory grin. Oh, god. He *was* her boyfriend. As usual, she was practically the last to know.

"Hi," he said to her. He looked off-balance, moving as if to kiss her, and then stopping himself. Awkwardly, he held up his palm, and just as awkwardly, Fern high-fived him.

"So. This is Matty."

"Matty. Hiya." Gregory was nervous, she realized. "It's good to meet you, man."

Man.

Matty gave a tight, polite smile. "Hello."

"So." Gregory rocked back on his heels, but the concrete step he stood on wobbled, and he pitched backward. "Shit." He righted himself before he fell. "Shit, shit. I mean, sorry for swearing. Fuck."

It couldn't have been planned, but it worked. Matty snorted. "Smooth. We have a swear jar, you know."

"How much?"

Matty cocked his head. "Five bucks."

Gregory got out his wallet.

"Matty! We don't have a — Where did you even *get* that idea from?"

"Mrs. Simms has one on her desk in math." Matty grinned. "Just kidding. I wanted to see if he would believe me."

"Of course he would. He already knows you don't lie."

"Yeah, I *never* lie." Matty rolled his eyes. "Ever."

Gregory laughed.

It was funny. There Fern was, having a funny moment with her son and her boyfriend. A fishing boat blasted its horn as it made its way around a small sailboat awkwardly tacking toward the cranes. A seagull complained cheerfully overhead. She wrapped her arms around herself and hugged because her arms needed to hug someone, and neither of the guys looked like he would appreciate her doing it to him. Not right now. Later, she'd hug both of them so hard they wouldn't know what hit them. Fern, the bus of love.

"Speaking of lying," said Gregory, "this was kind of just a ruse to get you both down here. I know a better place to get onion skins than begging all these vendors, one by one."

"You do?"

"You willing to take a chance?"

Matty lifted one shoulder and let it drop, but his face was bright, probably brighter than he knew. "I guess."

"Fern?"

"Okay?" *Don't hurt my boy.*

He held up three slips of paper. "When was the last time you took the ferry to the city?"

Dios. Matty had always wanted to ride the ferry, but on her days off she never had time to waste an hour going to the city and an hour back just to be on a boat. He'd been supposed to go to Alcatraz on a school field trip when he was eight, but he'd had strep throat that week. She'd never gotten around to making it up to him.

"Seriously? Mom?" Matty's eyes looked desperate, as if he thought she might say no.

"Are you kidding me? I can't fucking wait." It was a deliberate curse, one she could just afford. She dug the five-dollar bill out of her purse and handed it to him. "Here, take this for the boat instead of ye olde nonexistent swear jar. I think they have hot chocolate on board."

"Oh, *yeah,*" said Matty, and started off toward the ferry waiting area at a pace faster than a jog, slower than a run. His knees were stiff, locked as if he were a robot, which at that moment in his mind, he probably was. Matty was still young enough to pretend, and old enough to know he shouldn't tell anyone that's what he was doing.

Gregory took her hand. "What a nice kid." He pulled away, and her fingers felt cold immediately. "Crap. Is this okay?"

Fern glanced ahead — Matty was out of sight, on the other side of an orchid vendor. She turned to face him. She went up on tiptoes and kissed him. "Yes."

Gregory looked up at the blue sky overhead. "There's no fog."

"For once."

"We've never kissed outside before."

"I bet you're right."

"I'm not saying I have to kiss you all the way to San Francisco."

"Good."

He grinned, and Fern's stomach tightened. "But I'll want to. Just so you know."

"Good," she said again.

CHAPTER FORTY-NINE

Three weeks and three days after she'd left on her nontrip, on a sunny Saturday afternoon Abby finally managed to get out of bed and actually go outside. Her drip irrigation had kept the vegetables alive — the kale was still coming in even though it was warming up, and the parsley was growing as if its goal was to take over the yard. But something was eating the onions, and her hellebores had withered, as if they missed her daily pep talk. Her coreopsis was failing to thrive.

She knew the feeling.

There was a hole in the ground just to the south of the shed. It was a good, sunny spot. She'd been going to put in a pomegranate tree, planning to keep it small and espaliered. She'd bought a bare root one and left it in its burlap bag. Now it was dead, a dry stick with no promise left.

The hole was still there, though.

Abby stood on the edge of it, her bare toes dipping down. Loose dirt tumbled in. The hole wasn't bigger than a foot across. It wasn't good for anything but planting a tree in.

Or a phone.

Diego had texted her twice while she'd been "gone," sweet notes. Apparently his sister hadn't told him that she was off-limits, and Abby hadn't had a chance to. *Would love to see you again. I know that's crazy. But crazy can be good sometimes. . . .*

Kathryn had texted, too: *I thought you'd be back by now. Call me when you're home, I'll bring over some homemade granola, the crunchy kind you like.*

Abby held her iPhone above the hole. She could just drop it. That's all it would take. She could bury it, kicking dirt over it, scrabbling earth into the hole with her bare hands. In a year, a message tree would grow. It would look like one of those fake trees, the ones they put on hillsides, the ones that were actually cell phone towers made to look like trees (Abby always spotted them, the desperate evenness of their branches, the way no tree in the world would be so symmetrical). From its branches would flow voice mails of guilt, text messages of disap-pointment, e-mails of blame.

Abby sat, heavily, her feet shoved into the hole. Maybe if she waited long enough, someone would cover her feet with the extra dirt. They would fertilize her (no, wait, she was already fertilized). She would grow into something that looked more natural than a cell phone tree, but produced the same amount of dismay and disruption.

Her phone buzzed — she'd managed to silence it, but she hadn't figured out how to turn off its vibration. It was angry, a cursing wasp.

It was a photo text from Matty. His hat. It was still the light silver of the wool she'd given him, still undyed. And it was perfect. She could see, even at the small resolution, how well he was making his stitches now. His decreases were even and perfectly placed.

Her heart gave a thump that threatened to kill her right there, her feet still in the hole. He must have learned how to decrease like that from someone else. Or he could have learned from YouTube. She didn't know which would be worse. It was followed by another text that read, *I'm getting onion skins right now. I'm on the ferry!*

While she was looking at the phone's face, it rang.

Diego.

She hit ignore on the phone.

A minute later, she had a voice mail. *Voice* mail. It struck her as archaic — the voice, used as a communication device. Most people either e-mailed or texted when they needed something, but Diego had admitted to her that he wasn't good at spelling and that he'd always been self-conscious about it. On one of their two nights together, he'd held his hands up toward the ceiling and moved his fingers. "Good for nothing but gripping trees."

Abby had been able to think of a couple other things he'd already shown her his hands were pretty good at. "Don't you use gloves?" she'd asked.

"Supposed to."

"But you don't?"

"Sometimes you just need to feel the bark. These big old things can't type on a tiny cell phone. If I have something to say to you" — he'd turned to her with a grin — "I'll say it with my mouth. The mouth is the best thing for communicating there is." Then he'd moved down her body and proved it.

Now, her feet still in the hole, she listened to his voice. "I'm up a tree right now, pretty near your house, over by the new Catholic church they're building. They need a sick

471

poplar taken out. I just thought . . ." He cleared his throat. "I just thought if you were back in town, and if you got this, you could call me back. Or come see me. Maybe you can convince me you haven't changed your mind about being Fern and Matty's friend. 'Cause I think they might think that. And that — I gotta tell you, Abby — that would piss me off. I'm fine. You don't have to see me again if you don't want to. But them — anyway." The message clicked and went dead.

Abby's car coughed when she started it. She hadn't driven it in weeks. It felt funny to be behind the wheel. The seat belt was shorter now.

Diego's truck was in the dirt parking lot near the new church. She scanned the trees for the diseased poplar he'd mentioned, and she found his orange vest high up in a wildly overgrown tree, at least a hundred feet up.

It was probably for the best that Diego didn't text much.

I'm pregnant. Her text — invisible and dangerous — flew with a swoop out of her phone, across the dirt lot, over the construction, and up the tree.

She watched him. He was too far away for her to make out his features. She couldn't see his expression. But she could see his

472

limbs — she watched him swing sideways, reach an arm out to steady himself. He would be looking at his phone — he'd told her he kept it tethered to his body with a small bungee so that if he had to glance at it, he couldn't drop it and kill someone standing below.

His body stiffened.

The fuck.

She tapped a message back. *I don't want anything from you.*

The tiny orange figure swung wildly, legs kicking.

Is that u? In the parking lot?

What had she been thinking? What if he shimmied down — no, she could still hit the engine, peel out, beat him to her house, shoot the dead bolt, hide under her covers. *No.* A stupid, necessary lie. *I'm only telling you because it's the right thing to do. It won't stick.*

Her phone buzzed furiously in her hand. Of course he would call her. She was a fool for not thinking he might.

Abby hit the answer button. "It never sticks. This will be the fourth child I've lost."

"You know you could have *killed* me?" One orange arm was raised, as if he was shaking his fist at her.

"I'm sorry." She should have thought.

Why had it seemed like a good idea? She'd just wanted to watch him find out. . . . She hadn't thought further than that.

"We used condoms."

"Well, yeah. One must have failed."

"Failed? Shit. Are you sure it's mine?"

It felt as if his tree had fallen directly on top of her. She was smashed, flat, almost dead. But she supposed it was a fair question. Her husband had only been dead three and a half months. "Yes."

"You're sure. Because I've never knocked anyone up. I thought I couldn't do it."

"You can."

"Well."

It didn't sound like a question, but she answered it anyway. "That's why I took myself out of the equation. I'm just kind of . . . waiting. Just till it passes." *Maybe it wouldn't pass. Please let it not pass.*

"Abby." The orange figure swung back and forth slowly, a tiny plastic-looking pendulum. He'd taken his feet and hands off the tree and was hanging by his harness. "How can I help? Tell me what to do."

She was the same, dangling in midair. "Don't worry about it. Like I said, I lose babies. Give me another couple of weeks and I won't be pregnant anymore."

"So you don't want to be pregnant."

"I *do.*" Should she even admit that to him? How was that fair?

"What does the doctor say?"

"That I'm having a baby." The doctor was the only other one who knew. She hadn't even told Brook yet. She'd taken Tulip back and closed the door, refusing to say where she'd been. She didn't know what to say . . . not yet.

"Jesus Christ. When?"

"In December." It was a stark and impossible eternity of good luck away. "But it won't stick."

"That's what you keep saying. What do you want me to do?"

"Nothing. I don't want anything from you. You don't have to be involved at all."

"Then why the *fuck* are you telling me?"

Why was she? She touched the steering wheel lightly with her left hand. "Because."

"Great answer. How far along are you, anyway? Eight, nine weeks? That's how long it's been since you called me, by the way. And telling me now that the baby I might have fathered is about to die inside you, no matter what, am I getting that right?"

He was getting it right. Abby was the one who'd gotten it so very, very wrong.

His words were low and urgent. "The right thing to do would have been not to run away. The right thing would have been to let me help. A *baby.*" Something on the line crackled, either his voice or a branch. "What do you want me to do here, Abby?"

"Nothing. I'm sorry. I thought I had to tell you. . . ."

A heavy sigh. "Of course you had to tell me. But this was the wrong way."

He didn't say good-bye. The only thing she heard was a click and then silence. The distant orange man reattached his limbs to the tree, and started climbing upward, his tiny movements measured. Sensible.

And Abby, still sitting in her car, dropped through the air. Miles and miles of coldness opened beneath her and she had no harness.

There was nothing to catch her, nothing at all.

CHAPTER FIFTY

Matty talked about the ferry ride all the way home. "And then we saw the dolphin!"

"We weren't sure it was a dolphin, you know that, right? Take this corner slow, okay?"

Gregory nodded. John Prine's "Angel from Montgomery" crooned low from his stereo. *Just give me one thing that I can hold on to.*

"Because the Ybarra kids always play kickball on the sidewalk, and every once in a while, they pop out into the street like a Ping-Pong ball."

From the backseat, Matty laughed as if the words had been dirty somehow. "Ping-ping singsong," he said and laughed again. "Ping-poingy-poing."

Gregory grinned.

"I'm serious. Two of the kids have been tapped by cars already. Not hurt, *gracias a Dios,* because there's no other reason for it.

Their idiot parents don't tell them to stay out of the road. What if the bus ran here? Instead of a block away."

"Then they'd probably keep their kids out of the street," Gregory said lightly.

"Maybe."

"I'm being careful, Fern."

"I know." He was. He was a gorgeous driver. He would be good behind the wheel of a bus.

"Ping-Pong! Dolphin! The captain said it could have *totally* been a dolphin."

The man Matty had spoken to hadn't been a captain — he'd been the bartender, serving mochas and vodka tonics. But he'd worn a captain's hat, and had let Matty wear it for a minute, too. Matty was convinced he'd seen a dolphin leap near a leg of the new Bay Bridge, and Gregory, bless him, was backing him up now. "Coulda been. Looked like it."

Gregory had been good with Matty. Not in a creepy way, not in a dad way. Just in a guy way. Agreeing with him on the dolphin. Disagreeing with him on *Mad Max*. Talking to him like he was a person, not just some kid.

"And the wind! It blew that tourist's hat right off his head into the water. That was *hilarious.*"

Gregory pulled up in front of the house. She swore the front gate was even more crooked than it had been when they left — was it possible that gravity had a greater pull in this corner of Oakland? It would explain why nothing stayed standing in this neighborhood the way it did elsewhere. In Montclair and Piedmont and Rockridge, old houses just got old. They didn't slope and slant until they tipped right over. They held up. Here, it was like the earth quaked more. Harder.

"The wind didn't take *your* hat, though," she said.

Matty tugged it lower on his forehead. "That's because it's made good."

"That's probably it. And maybe because you never took your hand off it once." He hadn't — while they'd been up on the top deck, watching the city get bigger as if it were magically growing — he'd kept one hand on his head the whole time. Just in case.

"It would have stayed on, though. Even if I hadn't."

"I know." Stupid hat. What if her suspicion was right? What if Abby really never came back?

Matty *needed* her to come back. Why couldn't he just get hurt by an eleven-year-old girl at school? A simple Valentine's Day failure, a playground misunderstanding. He'd been hurt by his father for so long — it was beyond unfair that his first heartbreak by a woman might be by his father's wife.

But Abby would come back. She would.

Fern hated that she couldn't tell whom she was hoping it was true more for: Matty or herself.

"Look! Maybe he brought pizza!" Matty was out of the car and running up the walkway toward Diego before Gregory could finish putting the car in park. "¡Tío, Tío! Did you bring pizza?"

Diego nodded, and Fern's heart lifted. Pizza. Her brother. Beers on the front porch. Or in the kitchen, or in the backyard — it didn't matter where they hung out. She needed — wanted — to be with her brother tonight.

"Heartstopper from the Lanesplitter," he said.

"Yes," yelled Matty. "That's my favorite kind!"

"You sure this is still okay?" Gregory's voice was quiet next to her. "You don't have to introduce me to everyone in your life all in one day."

"I'm sure." For once, something was easy.

Gregory followed her up the walkway.

"Diego, this is Gregory. Gregory, my brother." She felt heat rush to the base of her skull. "Matty, go get some paper plates."

Matty boggled. "Really?"

She'd bought them for his ninth birthday party. The hundred-pack had been on sale at the SavMart. Fern hoarded them. Doing dishes was cheaper. But what else did she have them for?

"Go on." She looked at Diego. "Are Grandpa Wyatt and Elva here?"

"They are. But they went into Wyatt's room." Diego waited until Matty had run inside and then he switched to a stage whisper. "I heard a couple of things I wish I hadn't heard. I brought enough pizza for them, too, but I think we should wait a while. If you know what I mean."

"No, no, no. Stop talking. We'll stay out here. I hope Matty is quick."

Gregory sat on the top step. Fern sat on the swing next to her brother. Night was falling like purple velvet, a promise of the summer to come. Two of the Ybarra kids raced past the house, laughing, followed by two new white puppies. None of them spoke for a moment. It could have been an awkward silence, but it wasn't. She leaned companionably on Diego's arm, and Gregory looked upward at the rosy clouds. In another town, this would be the time for the fireflies to come out and dance. Here, they had mosquitoes and motorcycle exhaust, but those were just as welcome to Fern. This was *her* overgrown yard, *her* purple-and-red-streaked sky, *her* boys bumping around her, knocking into her knees, holding up her heart.

Matty ate pizza with his mouth open and told Diego about the dolphins and the captain and the fact that he had two entire grocery bags full of red onion skins from the vendor guy Gregory knew at the San Francisco Ferry Building.

"You're gonna dye that hat, huh? For your project?"

"Yeah!" Matty tugged it lower on his head.

"When's the science fair?"

"Three weeks."

Fern could almost *see* her brother thinking about Abby. She tapped Matty's woolen head. "We make a good team, this kid and me. He's been doing the knitting on his own with some help from YouTube, but I found the Web site on natural dyeing. We're good to go. I mean, just in case Abby doesn't get home from her trip in time."

"But she will," said Matty.

"Yep." Fern was the one helping Matty now. She'd even picked up a pair of needles, too, something she hadn't done since she was a kid. YouTube had reminded her that she still knew how to knit, and she was still pretty bad at it. Suddenly, her shoulders ached, as if she'd been carrying Matty's backpack all day instead of just the last few hours of their trip.

Diego grinned at Matty. "You're gonna show that old bitch of a teacher, huh?"

"Diego!"

"Come on. We all hate Mrs. Hutch."

Matty laughed. "Yeah, Mom. We all hate her."

"We're not supposed to admit that, though."

Gregory wiped his mouth with a paper napkin. "Even I hate her, Fern."

"Good man." Diego pointed a finger gun at Gregory and shot. Then he turned back to Matty. "But you only have the one hat? How are you going to set it up, like, so that she sees the original color, and then sees you dyed it red with the onions?"

"Technically" — Matty pronounced it carefully in four syllables — "it's going to come out closer to brown or orange, not red, like you'd think. It's chemistry. We tried it on a little bit of white yarn the other night. And I'm just going to make another hat. Maybe two more. To show."

"Just like that."

"Yeah, well, now I'm faster." The Ybarra kids and dogs ran past going the other way. Matty threw down his paper plate. "I wanna go see those puppies."

Fern sat up straighter. "Be careful. Don't run into the road."

"Not a moron, Mom." He clattered out the gate and chased after the pack.

He wasn't a moron. He was smart enough to get by. Like her. Like her brother. Fern bumped Diego's shoulder. "What did we do to deserve pizza, huh?"

She expected him to say something disparaging. Something funny to make Gregory laugh. Instead, he said, "Ah. You know."

"What happened?"

"Why do you think something happened?"

Her spider-senses went on alert. Something to do with Abby. It had to be. "Think? I know."

"Nah."

Gregory glanced at her. "You want me to take off?"

"Yes," said Fern, the word automatic. Worry juddered in her chest, and she didn't care that she sounded rude.

"You're cool, man." But Diego's legs jiggled and he thrummed his fingertips against the arm of the old porch swing.

"Yeah, well, I have a million midterms to grade and even though I've been damn good at keeping them out of my mind all day, I can't put them off much longer." He rubbed his hands on his thighs and stood. "Diego, man." They shook hands. "Good to meet you."

"I'm sorry —" Fern didn't waste time trying to make her words convincing. Something was wrong with Diego and she was irritated with herself that she hadn't noticed right off the bat. "Okay. I'll walk you out?"

At the car, she kissed Gregory hard, because she meant it, because she meant a lot of things she didn't feel like saying.

But he pulled back. "Who takes care of you?"

"What? Diego does." She tried to laugh it off. "He brought pizza. That's not bad, right?"

"I'm not going to wait forever."

It wasn't like she didn't know what he was talking about. "I know."

"I want to be with you. That means something to me. I fit into little pockets of your life, but I know I don't fit in here, with your family. That's been fine up till now. But someday it won't be fine."

Fern looked at the ground. "I'm sorry."

"I just need you to know. I'm pretty

patient. But I'm not a saint. Someday I'll want more." Gregory's eyes were impossibly, heartbreakingly kind. "Or I'll want less."

"I know." Her voice was almost a whisper. It was all the breath she could grab.

He said, "What about you, Fern? When do you get your turn?"

She would have said, *I'm good,* but she couldn't — she wasn't — so she tugged the strings of his A's hoodie and kissed him one more time, hoping he'd feel what she meant, what she couldn't say.

CHAPTER FIFTY-ONE

When she was back on the porch, Diego said, "I'm glad you didn't make me witness that good-bye." He smiled vaguely. "Kissing stuff. Super annoying."

Fern shook her head to clear it. She would have to worry about Gregory later. "What happened?"

"Eh."

"What did she do?" It was Abby. It *had* to be Abby.

"It's what we did." He blinked, and for a sudden terrifying moment, Fern thought her brother was about to cry. But then, the next second, there was nothing on his face but anger, so stark and white it scared her. "She's pregnant."

"The *fuck*."

He slumped. "Exactly what I said."

Fern hit him on the shoulder. She wanted to do it with her car. With her bus. "*¿Tu eres un idiota?* Seriously?"

487

"We used condoms."

"Then she can't be. She's lying." Oh, god. Abby had *tricked* her brother, like she'd been planning on tricking Scott. "Were they *her* condoms?"

"Does that matter?" Diego scrubbed at his face. "She said it won't last."

"What the fuck does that mean?" But Fern knew. *They didn't stick.*

"She said she'll have a miscarriage." For the first time, Diego met her eyes, and at that moment, Fern would have happily killed Abby for putting that kind of agony into his gaze. All her brother had wanted from his wife was a kid. Just one. "She sounded sad."

"Sounded? You didn't see her?"

"She texted me while I was up a tree. I called her back and she finally answered. She was in the parking lot across from the church construction. Said she wasn't, but I know it was her car."

The swing was moving too fast — Diego's nervous legs pumping it back and forth. Fern slid off and down to the top step Gregory had vacated.

A child.

A child she'd lose.

Oh, god, what if Abby didn't miscarry?

Math — it was math in her head, only this

time the numbers mattered more than they ever had before. A child. It would be Diego's son or daughter.

It would be Matty's cousin.

Forever. There was no getting around blood. It was okay that Abby had left them (no, it wasn't, it was *not* okay, but it was what it was) because she wasn't blood. Fern should never have let down her guard in the first place. She'd let the wrong person in, and then they'd been hurt, and that was the way life went.

But a baby would be forever.

Abby would get the family she'd been looking for. All built-in, tied up in a cute little package. Just like she'd wanted.

The problem was, that family was *Fern's.* If she could have dropped some kind of dome around the house, some kind of invisible shield, one straight out of one of Matty's comic books, she would have. No one in, no one out. She would give everything she had left (the box of coins, her less-than-five-year-old water heater, her health) to pay for it. If they starved to death together inside, they'd at least be together at the end.

"Where's Matty?" She needed him here, next to her on the porch, inside her imaginary shield. "Matty?" Her voice was too loud, too shrill.

"He's fine. He's playing." Diego's pupils were large in the darkening night. He'd had that look long ago, the first night their mother didn't come home at all. He'd had it again when his wife had left him.

"Matty!"

"I'm here!" The gate bounced open, and one of the Ybarra boys laughed. "What?"

"Nothing."

Matty gave her a suspicious look but then seemed to shrug it off. "Here, I got your mail." He dumped a pile of bills — always bills — into her lap. "I'm gonna go play WWE. *Tío,* you coming?"

"Yeah. Just a minute."

The door slammed shut behind him.

Fern didn't have the right words. She had no words at all. "Diego . . ."

"I don't know what to do."

His voice cracked, and Fern felt something in her chest crack along with it. "Do what you would do if she wasn't Abby."

"Like . . ."

"Like if she was just some girl you met at a bar. What would you do?"

"Offer to help."

"Did you do that?"

He glared at her. "Of course I did."

"I know you did. What else would you do?"

490

"Try not to fall in love with her."

Fern's heart ached. "Would that be hard?"

"I don't know. Depends on how much she ends up hurting you. Matty. Us. If she does, fuck her. But, Fernandita — I want the baby. I want the baby so bad I can't stand to think of it not working. Not *sticking.*"

It took all her courage to say the words: "Tell her, then." *If he did, if the baby stuck, if Diego chose her . . .* Fear was a solid wall hit at sixty miles an hour.

"What?"

Desperate to put something — anything — in order, she flipped through the mail, her fingers thick and clumsy. All bills, two advertisement flyers, one slim envelope addressed to her. She arranged them by size. "Tell her you want the baby."

"I can do that? I mean, I know I *can,* but that's . . . that would be okay?"

"Only if you mean it." She slit the smallest envelope with her first finger, ripping it.

"I mean it. I would fucking mean it."

Fern looked at the slim piece of paper in her hand. *"Que cabrón."*

"What?"

The silent explosion inside her head made her rock backward in pain. "It's a check."

A check, made out in Abby's clear hand. Five hundred and twenty one thousand dollars, fifty-two cents. It was drawn on a personal bank account. Not a money order, nor a cashier's check — nothing as secure as that. A fucking personal account.

The memo line didn't read *Take care* like Scott's checks had.

And it didn't read *Taking Care* like Abby had written cheekily on the one work-related check Fern had received.

In tiny, cramped handwriting that barely fit in the small space, it read, *I'm sorry I hurt you. I won't do it anymore. You're off the hook.*

"She just fired me."

The worst part was the knowledge of how much it was going to hurt later, like getting a burn that blistered from accidentally touching a hot stove. It stung badly at first, yes, but the fear — the knowledge — that it would get worse before it got better was the terrifying part.

Fern would deposit the money, because she would have to.

And if the baby was born full-term, she would have to see Abby sometimes. So she would have to be cordial.

To someone she'd thought was becoming a friend. A real friend.

This was why — Fern knew — *this* was why you kept the door closed. You had to keep it shut against the danger, against the potential damage. If you didn't, everything rushed in like a flood, stripping away everything you loved.

CHAPTER FIFTY-TWO

The pain came the next Wednesday morning. Abby felt it in her sleep, a low twinge that would soon translate to cramps and then to real pain. She didn't have to wonder what was going on — she knew.

What she wasn't prepared for was the weight of the sadness that parked itself on her chest, pinning her in place. The fear was bigger than Tulip and had the weight of a black hole. She'd thought she'd felt all of it in the past. No matter what happened, she'd thought, if this pregnancy turned into a loss, it couldn't be — it would never be — as painful as the first three she'd lost.

But she'd been wrong. This one cut deeper. Even though she'd tried not to let herself hope, she had. In deep and secret moments, just before she fell off the ledge into sleep, she'd thought about the heft of a baby. Nothing more concrete than that. Just how a baby would feel in her arms, a fat, happy baby that had spent a full forty weeks inside her body, a baby that was outside her body but in her arms, breathing air but drinking her.

She rolled sideways in bed, moving slowly to the edge. The pain was sharper. It would get worse, soon. In the bathroom, she wiped the first blood away.

She could have called Diego, if she'd handled it differently. But she hadn't. She didn't deserve his sympathy (or, worse, his possible relief).

Kathryn answered quickly, her voice hoarse with sleep. "Are you okay?"

"No." It was a sob, a scream, a wail, even though the word itself was almost inaudible.

"Oh, my girlie."

"Can you take me to the hospital?"

A pause. "What's wrong? Are you going to finally tell me? Are you sick?" Panic rattled at the edges of Kathryn's voice.

"I was pregnant. I'm quickly becoming unpregnant. Again." Abby wondered if Kathryn remembered the garden conversation they'd had, when Kathryn had told Abby to sleep with someone. Anyone. She had. And this was her punishment.

Another long pause. "Do you think you need an ambulance?"

She needed a lot of things. She needed a

god to pray to. She needed more time with the creature inside her, the tiny sea monkey she couldn't will to be any bigger. She needed her mother. (Fourteen years now she'd been gone — such a long time. Abby wasn't even sure what her mother would have said to her. She'd lost the sound of her voice years before.) But she didn't need an ambulance. "No, that's okay. There's no real hurry."

"You're bleeding?"

"It's not bad yet. Take your time. Get your coffee."

Kathryn lived fifteen minutes across Berkeley, near the tunnel. Abby knew she'd be pulling up in ten.

Abby dressed. She got her wallet, her medical ID, and the book she was reading. Raspberry leaves, in a small ziplock, for a successful pregnancy. It was already too late, but why not? She pulled out the bag with her knitting in it — if Kathryn insisted on staying (and she would), Abby would need something in her hands that she could fiddle with while Kathryn chatted with her. Darling Kathryn. She'd say light things, loving soft things. It would be unbearable, but the thing that was breaking in her body was worse.

In the car, though, Kathryn didn't say the

soft things Abby thought she would. "What the hell were you thinking?"

"What do you mean?"

"Not telling me?"

"I didn't tell anyone." It wasn't a good excuse, but it was all she had. "Except the father, but I told him not to count on anything, so he won't be disappointed."

"How long were you planning on keeping that up? Not telling anyone?"

"Until this morning came. Whenever that was."

"What are you talking about?"

"You know I don't keep babies. I'm not . . ."

"Not what?" Kathryn's voice was short.

"I'm no good at it." *Not enough.*

"Bullshit."

Abby shook her head and looked out the window, gripping the seat belt as she tried to decide if another cramp was coming.

Kathryn stomped on the brake harder than she needed to. "Not that you're not good at some things. That's for damn sure. You *suck* at some things."

Abby just stared at the red light, willing it to go green.

"Do you know how I felt this last month?"

"I'm sorry."

"No, you're not."

Annoyance brushed against Abby's skin. "I said I was. I meant it."

"I know you better than anyone else, you know that? I've known you since the day you first drew breath. I was the third person to hold you, and let me tell you this." Kathryn slammed the stick into first and lurched through the light. "You're better at hiding from yourself than anyone I've ever known."

"I don't know what you're talking about." Abby suddenly felt sixteen, caught sneaking out of the house to meet Robby Wilkens.

"Oh, honey." Kathryn took a deep breath, her voice suddenly softer. "Ever since your parents died, you've felt like you needed to make a family, instead of seeing that you have one already. Me. Rebecca. Brook. Your friends. I thought Fern and Matty might enter that category sometime, too."

Something cracked inside Abby's chest, higher than the cramping. "Kathryn —"

"But then you push everyone away when what you need is to trust them. To trust us. Who's the father?"

Abby took a breath and released it shakily. "Fern's brother, Diego."

"Jesus, Abby. Seriously?"

"No, it's okay. It's fine, really. I don't *need* him." All she needed was this to work, this tiny flutter of life to stay with her. "I swear."

Kathryn sucked in a quick breath and then rolled down her window. She turned left and pulled into the ER parking lot. "For the love of god, dear heart. That's what I'm trying to say. We all need people."

Abby hobbled the few feet into the doors of the hospital. Then came more pain, dull and throbbing, and then came the rote formality she'd been through before — signing the paperwork, sitting in the waiting room with her hands at her low belly. A man bellowed his way in, his fist wrapped in bandages, the blood dripping through and down his shirt-front. Some kind of machine accident. He was admitted quickly. Then a kid having an allergic reaction to milk — they pushed him right in, too. Everyone was having a higher-priority medical emergency than she was. That was okay. She wouldn't die from this. Not physically.

She sat in the hard plastic chair, her fingers knotted together at her waist. She should get out her knitting, or her book, something, anything, to take her mind off what Kathryn had said.

What if she already had enough?

It was a traitorous thought.

But yet.

A yellow heat flooded into her, moving

from the top of her head, all the way through her body, right down to her toes.

What would the knowledge that she was already enough feel like? Would it feel like the warmth that was rushing through her? Would it taste like relief?

A woman entered the waiting room. She was wearing a red head wrap and carrying a small child on her hip. Her head was high, but she was crying silently, tears dripping from her chin to her chest. Behind her, a man followed. At the desk, she whispered something to the triage nurse, who nodded and pointed to the entrance door, the one Abby still hadn't been cleared to go through. The woman turned and quietly transferred the child to the man, who spoke softly into the boy's hair, words Abby couldn't understand. Then the woman walked through the door into the next room. Her shoulders were straight, her neck long, her body tall.

She was alone.

Abby's own tears started. She watched the man put the child on a plastic chair and give him his phone to play with. The man swiped his hand over his stubbled mouth, then stared straight ahead, obviously lost somewhere else in thought. Maybe in his thoughts, he was in the next room with his wife, who was sick. Possibly very sick.

Maybe he was in his home country, resting on a bed more comfortable than he ever slept in here.

Abby, though. She was right there, in the same exact room with him, but they were both completely alone. The baby inside her wouldn't live to be that child's age. Abby would leave the hospital walking next to Kathryn, but they would both be alone as they passed under the EXIT sign.

The woman in the head wrap had gone in, alone, without her family.

And maybe that was okay.

Maybe it was enough, just being near one another. Maybe . . . that was the whole point. They were all enough by themselves, and a bit more, together.

The thought was big enough to make the ground shake, to make the building slide sideways, to make the sky crumble. Those things *should* have happened, but they didn't, and for a moment she was surprised, as she looked around, to see nothing had moved.

So Abby let it all go. It was an experiment, really. To see if she could. That's all it was.

She let go of her expectation. She let go of her hope, and her excitement, and her sorrow. She let go of the image she had of herself as someone strong enough to get by until she turned into the person she was meant to be. She let go of her need to be a mother. To have a child cling to her, to have a child to cling to. She set all of it down on the floor in front of her — invisible, vast, everything she'd ever thought she needed.

There was nothing to hold, nothing but emptiness. So she let it all go, and she was left with open space.

She was left with just openness, terrifying and brilliant and ungraspable. The experiment (because that's all it was supposed to have been) turned real.

When Kathryn finally came into the waiting room a few empty and equally glorious minutes later, Abby's tears had turned to incredulous wonder.

"Are you okay? Why are you still out here? They should get you in. I'll go talk to someone, all right?"

"I'm okay," Abby said in surprise. "I think I might be okay right here. As long as you're here with me. I'll be okay."

CHAPTER FIFTY-THREE

"No, Mom, you're doing it wrong." Matty leaned forward, pausing *Poltergeist*. They were working their way through the tamer horror movies because Matty said he wanted to be inoculated to, as he called it, the "hard-core stuff." Pointing out to him that he wasn't eligible to watch the rated-R stuff until he was eighteen had only earned her a beatific smile. "Unless a grown-up is with me. A supercool grown-up. Luckily, I know one of those." She knew he didn't mean her, and had answered that Diego wasn't actually *that* cool.

"Look," he said, pointing to the knitting in her hands. "That's totally wrong."

"What do you mean? Looks right to me."

"You're doing your stitches, like —" Matty grabbed at her knitting and peered at her stitches. "Dude, you're doing them backward."

Fern held it out and looked carefully at

her ribbing. "Dude. No, I'm not." She'd known how to knit, a million years ago, and it had felt like it was coming back to her. She'd learned at a friend's house when she couldn't have been more than ten. Her friend's aunt Rita, that's who had taught her. She remembered the feeling of the movement of the needles.

"Look at the leg of the stitch you're going into. That's wrong."

"But the finished stitch looks exactly like yours."

"It's still not the right way to do it."

From the kitchen, she heard Elva giggle. Grandpa Wyatt said something that sounded inappropriate, even though she couldn't quite make out the words. Then she heard, "Hey! My tooth! Not *that* hard! You sexy beast!"

Elva tittered happily. Matty snorted.

She hadn't told Grandpa Wyatt yet that his tooth would be paid for as soon as she put the check in the bank. He was phobic about the dentist (thus the break), but she'd made an appointment for him for the next Monday. She'd tell him that morning, right before she loaded him, yelling and protesting, into the cab that would be suddenly available in the tooth budget, too.

The box of old Mexican coins had been

her last hope. It shouldn't have been such a surprise, but it had still felt like a sick thud: they hadn't been worth thousands. The coin dealer had been nicer than he needed to be, surprisingly gentle. He'd probably seen her type before. Maybe he saw her type every day. "Look, these silver fifty-peso pieces?"

"Yeah?" Silver was silver, right? Always worth something.

"Silver plate. People always make that mistake." The guy had a waxed mustache, had probably had it decades before it was hip. He looked sad for her. "All ten of them are worth about twenty bucks."

Fern had dropped into the cracked leather chair on the other side of his desk. "Oh."

"But this," he hastened to add, "this one! The five-centavo? This is worth real money here. I'll check the rates, but I'm thinking at least two fifty." He clarified quickly, "Two *hundred* fifty." He turned his computer screen and showed her the resale sites. He seemed hurt by not being able to give her more.

All told, the box went for $472. Not even enough for the tooth. Fern kept her favorite coin, the silver 1945 fifty-centavo piece, even after she'd learned it was actual silver. She would need something to tuck in her palm to sleep with, once the rest of her treasure was gone, once she'd cashed the enormous check that would make them rich. The check that would hollow her out, leaving nothing but a husk of a woman behind.

Fern turned back to Matty, reaching for her half-knitted hat. "Explain to me how it is that if I'm getting the exact same result, you're still saying it's wrong?"

Matty tossed the hat back to her. "So . . . it's like when I get As on the math test but I don't do my homework? If I get the same results, it doesn't matter how I get there, right?"

"Smart-ass."

"You get what I'm saying, though."

He had a very good point. It was one she wouldn't admit, either. She'd try to do it his way, that was all. "Hey."

"Hey what?" Matty peered down at his own knitting.

"You never said what you thought of Gregory."

Matty set the remote on his thigh and jiggled it, obviously impatient to get back to the movie. "Yeah."

"Yeah?"

"He was fine, I guess."

"Can you be a little more neutral, maybe? I thought you'd liked that whole dolphin thing. And the fact that he got us all the onion skins we'll ever need for all our yarn-dyeing needs forever."

Matty shrugged. "Yeah, he was cool. I just figured he wouldn't come back, so I didn't bother spending any time on him in my brain." He tapped his forehead. "Very smart up here, you know. Lots to do." He switched to a robot voice. "PRI-OR-I-TI-ZING."

"Why did you think *that*?"

He raised his shoulders again and let them drop. "Because you don't let anyone in."

Her throat was tight, like she'd tried to swallow a dry dollar bill. "What?"

"You want me to hit play?"

"What do you mean?"

"HIT. PLAY," said the robot.

"I don't let anyone in? I let way too many people in." That was where she'd gone wrong with Abby, after all.

"Whatever. I just don't think he'll stick around."

Stick. "I invited him to spend time with you and me that day. That's no small thing, bucko." Matty didn't have to know what a big deal that was. She shouldn't have even brought it up. Her throat was tighter now.

Matty just rolled his eyes.

"What?"

He looked at her. "Come on. You let him

sit on the porch for like five minutes before you and *Tío* kicked him out, right?"

"Not fair." He was exactly right, and that was the worst part. Fern had already let Gregory too far into her circle. That was why she hadn't told him about the baby Abby was carrying. Gregory knew something was going on, but when she'd seen him on Monday, he hadn't even asked. They'd just had sex, and then he'd smoked his clove. They'd listened to Lyle Lovett and talked lightly about the singer's hair. Then he'd said he had more grading to do.

Fern yanked at her next stitch, making it too tight. She'd regret it on the next row. "Know what? It's time for bed."

"Hey!"

"It's almost ten. You're supposed to be in bed by nine."

"I have a *bedtime*?"

He was only partially kidding. They'd always laughed about the fact that she'd never enforced a bedtime with him, trusting him to sleep when he was tired. It had been a joke, except that she didn't think it was funny anymore. Yeah, he had a bedtime, yet another ill-chosen, arbitrary rule that Fern had made up in her head and then hadn't bothered to ever back up.

"This weekend we can work on trying to

dye the first hat, right?" He'd made two, one for contrast. He'd sped through the second like his fingers had been on fire.

"Sure. Hey, Matty?"

"Yeah."

"It's in three weeks."

"That's plenty of time."

"Abby might not come back . . . before then."

"It's okay. I bet she does come back in time. But even if she doesn't, I want to do it by myself. I've been Googling the onion dye baths and stuff. I can do it."

"We have no idea what we're doing. Maybe you can just turn in the hat. We'll make up some crap about something. Tying knots to change string into fabric."

"No. I'm going to do it *by myself.*"

"What about Mrs. Hutch? Is she still after you?"

"Mrs. Hutch already thinks I'm going to fail. It doesn't matter what I do or don't do. At least this way I'll be doing what I want to do."

"But shouldn't you aim for a good grade? If you can?"

Matty's body went seizure-rigid and he slid off the couch to the floor. *"Mom."*

Fern was tired. God, she was tired. And she had to work a split shift tomorrow.

"We'll finish the movie another night."

"Whatever," said Matty. "Not like I haven't already seen it at Jorge's."

Ow. "You have?"

"Twice."

His door slammed.

Shit. She'd managed to blow that, hadn't she? Again.

In her pocket, her phone vibrated.

I think she lost it.

For a second, Fern thought Diego meant Abby was losing her mind, and then she realized that the actual meaning of the words was even worse. Her fingers hovered over the tiny virtual keyboard. What should she say? What *could* she say?

She wouldn't wish that loss on anyone.

Shit. Are you with her?

It happened this morning, She sent me a text on her way to the hospital and now she's not answering me.

Oh, god. Keep me posted.

Fern's gut was even tighter than her throat now. She would *not* cry. Why on earth was she tasting salt water at the back of her throat? There was no reason for that. It was just a miscarriage. Without stopping to wonder why she was doing it, she pulled the circular needles from her stitches. Then she yanked on her working yarn, hard. She kept pulling. In three minutes, she'd destroyed the hat she'd been making. It was red, a bright, fire-engine red, and she had loved what she'd done so far.

In minutes, all that work was gone, a pile of crimped, forlorn yarn in her lap.

Fern tugged a few inches of it between her fingers. It was strong stuff, and even stronger when it was doubled. She had an urge to take the ball of it outside. She sat silently, her eyes closed, doing the math, estimating the length of the house, adding the width, doubling it, adding a bit for the laundry room extension. Judging by the yardage on the ball band (223 yards), she could wrap it around the house four times. Plus a little bit. Four-ply around the house? It would be pretty strong. It would be hard to open any of the doors if she did it right.

But it wasn't strong enough.

Oh, god. Poor Abby.

Poor Diego.

For one bone-achingly cold moment, she imagined that happening to her. Not getting pregnant with Matty would have meant no marriage, no house, no house payments. No tripping over Grandpa Wyatt's slippers. She wouldn't know that Elva cried every Memorial Day for her father. Fern would live somewhere else, maybe even in a different city. She might have ended up married to someone else, with different children.

The thought was so unbearable it made her chest hurt.

Matty was in bed, playing with his phone. He looked up, his eyes narrowed. "I'm *going* to sleep."

"With your phone in your hand?" It was an automatic argument, and she didn't mean to say it. "I'm sorry. I'm . . ."

Matty waited.

Fern perched on the end of his bed. "I'm sorry, *mijo.* You're right. I guess I do."

"Do what?" Still suspicious. Of course he was.

"Keep people out."

His face — his darling face, the one she loved more than any other face in the whole world — softened. "It's okay. It's just who you are."

"I guess. But I can try harder." She imagined Gregory at her kitchen table, listening to Grandpa Wyatt talk about the different towing capabilities of full-sized trucks. She knew he'd really listen, and that he'd want to. "I used to be less serious, you know. I was a grasshopper."

"Huh?"

"You know that story about the grasshopper and the ant?"

Matty rolled his eyes. "Yeah. You're totally an ant."

"No way. I've always lived in hope." Now she didn't have to. She could deposit the check, and hope would be a moat filled with dollar bills, keeping Matty safe. "Totally carefree."

Matty raised an eyebrow. Fern hadn't even known he could do that. Was that new? "Yeah. That's you all right. *Estamos completos.*"

Her throat ached. "What do you mean?"

"I just think if you were a grasshopper, you wouldn't mind so much when things change."

"I don't mind when stuff changes!" It was such a lie that she almost laughed. When *had* she gotten so serious? Was it when she met Abby?

No. If she looked at it truthfully, it had been when Scott had left. Maybe even before that. The moment she'd learned she was pregnant with Matty, maybe. That was when she'd become a worker ant.

And she hadn't even noticed.

"It's fine, Mom. We're good this way. We *are* complete."

"Mijito." If he was trying to make her feel better, it wasn't working.

"I thought Abby was getting in with us for

a minute, but then when she stopped answering her phone and stuff, I figured maybe it's for the best. Like with Dad, you know?"

"Dad?" Fern's fingertips went cold.

"I know he left because of whatever — like — I know you said it wasn't me and all, but I know you kept him out to keep us safe. To keep us complete, just like we were."

"Matty —" It was so terrible. And so true.

He plugged his phone in and set it on his bedside table. Then he tucked his hand in hers in exactly the same way he used to when he was little. "We're good, Ma. I like us, too."

Her voice was so thin she didn't recognize it as her own. *"Estamos completos."* Maybe if she kept saying it, it would be true.

He smiled and closed his eyes.

Fern stayed with him until his breathing slowed, trying not to listen to the ragged edge of her own.

When she went back into the living room, she moved to the front door. She turned the dead bolt, feeling it slide into place in her heart, knowing the metal might kill her and that if it didn't, the words surely would, but she whispered them to herself anyway. *"No somos suficientes."*

Then Fern sat on the couch and while she

stared at the frozen image of a woman screaming on the screen, she rewound the yarn into a ball.

Abby would be so sad.

Fern cast on again. One more time.

They were *not* enough, not the way they were. Not yet.

CHAPTER FIFTY-FOUR

For a guy who didn't like to text much, Diego was getting good at it. Abby's phone pinged every hour or so.

What about now?

Still pregnant.

An hour later: *Now?*

Still pregnant.

Every time she texted the words, her heart felt like it would pound right out of her chest in sheer happiness that could still break, but not yet — right now it was real.

She was still pregnant.

The ER doctor (fresh on his shift and as chipper as if he'd just slept for three days straight) said, "Well, this kind of thing is normal."

"I know."

"So go home. No special instructions for you."

She blinked in surprise. "No D and C this time?"

"No!" He'd grinned. "Sorry! Thought the nurse told you! Nothing abnormal in your ultrasound. Just a little spotting. Happens sometimes." He flipped a page or two. "Yep, you have some history. Looks like your OB is already watching you carefully. You can expect a call from her by the end of the day. But it looks like everything's good."

"The pain?"

He shrugged. "You're still feeling cramping?"

"No." She hadn't since she got out of the car.

"Happens."

"I'm still pregnant." Abby had looked toward Kathryn desperately.

Kathryn gave a bark of laughter and gripped both of her hands. "This one, girlie. *This* will be the one."

Kathryn took her home. Abby slept the afternoon away, then the early evening. She woke up and cooked a sweet potato from the garden. She ate the whole thing, along with four pieces of jack cheese and two apples. Then she went back to bed and slept until morning.

The next morning, her cell phone was full of texts, running over with them. Diego had gotten her text message late, and he was obviously panicked. Apparently he'd come by last night, but she hadn't heard him knocking.

I'm still pregnant, she texted. The phone made the sweetest sound as the words flew outward.

He was at her house within twenty minutes.

They talked. They'd talked and argued and he was right, and then she was right, and then both were furious and both of them were wrong.

Then they'd agreed.

They would do their best.

In the backyard, the morning sun was thin and clear. They kept their eyes fixed on the eucalyptus overhead.

Abby said, "It still might not work out."

"I know."

"There's no way to protect myself from that, though."

"Nope."

"You knew that already."

"Yep," he said. "Worrying about something doesn't make it happen. It doesn't make it not happen. And it sure as hell doesn't get you ready for it if it does. It just feels shitty."

Simple words. Abby smiled. "Yeah."

Diego took her hand. She let her fingers lace with his. His knuckles were thicker than

Scott's had been. They watched Tulip ravage a marrow bone. It was so big it had barely fit in the freezer, but in Tulip's wide maw, the bone looked almost dainty.

"What are we doing?"

Abby knew what he meant but asked anyway. "You mean us?"

"Yeah."

"I have no idea. What do you want to do?"

"I want to have a baby with you."

"But what if this —" She touched each of their interlaced fingertips with the pointer finger of her free hand. "*us* — doesn't work?" How could she possibly know what she'd feel in the coming months? She was still in shock over Scott. Diego felt amazing. But would that last?

He leaned his shoulder against hers, just enough weight. "What if we don't name it?"

She knew he wasn't talking about the baby. "Don't we have to?"

"I don't think we do."

"Then what do we do?"

"Whatever we want to. Maybe we date. I'd love that. I'll take you to your doctor's appointments and we'll go to matinees afterward. I'll buy you whatever you're craving to eat. Maybe we fall in love. Or maybe we just stay in like, and get ready to make a family together. A lot can happen in the next seven months."

A long time and she'd never keep this baby that long —

"Don't," he said. "Don't get that look. If we lose the baby, then we're both exactly in the same place we are now, right?"

He was right. "I'm scared."

"I'm fucking terrified," he said. "Tell me again what the doctor said."

Abby was happy to repeat the words. "That no one can know why I miscarried before, but that it might have been about the combination of me and Scott. Maybe this combination is a better one. There's no physical reason to think it won't work this time."

Diego's face was bright, and his shoulder was warm against Abby's, and something like peace rested just above her heart. "Ah," he said. "So good."

"Did you tell your sister?"

"All she knows is that last night you were at the hospital."

"So she doesn't know." That there was still a chance of a baby, a real child.

Diego shook his head. "I haven't talked to her yet."

"Let me tell her? Unless you mind?"

He took his eyes off the sway of the

520

branches overhead. "Why?"

"Because I owe her."

Chapter Fifty-Five

Fern could have sworn she saw her brother's truck pulling away from the curb at Abby's house, but by the time her Uber got to the driveway, the truck had sped away.

She stood next to the mailbox and dialed Diego's phone. She got his voice mail.

That was fine. She didn't want to talk this over with him, anyway. Not before she talked to Abby.

For a long moment, she stood in place, looking up at the house. An amazing-looking place, really. It *looked* like money, with its window that shone high and clean, its paint unchipped and not peeling. This part of Berkeley smelled like money, too, of fresh air and of someone else pushing the lawn mower.

But for the first time, Fern realized she didn't *want* anything better than the house she had. So her home wasn't in the best neighborhood. So it was kind of falling down. So it was small and sometimes smelled like curry, other times like rice and beans or sweat socks or burned toast.

It was hers, and it was filled with the people she loved.

This big house just had Abby.

Fern knocked.

Nothing sounded inside, not even Tulip's bark. Abby's car was in the driveway, though, so she was probably somewhere close by. She could call but didn't want the possibility of Abby hitting the ignore button.

Fern knocked again, then tried the door handle. Locked. Damn it. The gate was too high on the side of the house for her to climb. She looked up — there were open windows on the second floor, but with her luck, she'd fall on the brickwork below. On a hunch, she pulled back the doormat. Sure enough, a silver key gleamed underneath.

Of course Abby was lax about security. People who had a lot worried about everything less than those who didn't.

Fern unlocked the door and poked in her head. "Hello?"

Nothing.

She went through the foyer (perfectly tidy, fresh iris blooms in a crystal vase) and into the kitchen. "Abby? It's Fern."

The countertops were clear, the appliances wiped shiny and clean. The only thing on the long dining room table was a slim paperback.

Baby Names and What They Mean.

"Oh." Pain socked her, a thump to the chest. Before she'd gone to the hospital, she'd gotten out this book? Judging by the dog-ears and the creased cover, it wasn't new. Fern flipped the pages. There were red stars next to "Sally" and "Greta." "Dagmar" and "Rodney" were fervently crossed out. *"Dios."*

She put the book back exactly as it had been, open and facedown on the first page of G names.

She called up the stairs, "Abby?" Still there was no answer. And no Tulip.

Outside, then.

"Abby?"

There was a low, hoarse bark, and Tulip ran at her. He pushed his nose into her crotch ecstatically. "Hey, boy," she said. "Down. Quit it. Nothing to see here. Where's Abby? Hey, Abby?"

The door to the potting shed was ajar. Fern crossed the lawn.

At first she thought the space was empty, but as her eyes adjusted, she could see into the corner, just past the second long table.

Abby was down, lying on her back in a pool of red.

Red, red — god, blood? Adrenaline spiked through Fern and she reached for her cell phone as she plunged forward. "Abby! Jesus!"

But the red was a heavy blanket. And Abby, her eyes now open, looked perfectly surprised, round mouth, wide eyes. "Fern! What are you — ?"

"*You scared me.* Are you okay?"

"I got tired. I decided to lie down. I had just closed my eyes."

"Out here? You have a whole *house.*"

"But this is my favorite place." Abby sat up. "Your brother just left."

"Are you sure you're okay?"

Abby's radiant smile was as unexpected as an earthquake. "I'm wonderful."

"Sorry?"

"I'm still pregnant."

"Holy shit. But I thought —"

Abby patted her belly. "Yeah, we all thought. False alarm. I'm healthy. We're healthy."

Equal parts fear and joy flashed through Fern's limbs. She felt queasy. "Wow."

"Exactly."

Then Fern was being embraced by Abby in a hug so tight it felt like she couldn't breathe, but that was okay, because she didn't *need* to breathe. Not this exact moment. For a few seconds, she could hold her breath and hope as hard as she could.

"I'm so glad you came," said Abby in her ear. "I wanted to tell you myself. I'm so glad."

Fern pulled back, feeling awkward, her movements jerky. This gardening shed was, after all, the place she'd had her first seizure in years. Even though it smelled heavenly, of dirt and lavender and sunshine, she wanted out. "Can we sit outside?"

"Of course, of course. I was going to call you as soon as I took a nap. I'm so tired," said Abby. "And it's wonderful to feel this exhausted for a reason."

They sat in the Adirondack chairs that faced the garden. There were two long rows of something green growing, something with clear plastic that flapped.

"What's that?" Fern didn't actually care. She just didn't know what to say next.

"I'm experimenting with germinating early hyssop outside."

Silence dropped hard between them. Fear reared up again inside Fern and she wasn't sure if she'd be able to stay seated. "I'm really mad at you."

"I know," said Abby. "I would be, too."

"You sent that check."

"Is that why you're here? I won't let you give it back to me." Abby turned in her seat, pulling up her legs. Soon, Fern thought, she wouldn't be able to do that. Her belly would preclude that kind of graceful move.

"That's not why. You *fired* me."

Abby looked at her knees. "I was scared. It wasn't about you."

"It wasn't about us when Scott left, either."

"Sorry?"

"I know that now. It wasn't about us. It was just him. It was just Scott being Scott. The problem with him leaving was that I tried to fix things for Matty. That's all I did, for years. I tried to make things right, to make up for Scott being nowhere in the picture. It was exhausting, and in a perfect world, I wouldn't have had to do it."

Abby kept her lips closed. She nodded.

Fern felt her upper chest tighten. "You hurt my family. You left Matty wondering what he'd done wrong. You left him to finish the project alone. Who does that to an eleven-year-old?"

"Me," said Abby. "Apparently I do."

"You left *me* wondering what I'd done wrong, too. You know who else did this to us?"

"Scott."

"Yep."

Abby tilted her face to the sun briefly. Then she said, "I'm sorry. Those words don't sound like much, I know that. But I do mean them. I'm *so* sorry I hurt you."

"Yeah, well." Fern felt a tremor in her fingertips, but it wasn't an impending seizure. It was just fear, plain and simple. Big words — she had the *biggest* words to say to Abby, and what if she got them wrong? "Family does that to each other."

Abby's knees jumped, but her face stayed still, as if she were frozen. "Pardon?"

"I made you something last night." Fern dug in her purse. She gripped the red hat firmly but gently, like it was a kitten trying to escape a box. "Here." She felt stupid handing it over. She'd made a hat, using Matty's pattern, and she was giving it to a real knitter. What was she thinking?

"You made me a hat?" Abby's voice was thin as a penny pressed in a souvenir machine.

"It took forever. Like, almost all night. I couldn't sleep anyway. I thought it would go way faster than it did." Fern flexed her wrists and shook them out. "It has a couple holes that I couldn't figure out. And my hands hurt."

"I can't believe you . . . Why? Why did you do this?" Abby pulled it on. It made her look like an adorable elf.

"Matty told me. About the red scarf Scott had knitted."

"The one I lost."

"I thought maybe that meant you liked red."

"I do." A shine rose in Abby's eyes.

"Don't you dare cry."

"Wouldn't," said Abby. "No way."

Fern felt the feeling again, the one she'd felt last night, when she'd thought Abby was miscarrying. *Protective.* "You want my family."

"No, that's not —" Abby blinked. "Fuck it. Truth? I did. I do. I *do* want your family. I want Grandpa Wyatt to tell me tow truck stories. Matty says he has a million of them, all of them only half true. I want to eat Elva's cooking, no matter what it is. I want to be the cool aunt — or whatever I could pretend to be — when Matty needs to run away from your house when he's a teenager."

"Diego?" Fern prompted.

"I want him, too. I don't know how he'll fit. Neither of us do, but we're going to wait and see. And I want this baby." Abby's voice was as fierce. Ragged at the edges, just like any mother's voice. "Yeah, you're right. I wanted your family. I do want it. But I know I blew it."

Fern could barely speak around the lump in her throat. "You can have it."

"Pardon?" said Abby again.

"No chingues, you're so fucking *polite.* Who says *pardon?* You heard me. You can have my family. But look. You have to *be* there. You have to *stay."*

"Fern." It was a gasp. "I'll stay. I swear I'll stay. Is this about the science project?"

"Fuck the project. He's gone stubborn and wants to do it all himself."

"Is it about the job?"

"Honey, I'm going to deposit that big-ass check. I've gotten okay with it. It's the right thing to do, I guess. So I don't need the job. But I'll help you. If you want me to."

"I do. I do."

"I think I'm going to be one of those online business assistants. Gregory showed me a site where you can set your own price. I'll be good at it."

"No more driving?"

Fern shook her head. Her lungs felt tight. "Nope."

"I'm so sorry."

"It's not your fault." It would have been

so much easier if it actually had been. But it wasn't.

"Fern —" Abby leaned forward, but Fern interrupted her.

"You have to know this: I am never going to lie for you like I did for Scott. I tried like hell to make him sound like a stand-up, decent man whenever Matty asked about him, even while I knew he was a piece of shit for leaving his son behind. You, I won't lie for. You leave us, you hurt Matty one more time, I'll tell him exactly what I think."

"I won't."

"Won't what?" Fern needed to hear the words.

Abby was crying freely now, tears streaming down her cheeks, but she was smiling. "I won't disappear again. I won't hurt him." She rubbed at an eye and tugged the hat straighter. "I realized something in the hospital."

"What's that?" Fern tucked her hands between her knees, trying to still their trembling.

"I'm . . . okay. This way. Not a mother. I want to be one, but if I don't get my wish, it's okay, because it has to be. That's life. So I guess I'm saying that I understand. If you change your mind."

Fern shrugged, as if it were unimportant

531

(it wasn't — it was so important that she ached). "Why would I do that?"

"If I lose the baby. Family might be . . . family is maybe a bigger concept than I'd thought it was. And I understand I'll be . . . that you'll let me be part of your family — if it sticks."

Family as a bigger concept. Maybe that was true for Fern, too. She took a deep breath and then jumped. "Yeah, well. I figure you're ours even if it doesn't."

Abby stared.

"Scott had good taste. And don't say *pardon* again," Fern warned. She wouldn't cry. She would *not* cry. It ached so much, opening like this. Her chest creaked with it, and it was hard to remember the combination to open the locks she'd put around her heart. Which reminded her. "I can't believe you leave your key under the doormat."

"Oh, my god, you totally broke in."

"Is it breaking in if I have a key?"

Abby didn't say anything. She stretched out her legs to the grass and leaned back, then reached to take Fern's hand.

It felt weird. Fern was used to holding Gregory's bigger hand. Matty's small one. She held the hands of old women getting on and off the bus, their skin thin and brittle. Abby's hand was warm and dry, the same size as her own. Her fingers felt strong.

They both looked up into the sky. Clear, blue, and so bright. It might get too warm to sit here later.

But for now, they sat together in the sunlight.

CHAPTER FIFTY-SIX

Abby curled her fingernails into her palms and kept moving forward, her heart hammering so loudly the kernel growing inside her was probably dreaming of monsters. She'd known that the science fair was a big deal, but she'd had no idea how *very* big a deal it was.

The entire auditorium was full of *things.* Rows and rows of tables, each one holding something that squawked or moved or rolled or grew. Parents yelled as kids raced from row to row. Two young teachers with whistles around their necks looked almost ready to cry. Three people bumped into Abby within seven steps of the front door.

"Holy crap," she whispered to herself. Three grades of kids, the entire middle school, each kid with a project. And each of them with a family coming to view the work. How the hell was she supposed to find Matty?

And then, like she'd wished them into existence, Fern barreled through the main door with Grandpa Wyatt on one side, Elva on the other. Wyatt held a cane, and Elva's red dress was hitched up into her stocking.

Abby rocked on her heels, feeling more off-balance than she'd ever felt before. This was it. The test. The first time she'd seen Matty in long, long weeks. It was official. Abby had *never* been this particular kind of scared, not when she'd had her miscarriages, not even when she'd been on the floor with Scott, doing CPR, waiting for the medics. Those times she'd been scared of losing something — someone.

This new kind of fear was unfamiliar. She'd *already* lost these people. She'd pushed them away, and run from them when they tried to help her. They were allowing her in, and oh, god, she wanted to stay.

But no matter what, she would be all right.

It was her mantra now. *It will be okay.* The words helped her to breathe. For the last few weeks, the words had put her to sleep, and they were the first things she thought in the morning.

It would be okay.

If she really did lose the baby.

If she never got to look at Matty's dancing eyes again.

If she never got to hear Fern's laugh.

If Diego never sat next to her on the porch, if he never kissed her again.

She'd be okay.

But sweet baby *Cristo,* as Fern would have said, it was all right to *want* this.

"Hi," she said.

Fern smiled. That was all.

And it was all she needed.

"How many kids does this school *have*?" Grandpa Wyatt lifted his cane as if he wanted to joust with one of the students running past.

"All of them, I think." Elva had worn black kitten heels and was teetering slightly.

"Holy shitballs," said Fern. "How are we supposed to find him? He didn't tell us."

They moved forward together, one of a number of small clusters of people. Those clusters, Abby saw, were families, all clinging together. Like them. Happiness filled her like helium. If she spoke, she might sound like one of the Chipmunks.

"Here." Her voice didn't squeak. She pointed at a laminated poster at the end of the first row. "A map."

"Great," said Fern. "His class is row eight. Now we just have to get there. How are we supposed to get through this mess?"

A small robotic cupcake ran across the aisle in front of them, followed by a huge cupcake on wheels, driven by a kid wearing a frosting hat. Somewhere a rooster crowed. There was livestock in here? Maybe they should be thankful Matty had been only knitting and dyeing things for the last two months.

"Wait!" Grandpa Wyatt raised his cane and almost hit a woman in a green sweater in the eye. "I got an idea! Go with me on this. Give me your sunglasses."

"Oh, no." But Fern took them off the top of her head and handed them over.

They were too wide for Wyatt's narrow face. He swept the cane back and forth in wide arcs as he moved forward.

Without missing a beat, Elva yelled, "Blind man coming through! Step aside. Hello? Yes, you, please give way."

Fern looked horrified but followed in their remarkably wide wake. "Come on, Abby. Sorry, ma'am. Oh, *dios.* Sorry, sir," she said.

"Oh my god, he's amazing," said Abby.

"How are you?" Fern didn't look at her, just kept moving forward, her hands out as if Grandpa Wyatt might topple backward any second.

Abby swallowed hard. "Just entered week thirteen."

"Oh, damn." Fern grinned at her. "That's amazing."

"I know." Joy felt like the parade she was in right now, the wobbly line of people she cared about, cutting through the jostling of the crowd.

At row eight, Grandpa Wyatt made a sharp right turn. "Here we go," he said.

"He's healed!" said Elva.

"I'm assuming you've pulled this routine before?" said Fern.

"How do you think we get the best samples at Costco? There he is! My grandson! The scientist!"

Matty stood behind his table, next to four full-color signs. The first sign was hand-drawn knitting moves, cartoonlike and arrestingly clear. They showed the slipknot, then the first row of upturned loops, the way a knit stitch pulled out of its turn before tucking back in, the way a purl caught itself.

The next sign depicted an onion's growing season. Abby's heart tripped faster. Her favorite plant, drawn by Matty.

The third sign was a chemical description of what happened in a dye pot, and the fourth had three hats he'd knitted pinned to it: the first, undyed and simple. The second, dark tan, almost brown. The third was lighter, and a bit splotchy.

Three! He'd knitted three hats! And dyed them! He'd done all this himself! If Abby felt proud, how must Fern be feeling? But before she could turn to look at Fern, Matty leaped around the table like he was a baby goat. "Abby! You're here! You're here!" Then he looked behind her. "Did you bring Tulip?"

"Not this time," she said.

"That's okay." He flung his arms around her. "I knew you'd come. I told everyone you would."

Abby caught the sob where it started, at the back of her throat. "I missed you," she said. "I'm sorry I didn't help you more."

"It's okay. I wanted to see if I could do it myself. And I did. You can help me with the next one."

Abby felt baptized, newly born and perfect.

Matty hugged Fern and Elva and his grandfather. Then he quickly moved back into place, guarding a pot of steaming water propped over a can of Sterno. "Mom." His voice was suddenly desperate. "She won't let the water boil."

Matty looked like he'd gone right to panic as soon as he'd looked into the pot. "She said I have to blow out the flame when it starts to bubble." He flailed the way he had when he was small and frustrated. *"Safety."*

Fern looked around. "There's like a thousand people in here."

"What?"

She raised her voice so she could be heard over the clamor. "And there are little kids running around. She just doesn't want someone to get burned."

"You're on *her* side?" Matty was incredulous. "I'm going to fail. I fail everything with her. She hates me and I hate her, and . . ."

"Hello, Matias." Mrs. Hutch was dressed up in a blue dress exactly the color of the auditorium's walls, exactly the right color for creeping up on students.

"Hi." Bright pink lit Matty's tan cheeks. Watching, Fern felt the same heat light her own face. Her kid. This was *her* kid. She was so goddamn proud, and if Mrs. Hutch pulled a single thing, if she said one word against him or his work, so help her god . . .

Her arms crossed, Mrs. Hutch leaned forward to check the flame on the Sterno. "Not boiling, right?"

Matty poked miserably at the lukewarm onion skins. "No." Fern felt his misery creep into her own skin. Poor kiddo.

"Mrs. Ray-jus?"

Fern took an indulgent second to memorize the tightness of the teacher's voice so she could imitate it to make Gregory laugh later. He was taking all of them out to dinner. Somewhere nice, he said. He wanted to help Matty celebrate his project. And more than that, Fern was going to let him. "Yes?"

"Your son did a great job on this project. You should be very proud of him." Mrs. Hutch stalked away to terrorize the next table.

"Holy shit," said Matty.

"Hey! Language," said Fern. "But holy *shit.*"

"Dude!"

"Good job!" Grandpa Wyatt gave Matty a high five, but Matty's missed, as his gaze whipped to the right, toward Abby again. His eyes lit up in that way that sometimes made Fern feel like she could fly.

"Did you hear that, Abby? Are you going to stick around?" Matty asked. "Do you want to go to dinner with us later?"

Abby looked at Fern.

Fern nodded. It was okay. It was better than okay.

"I'd love to," said Abby. "Diego mentioned it to me, but I didn't want to accept without your approval. It's your day. He's right behind us, by the way. He had to drop off a chain saw at a job, but he said he'd be here soon."

Fern wondered what Matty thought about Diego and Abby, if he had any thoughts at all. Maybe over dinner, if it felt right, they could tell him about the baby. It was Abby's call, of course. She was the one most scared, most cautious, about sharing the news.

But Fern was scared, too. Terrified. There was *so much* coming up. Her family was bigger now, and it would probably keep getting bigger as the years went on. By choice. Abby had made the first move. She'd chosen them.

Then they had chosen Abby back.

Diego and Abby might not stay together. The baby might not live. Gregory might decide Fern wasn't worth the effort. Grandpa Wyatt's bad teeth might give way to heart problems. Elva might keel over in the kitchen and drown in her own soup. There was no safety, no guarantees, in any of it. Life came with no money-back guarantee.

But maybe it was like being on the bus. The passengers (like Fern, because that's what she was now, just a passenger peering out the side windows) didn't get seat belts, because statistically, they were safe enough without them. They dropped their thin coins in the fare box, then rode, hopeful.

Safe enough.

Safe enough, when it was combined with family, might be all anyone needed in the end.

Fern marched around the table and kissed Matty on the top of his head. He squawked like a chicken but didn't look displeased. Then she went around again, kissing Elva on her right cheek and Wyatt on his left. His stubble scratched and Elva's face lotion left her lips smelling like violet.

Then Fern wrapped her arms around Abby and gave her a hug, the kind Fern used to give all the time, the kind she wasn't going to forget how to give. A full-body hug, boobs to bellies to thighs. She planted a smacking kiss on Abby's cheek and then stepped back, folding her arms.

"Where's that Mrs. Hutch? I think I'm going to kiss her, too."

Epilogue

Life Science Project
by Matias Reyes for Mrs. Hutch

In our class this year, we talked about changing states of matter. Everything can change from one state to another (liquid to gas, gas to solid), even though it might take a whole lot of pressure or energy or extreme temperature to do it. In this experiment I'm not going to change a solid to a liquid or anything, I'm just taking one solid in one form, applying outside energy and heat and chemicals to construct a solid in another form.

Sounds fancy, right? *STICK AROUND BECAUSE IT JUST GETS BETTER.*

First, you need a ball of yarn. White is best, although my father's wife (not my mother), Abby, explained that it isn't really white, it's off-white, because that's the way it came off the sheep. In this case, it came off a Blue-faced Leicester, which is a kind of sheep, and it doesn't have a blue face (disappointing!), but the blue veins can be seen through its white hair on its nose, which is why it's called that.

Then get two circular knitting needles, size US 8. You can use YouTube to understand these directions because I'm supposed to keep it to three pages and I can't teach you to knit in that time.

Cast on 88 stitches and join them in a circle. Knit 2, purl 2, all the way around until you have a tube that's nine inches long. (This will take longer than you think, trust me on this one.)

Then the recipe (it's not called that, it's called a pattern, but it's basically a recipe for actions) goes like this:

Round 1: Knit 2, purl 2 together, repeat that all the way around.

Round 2: Knit 2, purl 1, repeat that all the way around.

Round 3: Knit 2 together, purl 1, repeat that all the way around.

Round 4: Knit 1, purl 1, repeat that all the way around.

Round 5: Knit 2 together all the way around.

Round 6: Knit all the stitches.

Round 7: Knit 2 together all the way around.

Round 8: Knit all the stitches (you only have 12 left or you messed something up, but if it looks like a hat, don't worry that much about it).

Round 9: Knit 2 together all the way around.

Then cut your yarn, leaving a long tail, thread it through a big tapestry needle (or you can make one out of a paper clip if you're that kind of creative person like I am), and pull it through all the stitches. Sew up the ends and hide them the best you can. It's not that hard.

GUESS WHAT? You used the *kinetic energy* of your hands (converted from the food and water you put into your body) to make something that didn't exist before. A hat!

Brag to your friends! But it's white (off-white) and that's no good for when you crash while you're skateboarding or when your friend is eating spaghetti too close to your head, so now is the time to use naturally occurring chemicals and heat to change the color, like magic, except it's *science*!

Go to the grocery store and get one of those plastic bags near the apples. Take all the red papery onion skin in the bottom of the red onion bin. If they ask you what you're doing, make your eyes really big and say it's for a science project. They won't charge you, because you're a kid and adults like kids who do science projects. The more you get, the better. I got mine from a cool dude my mom's boyfriend, Gregory, knows, but I bet you could get a lot just by going back a few times to the same store.

Put them in a pot (check with someone first, I used Elva's favorite pot and I got in trouble even though it was just *onions*). Boil, and simmer (that means little bubbles) for an hour. Take out the onion skins with a fork. Get the hat wet under the faucet (so it's not shocked by the water in the pot) and then, while it's still dripping, put it in the pot of water. Keep it simmering for about an hour, stirring and poking to make sure the dye gets all over all the strands. Whatever you do, don't forget you're doing this. You should stay in the kitchen and do your homework or watch TV or something. Abby told me once she forgot a dye pot and came back and her knitting was on fire. Turn off the heat. Let the hat cool in the pot along with the water. Overnight is best. And then let it dry! In the sink is best, since if it drips on the floor of your bedroom, your mom will be irritated with you. Ask me how I know.

Your hat will be an awesome brownish orange color, and NO ONE ELSE will have one just like it. And it's all natural, all organic, from a sheep and some onions and some water and the kinetic energy you put into it. And when you get an A on the project (HINT, HINT, MRS. HUTCH), you will smile and feel happy every time you wear the hat that reminds you of your family and how sometimes it's fun to learn.

(But don't quote me on that.)

ACKNOWLEDGMENTS

To my ever-excellent editor, Danielle Perez, thanks for always managing to see what I *mean* to do and helping me get there. To Susanna Einstein, love and thanks. You're the best agent in the whole wide world (with the cutest kids), and I'm glad we're on this wild publishing ride together. To AC Transit and the bus drivers who are superhuman in their kindness and dedication, thank you for letting me imagine what it would be like to be a part of your ranks. Any mistakes are mine, as are any liberties I took with the funeral industry and the valuable information I got from Oakland's Chapel of the Chimes. Thanks to my sister Christy Herron and my friend Rachel Harvey for sending me wonderfully detailed reference e-mails about what eleven-year-old boys are really like. Cheetos and underpants, check. Your boys' quirks and sweetnesses helped make Matty real. Thanks to my sister Bethany for being the best partner in playing hooky. As always, thanks to the friends I can't and won't do without. When I need to bury a body, Cari Luna will provide the dark, lyrically dense soundtrack, Sophie Littlefield will pour the Islay Scotch while using her iPhone as a torch, and Juliet Blackwell will wear something sexy and say something wise and comforting while we all take turns wielding the shovel. And always, to Lala Hulse, all my love. If we end up with a Great Dane, it will be only partially your fault now.

■ ■ ■ ■

CONVERSATION GUIDE: *THE ONES WHO MATTER MOST*

RACHAEL HERRON

■ ■ ■ ■

This Conversation Guide is intended to enrich the individual reading experience, as well as encourage us to explore these topics together — because books, and life, are meant for sharing.

A CONVERSATION WITH RACHAEL HERRON

Q. How did you get the idea for this book?

A. The original idea for any of my novels usually gets buried so deep that by the time I've finished writing, I can barely remember what the first idea was. This book, though, was different. The first scene *was* my original idea. A woman makes the agonizing decision to leave her husband, tells him, and then he drops dead.

Questions, naturally, follow that first idea. My first big question was, *How do you mourn a person you were abandoning?* My second question, the question that became the impetus for the rest of the novel, was, *What secret might you find in a desk drawer?*

Q. Do you always know the endings of your novels when you start them?

A. I wish! I know writers who know their

endings and aim for them like marksmen. Rather than apples to be hit with arrows, though, my endings are always asymptotes. I write toward them forever, getting closer and closer but never *quite* getting there. Usually I have to revise the whole book (minus the ending) a few times until I figure out what should really happen.

In an early version of this book, Scott was a philanderer. He was a hackneyed cliché, and he bored me to death. Abby's discovery of his affairs was certainly a good reason for her to leave him, but it was hard to understand why a smart, kind woman would choose a jerk like him in the first place.

When I realized that Abby's main focus was *family,* I nixed his cheating ways. Scott became who he was meant to be, a well-intentioned man who'd never quite pulled it together, the guy who'd never quite grown up. A secret vasectomy would, for Abby, be the ultimate betrayal, not an affair. Figuring that out made lots of other things drop into place. When those magical things shift around in a manuscript, writing becomes a purely joyful act.

Q. What might surprise a reader of The Ones Who Matter Most?

A. Writing the scene in which Abby is scrabbling through the rolltop desk's drawers was a special treat. Writers are incorrigible thieves, stealing bits and pieces of their lives to provide sparkle and heft. We can't help populating our books with parts of ourselves. I share Abby's optimistic naïveté as much as I do Fern's ruthless practicality.

But beyond the stolen personality pieces, we steal actual objects. In my first novel, I borrowed a Canadian friend's cat, Duncan. I lifted him, huge and orange, out of my mind's eye and plopped him into the book (and, at one memorable point, into a bathtub). I absolutely forgot that's what I'd done until the book was published, eighteen months later. I got a congratulatory e-mail from my friend, who said, "Good book. But is that my *cat*?" In another book, I put my incurably horrible (and dearly beloved) cat Digit on a boat, because I'd always thought he'd like life at sea. He was a tuna guy.

For the book you're holding, I stole even more from myself (always a little safer than stealing from other people). That's my desk in Scott's office. As Abby explores the many small drawers, Abby wonders why they aren't being made *useful.* They could hold hair bands and gum and those wonderful yellow Paper Mate pencils. In my office, those drawers *do* hold those things. Found in an antiques store in a defunct chocolate factory in Oakland, my desk waited for me to stumble over it. As my eye fell on it, a solo spotlight hit its polished oak highlights and a heavenly choir sang one high, perfect note. I hadn't been looking for a rolltop desk, especially not one as unwieldy as a drunk cow. It was in my office the next day.

I have a wee drawer just for shawl pins. I have one for stamps. There's one for Sharpies, and one for Post-its (that's my favorite drawer). One of the side drawers has a *fake back.* I could totally hide something behind it! Well, now I can't, since I've told everyone about it right here. But the fact remains that I could. It made me happy to plop that desk, candy drawer and all, into Abby's house.

Another stolen shiny object is the café Abby and Fern meet in. I've written parts of each of my books at that exact café in San Leandro. I adore the kids who run it (as soon as you hit forty, you can call the twenty-somethings kids, right?). It closed for a while, and the whole community was bereft because we treated it like our living room (we put our feet up, Skyped with family, sang Christmas carols by the tree). Then Sarah bought it and reopened it, leaving it exactly the same (only better! Beer and wine now on the menu!) and it's our place again. It's a family there, and I'm so proud to be a part of that community that it's a joy to bring it into this book.

Dropping pieces of nonfiction into fiction creates a small, tangible connection: real life intersecting with the imaginary. Characters meeting "characters." The whole book, of course, is mine. It came out of my head, so it belongs to me (and really, I belong to it). But those tiny real-life cameos can help bring books to life.

Q. If you based a couple of past cats on real cats, is Tulip the Great Dane based on a real dog?

A. No. No, no, no, no. Nope!

Of course, my wife *just* e-mailed me a picture of a partially blind four-year-old black-and-white Great Dane who needs a forever home.

THIS MEANS NOTHING. (Although I can't get over the image I have of a Great Dane carrying our elderly five-pound Chihuahua in a wee backpack . . .)

No. No, no, no.

Hmmm.

QUESTIONS FOR DISCUSSION

1. What role does Kathryn play in Abby's life? How has she helped shape Abby's life trajectory?

2. Do you think Abby will be able to carry this pregnancy to full term? What echoes do her past miscarriages present in her current life?

3. "Chosen family" is a theme of *The Ones Who Matter Most*. What other themes do you see in this novel?

4. How has Abby changed by the end of the novel? Is it for the better? How do her decisions as the book progresses affect this change?

5. Same question for Fern: How has she changed? Is it for the better? Is life pushing her? Is she pushing life back?

6. Fern thinks of herself as stubbornly independent and actively wants Scott to stay out of her and Matty's life, yet she's been taking checks from him since he left. Is this a contradiction? Why or why not?

7. Matty learns several skills through the course of his science project. What's the most important thing he learns? What will serve him the best as he grows up?

8. What do you think Matty will be like at sixteen? At twenty-five? At forty?

9. When Scott left Fern and Matty, his father, Wyatt, chose the ones left behind. Do you think he made the right decision? Why?

10. *Estamos completos:* "We are complete." Is there a complete family by the close of this novel? Is this something a family can truly attain, or is it a dream on Fern's part?

11. Is most of your family related to you by blood or by choice? Of course you wish for health and happiness for your family, but what else do you wish for the ones who matter most to you?

ABOUT THE AUTHOR

Rachael Herron received her MFA in English and creative writing from Mills College and when she's not busy writing, she's a 911 medical/fire dispatcher for a Bay Area fire department. She is the author of *Pack Up the Moon* and *Splinters of Light* as well as the Cypress Hollow romance series and the memoir *A Life in Stitches.* She is an accomplished knitter and lives in Oakland with her wife, Lala, and their menagerie of cats and dogs.

The employees of Thorndike Press hope you have enjoyed this Large Print book. All our Thorndike, Wheeler, and Kennebec Large Print titles are designed for easy reading, and all our books are made to last. Other Thorndike Press Large Print books are available at your library, through selected bookstores, or directly from us.

For information about titles, please call:
  (800) 223-1244

or visit our Web site at:
  http://gale.cengage.com/thorndike

To share your comments, please write:
  Publisher
  Thorndike Press
  10 Water St., Suite 310
  Waterville, ME 04901